WAITING FOR WREN

BOOK FIVE IN THE BODYGUARDS OF L.A. COUNTY SERIES

CATE BEAUMAN

Waiting for Wren

Visit Cate at www.catebeauman.com
Follow Cate on Twitter: @CateBeauman
Or visit her Facebook page: www.facebook.com/CateBeauman

First Print Edition: October 2013

ISBN-13: 978-1492159278
ISBN-10: 1492159271

Editor: Invisible Ink Editing, Liam Carnahan
Proofreader: Kimberly Dawn
Cover: Streetlight Graphics

DEDICATION

To my friends Jen Helmer and Ashley Nickel, two of the strongest women I know.

ACKNOWLEDGMENTS

A big thank you once again to my good friend and fellow author Rachelle Ayala for your thoughts and encouragement while writing *Waiting For Wren.*

☙ Chapter One ❧

Park City, Utah
July 1999

STARS TWINKLED ABOVE AND THE MOON GLOWED bright as Tucker took the mountain curve a little too sharply. Cool air blew through the open windows and music blared from the speakers as he approached the next twist.

"Take it easy, Tucker," Staci shouted from the backseat.

He turned up Will Smith's *Wild Wild West* louder, grinned at his sister in the rearview mirror, and gunned the engine into the next wind in the road.

Staci and Jasmine screamed, and Tucker and JT let loose enthusiastic whoops, as the black Mustang fishtailed closer to the guardrail than Tucker had planned. Heart thundering, Tucker eased off the gas and gripped the wheel tighter until he had full control of the vehicle again.

"Damn it, Tucker, knock it off or I'm telling Mom." Staci gave him a smack on the shoulder.

"Chill out," he smirked, slowing as they approached the neighborhood of large summer houses scattered among the trees. Staci wouldn't really tell Mom—at least, he didn't think so. He was just showing off a little. It wasn't everyday Jasmine Smith sat in the front seat next to him. Staci *knew* how much he liked her. He and Staci never told on each other. Tattling on your twin went against every rule in the book.

They approached JT's rambling stone-and-glass house, and Tucker rolled to a stop. Jasmine opened her door and slid out. She swiped a golden lock of her chin-length hair behind her ear and gave Tucker a smile as she pulled on the lever, sending the seat forward. Tucker smiled back and snuck a glance at the lush, tan breasts peeking from Jasmine's spaghetti-strap sundress. JT unfolded his long, well-built body from the back, stretching as Jasmine sat again. Crouching down, he leaned his arms against the window frame. "Good movie tonight. We still planning on baseball and swimming tomorrow?"

"We'll be by to pick you up—ten sharp. Be ready to kick some ass."

"Better believe it. Fucking Johnny Simmons," JT said with uncustomary venom. "His bragging's really starting to piss me off."

"No shit. He turns into a bigger tool with every passing summer."

"Guess we'll have to show him a few things."

"We have nine innings to shut him up."

"Maybe he'll end up falling on his way to second base, like Nick did when Johnny's foot 'accidently' tripped him. Payback's a bitch." JT extended his hand through the window, and Tucker gave him a high five. "I'm looking forward to it." He rose to standing. "See you guys in the morning."

"Bye," Jasmine and Staci said in unison.

"Later." Tucker waved and drove the quarter mile to Jasmine's house.

"Go ahead and drop Staci off first if you want. You can walk me home." Jasmine bit her lip and looked up from under her lashes.

Tucker swallowed as his hormones immediately shot into overdrive. He accelerated, wanting to park the Mustang and get on with the evening. Curfew was forty-five minutes away, and Jasmine had just given him the invitation he'd been waiting for all summer. He drove another eighth of a mile past four more houses and turned into the U-shaped lot, circling around and coming to a stop in front of the massive double pine doors of the Campbell summer estate. He opened his door and almost forgot Staci in his rush to be on his way with Jasmine.

"Hey."

He stopped the door mid-swing and released the front seat. "Sorry."

"What's your hurry?" Staci smirked as she got out and drilled her finger into his stomach, understanding full well where his mind was. "Don't stay out too late. I don't want to have to cover for you again."

"I'll be home by midnight. Promise." He tugged gently on a lock of her shoulder-length black hair as he stared into dark hazel eyes, which were exactly the same as his own.

She pulled the keys from his hand and pocketed them in her jean shorts. "Oh, and I get to drive to the ball field tomorrow. It's my day. I call it."

"But—"

"You're hogging the car. Dad said we have to share."

He huffed as he held her gaze. This sharing-the-car crap sucked. They'd only been driving for four months, but it was hard to take the passenger seat after getting used to having his own wheels. Less than thirty days until they went back to Monterey, then they would have their own vehicles back. He tugged her hair again. "Brat."

"I'm driving to the resort too and home and wherever else we decide to go."

He shrugged. "We'll see."

Her brow shot up in challenge. "I guess we will. I'm going to sit in the hot tub for a while."

"Later." He walked over to Jasmine and took her hand as they started down the drive. Tucker waited until the front door shut behind his sister, then looked over at Jasmine and smiled in the bright moonlight. He'd dreamed of this moment since Staci brought Jasmine to the house almost a month ago. Jasmine was extremely hot, and athletic too—a perfect package. She didn't pretend to know about baseball or football the way other girls did; she actually *knew* what she was talking about. He was pretty sure he was half in love, and he wasn't about to blow it. He'd been out with plenty of girls now that he was allowed to date, and Kimberly Hastings had let him get her off in the theater while they pretended to watch 'The Matrix.' He knew what to do; he had moves. He just had to keep cool. "So, what did you think of the movie?"

"It was pretty good. I love Will Smith."

"He's a great actor."

"And a good musician too."

They fell into silence as they passed the first three driveways, then the fourth, and strolled onto hers.

"Thanks for walking me home."

"No problem. It's a nice night—not too cool." With every step, they came closer to Jasmine's front door. He was going to miss his chance to ask her out if he didn't hurry up. "Hey, um, do you want to go to the lake with me tomorrow night? We could start a fire and roast some marshmallows or something." He was counting on "or something." He wanted to spend a couple hours rolling around with Jasmine on a blanket by the water.

"Tomorrow?"

"If that doesn't work, maybe we could go another night."

"No, tomorrow's good. I have to ask my parents, but I'm sure it's fine."

Yes! "We can play some ball with everyone in the morning and go swimming, then I could pick you up here at six." Shit. It was Staci's turn to have the car. He'd have to work around that little issue. She could use the Mustang free and clear for an entire week, heck two weeks for all he cared, if she agreed to give it up for one night. He would explain how important this date was, and she would be okay with it. Nobody understood him the way his sister did, and vice versa. Mom called it a 'twin thing.'

"I'll talk to my mother."

"Cool." They took the three steps to the front door and faced each other in the dim outside light.

Jasmine licked her lips. "Thanks for inviting me tonight. I thought spending the summer in the mountains was going to be boring. You, Staci, and JT have made Park City pretty fun."

"I love coming here. We've come every summer since Staci and I were babies. This is the only place my dad can get away from the hotels."

She smiled. "Didn't he just leave on a business trip?"

Tucker shrugged, grinning. "There was a problem in Boston. He'll be back in a couple days."

"It must be cool to have a hotelier for a father. Luxury resorts all over the world."

He jerked his shoulders. "It's okay. If you've slept in one bed, you've slept in them all. *Your* father's a producer. Now that's cool."

"I guess." She licked her lips again as the easy conversation died away into nervous anticipation.

He glanced at his watch—quarter to midnight. "I should probably get going."

She held his gaze. "Okay."

He took a step closer, until his chest brushed her firm breasts. "Thanks for coming tonight," he whispered as Jasmine closed her eyes and he moved in for the kiss. His heart pounded as glossy, strawberry lips pressed against his, and silky tongues collided. She wrapped her slender arms around the back of his neck, and he dove deeper. The outside light blinked off and on twice, and he eased away, staring into her beautiful blue eyes. His stomach clenched as waves of lust erupted through his system. Kissing Jasmine was even better than he'd imagined it would be. He'd never felt like this before. This had to be love.

"I guess I should go in."

"I'll—I'll see you in the morning. Staci and I will pick you up around nine thirty."

She nodded, twisted the doorknob, and let herself inside. "Bye."

He gave her a wave and looked down just in time, catching himself before he fell down the stairs. "Bye."

Smiling, Jasmine shut the door behind her.

Tucker started toward the road in a daze. He'd kissed several girls over the last two years, but it had never been like that. Jasmine was different. He twisted his wrist to look at his watch, then heard the snap of a branch among the trees along the driveway. He paused, peering into the shadows. More twigs broke as something took another step. Cold sweat beaded on his forehead. Ms. Hayes said mountain lions were spotted in the area a couple days ago. Tucker walked backwards, scrutinizing the thick mass of pines, waiting for a huge cat to pounce. His breath puffed out as he shuddered, and it no longer had anything to do with a kiss under the stars.

There was another crack somewhere in the woods, further away this time, but he wasn't about to wait around to find out what was lurking in the brush. With little pride, Tucker turned his athletic body and sprinted the eighth of a mile home. He'd never been so happy to see the timber-and-glass work of art, designed by his father, tucked among the trees. Breathless, he slammed the door behind him and pressed his head against the heavy wood, groping for the lock and twisting it into place.

"Tucker?"

He swiped at his sweat-soaked face with his forearm. "Yeah, I'm home, Mom," he hollered to the other side of the house.

"Lock up, honey. I'm already in bed. I'll see you in the morning. Love you."

"I did, and I love you too." Adrenaline still rocketed

through his veins as he moved through the large open-concept living room, dining area, and kitchen to the left wing he and Staci shared. He knocked on her bedroom door. There was no answer, so he walked down the hall to the glass doors and outside to the brick terrace his father had dug into the side of the mountain several years back. The large jellybean-shaped pool glowed blue. Staci sat in the bubbles of the adjoining hot tub, which was big enough for at least ten, looking up.

"Spot any aliens tonight?"

She turned her head, smiling. "No. Just three shooting stars." She sighed. "I love being here. Summer's going by so fast. Before you know it, we'll have to go home."

He stepped into the warm water and sat on the brick edge, staring out at the bright lights of downtown Park City miles in the distance. "Maybe we can talk Mom and Dad into coming for Christmas. We could ski and go tubing like we did a couple years ago." That was his favorite Christmas. He couldn't remember another time he and Staci laughed so hard, their tubes colliding as they careened down the steep mountain trails.

"Maybe, although I think Mom has her heart set on Paris."

He rolled his eyes, huffing. "I don't see what the big deal is. We've been there a million times."

Laughing, Staci drilled her finger into his stomach. "You're so basic, Tucker."

He grinned, shrugging. "One of us has to be. You and Mom could bankrupt us the way you burn up the plastic."

"I'm happy to spend the money you don't."

He snorted. "So dedicated."

"Darn right. I'm the best part of both of us."

He chuckled, but she was right; she was definitely the better half of the Campbell twins. He would never love anyone more than Staci. "But I'm older."

"By two minutes," she scoffed. "You're always in a rush. I've always chosen to be fashionably late."

"Don't I know it." He tugged on her ponytail. "I need to talk to you about something before you start listing off all of your inflated virtues."

"What?"

"I need the car tomorrow night."

She plopped her hand back in the water, sending small droplets flying over his legs. "It's my turn, Tucker."

"I have a date with Jasmine."

"So?" She leaned her head against the bricks.

"Come on. She's really...important. I've never felt like this about anyone."

"That's what you said about Denise Gordy."

"This is different. When I kissed her, my stomach got all... weird. Please, Staci. You can have the car for a week."

"A week?" Her brows arched as she sat up. "You have my attention."

"I want to take her to the lake. We'll roast marshmallows or something."

She scrunched her nose. "I don't want to know about the 'or something.'"

"Two weeks. You can have the Mustang free and clear for two weeks."

"Deal."

"Yes! This is going to be great."

"I bet." She settled her head again and closed her eyes.

He glanced at his watch. "It's twelve thirty. We should call it a night."

"I'm not tired."

"I'm going in." He stepped from the water and grabbed a towel for his legs. "Make sure you're ready to go by nine thirty. JT and I have to kick some ass on the ball field."

"Good night."

"Night. Lock up on your way in."

"Got it, Dad."

"I've gotta take care of my girls." He imitated Dad's Massachusetts accent perfectly as he repeated what his father had said to him every time he'd gone out of town since he and Staci were little. *Take care of our girls, Tucker*. Tucker reached for the knob.

"Hey, Tucker."

He paused and turned back. "Yeah."

"If you ever drive like that again, I *will* tell Mom. You scared me. I'd like to live to see my seventeenth birthday, and since I love you, I'd like for you to see yours too."

A wave of guilt swamped him as he thought of the way she had screamed. "Sorry. I won't do it again."

"Good."

He reached for the knob again.

"Tucker?"

"What?"

"I would've given you the car for free. I know how much you like Jasmine. You two make a cute couple."

He brightened. "So, deals off?"

"Forget it." She grinned.

"Brat." He grinned back. "See you in the morning."

"Love you, Tuck."

"Love you too, even though you're a brat."

He shut the glass door behind him and glanced at Staci once more before he went to bed.

"Tucker, you need to get up."

He blinked his eyes open in the bright sunshine and pulled off his headphones, which were still belting out Pearl Jam as he looked at his mother. She was all done up for the day in her designer skirt and top. He and Staci had her eyes and black hair, but the rest of their looks were definitely Campbell traits. "What time is it?"

"Just about nine, honey. I'm on my way out. Linda and I are meeting with the interior designer to get some ideas for the living room, then we're going to have lunch. I should be back around two."

His mother redecorated the house every other summer. Mr. Sphen would blow in here in another week or two and rip the rooms to shambles before he set them right with something new.

"Ms. Hayes already brought the groceries by this morning, so there's plenty of food in the fridge."

He sat up. "Good. I'm starving."

"Well that's nothing new." She winked and kissed his forehead. "Have fun today. Dad will be home tomorrow. We're having dinner as a family, so don't make any plans."

"Got it. I'm busy tonight though. I'm going out."

"Isn't it your sister's turn to have the car?"

"Yeah, we made a deal. She gets the Mustang for the next two weeks."

His mother blinked her surprise. "Must be something special." She tossed a pair of dirty gym shorts in his hamper. "Where are you off to?"

"Baseball and swimming." He knew she wasn't asking about what he and Staci were doing today.

She paused as she reached for a wrinkled cotton t-shirt on the floor. "Where are you going tonight, Tucker?"

He threw the covers back and stood. "Oh, I'm taking Jasmine on a date."

"Jasmine? Staci's friend down the street?"

"Yeah."

"She seems like a nice girl. She's very pretty."

"Yeah," he said again, not wanting to have this conversation.

"What do you plan to do?"

"Probably catch a bite to eat or something." He avoided his mother's stare and reached for his towel on the back of the door. He wasn't stupid enough to tell her he was taking Jasmine to the lake so they could...do whatever.

"Well, you make sure you mind your manners, sir. I'm raising a gentleman."

"I will." He'd never planned to be anything but.

She looked at the clock on his bedside table. "Shoot, I need to go. I'll see you this afternoon. Wake your sister. Tell her I said I love her and to have a good day and I'll take a dip with her after dinner—a girls' night in."

He frowned. "She's not up yet?"

"No, I haven't seen her. I guess she decided to sleep in. Bye, honey." She left.

"Bye." His frown deepened. Staci never slept in. She was always up at dawn, no matter how late she went to bed. He walked from his room to the next door over and rapped his knuckles against the wood. "Stace, time to get up." He turned the knob, opening the door a crack. "Get up, Stace. We're going to be late."

Tucker continued down the hall to the kitchen, opened the bag of bagels on the counter, and pushed the plastic lever down. He shoved another in the slots for Staci and got out the cream cheese. Breakfast, a quick shower, then they had to leave. Moments later, the smell of toasted bread wafted through the air, and the bagels popped up. He spread lavish amounts of soft cheese around the doughy disks and licked the edge of his thumb, then he sandwiched Staci's pieces together, took a huge bite of his own, and started toward their wing.

He stopped outside Staci's room, expecting to hear the shower running and Staci's off-key singing, but there was silence instead. "What the hell? Come on, Staci, get up." Annoyed, he barged in. "We're going to be—" He stopped, gaping at Staci lying on the floor, pale, naked and spread eagle, her dark purple hands raised above her head.

"Staci?" Tucker dropped the food and rushed to kneel at his sister's side, staring in horror as his heartbeat throbbed in his skull, struggling to take in the milky green hue of her once-dark hazel eyes and the pinpoints of blood marring the whites. Bruises on her cheekbones and wrists blackened her usually creamy skin. A deep violet indent circled her neck, and a line of dried crimson trailed from her bluish lips to her ear and kept going. Cold sweat beaded his forehead and dribbled down his back as he reached out. This was wrong. Everything about this was wrong. He wanted to shake her and make her blink and breathe, but her long, slender neck was gouged with the ugly purple marks. “Staci?” he shuddered out again as he touched her shoulder, flinching as his trembling fingers made contact with her icy skin. He jerked away, wanting to scream, but the sound stuck in his throat as his stomach revolted. He turned, puking up his bite of bagel and bile, then looked at his sister and hurried from the room for the phone.

He didn’t remember picking up the receiver or dialing 9-1-1, but a woman’s calm voice echoed in his ear like a loud buzz. He walked back to the room, unable to clear the fog from his mind while he stared at his sister’s lifeless body and crouched down, holding her cool, rigid hand. “My sister’s dead,” he said dully. “Staci’s dead.”

☙ Chapter Two ❧

Los Angeles
October 2014

Chaos reigned at the Cooke estate, but that was nothing new. Children ran about—two bullets with blonde hair, screaming and laughing as they dashed from room to room. Beautiful women in different stages of pregnancy or parenthood held pretty-eyed babies, standing in noisy herds, chatting away. The men of Ethan Cooke Security hid from the pandemonium, playing a round of poker on the windblown deck as waves crashed against the cliffs below.

Tucker sipped his beer, glanced at his crappy hand, and continued his study of the sassy black-haired goddess cooing at Morgan and Hunter's new son, Jacob, in the living room. No one wore a pair of jeans the way Wren Cooke did. Her slim, petite body was a work of art. She grinned at something Morgan said as she handed Jacob back to his eager mother, and her gray eyes met his through the panes of glass. Her smile faded as he held her gaze. Seconds passed before she looked away. A small smile touched his lips, and he took another sip of the dark brew, focusing on the game and his friends crowding the table.

"You in?" Ethan asked.

Tucker glanced at his pair of threes. “Nah, I’m folding.” He set his cards face down and leaned back in his chair, watching as the hand played out. He didn’t have jack shit to work with; neither did Jackson, he could tell. His fellow bodyguard kept sliding his shiny wedding band round and round with his thumb. Ethan appeared to have something. He licked his lips like a damn lizard—little darts here and there—whenever he had good cards. Hunter, however, had a champion poker face. He wasn’t giving anything away. Tucker had been scrutinizing his pals’ ‘tells’ for the last hour. Never hurt to keep them in mind for the next time.

Hunter threw another chip to the center of the table. “I’ll raise you.”

Austin sighed and set down his hand. “I’m out.”

Ethan chuckled sinisterly and tossed in two more chips.

“Son of a bitch.” Jackson shook his head. “Folding.”

“Call it,” Hunter said smirking as he laid out a royal flush.

“Fuck.” Ethan set down his four-of-a-kind and Hunter snickered as he pulled the tidy pool in his direction. “One of these days you’ll beat me, Cooke. Maybe.”

“Kiss ass, Phillips.”

Kylee and Olivia pounded on the window, smiling and waving at their fathers. Jackson and Ethan smiled and waved back. Then the girls took off again.

“Looks like they’ll sleep well tonight,” Jackson said.

“Sleep? What’s that?” Hunter stretched and peered through the glass, staring at his wife and infant son. “Jake’s up every two hours pooping and snacking.”

“It’ll get better,” Ethan assured him. “Couple more months and you and Morgan will be catching a solid six or seven. Emma’s sleeping again now that those teeth finally poked through. The last few days sucked around here.”

Hailey’s laugh carried through the air, and Austin glanced toward the bright lights of the living room. “I just want my wife back. Her emotions are all over the place. One minute she’s smiling, the next we’re mopping up tears.”

"Four more months," Hunter reminded Austin. "Four more months and things will be normal again." He smiled at Morgan. "Actually, they'll be better."

"Thank God," Austin said as he picked up his Corona and took a swig. "So, we had our ultrasound yesterday."

"And?" Ethan restacked his chips.

"It's a boy." Austin beamed. "We're having a boy."

Jackson paused mid-shuffle and grinned. "Congratulations, man."

Hunter slapped Austin's back. "Way to go. We've gotta even things out around here. The females are taking over. Jake's going to need a playmate."

Jackson dealt out the next round. "Alex and I might be able to help out, unless we have another girl."

Tucker reached for his cards, stopping midway. "Alexa's pregnant?"

"Ten weeks yesterday. Alex finally gave me the okay to tell people. My parents are going ape shit, and Liv can't wait to be a big sister."

"Good stuff, man." Tucker bumped his knuckles. "Damn good stuff." He knew how much Jackson wanted this. Things were finally settling down at the Matthews household. Abby got a place of her own shortly after the wedding in August. Even though security was still a priority for the Matthews/Harris women, life appeared to be moving in the right direction.

Tucker reached for the cards again as he caught sight of Wren talking to her Ken-doll date. Then she started down the hall toward the kitchen.

"I'm going to sit this round out and grab another beer," he said. "Anybody else want one?"

Hunter grunted, Ethan and Austin shook their heads, and Jackson flat-out ignored him while he swiped a hand through his hair. Tucker grinned. Matthews actually had something this time.

He strolled down the long deck and opened the French

doors to the spacious kitchen. Loaded party platters, chafing dishes, soft drinks, plates, napkins and utensils cluttered every available inch of marble countertop. The Cookes knew how to entertain. He scanned the leafy green salads and mounds of fruit in a bowl, then zeroed in on what he really wanted.

He studied yards of wavy black hair cascading down a slim back, a small firm ass in snug jeans, and a fitted black blouse hugging generous curves while Wren stood on her tiptoes, struggling to free something from the refrigerator.

"Come on. Being short really sucks sometimes," she muttered.

Never one to miss an opportunity, Tucker walked up behind her, enjoying the sexy French perfume that immediately invaded his nose. His body brushed hers as he reached for the dill pickles crammed in the back on the top shelf.

Gasping, Wren whirled and looked up. Her perky breasts pressed against his solid chest, and her generous lush lips he wouldn't mind tasting firmed in disapproval. He stared into her striking pale gray eyes, which were accentuated by dark rings, watching her straight black brows furrow as she frowned. "What are you doing?"

"Helping you out." He leaned forward, pushing their bodies closer. He stared at her mouth as he grabbed the pickles. Electricity hummed and snapped, vibrating through his body as her breath shuddered out once, twice. "Here you go."

"I—" She took the jar. "Thanks."

"No problem."

She gave him a one-handed push to the chest. "Back up."

He took a step back as he continued to study his boss's baby sister—the female replica of Ethan Cooke, except Wren's cheekbones were sharper and her nose smaller and more feminine. The Cookes were no slouches in the looks department. "Ethan should get a stool in here."

Her eyes narrowed a fraction as she smiled and stepped forward, closing the gap between them. "Who needs one when I'm surrounded by so many fine studs?" She traced her well-manicured finger down his chest.

He clenched his jaw as her smoky voice caressed his libido—as did her finger still traveling south. He grabbed her wrist, stopping her an inch above the button on his jeans, and held her gaze. "Easy, Cooke. I'm not that kind of guy. I like to be wined and dined before I move to the bedroom." Like hell. He'd clear the counter off here and now. They rarely saw one another—barely knew each other, but there was something about Wren Cooke that got his blood moving. He'd been attracted to her since the first moment he'd laid eyes on her several months before.

She shot him a sly smile as she scoffed and pulled her arm free. "I bet." She walked over to the small sandwich station, which held a large variety of meats and cheeses to choose from. "You don't strike me as a strawberries and champagne kind of guy."

He followed her and leaned against the countertop. "Maybe not, but I'm willing to try anything once."

She glanced up from the roasted turkey and avocado on whole wheat she was building, then looked back down.

He smiled.

She peeked up from under her long lashes, and his smile turned into a grin.

"Why do you do that?"

"What's that?" He grabbed a piece of Colby Jack from the platter, folded it in half, and bit in.

"Stare at me. Every time I see you, you're staring in my direction."

He shrugged.

"If you didn't work for my brother, I would think you were a creep, but he screens his guards too well for that to be an option." She started laying ham slices on a thick cut of rye.

"Maybe you fascinate me."

She paused with another piece of meat in her hand, then continued her work. "Maybe you're full of crap."

He certainly wasn't—not in this case anyway—but he grinned again when her movements turned jerky as she piled cold cuts too high. Damn, there was something about her.

"And that. Why do you have to do that all the time?"

He shook his head. "You lost me."

"Smile that smug smile."

He chuckled this time. "What can I say? I'm happy."

She muttered something under her breath as she smooshed the top piece of rye onto the gargantuan sandwich.

"That's quite a sandwich. You make that for me?"

"No." She picked up the pickle jar and struggled with the lid.

He pulled the damp glass from her hands, popped the top with little effort, and handed it back.

Her fingers brushed his as she yanked the jar away, and green juice sloshed dangerously close to the top. "I would've gotten it eventually."

"You're welcome."

She huffed as she stabbed a fat pickle with a fork. "Aren't you playing poker?"

"I think I'm talking to you." Christ, this was fun. "You were going to tell me who that sandwich is for."

"My date. I made it for my date."

He nodded. "New guy since the last time. In fact, I've never seen the same man twice."

"So?"

"Just an observation."

She glared. "Are you trying to insinuate something?"

He arched his brow, surprised by how defensive she was becoming. "No."

"Let me clue you in on a little secret. This is 2014, mister. I'm a successful businesswoman and have no desire to settle down. I don't believe in soul mates, and I think marriage is a bunch of crap—for some people, especially people like me. I realize I descend from the infamous Grant and Rene Cooke of Beverly Hills, but my parents don't define me. I date around, but that doesn't mean I sleep around. Got it?"

He winced. Sensitive subject. "Easy, tiger. I just came in for a beer and conversation. I didn't want to start World War Three."

She picked up the two plates and turned, but not before he saw the flash of misery in her eyes.

He grabbed her arm, turning her back. "Hey, I don't care who you date. It's none of my business."

"I agree."

"So what gives? You don't strike me as the type of woman who gives a shit about what other people think."

"I don't."

But she did—clearly. "Good."

She gave him a small smile. "I should go." She started toward the door.

"Hey, Cooke, wanna grab a bite to eat sometime?" Never hurt to ask.

She stopped in the doorway. "I don't date cops."

"I'm not a cop."

"You were. Besides, I'm happy with Mark."

He frowned. Who the hell was Mark?

"I think we have something going—a connection. We just met a week ago, but he's...important."

Bullshit. He didn't know her very well, but he'd figured out a while back that Wren didn't let men become important. He grinned. "Got it."

"See you around." She took a step.

"Hey, Cooke."

She stopped.

"His name is Mike."

"Huh?"

"You're date. His name is Mike."

His eyes held hers as she turned and walked away without another word.

Mike pulled into the driveway and rolled to a stop behind Wren's sleek Mercedes Roadster. The ten-minute drive from Ethan's had been long enough for him to start his spiel on capital gains and investing. She tried to focus on the conversation, but her mind kept wandering to dark hazel eyes and a slow, sexy grin. She remembered the way Tucker sandwiched her between the cool air of the refrigerator and the sizzling heat of his tough, muscular body. Wafts of his cologne still tickled her nose, curling her belly into a tight ball of lust.

"...best option was to sell."

She came to attention as Mike smiled. What did he just say? "Sounds like a good plan," she tried, hoping that was the right answer.

"I agree."

She sighed her relief when that response seemed to work and opened her door.

Mike met her at the hood and walked with her to her front entryway. "I really like your friends and family."

"Me too. They're pretty great."

"Thanks for bringing me along."

"No problem. I'm glad all the noise didn't scare you away." Although that might have been the plan. As much as she hated to admit it, Mike bored her cross-eyed. He was more of a cigar jacket and Chopin kind of man, and she wasn't interested.

He smiled and leaned in for a kiss.

Warm lips touched hers, but she felt nothing. Her heart didn't beat faster. She didn't see stars. The mocking hazel eyes of another taunted her, and she put a little more effort into the embrace, pulling him closer with her hands on his shoulders, but it was no use. Michael Collins was a dud. Wren eased back. "Thanks for coming along. I should get inside. I still have work to do."

"Okay. I'll call you soon."

No, he wouldn't. She'd played this game too many times not to recognize the disappointment in his eyes. He wasn't feeling anything earth-shattering either. "Mike, I think we should probably think about keeping things friendly. I'm not really looking for anything romantic."

He blinked. "You're not?"

She shook her head.

"That's great. God, that's great." He winced and patted her arm. "Sorry."

"Don't be. You're a nice guy, but I don't think we have a lot in common." She took his hand. "It was nice meeting you."

He gave her fingers a gentle squeeze. "You too. Maybe I'll see you around some time."

"Okay. Bye." She pulled her keys from her purse as Mike walked down the lighted path, letting herself into her spacious four-bedroom, five-bath masterpiece she'd painstakingly redesigned herself. Bold, jewel-toned colors welcomed her, a perfect match for her personality. She set her Gucci bag down on the solid wood entry table, slipped off her heels, and wrinkled her nose as she looked at the alarm system she'd once again forgotten to arm. If Ethan found out, she would never hear the end of it. She punched her code into the panel and glanced at the clock in the living room, groaning. Ten-thirty and she had at least two more hours of work to plow through before she could call it a night.

Whining wasn't going to get it done. She walked in the dark to the kitchen and poured herself half a glass of red wine, then took the stairs to her home office. She booted up her computer, pressed the button on her phone to retrieve her voice mail, and made herself comfortable in her soft leather chair. Leaning back, she closed her eyes and flexed her aching toes while she listened to her assistant list off her schedule for the upcoming day. Patrick had jammed each hour full as usual—the price of a thriving business. Thank

God she loved it. She could do without the fifteen-hour days on occasion, but they came with the territory. Patrick clicked off and the next message started. "Hey, Wren. Rex here."

Her eyes popped open and she rolled them as the deep, gritty voice filled the room.

"It's been two weeks and you haven't called me back—still. I know I had a little too much to drink and acted like a jerk, but I want to make it up to you. I—"

She skipped to the next message, cutting him off. "Buy a clue, buddy, and stop calling." He'd called every day for the last two weeks. She had no intention of seeing Rex Richardson again. He was handsome and successful. His grandfather was Los Angeles's infamous hard-hitting DA. Too bad Rex didn't inherit DA Richardson's manners and integrity. Instead, he was a slimebag who didn't understand that dinner out didn't automatically lead to a romp in the sheets. An elbow to the solar plexus and a knee to the balls had cleared that up when a simple 'no' hadn't done the job. Ethan taught her how to take care of herself long ago. She'd never had to defend herself before, and hoped she wouldn't have to again.

She logged on to her computer as the next deep voice filled the room.

"Hi, Wren. It's JT Cartwright." He cleared his throat. "Uh, I don't want to be forward. Okay, yes I do, or I wouldn't be calling..."

She stopped scanning her mile-long list of unopened e-mails and smiled at his friendly candor.

"I was wondering if you might want to grab a meal together sometime this week. I've enjoyed talking to you over the last couple months. I'd like to get to know you better. It's getting pretty late, so I'll talk to you tomorrow. I'll be at my parents' estate for most of the morning. I'm sure I'll see you there. We can talk then. Bye."

JT Cartwright, son of one of her biggest clients. He was sweet, good looking, and one of the city's top defense attorneys. And she wasn't the least bit interested. Sighing, she pressed her fingers to her temple. "What's *wrong* with me?"

She caught another whiff of cologne and covered her face with her hands. "No," she scolded herself. Tucker Campbell was *not* the issue. His in-your-face sexy barely affected her. That slow grin and powerful underwear model's body of his was no big deal. "Damn," she murmured as she lied to herself.

How long would it take her to get him out of her mind this time? If she had known Tucker was going to be at Ethan's tonight, she would've bowed out of the evening. His broody distance, thick black hair, and firm chin constantly darkened with five o'clock shadow should've been considered a crime against humanity. No one had the right to be so devastatingly...hot. He was downright irresistible, with his subtle, wounded charm and lips that begged to be kissed. And he *knew* it. He *knew* he made her jittery when he stood too close and stared at her the way he did. "No," she said louder as she opened the first set of pictures Patrick had taken of her newest client's bedroom and bath. This is where she needed to focus: on her job.

She clicked from photo to photo, and visions of how the drab rooms could be transformed overshadowed her unsettling inability to forget about a man she didn't want to be interested in.

☙ Chapter Three ❧

Wren studied the inventory sheet she pulled from the FedEx box and grinned. "Perfect." The final touches she ordered for the Cartwrights' fireplace had arrived. She had put a rush on the antique gold mantle clock and matching candleholders, thankful her supplier had come through again on short notice.

Lenora Cartwright decided at the last minute to throw a gathering in her newly decorated library, despite Wren's not-so-subtle hints that she wasn't ready for the big reveal. Lenora assured her a piece missing here and there wasn't a big deal. The space was beautiful—everything Lenora had hoped for—and she wanted to show it off, but Wren's vision wasn't complete, which meant it wasn't perfect. Cooke Interiors accepted nothing less than perfection for their clients.

She glanced at her watch and winced. She had two hours to make everything right before the florists and caterers invaded the mansion. With time ticking away, Wren cut the tape from the largest box and pulled the flaps back. She gasped as she freed the gorgeous, overly extravagant timepiece from layers of bubble wrap. "I knew it. This is exactly right." She stroked the gold leaf, which had just a touch of old European flair, then set it gently down and dove in the next parcel for the rest of the contents. Gasping again, she suppressed the need to do a victory dance as she caressed ornately twisted candlesticks. "Wait 'til Lenora sees this. She's going to flip."

She brought the delicately feminine clock with her to the old-fashioned fireplace and set the piece dead center on the custom-made white marble mantle. Eyes narrowed, she took a step back, scrutinizing the enormous painting of an elegant English tea garden occupying several feet of the huge wall, the oriental rugs she'd chosen, and the newest gold accents pulling all the pieces together.

Mrs. Cartwright wanted her library to reflect her passion for old world Europe, and she was getting it in spades. This one room had taken Wren months to design from demolition to candlesticks. It was hands-down one of her best accomplishments. She blinked back tears of pride as she walked to the table and placed tapered candles in leafy holders, finishing the job once and for all.

"Wow."

Her gaze flew to the door, and she stared in utter surprise. What was he doing here?

"Look at this place, Cooke. It's incredible." Tucker strolled through the book-laden room in black boots, snug, dark blue designer jeans, and a form-fitting white long-sleeve shirt rolled halfway up his powerful forearms. Holy God, he looked amazing. And she could already smell hints of his cologne. Two encounters in less than twenty-four hours was completely unacceptable.

Frowning, she gripped the slim, tapered wax too tight. "How did you know I was here?"

"Oh, when I'm not working, I'm a part-time stalker." He sent her one of his slow grins.

She stabbed the last candle in its designated spot and turned with the candlestick in hand. "Why are you here, Tucker?" She set the heavy antique on the right side of the mantle and hurried back for the second as her euphoric moment from a job well done quickly nosedived into lustful nerves.

"Sarah asked me to drop something off."

"Sarah?" She frowned again as she set the accent in place. "Why would Sarah ask you to drop something off at my client's home?"

"Technically, Ethan did—sort of. I stopped by the house—forgot my wallet last night. Sarah was running around trying to get the girls ready for their checkups when she remembered she never gave you the earrings you wanted to borrow." He held up a small felt jeweler's case. "Ethan was on his way out the door. He handed me the box, hollered an address, and told me to bring these to you."

She'd forgotten about the diamond dangles herself after her encounter with Tucker in the kitchen. She'd thought of little else while she tossed and turned throughout the night, showered this morning, ate her breakfast, and drove to work. Lenora's impromptu party and her scramble to come up with the final missing accents had been an excellent distraction. She'd been back on track, then he walked in here smelling like sin, fuddling her brain once more. "Thanks." She turned back to her candlesticks, dismissing him, hoping he would get the hint as she moved the chunky gold ever so slightly. One of the tall tapers fell, and she reached out, catching the candle mid-flight.

"Good hands."

Ignoring him, she stood on her tiptoes, struggling to put the smooth white wax back where it belonged.

Strong hands wrapped around her waist, lifting her off the ground. She gasped, glancing over her shoulder, finding herself eye to eye and inches from Tucker's firm, kissable lips. "What are you doing?"

"Helping you out."

She turned back and placed the candle in the empty space. "All set."

He lowered her the six or so inches to the floor, and she turned to face him. "You didn't have to do that. I would've gotten it."

He nodded. "I'm sure. This place has plenty of ladders and stools, but this was faster." He studied the two-thousand-square-foot space. "Why the hell does anybody need something so big? Three floors' worth of books. There's gotta be at least two million volumes in here."

Sometimes she wondered the same thing, but how people spent their money wasn't her concern. "Good tax write-off I guess."

He zeroed in on the fireplace and took a step back, measuring the space with narrowed eyes.

"What?"

He shrugged. "The gold doodads and fireplace are foo-fooey and kinda ugly, but somehow they complement each other and work really well. You did a nice job."

She met his gaze and her brow winged up. "'A nice job?' I did an *excellent* job. I've eaten, breathed, and dreamed of this room for the last five months of my life, and I still have the pool area, the master suite, six bedrooms, and the ballroom to handle."

"How big *is* this place?"

"Twenty-two thousand square feet, including the twenty-car garage."

He whistled through his teeth and rubbed his index, middle finger, and thumb together. "The insanely rich. Good stuff."

"Good enough."

He glanced at his watch. "It's past lunch time."

Her stomach grumbled. The bowl of yogurt she'd scarfed down at five a.m. was no longer doing the trick. "I know. I'm starved."

"I was going to grab a sandwich. Wanna come?"

"No." She smirked. His physique in that outfit and cocky hazel eyes had already packed all the punch she could handle for one day. "I brought a salad."

"No to dinner. No to lunch." He sniffed his pits. "Do I

stink or something?"

She bit her cheek to hide her smile. She would not give in to his charming persistence. "You smell fine. I'm just not interested."

He sat on the edge of a study table. "I'm not sure I believe you, Cooke."

She didn't believe herself, so she clung to her favorite excuse. "I've already told you, I don't date cops."

"Ah, that's right." He crossed his arms at his chest, settling in. "Is it LAPD or all officers in general?"

She didn't actually have a problem with the police. She'd made the whole thing up months ago when she rushed into Sarah's temporary hospital room and spotted Detective Tucker Campbell perched on the side of her sister-in-law's bed, interviewing her after her horrifying experience with her stalker. He'd turned his head, met her eyes, and effectively knocked her breathless with one look. She'd never experienced such a raw, primal attraction to anyone the way she did Tucker. The moment had shaken her up, but she'd dismissed the entire thing, certain she would never see him again, until Ethan shared with her that Tucker had quit the force to join the staff of Ethan Cooke Security. Her 'cop rule' had been implemented right then and there—present officers, retired officers, but more importantly, detectives. Policemen were officially off the list of potential candidates for a night out on the town. "Pretty much all boys in blue."

He tilted his head. "Why?"

Why? Crap. What was she supposed to say? "You have god complexes." Yeah, that was it.

"God Complexes?"

"Mmhm. You're used to giving orders and having them followed. Most of you think you're above the laws you work so hard to enforce." She cleared her throat, looking away as she realized how lame she sounded.

Tucker grinned. "I see. What if I promise to put my complex on hold for a couple hours?" He yanked her forward with his hands on her waist, nestling her between his legs.

Surprised, she stared in his eyes. Their mouths were inches from one another, and they breathed each other's breath.

"Come on, Cooke." His gaze darted from her eyes to her lips and back again as his thumbs traced slow circles along the bottom of her ribs. "I won't even frisk you—unless you want me to."

Delicious tingles traveled from her spine, to her tummy, to her center. Tucker Campbell would be a hell of a frisker. She moved her hands to rest on his firm shoulders. "I—"

"It'll be fun," he whispered. "Promise."

She licked her lips, craving his. One lunch. How bad could one lunch be? "I—"

Someone cleared their throat, and Wren looked toward the doorway. Her sexual fog dissipated enough to recognize the Cartwright's son.

"JT!" Shaking her head, she sprung away from Tucker and grabbed hold of the distraction like a lifeline. "JT, come on in."

"Sorry to interrupt." He smiled.

"No. You weren't. You weren't interrupting anything," she said too quickly as she glanced at Tucker.

He grinned and stood.

She pressed a hand to her temple in an attempt to gather her scattered thoughts. "Um, Tucker Campbell, this is JT Cartwright."

Tucker's grin vanished into a look of surprise. "JT? Son of a bitch." He walked forward and held out his hand. "I didn't recognize you."

"Well, what do you know?" JT grabbed Tucker in a quick "guy hug." "My man, Tucker."

Wren frowned at the odd combination: Tucker, with his sinful bad boy looks, and JT with his horn rims, slightly receding hairline, and two-thousand-dollar designer suit. "You know each other?"

"Tucker and I go way back."

"Oh."

"We used to spend summers together in Park City—played ball, went to movies, had a hell of a time," JT supplied.

Tucker shoved his hands in his pockets. "Yeah."

"How're your parents?"

"Pretty good."

Wren studied Tucker. Something was wrong. Something had changed. Tucker's cockiness had vanished.

Tucker peeked at his watch. "I should probably head out—gotta work tonight."

"Detective, right? Mom said she ran into your dad a couple years ago."

"No. Bodyguard. I work for Wren's brother."

"Huh. We should grab a beer sometime and catch up." JT pulled a business card from his slacks and a pen from the table and scribbled something on the back. "That's my cell. Give me a call."

"Definitely." Tucker pocketed the card. "See you around." He looked at Wren. "Later, Cooke."

What just happened? "Uh, excuse me for one second," she said to JT and dashed after Tucker as fast as her snug pencil skirt and suede pumps would allow. "Tucker." He kept going. His quick strides caused her to pick up her pace even more. "Tucker, wait."

He stopped but didn't turn.

She skirted around him, coming to stand in front of him. "Are you okay?"

"Yeah, fine." He looked her in the eye as he answered, but his words were stiff and his shoulders tense.

"Tucker?" She grabbed his hand.

He pulled gently away. "I've gotta split." Pivoting, he walked out the door.

She stared after him for several seconds, struggling to unravel the mystery of Tucker Campbell. She'd seen that distant, wounded look a couple times before and wondered about him then as she did now. She preferred smug over sad any day.

Her phone rang, vibrating against her hip. What did Patrick want now? He'd called at least a dozen times throughout the morning with client concerns, demands, and schedule adjustments. Sighing, she pulled her cell phone from the sleek leather holder she wore when she was out at a site and groaned, recognizing Rex's number.

As if the evening calls to the house weren't enough, now he was moving to her business line? Pathetic. "Keep waiting, pal, and hold your breath while you're at it," she muttered, shoving the cell back in the case as she walked to the library, quieting her steps as JT spoke on his cell phone and fiddled with one of the candlesticks on the mantle.

"I'll need that file scanned over to me as soon as you can. Thanks, Charlotte." He hung up and turned.

Wren's phone beeped, alerting her to a voicemail. "Give it a rest, jerk."

JT sent her a questioning glance. "Everything all right?"

"Yeah." She huffed out a breath. "Someone's having a little trouble understanding that I have no desire to repeat a disastrous evening out. He keeps calling my house and has decided to give my business line a try today."

"That's harassment. I can take you down to the police station if you want. We can file a report."

"I think I'm good. He'll get the point eventually."

"Are you sure?"

"Yeah, but thanks for the offer."

"No problem." He cleared his throat and rocked back on his heels. "Wren, I'm sorry. I feel like an idiot. When I asked you out last night... I didn't realize you were seeing someone. You and Tucker..."

"Oh, we're not."

His well-sculpted brow winged high.

She could only imagine how their little...embrace had looked. "He works for my brother. We're just...friends." That wasn't the right word. She had no idea how to categorize herself and Tucker, but ‘friend’ would do for now. “But I think we should talk.”

He winced. “Uh oh. ‘Talk’ is never a positive sign after you’ve asked someone out.”

She smiled apologetically. “I’m flattered by your offer, JT, I really am. I’m just not in a place where I’m looking for a relationship.”

He nodded. “Okay. No biggie.”

“You sure?”

“Absolutely.”

“Good, I don’t want things to be weird. I’ll be spending a lot of time here during the rest of the remodel.” Guilt swamped her as she stared into his kind brown eyes. “Are you going to Tatiana Livingston’s ‘End Famine Now’ gala on Friday?”

“Wouldn’t miss it.”

“Would you like to be my date? I would love to spend the evening with a friend.”

“I’ll pick you up at eight.”

She smiled. “Let me give you my address.”

He crept up the stairs in the dark, even though he knew he was alone. Sneaking around somehow heightened the moment as he breathed in Wren’s scent and wandered from guestroom to bathroom, master suite to office, touching her things—the pricey vase set atop the fancy table, the sweeping curtains on huge windows overlooking the well-tended back yard.

She had expensive taste. Her home was classy and beautiful, with a subtle hint of flair—just like Wren. Her looks alone filled him with desire, but these delicious new developments made her downright irresistible. He had to have Wren Cooke—*had* to.

It had been so long since he’d played this game. He was

ready to try again. Getting to work, he walked about the pretty space, unsure of what he was looking for. But he would know when he found it. He sat in the soft leather chair, opening the desk drawers, the filing cabinets, pressing play, listening to numerous voicemails, when Wren's leather-bound planner caught his eye. He flipped through the last couple months, noting several dinner dates among the meetings and various other activities. He smiled as he read 'Rex Richardson' penciled in toward the end of September, Michael Collins this past Sunday, and JT Cartwright as her guest for tomorrow night's Gala.

He sat back, steepling his fingers, thinking of all the ways he could officially introduce himself to Wren. She was about to get to know him in a way she never had before. Grinning with the rush of anticipation, he studied the framed picture of Wren's brother and his happy little family posed in blue jeans and crisp white shirts with the ocean in the background. He chuckled as he zeroed in on Ethan Cooke's wife, knowing how the festivities would begin. Some things were just perfect.

He dropped his hands and settled himself more comfortably, then rushed to his feet as the beam of headlights cut across the wall. He hurried to the edge of the window, peeking out as Wren stepped from her pretty little Mercedes, talking on her phone, reaching for her bags. She was stunning in her tailored slacks and blouse. It was tempting to stick around and greet her, but that would be for another day.

He hustled down the hall to the master suite and let himself out the back, as Wren opened the front door, coming in for the night.

☙ Chapter Four ❧

Somehow Monday had turned into Friday. Consultations, virtual mockups, and buying trips for several clients' homes consumed every hour except for the five or six Wren allowed herself for sleep. That's what she wanted to do now more than anything—take a shower, slap together something quick to eat, and pull the covers up on her king-sized bed, but oblivion would have to wait. JT was due to pick her up in forty-five minutes. Canceling with less than an hour's notice wasn't an option. Sighing, Wren punched 'one' on her cell and listened to it ring.

"Cooke."

"Hey, big brother."

"Who's this?"

Confused, she pulled the phone away from her ear. "It's Wren."

"Wren... Wren... That name sounds vaguely familiar."

She smiled. "I get it. I've been a stranger."

"A guy starts to take it personal when he doesn't see or hear from his baby sister from time to time."

She rolled her eyes. "Give me a break. You're just as busy as I am, with my beautiful nieces, your lovely wife, and a somewhat successful business."

He chuckled. "Wanna compare profit margins?"

Ethan Cooke Security blew Cooke Interiors out of the water, but she was still doing just fine. "Not really."

"Did you change your mind? Are you coming to Hawaii with us?"

"I wish I could, but I can't. I figure at this rate, I'll be able to take a week off when Kylee's ready for college."

"Hmm... We'll have to find a way to do better than that. Why don't you hire another designer to help with the load?"

She'd been toying with the idea of taking on an associate; eventually she would have no choice, but she liked seeing to every detail and bringing her clients' dreams to life on her own. "Maybe some day."

"We're going to miss you. The whole gang's going—Morgan and Hunter, Hailey and Austin."

"Don't rub it in. I have too much work, especially with the Portland Project coming up. And *someone* from the Cooke clan should be here for Abby's fashion debut next Thursday. It's a good thing I'm willing to pick up your slack, big brother."

"I appreciate it. Sarah already arranged for a flower delivery."

Wren slowed and pulled in her driveway. "Ethan, I just got home. I'm going to have to cut this short. I need to get ready for the gala."

"Tell Tatiana hello from Sarah and me."

"I will." Holding the phone with her shoulder, she gathered up her briefcase and laptop bag.

"We'll be gone for the month with Sarah's photo shoots and the renovations."

"I talked to your contractor myself this morning. Let Sarah know I'll send over the preliminaries for the new studio and guest rooms tomorrow."

"Will do. Hunter and Austin will be with me for the next couple of weeks, but Jackson, Tucker, and Jerrod are still around if you need anything."

A wave of love consumed her as she got out of the car

and closed the door. Ethan was a great big brother—the only family member she'd ever been able to count on. "Thanks, but you don't have to worry about me. I want you to have fun. Hug Sarah for me and give the girls a kiss from Auntie Wren."

"You got it. Love you."

"Love you too. Bye."

"Bye."

Smiling, she hung up and made her way toward the house in the dark. She'd forgotten to leave the porch light on again. If Ethan ever found out she deactivated the motion lights he'd installed after Sarah's issues with her stalker, he would kick her butt.

She took the first two steps to the entry and reached forward, feeling around for the knob, sending the key into the lock. She opened the door and barely missed stepping on an object on the top step. Squinting, she bent closer, recognizing the mystery item as flowers. Her clammy hand fell away from the cool brushed nickel, and her heart skipped a beat as she stood slowly. Blue roses.

Trembling, she looked over her shoulder and hurried inside, slamming the door, locking it, turning on every light with the security panel at her side. Why were blue roses laying on her steps? She pressed her back to the solid wood as her eyes darted toward the living room, kitchen, and up the stairs, half expecting to see the sick freak who had tortured Sarah. *Ezekiel Denmire is dead,* she reassured herself.

She set her bags down with a thud and pressed 'one' on the cell phone she still clutched tight, her breath shuddering out as the phone rang.

"Cooke," came her brother's familiar voice.

She could hear Kylee laughing in the background. "You can't get me, Daddy."

"Hold on, honey. Wren?"

Another fit of laughter filled her ear, and Wren took a deep breath. Ethan was busy with his family. "Whoops. Hit the wrong number." She closed her eyes and opened them just as quickly, willing the terror away. All she had to do was say come and he would be here.

"You okay?"

"Yup." She glanced wearily at the dark beyond the windows. "Meant to call Patrick. He's number two on my speed dial. Sorry."

"Guess I'll talk to you later then. Bye."

"Bye." She ended the call, and her phone vibrated, alerting her to a new text. On edge, she jumped as she glanced at the sender. She didn't recognize the number but opened the message anyway.

Do you like them? They're just for you. I'm still waiting. Nineteen days.

Her heart accelerated to a dizzying beat as fear and anger warred inside her. She stared at the screen in disbelief. "You sick bastard. Keep it up and you'll be on a fast-track to a jail cell." She'd thought she was finished with Rex. This was his first attempt at contact since his call to her business line on Monday. More pissed off now than afraid, she saved the message, yanked opened her door, and snapped a picture of the disgusting 'surprise' Rex left her. She grabbed up the dethorned stems, slammed the door behind her, locked it, and headed for the trash, shoving the flowers into the Glad bag with vengeful purpose. She'd be damned if she was going to think about his sick games for one more moment. JT would be here in less than half an hour, and she would be ready. Rex Richardson had another thing coming if he thought she was going to cower to his foolish tactics. She passed the alarm panel on her way up the stairs, hesitating, backing up, then punched in her code, waiting for the red light to flash. Then she resumed her path toward the shower.

Twenty minutes later, Wren hurried downstairs in her fitted spaghetti strap cocktail gown. The A-line cut in pretty powder blue accentuated her slim figure and subtle curves, while the severe slit up the right leg showed off plenty of thigh and her fabulous strappy ice-pick heels—her favorite part of the entire ensemble. She'd spotted the shoes at Sarah's mother's boutique, fell in love, then found the dress to go with them.

She stopped in front of the hallway mirror and slicked her lips with light pink gloss seconds before the doorbell rang. She shoved the tube of lipstick in her small bag, gave herself a final once-over, and headed for the door, ready to get this evening over with. Hopefully she and JT could dance a few times, mingle for a bit, then leave. Her flight left at eight tomorrow morning, and she had yet to pack.

She reached for the knob, pausing as she thought of the blue roses, and peeked out the window, spotting JT done up in a tux. She sighed her relief, unarmed the alarm for the time being, and opened the door with a smile. "Hello."

JT's eyes widened. "Wow, Wren, you're a vision." He pulled a single white rose from behind his back. "I'll be the luckiest guy in the room."

She smiled again, accepting the sweet gesture, wishing the pretty bloom could be any other flower. "Thank you. Come on in while I put this in water."

JT stepped inside, walking with her to her spacious kitchen she'd redone in whites, creams, and stainless steel. "Very nice space."

"I like it." She unearthed a bud vase from below the sink, setting the delicate glass on the black marble countertop while she studied JT's attractive face and boxer's build accentuated in his tuxedo. "Something's different."

He pointed to his brown eyes. "Contacts for the big event."

She nodded as she filled the glass and placed the rose in water. "Aha. That's it. You're quite handsome, Mr. Cartwright."

"Thank you." He extended his arm. "Are you ready to go?"

"I am." They made their way out the door, and she sent

her key in the lock, stopping. "Hold on. Let me set my alarm." She dashed inside, dealt with the panel and activated the motion sensors for good measure. She pressed another function, overriding the silent setting. If Rex came back, the state-of-the art system would give him one hell of a jolt, along with most of the neighborhood. She smiled as she stepped into the cool October evening. *You're messing with the wrong woman, Rex Richardson*. "Let's go have some fun."

Tatiana Livingston and Jam, America's current chart-topping pop band, kept Tucker and half-a-dozen of his pals scrambling for the first hour-and-a-half of the End Famine Now fundraising event. They'd more than earned their pay while they dealt with one mishap after another—breaking up fights between the lead singer and the drummer, dealing with the bass guitarist's hysterical wife when she barged in on her husband bopping a couple of the groupies, but the *coup de gras* had been two fans rushing the stage during one of Tatiana's live televised spiels, encouraging viewers to call in with their pledges to end world hunger. Cameras continued to roll while Tucker and Jerrod sent the over-enthusiastic men sprawling mere feet from one of Hollywood's biggest stars and dragged them away, handing them over to the waiting police.

With the worst behind them—he hoped—Tucker waited for Tatiana to make her way back from her home in The Hills to partake in the dinner portion of tonight's event. Now that Tatiana would be in a fairly controlled environment, the evening had the potential to be boring at best, and that was fine by him after the concert from hell.

"We should be pulling around to the side entrance in about five minutes," Jerrod's voice echoed in Tucker's earpiece.

"Everyone's in place," Tucker responded as he stood at the

back of the Beverly Hills Hotel's Crystal Ballroom. "Things are in full swing around here and uneventful."

Box-office celebrities, rappers, pop artists, and a few of LA's most wealthy mingled in the grand room, all done up for the five-thousand-dollar-a-plate party, and Tucker wasn't impressed. People were people whether they stood in front of a camera to make their money or served a side of fries with a burger and shake.

He continued his scan of the noisy space as six familiar voices buzzed in his earpiece with updates on who was where, whom they were with, and the occasional muttered snide remark about one of Tatiana's guests.

"Damn," Collin Michaels whistled subtly. "I've never been so happy to pull door duty. Wait 'til you get a look at what's headed your way, boys. Fucking fantastic."

Smiling, Tucker looked to the pocket doors, waiting to check out Collin's version of 'fucking fantastic' and lost his breath when Wren walked in. Michaels couldn't have been more right. He'd never seen her as beautiful as she was now. She'd done something different with her hair; some of the shiny black twisted up in a fancy knot while the remaining riot of curls flowed free. Her light blue dress clung in all the right places, and the slit up the side showed off a teasing sample of smooth, glorious leg. And those eyes...

Wren turned as someone spoke to her, and Tucker swallowed. "My God," he whispered between clenched teeth. The powdery blue plunged dangerously low, exposing her slender back. It was all he could do to stay where he was. He physically ached from his need to touch her. Wren had him by the throat, and she didn't even know it.

She turned again, and her gaze locked with his. Pure heat sizzled between them, then she looked away as a man sidled up next to her, carrying a glass of champagne. JT Cartwright. JT touched the small of her back, and she smiled, locking her arm with his as they strolled further into the room.

What was she doing here with him? Tucker didn't have

anything against the guy personally—or maybe he did now that his childhood friend had his hands all over the woman he wanted. Clenching his jaw, he conceded that below the torrents of jealousy, JT was a good person. He'd been there for him during the darkest hours of his life. And that was part of the problem. He didn't like revisiting the summer of 1999. The pain still consumed him if he let it. Staci was dead, her killer was free, and life had carried on, despite the injustice. He'd cut himself off from memories of Park City, including anyone and anything that triggered thoughts of his sister.

Minutes ticked by, and one hour turned into two while Tucker watched Wren dance, laugh, and converse with Hollywood's A-list. He wanted to hold her against him while sexy notes poured from the live band's saxophones, the way JT did now. JT stopped suddenly, said something to Wren, then answered his phone. He signaled to the hallway and walked quickly from the room, disappearing down the hall.

Wren glanced in Tucker's direction as she had several times throughout the evening, but this time she started toward him through the crowd. She stopped in front of him, smiling. "Hi."

He fisted his hands at his side as he breathed in her exotic scent. "Hi."

"Are you having fun standing in your corner?"

"Best time ever."

She smiled again. "I thought I would come say hello before I leave. How are you?"

She was different without her sassy shield. He'd never had a conversation with her without it. "Good."

"Are you—are you okay?"

He knew she was asking about his abrupt departure from the Cartwright mansion the other day. "Never been better."

"I've been thinking about you. Monday... You were upset."

He shrugged. He wasn't bringing up his past among a crowd of strangers, especially not when her eyes were all soft and gorgeous and full of concern.

"I wanted to be—"

"You look good, Cooke." Unable to fight it any longer, he reached out and touched the diamond dangle at her ear, effectively changing the subject. "Damn good."

"Is that your way of telling me to mind my own business?"

"No. It's my way of saying I think you're a beautiful woman." Holding her gaze, he took a step closer and slid a teasing finger down the silky skin of her arm, testing them both.

She shuddered as her eyes darted to his mouth, then met his again.

"Have dinner with me," he murmured as he played with her fingers.

"I can't."

"Why? Because you don't date cops, or because of JT?"

"Because I'm going out of town tomorrow for most of next week *and* because I don't date cops. I'm not getting mixed up with you, Tucker."

He grinned as her fingers clung just as tightly to his.

"Why are you smiling?" She pulled her hand free. "Why is that amusing?"

"Because we're already mixed up."

"For a guy who keeps getting shot down, you're awfully sure of yourself."

"You just said you've been thinking of me."

"You're unbelievable." She shook her head and took a step back. "I was concerned, which was clearly foolish and misplaced."

He grabbed her arm before she could walk away. "No, it's sweet."

"Let's get something straight, right here and now." She stepped closer. "You don't interest me—not in the least. I don't want to go out with you now or ever. If you were the last man on earth, I *still* wouldn't choose you." Her gaze darted to his lips as she spoke.

"You think so?"

"Oh, I *know* so, buddy."

If he wasn't on duty, he'd have proved her wrong right then and there. Under the layers of cool disdain was an inferno ready to burn, and he sure as hell planned to ignite it. "Guess we'll have to wait and see."

"You'll be waiting a long time. Of all the—"

"Your date's back." Tucker spotted JT staring in their direction as he stood by the ballroom entrance.

"Huh?" She shook her head as he cut her off mid-rant.

"JT's back."

"I can't—I can't keep up with you."

And that's exactly the way he wanted it—Wren off balance. She was too used to calling the shots. "Guess I'll see you around."

She held his gaze another moment, then turned and walked away.

ೞ Chapter Five ೲ

WREN CRUISED NORTH ON THE 405 AFTER A MISERable flight home from Oregon. Her stomach still churned and her jaw ached after two hours and forty minutes of uninterrupted turbulence. The quick jerks and deep dips had tossed her and a hundred other passengers about mercilessly. The jet had touched down smoothly half an hour ago, sending up a cheer, but her relief was short-lived. She was home—thank the Lord—but she was behind, a good three hours at least, and that was being optimistic. Catching up on e-mails and the million other things she needed to do wasn't possible on the plane. She'd been too busy clutching her seat, concentrating on keeping the banana she'd snacked on in her stomach, where it belonged.

She *had* to get to work on the Cartwright project, ASAP. Lenora had called countless times in the six days Wren had been away dealing with the complete redesign of one of the more affluent law firms in downtown Portland.

She'd planned to create the virtual mockup for the Cartwright's pool house and surrounding area while she coasted at thirty thousand feet, but that didn't happen. Her cell rang, and she tipped the phone forward, glancing at the readout. "Oh my God. You're the client from *hell*." She let it ring twice more, then reluctantly pressed "talk." "Wren Cooke."

"Hello, Wren. It's Lenora."

"Hi, Lenora. What can I do for you?"

"I was wondering how the mockup came out. I'm hoping you can send a copy of the file over so I can take a look. I know you said you were going to work on it today."

Wren rolled her eyes. *Why, why* did she tell Lenora she was ready to start on the next phase of the design? "Actually, we hit turbulence on my flight home, so I wasn't able to get started."

"Oh. Well, I can't say I'm not disappointed. I hope I can still count on you to complete this job... You did say our needs were your first priority."

It was tempting to roll down the window and toss her cell phone out. "They certainly are. I'll have the mockup ready by nine tomorrow when we meet." She could create the preliminary designs tonight, but she needed to stop by Abby Harris's Fall Fashion reveal at Sarah's mother's boutique, then come home and sleep off the grinding nausea and brewing headache left behind from her flight.

"I had some time to think about the renovations while you've been in Portland, and I've come up with an idea or two of my own."

No! Anything but that. They'd gone through this with the library. After three weeks of Lenora changing her mind over every little thing, Wren had been ready to throw in the towel. Out of self-preservation, Wren yanked the Mercedes over two lanes and took the next off-ramp. "Lenora, I'm going to stop by. I'm about twenty minutes from your house. I have a couple of sketches ready to go and several swatches for you to look at. I also have three or four color pallets I want you to consider for the walls. They'll all work well with what I have in mind. You can start playing around with those and give me your thoughts when I come by tomorrow." The sheer volume of sample fabrics would keep Lenora busy for hours. Hopefully she'd just bought herself an evening of silence. "And I'll leave a couple of catalogs with different selections of the furnishings I was thinking about. The pages are marked."

Lenora squealed on the other end. "What an excellent idea."

Yes. Yes, it was. "I'll be by shortly."

"Okay. See you soon."

Thirty-five minutes later, after maneuvering through the stop-and-go traffic on Wilshire, then Santa Monica Boulevard, Wren finally turned on the Cartwright's street and pulled up to the security gate. She pressed the button and was buzzed in.

Wren circled around the drive, not bothering to park in her typical spot by the garage. This was going to be a quick in-and-out, by God. She needed two Tylenol and oblivion... after she went to support Abby.

Sighing, Wren gathered the catalogs and two thick books of swatches to occupy her nightmare client. She walked toward the front entrance in the lamplight and smiled when JT opened the door, dressed relaxed in blue jeans and a gray sweater that accentuated his sturdy boxers build.

"Welcome home."

"Thanks. All finished with work for today?"

"Yeah. Dad and I took a couple of clients out for a late lunch, and now we're catching up on a few details upstairs." He studied her face. "You look a little green."

"I feel a little green. Bad, *bad* turbulence on the flight back."

"Sorry to hear that. You must've caught one of storms heading in off the Pacific. They're saying the fronts are wreaking havoc in the mountains—lots of snow. Utah and Colorado are catching the worst of it."

"That's why we live in Los Angeles. I'll stick with the rain—when we actually get it."

He reached for the items in her hands. "Let me take those."

She handed over her heavy load. "Thank you."

"We're about to eat—pan seared scallops and tiger shrimp, if you want to join us."

She gave his arm a gentle squeeze. "You're very sweet, but my stomach's a little raw, and I have to go to my friend's show this evening."

"Why don't you head out? I'll give these to my mother."

"I should probably—"

"Wren, go home. Let me save you tonight. If she sees you, she won't let you leave for hours."

He had a point—a very good point. "I hate to do that, but I will this time. I owe you one."

"How about lunch sometime next week?"

"Oh..." She didn't want to send mixed signals.

"Friends."

She smiled. "Okay. Pick a day, and I'll make sure Patrick works it into my schedule."

"Tuesday good for you?"

"It will be. I'll be here for a couple hours in the morning. I can stop off and get us a muffin and coffee if you think you'll be here."

He shook his head. "I wish, but I have a huge case coming up. The State of California versus... Well, I can't tell you that—attorney-client privilege."

"That's okay."

"I won't be around much for the next month or two. I'll actually have to work at the office downtown. No more bumming meals off my parents."

"I'll miss seeing you."

JT stood up straighter. "She's coming," he whispered. "I can hear her heels down the hall. Go. Run."

He didn't have to tell her twice. "Okay. Bye." She hurried to her car and waved as she got in.

He gave her a salute, smiled, and closed the door.

Wren pulled out of the gate and started the long drive to the Palisades through Thursday night rush hour. JT saved her butt—big time. He was a sweetheart, the type of man a woman could settle down with and depend on. It was too damn bad she wasn't interested. He was certainly intelligent and attractive; he just wasn't her type—not that she actually had a type, per se. "A type" was meant for those looking to find a perfect partner to spend their life with. "Perfect" didn't exist, and rarely did a lifetime with one person. Marriage was a crapshoot, a contractual joke that worked until someone got itchy. Then it turned into a nightmare where said "perfect partners" fought over who got to keep the potted fern in divorce court, or worse, they stayed together and cheated and lied year after year. She wanted nothing to do with the bondage of marriage—never had.

She rolled to a stop at the light, and her mind wandered to Tucker and their last conversation at the gala. *Conceited jerk.* Even as she shook her head in disdain, he consumed her thoughts. He was there—almost always—distracting her. She had hoped the chaos of her six-day trip would lessen his effect on her, but that didn't appear to be the case. Those eyes and that slow grin of his were lodged in her brain like a thorn. Tucker Campbell *definitely* wasn't her type. Despite what he thought, they were *not* mixed up.

Desperate for a distraction, she lifted her phone from the passenger seat and pressed Patrick's number on her speed dial.

"Patrick Stone."

"Hi."

"Welcome home."

"Thanks."

"Did Lenora Cartwright get a hold of you?"

She groaned. "Which time?"

"Do you think we can bring her up on harassment charges? I mean really, Wren. The woman's *impossible*."

"You're not telling me anything I don't already know. I told her I don't have her mockup ready for the pool house." She chuckled at Patrick's quick intake of breath. "I'm pacifying her with pallets, swatches, and furniture magazines. I have to believe that's bought me some time. My plan is to punch it out first thing in the morning."

"The mockup or her?"

"Tough call. What's my schedule looking like for tomorrow?"

"Jammed full as usual, darling."

She closed her eyes for a second as she stopped at another red light. "I'm sorry I asked."

"I have you down for a consult with Lenora at nine. The furniture and accents are ready for the Fowler Estate. Delivery's at eleven. You're booked over there from ten-thirty to two o'clock. Don't forget your tools for the window treatments this time. I can't be flying all over Beverly Hills saving your fabulous ass."

"One little mistake..." She accelerated and turned on the Pacific Coast Highway.

"Until the next one," he teased. "Anywho, you have back-to-back new client consults booked until five, then you're free. I blocked out the rest of the evening for paperwork and whatever else you need to do."

"That's not too bad." She needed a couple of easy days. Her relentless schedule was starting to take a toll. "I'm having lunch with JT Cartwright on Tuesday. Can you set something up?"

"Lenora's defense attorney son?"

"One and the same. He's nothing like his mother."

"Let me look." He tsked. "Oh, that's going to make Tuesday messy, honey, real messy."

"That's why I have you, Super Assistant."

"Hold that compliment. Someone's here." Patrick gasped. "Oh, look at these—stunning. You got flowers, girl. Big beautiful roses."

She clutched the steering wheel. "Roses?"

"Mmhmm. A dozen blood-reds. They smell fabulous."

Her already-queasy stomach shuddered. "Is there—is there a note?"

"Sure is."

"Can you read it?"

"Thought you'd never ask. Let me open it up." She heard the sound of paper ripping, then Patrick cleared his throat for effect. "It says 'Welcome Home.' Then there's a twenty-five. Not sure what that means."

But she did. Today was the twenty-fifth day since her disastrous date with Rex Richardson. He'd texted her from a different number at some random time every day since the night he left flowers on her doorstep. Six days in Oregon hadn't stopped his harassment as she'd hoped it would. And now he knew she was home. She snapped on the heat as her blood ran cold. "Throw them away."

"What?"

"I don't want them," her voice shook. "Throw them out." How did Rex know she was back? Better yet, how did he know she'd been gone? "Did anyone out of the ordinary call looking for me while I was away?"

"No, not that I can think of. All current clients were patched through to your phone. New clientele set up appointments with me."

"Did you give anyone my travel itinerary?"

"I'm going to pretend I didn't hear your question."

She sighed. "Of course you didn't. I'm sorry." For the first time since this all began, she was truly afraid. The daily texts and even the blue roses were more annoying than anything, but Rex seemed to know her every move. Texts could be sent from anywhere and flowers delivered to a doorstep, but now she realized he was actively watching her. She glanced in her rearview mirror at the row of headlights behind her and wondered if Rex was following her now.

"Wren, are you all right?"

No. "Yes. Yes, I'm fine. It's been a long week, and the plane ride sucked. I just need to get some rest."

"I can cancel your nine o'clock. You can sleep in."

Lenora would have a heart attack if she had to wait another day for her damn mockup, and she needed to stay busy. Fear would be keeping her up no matter how her body craved rest, so it was better to carry on as planned. "No, I'm already behind. We need to keep my schedule."

"Are you sure?"

"Positive. I'm just about home. I'll call you tomorrow morning."

"Okay. Bye."

"Bye." She pulled in her drive, dropped her phone, and gripped the wheel with trembling hands as heat from the vents rushed over her. She stared at her darkened front steps in the shadows cast about from the neighbors' tall trees. What if he was here? His texts weren't threatening, and technically neither were the flowers, but Rex wasn't healthy. In the two years she'd owned her home, she'd never been terrified to get out of her car and go inside like she was now.

This is what he wants. He wants you to be afraid while he plays his games. Steeling herself, she grabbed her phone and got out with her key fob clutched in her unsteady hand. The cool rush of wind tossed her hair in her face, and she swiped wavy locks behind her ear as she strained to hear over the rustling leaves. She walked quickly, her eyes darting everywhere.

She just had to get to the door and step inside. The panic button was in the entryway if she needed it. The police would come help her, along with whoever was fielding calls at Ethan's company tonight. "I'm almost there. I'm almost there," she whispered, flinching, blinking, startled as the sensor lights flashed on to brighten the walkway. The security lights. It was just the security lights. She forgot she reactivated the feature the night of the gala. She took another step forward and saw the blood by the pretty pot of red mums. "Oh my God. Oh my God." A black cat lay on her step, decapitated and bloated in a pool of dark, congealed crimson. "Oh my..."

Her breath rushed in and out as she stumbled back. The cell phone in her clammy hand rang, and she screamed. Blindly, she pressed "talk." "Hell—hello?"

"Do you like it?" someone whispered.

She whirled, scanning, searching for Rex. He was here, somewhere. He had to be.

"Why won't you call me?" The whisper turned into a pathetic whine. "Why won't you call me, Wren?"

"Stop," she shuddered out as she hurried to her car, looking over her shoulder from time to time, sure he was waiting to pounce. "Stop doing this. I'm calling the police."

The whining stopped abruptly and turned into mad, riotous laughter. "They won't believe you! They won't believe you!"

"Leave me *alone*!" She hung up, gasping for air. Tears poured down her cheeks, and her hand shook as she opened her door, took her seat, and locked herself in. She had to get out of here. She had to get away. It took her two tries to shove the key in the ignition as she glanced at the bloodstained step once more and backed out with a squeal of tires. She sped off, heading toward Ethan's until she remembered he was gone and a quarter of his house had been gutted for the new edition. All of them were gone—Ethan, Hunter, and Austin. She pressed 'one' on her speed dial, listening to the repetitive ringing. Ethan's smooth voice told her to leave a message, but she hung up instead. She turned down another street, taking her farther from her home, and punched in Ethan Cooke Security's twenty-four hour assistance line.

"Ethan Cooke Security. This is Mia."

"Mia, it's Wren."

"Wren, are you okay?"

"Yes." Her voice broke, and she shook her head as she clutched the wheel with one hand. "No. No, I'm not. There's a dead cat on my porch."

"Oh."

That didn't exactly describe the horror she'd just backed away from. "Someone killed a cat and left it on my front step."

"Oh my God. Where are you?"

"In my car." She sniffed. "Driving around. I don't want to

go back to my house alone."

"Of course not. Let me patch you through to Tucker Campbell. He's on call."

Tucker? "No, wait—" But it was too late. Soothing music played in her ear.

"Wren?" Tucker's deep voice hummed with concern.

Her lip wobbled, and tears began to fall again. "Yeah, I'm here."

"What's going on? Mia said something about a dead cat?"

"Someone chopped some sweet cat's head off and put the body on my front step."

He muttered a swear. "Are you there now?"

"No, I'm in my car, driving around. It freaked me out. I don't want to be at the house by myself."

"I don't want you there either. Come to my place until we get this figured out."

If choking fingers of terror didn't have her by the throat, she would've refused, but Tucker was offering his help. She needed help. "I don't—I don't know where you live."

"Ocean View Apartments, off Highway One."

"What if he follows me? He might be following me right now." She glanced in the rearview mirror and cringed as headlights trailed behind her.

"Who?"

"Rex."

"Who the hell is Rex?"

"The crazy bastard who left the dead cat on my porch."

"Son of a bitch, Cooke. Don't stop. Don't pull over. Drive on a flat tire if you have to. Just get here. I'll be waiting outside."

"Okay," she sniffed, too afraid to be prideful. "I'm about ten minutes away."

Tucker hung up, shaking his head. What the hell kind of

trouble was Wren in? Dead cats and a guy named Rex who might be following her... Did Ethan know about this? He doubted it. Ethan wouldn't have traipsed off to Hawaii without mentioning his baby sister's problems. Tucker would hear Wren out, find out what was going on, then call the cops and her big brother.

Tucker shoved his phone in his back pocket and hurried around his disheveled living room, gathering up dirty dishes and the numerous fitness magazines he never had time to read. He grabbed the sweaty shirt he'd yanked off and thrown to the floor after his workout and swiped at the coating of dust on the ratty coffee table he'd bought off the young couple living downstairs a few years ago.

He tossed the magazines on the mismatched side table, set the plates and cups in the sink with a clatter, and walked to the chest of drawers in his bedroom for a clean t-shirt. Wren would be here any minute. He wanted to be outside when she arrived. It was dark and she was afraid. He couldn't blame her. This Rex character seemed to be playing a dangerous game.

Tucker took the stairs in twos to the lobby, then stepped out the glass front door. Wren's pretty red Mercedes pulled into the lot seconds later. Stopping, she rolled down her window as he circled around to the driver's side. Subtle hints of her French perfume and a blast of hot air from the heater greeted him.

"Where should I—" She cleared the tremor from her voice as she adjusted her white-knuckled grip on the wheel. "Where should I park?"

"Take the spot next to mine." He noted her blotchy cheeks and still-damp eyes as he pointed to his black Jeep Wrangler Moab.

She nodded and turned into the empty space twenty yards ahead. The cool and unshakable Wren was on edge—understandably.

He walked to her car, scanning the area, watching for

anything suspicious while she slid her briefcase strap and leather laptop bag on her shoulder, got out, and locked the door. Her gaze darted left and right, then met his.

"I don't think anyone followed you."

She folded her arms across her middle, her hands clutching her elbows. "Are you sure?"

"Not one hundred percent, but he's not here now. He didn't pull in the parking lot, and he sure as hell isn't sitting idle on West Sunset. He'll get creamed. Let's go inside."

She nodded. "I'm freezing."

They walked to the lobby door and he let her in first. "Up the stairs and hang a left. First door on your right." Wren started up in front of him. He studied her amazing ass in her khaki wide-leg trousers, her tiny waist in a trim, long-sleeve white blouse, and her stylish leather heels. "Didn't you fly today, Cooke?"

She glanced over her shoulder as they took the last step to the second floor. "Yes, I got back a couple hours ago. Why?"

"Ever hear of comfort while you travel?"

"I am comfortable. I had an eleven-thirty meeting with my clients before I headed to the airport. I couldn't go to a law firm dressed in ratty gym shorts and a t-shirt." She looked him up and down with scathing, red-rimmed eyes.

He grinned. She was shaken up, but she'd pulled herself together enough to throw a jab or two his way. Good. "Right here. 2A." Tucker shoved the key in the door and opened it for Wren to walk in first.

She took two steps in and stopped. "This is—this is where you live?"

"Yup." His beat-up leather couch, mismatched tables, and large flat screen TV were all that graced his mostly empty living room.

Wren turned with what could only be horror in her eyes.

He smothered his chuckle with a cough. Damn if she wasn't just what he wanted. "You gonna pass out on me?"

"I don't—I don't even know what to say. I offer all of

Ethan's employees free consultations and deep discounts on furnishings and accents with my connections." She walked over to the ugly burnt-orange curtains that had been on the windows when he moved in and batted at them with the tip of her fingernail. "Tucker, this is..."

"Awful?"

"That's putting it lightly."

He shrugged. "There's food in the fridge, my TV works, and the couch is comfortable."

"But free consultations and deep discounts. Surely Ethan told you."

He shrugged again. "I'm never here."

"But—"

"Cooke. It's not that big a deal."

"It is. This is your *home*."

"I guess. I think of it more as a place where I crash from time to time. I sleep here two, maybe three times a week—if I'm lucky."

She scrunched up her nose. "Lucky?"

He laughed. "I'm on duty a lot."

"What about when you bring a date home?"

"White walls and ugly furniture isn't usually the topic of conversation." He grinned and wiggled his brows. "Haven't had any complaints yet."

She scoffed and tossed him an eye roll. "Consider this your first. Have you always lived here, even when you worked for the police department?"

He nodded. "Wasn't around much then either. Homicide keeps a man busy."

She batted at the curtain once more and stepped away. "Did you always work homicide?"

"Nah. I was a beat cop for a while first."

"Did you deal with crazy men who left dead animals on doorsteps?"

He didn't typically start working a case until dead animals escalated to dead people. "Sometimes."

"Why did he do it? Why did Rex hurt that poor cat and leave it for me to find?"

"What's your impression?"

"I think he wants to scare me." She clutched her arms across her chest again as the little color left in her face vanished. "And it's working."

"Come sit down." He walked into the bedroom and unearthed the sweatshirt he'd worn earlier. "Here. Put this on."

"Thanks." She pulled on the extra-large gray hoodie and sat on the edge of the leather cushion.

He studied her, tense and stiff on his ugly couch, dwarfed in the soft fleece of his exercise clothes. Her pale cheeks and haunted eyes bothered the hell out of him. Her fire was gone. "Do you want something to drink?"

"No." She shook her head as she pressed a hand to her stomach. "No, thank you."

He took a seat next to her. "Tell me what's going on."

"Rex left a decapitated cat on my doorstep."

"Rex who?"

"Rex Richardson."

"The name's vaguely familiar."

"I'm sure it is. He's the DA's grandson."

His brow rose in surprise. "The Junior Vice President of Vera Corporation left a dead cat on your doorstep?"

She nodded.

"Why would he do that? How do you know it was him?"

"Because I do."

"That's not particularly helpful, Cooke."

She huffed out a breath. "You don't believe me."

"I'm not saying I don't believe you; it's just a little hard to swallow. I've met Rex a time or two. I never got a creepy vibe from him."

She huffed again and started to stand.

He pulled her back to her seat. "Don't be like that. For all I know, he's the scum of the earth."

"He is. Trust me on that."

"He may very well be, but he's also the DA's grandson. Politics are going to come into play when the police take a look at this."

She rubbed at her temple, then pressed her palms to her forehead. "He told me they weren't going to believe me. He'll keep right on doing what he's doing, because they won't listen to a word I'm saying."

"When?"

She looked at him, frowning. "When what?"

"When did he tell you the cops wouldn't believe you?"

"Tonight, when he called."

"He called you?"

"Yes. Tonight he actually spoke to me. Usually he texts once a day. He also had roses delivered to my office."

"When were you going to tell someone about this?"

"I was hoping he would get bored and stop if I didn't acknowledge him, but it keeps getting worse." Her lips quivered, and she pressed them firm.

"Cooke, you're being stalked. Ignoring the situation won't make it go away."

"So I've noticed. He's crazy, absolutely crazy." Her voice trembled, and she shook her head as she stood and walked to fiddle with the orange curtain.

He hated seeing her like this. His first instinct was to pull her into a hug, but the cop in him wanted answers. She was vulnerable and willing to spill. Her pride wouldn't get in the way of the details. "Tell me about tonight. Start from the beginning."

"I flew out of Portland at three. The flight was awful—turbulence the entire way. I landed around five forty-five and started home."

"In your vehicle, or did you take a cab?"

"My car. I left it in long-term parking."

He nodded, encouraging her to continue.

"I was on my way home to change. Abby's show is tonight. I was supposed to go."

"She'll understand."

"I hope so. This is her debut. She's been through so much. I wanted to be there."

"Abby has a whole bunch of people supporting her. We need to get this situation figured out. Tell me what happened next."

Wren walked back to the couch and sat. "Lenora Cartwright called when I was on the 405, asking about her damn mockups for the millionth time, which I still haven't gotten to."

"Eager client."

She sent him a wry smile. "You could say."

"I think I remember her being a little demanding."

"That's right. You know the Cartwrights. I keep forgetting."

They weren't circling around to his association with the Cartwrights. "What next?"

"Out of desperation, I told her I would drop off swatches, color pallets, and furniture magazines."

He grinned. "Shut her up for a while."

"It was either that or kill her." She chuckled. "I didn't think I could laugh at a time like this." She touched his hand. "Thank you."

He reversed his palm to hold hers. "Laughing is better than crying."

"I agree one hundred percent. I hate crying. It makes me feel weak and foolish."

"Nah." He imagined Wren rarely gave in to her tears.

She squeezed his hand, then put hers back in her lap. "I went by the Cartwrights to drop off Lenora's stuff. JT met me at the door and saved my life."

He frowned. "How's that?"

"First he offered me dinner, but my stomach was upset from the turbulence, then he said he would head his mother off so I could go home and rest."

"A real night in shining armor." Wren's blatant admiration for JT rubbed him the wrong way.

"He really is. We're having lunch on Tuesday—my treat—for saving me undue hours of pain and suffering."

He didn't want to hear about Wren's lunch date, especially when she refused to have a simple meal with him. "So JT came to your rescue. Take the story from there."

She stared at him for several seconds, then kept going. "I started home through the insane traffic and decided I should check in with Patrick."

"Who's Patrick?"

"My assistant."

"What's his last name?"

"Stone. Why?"

He shrugged. "Curious. That's all."

"Patrick is *not* my stalker. Trust me. He'd find you more attractive than he does me—promise."

"Stalking isn't about sex. It's a need for control over another person."

"It's Rex, not Patrick."

"I like to keep my options open."

"Do what you think you need to, but you're wasting your time on one of the people I know and love best."

Tucker had never been so envious of another man. What would it be like to rate Wren's absolute adoration and trust? At most, he and Wren were tiptoeing around a cautious friendship. "Better to look and eliminate than wish you had all along."

"I'll let you be the cynic."

He shrugged again. "Keep going."

"Patrick and I ran through my schedule for the day. While we were talking, a delivery arrived—blood-red roses and a note that said, 'Welcome Home'. There was a number twenty-five on the card as well."

"What does it mean? The twenty-five?"

"Today's the twenty-fifth day since my first and only date with Rex."

"What did Patrick do with the flowers?"

"I told him to throw them away. I didn't want them."

"He should've called the cops."

"He doesn't know. I haven't said anything to anyone." She shook her head. "It doesn't matter."

"Yes, it does. If you get anything else, you call the cops right away."

"I know that now. I had no idea one bad date would end up like this." She plucked at the leg of her pants.

"We're going to figure this out."

"I hope so."

"We will." Though he knew it was bound to take a while, especially with the DA's family potentially involved. "Tell me the rest."

"Patrick and I hung up as I pulled in the drive. It was dark and I was afraid." She looked up from her jerky tugging movements, meeting his gaze. "I was terrified he was waiting for me. He seems to be watching my every move. I got out of my car and hurried toward the door. The security lights flashed on and I saw the cat." She laced her fingers, clenching them together. "I knew it was a cat right away. He had a black body, but something looked funny about him, and then I realized he was missing his head. There was blood everywhere." Her breathing came faster, and she closed her eyes.

"Take your time."

"I wanted to run and scream, but I kept staring. My cell phone started ringing. I don't remember answering. Somehow the phone was up to my ear, and he was whispering. He asked me if I liked it. Then he started whining like a spoiled child. He wanted to know why I wouldn't call him back. I told him to stop and that I was calling the cops. He started laughing." She shuddered. "His laugh was scarier than the cat and the flowers and the dark. He said they weren't going to believe me." Her voice broke, and she covered her face with her hands.

Enough was enough. He scooted over and wrapped her in

a hug. "It's over now. You're safe. You're safe here with me." To his surprise, she leaned against him and rested her head on his shoulder.

"Why is he doing this?"

He breathed in the bold scent of her soft hair as strands of wavy black tickled his cheek. "I don't know."

"Maybe he's paying me back for damaging his pride when I hurt him."

"Cooke, you're sexy as hell, but there's typically more to something like this than a bruised ego." He rubbed his hand up and down the sleeve of her arm. "Not always, but usually. Rex is the Junior VP of one of the richest companies in the world. He'll find another date."

"No." She pulled back. "I really hurt him. I knocked the wind out of him and kicked him in the balls."

He stared at her, shocked and speechless. She was no taller than five-three and weighed one-ten if she was lucky.

"He didn't understand 'no,'" she continued, "so, I helped him out."

"Good for you, Cooke. Sounds like he's a first-class pig." Maybe Rex did have his hand in this. Wren had humiliated him, and he was paying her back by terrorizing her. The tactics seemed petty and out of character for the man he'd met on more than one occasion, but it was definitely worth looking into. "I'm going to phone this in."

"Whatever you think we should do."

The police came with their badges and barrage of questions and left two hours later. Tucker's murmurs mixed with the cops on the other side of his front door, while Wren rested her head on the arm of the surprisingly comfortable leather couch. Her skull throbbed and her stomach twisted with nerves and outright fear. The detective took her statement and asked what he needed to ask, but Rex had been right. They didn't believe her, even after the officer flipped through several saved texts and the picture of blue roses placed at her door.

The officers were heading over to her house to make a copy of Rex's initial voice mail, which she hadn't erased, and to photograph the dead cat. Detective Owens sent someone to Patrick's for a statement regarding the flower delivery. The detective told Tucker he and his partner would stop by Rex's and ask him some questions, but an investigation was unlikely to go much further. His lawyers were top-notch, and at this point, nothing Wren had showed them was a direct link back to Vera Corporation's VP. In short, the good ol' boy network was alive and well.

Wren pressed her fingers to the throb in her temples and sighed. Now that the police were on their way out, she could try to put this away for the night. Tucker had insisted she stay there minutes before the officers arrived, and she hadn't been stupid enough to refuse. She glanced around at the stark white walls, wretched orange curtains, and enormous flat screen filling up most of the wall. Despite Tucker's butt ugly living space, she felt safe here.

The door opened and she shot up, still on edge.

"Relax, Cooke. It's just me."

Her heart settled as Tucker twisted the lock. "They don't think Rex is doing this."

"They're looking into it."

"So they say."

"I worked with Owens for years. He said he's going to look into the situation, so he will."

She held his gaze. "Obligatory glimpse maybe. He was ready to close the book on this before he even turned a page."

"Give him a chance. He'll give this more than a glance, because it's the right thing to do, and because I've asked him to."

"You're not one of them anymore."

"I was for seven years. Loyalty goes a little deeper than

that. Brothers for life."

They'd see about that. She rested her aching head on the arm of the couch again.

"You left out the blue roses when we talked."

"You asked about tonight." She closed her eyes in defense against the naked light bulb shining from his ceiling. "Believe me, I'm not trying to keep secrets."

"All the pieces are important. From now on, you share everything."

She opened her eyes and met his cool, serious gaze. "Why are you getting upset with me? I just told you I didn't leave out the roses on purpose."

"I can't help you if I don't know what I'm dealing with."

She'd never seen him like this. He was usually too busy being smooth. "I'm sorry. Like I said, I didn't leave the roses out on purpose."

"When was the last time you had something to eat?"

And just like that, the tense moment was over. She scrunched up her nose at the thought of food. "I'm not hungry."

He grunted and walked to the kitchen, opened a cupboard, and something clattered moments before the microwave hummed and a pan scraped against one of the burners. Minutes later, he came back. "Here."

She opened one eye and peeked at the perfectly golden grilled cheese on the plate and the poop-brown coffee cup in his hand. He'd cooked for her. She stared up at him, more than a little surprised. "What's in the mug?"

"Decaffeinated green tea with honey."

Who was this sweet, sexy god with the amazing body and gorgeous face? Her stomach fluttered from his kind gesture, and she ruthlessly ignored the uncustomary hitch as she reached up and took the dish. "Thank you."

He set the cup on the coffee table. "Go ahead and take a bite. You look like hell."

And Tucker Campbell was back. She put down the sandwich she'd picked up. "Stop with all the flattery. I can hardly take it."

He grinned. "Just eat. We'll both feel better if you do."

She grabbed the half and shuddered as she brought it to her mouth. Food was the last thing she wanted. She darted him a glance from under her lashes as he stared down at her. Trapped by manners, she nibbled at the buttery whole wheat and gooey cheddar jack. She chewed, swallowed, and bit in again, oddly comforted by the simple meal. "It's good."

"There's probably more calories in that sandwich than you eat in a week."

She frowned. "I eat. I eat plenty, thank you very much. I just choose healthy options."

"Your luggage still in your car?"

She picked up the other half after devouring the first. "Yes."

"I'll go get your stuff."

"No," she said quickly, thinking of Tucker alone in the dark parking lot.

"I know we're mixed up and everything, but I think it's too soon for you to be walking around my apartment naked."

She snorted out a laugh. "You wish."

He sent her one of his slow grins. "Maybe." He took a step toward the door.

"Wait."

He turned. "What's wrong, Cooke?"

She thought of the dead cat and the moonless night. "What if he's out there? What if he hurts you?"

He winked. "I'll be okay."

She studied Tucker's white cotton t-shirt hugging his broad shoulders and impressive arms. His navy blue gym shorts hinted at his powerful thighs and showed off his well-shaped calves. He could definitely take Rex if he needed to. She shrugged her embarrassment away and focused on her dinner.

"Keep this up and I might start thinking you're actually

sweet on me."

"Dream on," she said without heat, answering his teasing smile.

Tucker's cell phone rang. He glanced at the readout. "It's Ethan."

She winced. "I didn't want to tell him about this yet."

"Too late." He pressed "talk." "Campbell. Yeah, she's right here. She's shaken up but fine. I was going to call you." He tossed her a scathing look.

Wren could only imagine what Ethan was firing in Tucker's ear. She sent him an apologetic smile.

"They just left," he continued as he held her gaze. "I'm sure he is. She's staying here tonight. I need to get her luggage from her car. I'll have her call you back in five. Bye." He hung up.

She set the remaining quarter of the grilled cheese on her plate. "Ethan's pretty worked up, huh?"

"Good guess. He's going fucking bananas. The DA called him. He ripped Ethan a new asshole, wondering why his sister's making wild accusations about his grandson leaving dead cats on her doorstep. Ethan wants you to call him. You can deal with your brother for now. I'm sure I'll have another turn later." He pulled her car keys from the top of her purse and grabbed his own from the peg on the wall. "Don't open the door for anyone. I'll let myself in." With that, he shut the door behind him and was gone.

Wren stared after Tucker in the silent room. Her stomach felt surprisingly better, and her headache was down to a dull roar. Sighing, she picked up her phone and prepared herself for a grilling from her worried brother.

ꕥ Chapter Six ꕥ

WREN SAT AT THE STUDY TABLE IN THE CARTWRIGHTS' library, staring at the sunny yellow palette and green and white striped fabric swatches Lenora liked best. Thank the Lord they finally agreed on something. She squeezed the bridge of her nose and closed her eyes. The day had passed in a whirlwind. Between the schedule changes to accommodate Jackson and Jerrod's ability to drive her to her worksites, meetings with potential new clients, and her late-afternoon go-around with Lenora, she was toast.

Typically she handled chaos with ease. Bedlam came with the territory. Her career revolved around the wants and needs of wealthy and often spoiled adults who believed their whims were her top priority. And usually they were, but not today. Today she struggled to keep everything—including herself—together. Her head ached as it did last night, and her stomach churned with unshakeable worry. Tylenol and Saltines weren't doing the trick, nor were her silent pep talks to herself or the deep breathing techniques she relied on when the pressure became too much.

Sighing, she pulled her laptop closer and punched in the first few adjustment codes to update the original mockup she'd made for the Cartwright's pool house. Now that the foreman had gotten back to her with firm dates for phase one's completion and Lenora had given her the go-ahead, she could begin placing orders for custom-made furnishings, paints, rugs, and the numerous accents they would use throughout the space.

The next step was to get the reluctant head gardener involved with the landscaping overhaul. Wren had noticed that Romeo did everything in his power to avoid interactions with Lenora. She couldn't blame him, but he would have to get over it. If she could handle 'the lady of the manor' for a few hours, so could he. Still trying to find her groove, she flipped screens and e-mailed Patrick. It would be better to get the meeting over with sometime in the next couple weeks. They could turn the dreaded occasion into a breakfast or luncheon. Food seemed to be important to the somewhat portly Romeo. She would soothe ruffled feathers with a nice meal. "What can I say? I'm a genius." Chuckling to herself, she returned her attention back to the mockup.

She punched in the color adjustment as her cell phone rang. Wren glanced at the readout, smiled, and answered. "I'm still fine. In fact, I haven't moved from the study table I've been sitting at since the last time you called."

"Don't piss on protocol, Cooke. Every hour on the hour until I can come pick you up."

"Lucky me. And how much longer will we play this game?"

"Ethan's still rearranging schedules to get you full-time coverage for a while. You just keep answering when I call and stay where we left you. I'd like to avoid any unnecessary confrontations with your riled-up and very cranky brother."

"What can I say? I inspire love and loyalty wherever I go."

Tucker snorted into the phone. "You think so?"

She grinned. "Definitely."

"I'm stuck in traffic. I'll be there in about thirty minutes."

"Ten-four, boss."

"Since you seem to be handling the situation better today, it's your turn to cook tonight. You can cook, right?"

"Very well, actually." Ms. Willa had insisted she and Ethan

learn to handle themselves in the kitchen. "I'm a jack of all trades."

"Stay put until I get there, Jack."

"Yes, sir."

"Smartass."

The dial tone buzzed in her ear, and she chuckled. Tucker's hourly calls had annoyed the hell out of her for much of the day until she decided to have fun with them. After all, he was doing what he was told. Ethan was stuck in Hawaii for the foreseeable future with his family. His trip to the islands wasn't only for pleasure; he, Austin, and Hunter were attending several conferences in between pulling duty for two Hollywood families on vacation and helping out with the Phillips/Cooke kiddos when Sarah left for her photo shoots.

During their endless phone conversation last night, Ethan insisted she hop the next flight to Hawaii, but she refused. The island brood already had their hands full, and she had a job to do. More than that, she wasn't about to burden her family with her problems or risk involving Ethan and Hunter's children. Besides, Rex was likely to lay off now that the police were involved.

Having a round-the-clock guard was probably overkill, but that's the compromise she and Ethan made. He'd tried to flex his big-brother muscles and demanded she work from his office for the next little while; she'd promptly told him to go to hell. Her business would not suffer because some sicko had a vendetta to settle. She'd worked too damn hard to make Cooke Interiors one of the top design firms in LA. She'd be damned if Rex Richardson was going to ruin her reputation for client-focused service at its best. She and Patrick would continue to run the company just as smoothly as always, with a few minor adjustments.

She understood her situation and was being a team player. She'd slept overnight in Tucker Campbell's apartment, breathing in his sexy scent while she lay in his bed. And she'd rearranged her schedule to fit Jackson, Jerrod, and

Tucker's, staying put, locked behind her client's gated fortresses, hadn't she? But tomorrow life got back to normal—whatever that was.

"Hey."

Wren whirled, almost falling out of her chair. "JT," she whispered, closing her eyes as her heart slammed a jittery beat.

"Sorry. I didn't mean to scare you."

She took a deep breath. "That's okay. I'm a little on edge today."

"I heard."

Her brows winged up. "You did?"

He nodded and walked further into the room, wearing his fancy courtroom duds. "Kinda hard to keep that sorta news out of legal circles. DA Richardson is pretty riled up."

"As he should be. His grandson is a nut job."

"Is there anything I can do to help?"

"No..." She stood and leaned against the table. "Actually, yes. I would love some straight-up honesty."

He nodded. "Okay."

"What's the likelihood the police are going to make an arrest?"

"Probably not great."

She puffed out a breath and looked to the ceiling. "And why am I not surprised?"

"I did a little digging after I found out you were involved. Rex Richardson agreed to meet with the police last night with his attorney present. They questioned him for less than half an hour."

"Unbelievable. They grilled me for two."

"Other than the voicemail he left on your home phone, there's no hard evidence linking him to the rest. His attorney called the entire situation 'ridiculous, baseless, and completely insulting to Mr. Richardson's exemplary character.'"

Her jaw clenched as she thought of the month-long harassment she'd endured. "Now that's ridiculous. Did they expect him to have a moment of conscience and confess to everything?"

JT's cell rang. He glimpsed at the readout. "Damn. I have to take this. I'm sorry. I'll be right back."

"Take your time." She needed a few minutes to gather the tethers of her temper. Rex was harassing *her*, yet somehow she had become the villain and he the victim. She walked to the window and stared out at the lush grasses of the manicured lawn while JT's murmurs echoed from the hallway. Her phone chimed on her hip, alerting her to a new text. She yanked her cell from the leather holder and gaped at the two-word message.

Nice try. 26.

Her hand shook as she read and reread Rex's latest message. "No," she whispered. "No." This wasn't happening.

"Wren? Are you okay?"

She turned slowly to JT as reality blindsided her. "He isn't going to stop."

"What happened?" He walked to her and rested a supportive hand on her arm. "What's wrong?"

She held up her cell phone. "He sent me another one."

He took the phone. "Let me take you down to the police station."

"I—"

She heard someone knock against the doorframe. "Hey, JT. Cooke, you ready to go?"

She glanced over to where Tucker stood, wearing khaki slacks and a navy blue polo top. "Tucker." She pulled the phone from JT's hand and hurried to him. "Another one. He sent another one."

Tucker frowned as he studied the screen she held up.

"I thought his 'date' with the police would put a stop to this—at least for a little while." She shook her head. "But it won't. He'll keep doing this, because he can. No one's going to touch him, and he knows it."

"We're going to handle it."

"How? By calling the cops so they can question him with his lawyer at his side, then tell him he's free to go? Not even twenty-four hours, Tucker, and he's back to his games."

He took her chin between her fingers and held her gaze. "We'll handle it. Trust me."

Something in his intense stare made her believe him, and she nodded.

"Let's get out of here."

"I have to get my stuff." She turned toward the table and jumped, having forgotten that JT was still there.

"Are you sure there's nothing I can do to help?"

"I don't—I don't think so." She looked to Tucker for confirmation.

Tucker shook his head. "The cops are going to have to handle this one. Wren will have protection until this bastard makes a mistake. And he *will* make a mistake." His eyes left JT's to capture hers. "They all do."

Wren secured her laptop, then gathered her catalogs and other items, tossing them in her briefcase. She wanted out of there. She wanted to go home and pretend this wasn't happening.

Tucker walked over and slid the straps of her laptop case and bag on his shoulder.

"Wren, I'm sorry for what you're going through. If you think of anything, anything at all..."

She nodded, took JT's hand, and kissed his cheek, fighting against the tears pooling in her eyes. "You're a good friend. I'm lucky to have you."

He patted her shoulder. "Be safe."

"I will." She stepped back, blinking the worst of her emotions away, refusing to allow Rex Richardson to upset her any further.

"Come on, Cooke. Let's get you home. Later, JT." Tucker wrapped his arm around her waist.

The solid strength in his gentle hold comforted her. As much as she wanted to depend only on herself, she leaned into him as they left the library and walked out the front door.

Amazing scents wafted from Tucker's humble galley kitchen as Wren thwacked and chopped away at an assortment of vegetables. Hints of garlic, thyme, and rosemary teased his stomach as he sucked in a breath with his next arm curl. The gym wasn't an option with the current situation, and Wren's silence on the ride home had been a none-to-subtle hint that she wanted to be left alone. Her stalker's latest text had shaken her—enough that she'd been willing to take the comfort he offered on their way out the Cartwrights' door.

She didn't want to be afraid, she didn't want to need him, but she was and she did. Wren was going to have to get used to him being around for a while. Ethan had assigned him to the sassy package in the next room until they got this situation figured out.

They had a long way to go. He'd called in the new text to Owens as soon as they arrived at the apartment and sent a copy of the message via e-mail to the station. There wasn't much else he could do; he and Wren both knew it. She'd held his gaze for several seconds after he hung up, shook her head in disgust, then marched herself into his kitchen and started pulling food from his refrigerator at random.

Beads of perspiration tracked down his face and chest as he finished his last rep. He set down the thirty-five pound dumbbells and wiped at the sweat with a tattered gym towel. He took a deep breath and stretched his biceps. That last set was a bitch.

Bending at the knees, he reached for the weighted ball, and suddenly his bedroom window smashed. Tucker dropped, rolling automatically as a slice of heat grazed his temple and something landed on the floor next to him with a heavy *thump*. He lay on the carpet among the shards of glass, blinking several times, then rushed to his feet as reaction set in. His heart jackhammered and adrenaline coursed through his veins as he ducked past the window yelling, "Wren!"

Her small frame crashed into his as they collided in the hallway. He wrapped an arm around her and turned, taking the brunt of the force as they slammed into the wall.

"Are you okay?" they asked at the same time. "I'm fine," they spoke in unison again.

He gripped her upper arms, studying her for himself. "Are you sure you're all right?"

"Yes, but you're not. You're bleeding." She pulled out of his hold. "Let me get a towel." She dashed away.

He was bleeding? And then he felt the warm drops dribbling down the left side of his cheek. He touched his fingers to the throb at his eyebrow and temple and looked at the considerable mess covering his hand. "Son of a bitch." He wiped his bloodied palm on his shorts. Injuries would have to be dealt with later; he needed to figure out what the hell just happened. He hurried back to the bedroom, cautiously peeking from the side of the gaping hole in the window, then searched for the object that had busted out the entire bottom pane of glass. He crouched in front of a brick wrapped in duct tape next to the edge of his bed, studying the bold black letters written in permanent marker: *SHE'S MINE!*

"What happened?"

His gaze flew to Wren standing in the doorway. "Stay there. I don't want you messing up the scene." Or seeing what was there to see.

"Was it a rock?"

"A brick."

"Oh my God. You're lucky you weren't killed."

He walked back to where she stood in the hall. "We need

to call this in."

"In a minute. Come here." She grabbed his still soiled hand and pulled him to the living room. "Sit down. You're bleeding all over the place."

He settled on the couch and winced as she applied pressure to the ache along the side of his head. "Easy."

"You're bleeding pretty good."

"Hurts like hell."

"I'm sure. I'll be right back." She dashed toward the bathroom.

"Don't even think about pouring that stinging shit on my face." He would sit on her before that happened.

She came back with another clean towel and a dripping washcloth, kneeling in front of him again. "Let me see."

He leaned further into the cushion as he eyed the cloth wearily. "What's on that?"

"Water. Now let me take a look." She pulled his hand and the bloodied towel away from his temple and sucked in a sharp breath. "That's pretty deep. I'm going to clean your wound some—make sure there isn't any glass in it, then we'll apply pressure and get the bleeding stopped."

"You keep surprising me, Cooke. I had no idea you were a nurse, too."

"My parents are doctors." Brows furrowed, she moved in close, settling her body between his thighs, dabbing gently at his wound.

"Must be in the genes." He hissed out a breath as she continued her painful work.

"No. I went through a long disappointing phase where I thought that if I tried to be interested in something my parents were, they might pay attention to me."

"Didn't work, huh?" He wanted to reach out and play with her long, wavy strands of silky black hair.

"Nope. Nothing did. I tried learning about medicine, being extra good, even extra bad. When I was ten, I woke up and smelled the coffee and realized Grant and Renee were too wrapped up in themselves to have time for their children."

She said what she did so matter-of-factly. He studied the exotic beauty carefully tending his wounds and finally understood a small piece of Wren Cooke. Under the layers of self-confidence and success remained the remnants of an unhappy childhood. The Cooke children had grown up in the lap of luxury, much like he did himself. The only difference was he and Staci had been lucky enough to have parents that gave a damn.

"Doesn't look like we have to worry about flushing out any glass. You're going to have a heck of a bruise though. How do you feel about stitches?" She set the clean cloth on his cut. "I think you're going to need them. Here, hold this." She took his hand, settling it on the towel against his gash, then folded the unsoiled edge of the washcloth and swiped at the drying blood on his pecs and stomach.

He grabbed her wrist, stopping her movements. "They're stupid."

She frowned. "Huh?"

"Your parents. They're stupid for missing out on something special."

She held his gaze, swallowing, and stood. "We need to—"

Something crashed through the living room window, and Wren screamed. Instinct had Tucker gripping her arm and yanking her to the floor. He covered her body with his, protecting both their heads with his arms. The sound of Wren's rapid breathing filled his ears, though he could still hear cars rushing by on West Sunset. He gained his feet, hurrying to the edge of the window. No one was there. Tucker turned back and spotted another brick wrapped in duct tape by the couch. He could see the words *YOU'RE MINE!* from where he stood.

"It's getting worse." His gaze whipped to Wren, who was staring at the message sent for her.

"It's going to get worse every time." She glanced at him,

then at the darkness boring in through the busted window as she curled her arms around her legs. "How does he know I'm here?"

Tucker had his theories. He walked to her, crouching in front of her, resting his hands on her knees as her phone jingled with a text alert.

She looked at the cell as he picked up the phone from the coffee table and read *I'm just getting started.* Tucker clenched his jaw against the ball of helpless rage icing his stomach.

"What does it say?"

"I'm going to call Owens."

She gripped his wrist. "What does it say, Tucker?"

He puffed out a breath as he met her eyes. "'I'm just getting started.'"

She nodded. "He's never going to stop."

"Yes, he is." He gave her knee a gentle squeeze.

She picked up the bloodied cloth on the floor and pressed it to his temple. "You're still bleeding."

"We're going to get him."

She said nothing.

"We're going to get him, Cooke."

Forty-five minutes passed in a blur of questions and answers. The Crime Scene Unit packed away their cameras and aluminum fingerprinting powders while Tucker stood in the hallway close to his open front door, listening with half an ear as Detective Elena Revas spoke with Wren on the couch.

"We found the devices," Owens said. "One on Ms. Cooke's vehicle and another on yours."

Tucker nodded. "Figured as much. We'd only been home half an hour when the first brick came crashing through the window, and I know he didn't follow us home—I took the long way and didn't spot a tail."

"Seems like you've got a bead on this guy."

He shrugged. "Just makes sense. Wren typically works 'til seven at least—usually at her office the last half of the day—hence the late flower delivery to Cooke Interiors yesterday evening. We cut out early this afternoon when she got the last text. He knew she was here at my place—a deviation from her pattern—a good two hours earlier than she should be. If he didn't follow us physically, he followed electronically."

"Never should've left the force." Owens shook his head mournfully. "We'll see if we can get the GPSs linked to an e-mail address or cell phone."

They wouldn't, but Tucker nodded anyway. Whoever they were dealing with was too smart for such a stupid and obvious mistake.

"Looks like this case is escalating quickly."

"Maybe you'll start taking it seriously."

"Fuck off, Campbell."

"Look, I understand the situation you're in and I don't envy you, but we've got a serious problem on our hands."

"On two fronts. I've got the DA on my ass pressuring me to wrap this up before the media grabs hold, then I've got a woman being threatened who insists Rex Richardson is responsible for the whole damn thing and there's not a fucking shred of evidence connecting him in any way."

"Rex groped her on a date and left a message admitting he was a jerk."

"Let's lock him up and throw away the key," Owens scoffed. "Give me a fucking break, Campbell. You haven't been off the force long enough to be firing bullshit like that back at me."

Tucker squeezed at the back of his neck, knowing Owens was right. They didn't have jack shit to work with.

"I'll drag Rex's ass into the station, but we both know how it's going to end."

"Yeah."

"Excuse me, Detective Owens." A beat cop stepped up next to him and Tucker. How the hell was this kid old enough to wear a badge? He had rookie written all over him. "Can I speak to you for a moment?"

"This about the Cooke case?"

"Yes, sir."

"Go ahead."

The young officer glanced from Owens to Tucker. "Okay. Uh, the alarm just activated at Ms. Cooke's home."

Tucker's cell started ringing as the newbie finished his sentence. He stepped away and answered. "Cooke."

"Tucker. It's Mia. We've had an alarm activation at Wren's house. The police are on their way now and I've let Jackson know. He's heading over."

"Tell me what's up with the sensor panels."

"Looks like the upstairs double doors are the point of entry."

"Upstairs," Tucker muttered to Owens and the Rookie.

Owens held up his finger in a "wait a minute" gesture. "Find out who's taking the call," he said to the rookie. "Discreetly. I don't want anyone overhearing." He gestured to Wren.

"Hold on one second, Mia," Tucker said as he waited for the answer.

The rookie turned away and radioed in. "Who's responding to the alarm activation on Costas Drive?" The dispatcher responded and the officer turned. "Lou and Smitty."

Wren stood with Officer Revas, shaking the officer's hand. *Shit*. "Mia, I'll call you back."

"Okay."

Tucker hurried into the apartment, heading Wren off. "Hey. Did Elena get your statement?"

"Yes. What did Detective Owens say?"

"Honestly, not much."

She huffed. "I figured. Officer Revas said we can start cleaning up." She glanced around at the mess on the floor.

"Where's your vacuum?"

Wren seemed steadier than she did an hour ago. "You don't have to clean my apartment."

"Did you call your cleaning crew?"

He grinned. "Yeah, they said they wouldn't be able to make it."

She chuckled and stepped closer, raising herself on her tiptoes to examine the butterfly stitches and Band-Aids the paramedic had placed over his cuts. "Looks sore. Lots of bruising. Do you have a bag of peas?"

She smelled so damn good. "Probably."

"When everyone leaves, we'll get that iced, and I'll start dinner again."

"My own personal nurse." He winked. "How do you feel about sponge baths?"

She laughed, her full-out laugh he hadn't heard since the last gathering at Ethan's.

He skimmed his finger along her chin. "Not gonna lie, Cooke. I love that sound."

She sobered instantly and stepped back. "Where's the vacuum?"

"Hall closet."

"Campbell." Owens popped his head in the doorway. "Can I talk to you for a minute?"

"Yeah. Be right back," he said to Wren as he followed Owens to the stairwell. "What?" Whatever it was, he already knew he didn't like it. Tension tugged at his shoulders with a vengeance.

"Cops are setting up a scene at Ms. Cooke's house. Looks as though someone helped himself to her underwear drawer. Her panties were sliced at the crotch and strewn about the bed."

Tucker's stomach curdled with a rush of anger. "Get your ass down to that station and bring the fucker in before I go find him myself."

"Take it easy, Campbell. You know there are procedures

we have to follow."

"*You* have procedures you have to follow. I play by a different set of rules now. I better not see him anywhere near her, or I'll take care of things my own way."

"Don't say shit like that. Something happens to him and I'll have to come looking for you."

"Guess you'd better get to him first."

Owens eyed him as he took a step toward the lobby. "I'll keep in touch."

"We're leaving," Tucker said, as he officially made the decision he'd been tossing around since this afternoon. This was the best solution until he and Ethan could think of something else. "I'm taking her away for a while."

"Where?"

"Colorado. Ethan has a safe house in the mountains. We'll hunker down there for a couple weeks or so until we can figure some of this out."

"You'll have your cell, right?"

"Yeah."

"I'll keep in touch."

"Thanks."

Several officers walked by with their kits, following the detective out.

Tucker heard the vacuum begin to hum in his apartment. He closed his eyes and rested his forehead against the wall, instantly regretting it as a deep throb shot through his skull. "Damn it." He righted himself immediately and clenched his fist at his side. This was no longer harmless harassment. Texts, flowers, and a dead cat hinted at trouble. Tracking devices and break-ins to screw with someone's underwear screamed lethal obsession. It was time to pack Wren up for a while and get the hell out of LA. He pulled his phone from the elastic waist of his gym shorts and punched in Ethan's number.

"Cooke."

"It's Tucker."

"What's going on?"

"We need to go. We're heading to Colorado."

"What's going on, Campbell?"

"They found a tracking device on her car, and mine. He threw two bricks through my windows with messages letting me know she's his, and he broke into her house about fifteen, twenty minutes ago." Tucker closed his eyes as he hesitated with the rest. "He ripped up her panties and threw them all over her bed."

"Fucking bastard," Ethan spat.

"Let me grab some clothes and my toothbrush and we're outta here. I'll call Collin or someone else to drive us to the airport. Jackson went to the scene. I'll check in before we leave. And it wouldn't hurt to have you book our flights under the business. This guy's going to hunt for her when he figures out she's gone."

"You can't go to Colorado."

"Why the hell not?"

"The snow's made the roads impassable, not to mention the plumbing issues. George checked on the place last week before the blizzard hit. The pipes in the downstairs bathroom burst. He had to shut off the water completely until he can get it fixed."

"Well it's a good thing we don't have a crisis on our hands or anything." He ran his fingers through his hair in utter frustration.

"I'm looking into another house out East."

"Doesn't help us much now."

"Bring her here. We'll keep her—"

"That's not a good idea, and you know it. Last thing we need is to get one of the kids mixed up in this. Think like the CEO of a security firm and not like her brother."

"Fuck, man, this is my *sister*. How about Europe? We have connections—"

"Arrangements to Europe will take too long. This needs to happen now. I know where I can take her." He clenched his jaw, wanting to rescind the offer even as he said it.

"Tucker?" Wren stepped into the hall.

He didn't hear the vacuum shut off. He turned to face her.

"Are you okay out here?"

He stared at the gorgeous woman who was wearing his gray hoodie—the woman who'd cleaned up his house, offered to ice his cuts, and fix him dinner again after the last forty-eight hours from hell. "Yeah. Just finishing up a call and I'll be in."

"Okay." She went back inside.

"What's going on?" Ethan asked.

"Just waiting for Wren to go back in the apartment."

"What were you saying?"

He sighed. "I said I know where I can take her."

"Where's that?"

"Park City. My parents have a home in the mountains. We'll be safe there until we get things figured out around here."

"I'll book your flights and call you back. I don't know how to thank you, man."

The weight on his shoulders grew exponentially as he thought of the summerhouse in Utah. He hated that place.

"Take care of her for me."

"You know I will." He ended the call and made his way back to the apartment. Wren wasn't going to be any more excited about the idea than he was.

☙ Chapter Seven ❧

Tucker drove the rental Jeep over the snow-crusted roads of downtown Park City. More than a decade had passed, yet so much was the same. The lights shined bright along the busy strip while tourists walked about, perusing numerous restaurants and shops. Ski trails were ablaze in the distance as grateful resort owners and skiers alike capitalized on the gift of late-October snow. The back-to-back storms had dropped five feet over the last week, and no one appeared sorry...except for his silent passenger staring out the window.

Wren hadn't been pleased when he told her they were leaving LA as soon as possible. She'd argued her need to stay for her business, but her pleadings had fallen on deaf ears. Safety came before profit—the end. He'd wanted to drag her to the airport immediately after hanging up with Ethan, but fate had been on her side when all outgoing flights were booked last night. She'd had most of today to make hurried arrangements with Patrick via phone and Skype for her abrupt departure while they hunkered down in Hunter and Morgan's house, waiting for Collin to pick them up and drop them off at LAX for their four o'clock exit.

Wren spent every available second on her newly issued cell while they waited to board at the gate. The two-hour flight was dedicated to feverishly putting together mock-ups and orders. She'd fought to appear calm as her fingers flew over the keyboard, but her bopping leg and clenched jaw gave away her inner turmoil. Wren's life was unraveling before her eyes, and there wasn't a whole hell of a lot they could do to change it until Rex Richardson was stopped.

"We're about five, maybe six minutes away." And he was dreading every second. The pretty lit up buildings of Main Street brought back a flood of memories he didn't want to deal with. Park City represented such a huge piece of his life.

"Mmm," was her answer as he turned on Mountain View and started the climb to the top. He passed the sharp twist in the road, and Staci's scream echoed through his head as she begged him to slow down. The Cartwright home, long since sold, appeared on the left, then Jasmine's house on the right. He counted off the drives, one, two, three, four, then turned into his own. The grand wood-and-glass structure was lit up like glory, and smoke plumed from the chimney. A white pickup with snow tires sat in the drive close to the garage—Ms. Hayes's he imagined. He killed the ignition and stared at the heavy pine doors. How many times had he walked in and out of those, taking everything for granted?

"This is your cabin?"

"Huh?" Wren's question pulled him back to the present.

"This gorgeous work of art belongs to you?"

He shook his head. "My parents."

"This isn't a *cabin*, Tucker. This is a full-fledged house, and it's spectacular."

He shrugged as the front door opened and Ms. Hayes hurried toward the Jeep. The sweet, blue-eyed housekeeper had aged some in the years he'd been away. Her short brown hair was mostly gray, and the slight hump on her back had worsened.

Tucker smiled as she waved, and he was instantly consumed by a flood of love. She'd been a part of their family for as long as he could remember. He opened his door and caught the tiny bundle in his arms.

"Tucker Campbell. I've missed you so."

She smelled the same—like lavender and lemons. He closed his eyes and swallowed over the sudden lump in his throat, then cleared the emotion away. "I missed you too."

She eased back, smiling, and touched his cheek. "And look at you. So handsome, so beautifully handsome even with a nasty bump on your head. You always have been. How are your mom and dad?"

"Good. Mom stays close to home, but Dad still travels quite a bit."

She nodded, understanding perfectly that life had never been the same for his parents after Staci's death.

"I'm so glad you're here, honey." She handed him a key.

The passenger door shut, and Wren walked over to join them.

"Oh my, look at you, dear. Aren't you a vision?"

Wren had pulled off sexy winter chic in her brown leather jacket, cream-colored scarf tied at her throat, and matching beret placed atop the mass of flowing curls. "Ms. Hayes, this is my friend, Wren Cooke."

Ms. Hayes took Wren's outstretched hand and pressed her palm to her cheek. "It's so good to meet you, Wren. You must be special if my sweet, handsome Tucker brought you here."

Wren smiled as she sent Tucker a curious glance. "It's nice to meet you too, Ms. Hayes."

"Now, everything's all set up for your stay. I made corn chowder for your dinner and stocked the fridge. Tommy, my grandson, brought in plenty of firewood to keep you both comfortable."

"That's very sweet of you." Wren smiled again. "Will you stay and have a bowl of chowder with us?"

"Aren't you a doll baby? I wish I could, but Henry's waiting for me to eat a dinner of our own. I'm going to be on my way. It sure is lovely to meet you, Wren."

"You too."

Ms. Hayes let Wren go and turned back to Tucker. "I'll be by to check on you in a few days. Call if you need anything." She leaned in close. "It's still a good place, honey, once you sweep away the sad. So many wonderful things happened here." She gave his cheek a gentle pat, and he nodded.

Ms. Hayes's intentions were well-meaning, but he would never be able to "sweep away the sad." "Say hi to Mr. Hayes for me."

"Will do, honey." In her sturdy winter boots, Ms. Hayes made her way to her truck, took her seat, and left.

The vehicle vanished down the road, and the world was suddenly silent. Wren stared at him in the crisp air. He didn't want to answer the questions burning in her eyes any more than he wanted to step through the doors of the house he hadn't been in since the coroners wheeled his sister away in a body bag. "We should get our stuff."

"Ms. Hayes is very sweet. I like her already."

"She's the best." He walked to the trunk.

"Sounds like you've known her a long time."

He pressed the key fob and the back opened. "Yup."

"How long have your parents had this place?"

"Since I was a baby." He gathered up the large duffel bag he'd packed on the fly and waited for Wren to grab the luggage she still had from her trip to Oregon. He slammed the trunk closed and met her curious gaze.

"I feel like there's a story here and I'm missing most of the chapters."

He couldn't talk about it. He couldn't be here. Why did he bring Wren to his own rendition of hell? Ten minutes in his old driveway had ripped away every layer of emotional protection he'd shrouded himself in. Fourteen years of turmoil swooped in to buckle his knees and swallow him whole. "Let's head in. It's cold."

She stopped by the passenger's side, grabbing her laptop and briefcase, then followed him to the house.

His boots crunched in the crusty snow as they made their way to the entrance. Tucker gripped his bag tighter with sweaty hands and swallowed against the burn of icy air assaulting his throat with each rapid breath. Through the open doorway, he caught glimpses of his past frozen in time. He stopped abruptly.

Wren halted next to him. "What? What's wrong?" Her voice trembled with fear as her eyes darted about.

"Nothing. Go ahead in." He set his duffel down, suddenly terrified he wouldn't be able to step over the threshold. "I'm going to pull the Jeep in the garage, then get some more firewood."

"But Ms. Hayes said her grandson brought in plenty."

"I should probably get some more anyway." He walked off, leaving Wren staring after him as he made his way down the small embankment to the stacks of wood in the shadows of the house, wondering how the hell he was going to make himself go through with this.

Wren frowned as Tucker disappeared in the dark. What was going on with him? At some point during the drive from Salt Lake City, Rico Suave vanished and Moody, Broody Bummer Man appeared. She wanted Rico back.

With a shake of her head, she eased the heavy pine door open and gasped. Tucker's parents' "cabin" was a testament to amazing architecture and serious wealth. Gorgeous marble flooring gave way to hardwood floors and elegant area rugs that cost a small fortune. The large open-concept space was a masterpiece, with views of Park City visible through the acres of glass. The bright lights of town in the distance and ski trails lit in the true country dark were as breathtaking as Ethan and Sarah's view of the Pacific and LA beyond.

She stepped farther into the house, closing the door behind her, and stopped, scrutinizing the area again with a curious and professional eye. Now that the initial shock had worn off, she realized the furnishings and style were at least a decade behind. The stunning space was stuck in a late-90s time warp. Why hadn't the home been updated to reflect the current trends? Clearly the Campbell family could afford it. Wren itched for her sketchpad, color swatches, and catalogs. Two months. Two months is all she would need to bring this place around to its present-day potential.

She set their luggage to the side, pulled off her beret, scarf, and jacket, and wandered from the spacious living area to the kitchen. Granite countertops in blue pearl complimented shiny appliances and glass-fronted cabinetry. Wren walked to the top-of-the-line stove, which was keeping Ms. Hayes's corn chowder hot under the low gas flame, and breathed deep. The creamy soup smelled like heaven.

She glanced around at the new espresso maker, stocked wine fridge, and fresh bread from the deli. There was no shortage of creature comforts here. When Tucker told her he was taking her to his parents' cabin in the woods, she'd been expecting something small with questionable plumbing and a mom-and-pop general store fairly close. She'd hoped for at least a dialup, but here she would have Wi-Fi, scanning capabilities, and whatever else she needed. Running her business from this miniature palace would be slightly easier, but she still worried. Patrick was going to be dealing with most of the burden—face-to-face meetings, picture-taking for room assessments and consultations, curtain, furniture, and accent installs... *everything,* while she handled her clients through e-mail and Skype. Tucker had confiscated her cell phone, giving it to Detective Owens for monitoring, and replaced it with an Ethan Cooke Security phone to use for communication with Patrick only. How long would her clientele put up with the inconvenience? What would happen when word spread that Cooke Interiors was being run by Wren Cooke's assistant while she hid herself away in some undisclosed location for 'personal reasons'?

Tucker and Ethan didn't even let her tell Patrick where she would be going. If Patrick needed to send her fabrics, catalogs, or anything else, he had to drop the items off at Ethan's office for Mia to handle—just one more inconvenience she and her partner couldn't afford. Her reputation would be in tatters by mid-November at the latest, and her business bankrupt. Five-and-a-half years of hard work would be ruined, while Rex Richardson sat in his corner office on the fifty-fourth floor, laughing his ass off.

Wren pressed her lips firm as her stomach sank with the thought. She would have to make the best of the situation and do everything in her power to keep her company in the black. Failure was not an option.

The front door burst open, and she flinched, still jumpy after last night's brick incident.

Tucker walked in with a large pile of wood, kicking the door closed behind him. He stomped the snow from his feet and stepped from his boots after a small fight with the rubber soles.

"Need a hand?"

"No. I'm good." He settled his armload on the side of the large stone fireplace crackling with beautiful sweeps of orange flame.

"Between what you've brought in and Ms. Hayes' grandson, we'll be set for days." Hopefully they'd be heading home in no more than two or three.

"Should be."

She crossed her arms, leaning against the countertop, studying him through the opening among the cabinetry that sectioned the kitchen area from the living room and dining space. "Are you always a man of few words when you're on duty, or are you angry that I dragged you away from your couch and big screen to suffer in a dump like this?" She'd expected one of his slow grins, but he stared into the flames instead. "Tucker, what's wrong?"

"Nothing."

"I don't think either of us believes that."

He looked away from the fire, meeting her stare. "Let it go, Cooke."

She nodded. "Got it."

"Don't be like that. I said I'm fine, so leave it alone."

She blinked, surprised by the edge in his voice. "Who *are* you?"

"Same person I've always been," he muttered.

"No. Not even close. The Tucker Campbell I know is a slick-talking bodyguard who lives in a dumpy apartment in LA. This guy," she made a sweeping gesture in his direction, "whoever he is, is some broody, heir apparent with his boxers in a twist."

He said nothing as he continued to hold her gaze.

Jerk. She turned away from his impenetrable stare and started toward the left wing of the house, the only hallway that was dark.

"Where are you going?"

"Haven't a clue. I guess I'll check out the rest of the place on my own, since your hosting skills suck."

"Those rooms are off limits."

She scoffed and kept going.

"Hey," he snapped sharply. "I said off limits."

Shocked to her core, she stopped in her tracks, turning slowly to face him. Why was he acting like this? The man staring at her was a stranger, and she didn't want to be anywhere near him. Not knowing what else to do, she went back to the kitchen to begin dinner preparations. She no longer had an appetite for the pot's deliciously creamy contents, but she wanted to be busy. Nerves were easier dealt with when there was a task at hand. Tucker's sudden mood swings were something she'd never expected. She'd had more than her share of unsettling surprises over the last couple weeks.

Standing on her tiptoes, she opened cupboards at random until she spotted soup bowls deep in the recesses on the second shelf. She scooted closer, brushing the dishes with the tips of her fingers, but her efforts were no use. *Damn* her height.

Tucker came up behind her. His chest and stomach pressed against her back as he grabbed two bowls.

She turned as he set the dishes on the granite.

"I'm sorry for being pissy."

"No big deal." She averted her eyes and tried to scoot away, but he kept her boxed in against the counter.

"Yeah, it is. I was rude. The west wing of the house doesn't get used—my mother's wishes."

She bit her tongue, stopping herself from asking why. What was it about this place that set him so on edge? "I didn't mean to invade her privacy."

He shrugged. "You didn't know."

His voice was strained, his eyes troubled. She wanted to help him, but he'd made it clear he'd rather be left alone. She gave him a gentle push to the chest, freeing herself from his trap, and made herself busy with the deli bread, a serrated knife, and a cutting board. Attempting some semblance of normalcy, she cut thick slices of doughy Italian. "This really is a beautiful home. Do your parents come here often?"

"No, not anymore." It was his turn to lean against the counter. "My dad lets his business associates use the place when they feel like getting away. Someone's usually here every couple weeks or so. Do you want some wine?"

"Sure. I'll take half a glass of white." She set the bread on a plate. "What does your father do?"

Tucker twisted the wine key into the cork and pulled. "Travels mostly."

She frowned, confused. Tucker told Ms. Hayes his mother stayed close to home, but his father traveled a lot? Maybe they had an unhappy marriage. "Oh." She turned to the stove and flipped the burner to 'off.' "How hungry are you?"

"Not very."

She had no interest in eating either. Tucker's blatant evasions were frustrating and unnecessary. If he didn't want to talk, they didn't have to talk. He could keep his mysterious family and secret rooms to himself for all she cared. Tucker typically intrigued her—reluctantly so, but this Jekyll and Hyde routine of the last couple hours was already old. "I think I'm going to pass on dinner." She made her way to the foyer and grabbed her luggage. "Which room is mine?"

"I'll show you."

"I can find my own way if you just tell me."

He shrugged. "Down that hall. First door on your right."

Wren started down the lighted wing, stopped, and turned. "You know, Tucker, Collin can take over my protection if this isn't working for you. I could've stayed in LA for another week and waited for him or someone else to bring me to London. If you don't want me here, say the word and I'm gone."

He held her gaze for several seconds before she shook her head in irritation and walked away. She didn't have time to play games with the cold, miserable man in the kitchen who was so adept at pushing her buttons. Mockups and orders waited to be created in her room for the time being. She had a business to keep afloat. Tucker could brood all by himself.

☙ Chapter Eight ❧

TUCKER ROLLED OUT OF BED, BLINKING AGAINST THE rising sun. He stood by the huge panes of glass in his room, scrubbing his hands over his cheeks and rubbing at his tired eyes, carefully avoiding the bandaged gash that still hurt like a son of a bitch. He'd tossed and turned all damn night, watching the hours tick by on the digital clock. Years ago, the country dark and silence of the woods had soothed him; now they left him edgy. He was used to city noise—traffic rushing by, car alarms, and the squeal of tires. He wanted the urban clamor back. Anything was better than the racing thoughts and haunting memories that had plagued him since they'd set off for Park City.

He stared out at the bold pinks and purple of the spectacular sunrise, the dark green of tall pines, and the pure white snow coating the rooftops downtown and gray mountaintops beyond. He'd seen this breathtaking picture on many Christmas vacations—and would have been content to never see it again.

He turned away from the view, as if doing so would somehow banish the pain, and pulled on a pair of black pajama pants over his boxers. He sat on the edge of the bed and lay back, running his fingers through his hair. What the hell was he doing here? Why did he think bringing Wren to the summerhouse would be okay? They had to go. Maybe he could take her to one of the resorts. They could use assumed names...and constantly look over their shoulders.

He clenched his jaw, knowing the idea wouldn't work. Rex Richardson, along with numerous others, knew he was heir to the Campbell Empire. And if he didn't, it wouldn't be hard to find out. Once Wren's stalker realized she'd left LA with him, his father's hotels would be a plausible place to search for her. There were Campbell Resorts all over the world. Hunting for Wren would take considerable time and effort, but her stalker's escalating behavior proved he would look anywhere and everywhere until he found her. What if the resort he took her to was the one Rex chose—if it was even Rex to begin with...

That's why he'd brought her here. Hardly anyone knew of the house in Utah. Most people assumed his father sold the family getaway after Staci's death. Deep down, below the well of misery, he recognized he'd made the right call. Now he had to deal with it. The sooner the police took care of Richardson, the faster they could go home.

Tucker glanced at the bedside clock. Eight on the dot. Ethan was up...or he would be when his cell phone started to ring. Tucker grabbed his cell and dialed.

"Cooke."

"You're up."

"I have a ten-and-a-half-month-old and a four-year-old. Sleeping in doesn't happen around here." Kylee screamed in the background, and Emma's gibberish echoed through the phone.

"Guess not."

"What's up?"

"I wanted to see if Owens shared anything with you while Wren and I were en route to Utah. Thought I'd be merciful and let the guy sleep awhile. He was probably out working a scene until God knows when. Gotta love Saturday nights in LA."

"I was going to call later when I was sure you and Wren were up and around. I imagine you haven't slept well the past couple nights."

Ethan had *no* idea. Sleep was something Tucker had done without since Wren walked through his front door. He'd tossed and turned on his couch Thursday night, torturing himself with thoughts of Wren's glorious body curled up in his sheets. Friday, he settled for a cot at Morgan and Hunter's, lying in the same guest room as Wren. They'd both been awake, mere feet from each other, listening to every creak and crack the house made. "Not particularly."

"Owens and I spoke briefly. They got word on the GPSs. The tracking systems found on both your vehicles linked back to a pay-as-you-go phone. The serial number didn't connect to a credit card on file, so whoever bought the devices paid cash, which leads us nowhere."

Tucker didn't expect anything less. "Does Rex have an alibi for Friday?"

"Owens said they had him in for questioning for quite a while yesterday. He's insisting he didn't do any of this—gave Owens his whereabouts for every evening since his first and only date with Wren. He, his lawyers, and grandfather want this put to rest ASAP. Apparently he's been laying low for the past few days. He took a little time off this week after the board members at Vera Corporation found out about the whole thing. According to his attorneys, he was making arrangements to head out of town Friday afternoon—at their advisement until this blows over, but he was called into an emergency meeting on his way to the airport. He was teleconferencing with Beijing well into the evening. Several witnesses confirmed he was in his office when bricks were crashing through your windows and someone was helping themselves to my sister's underwear."

"Doesn't mean anything. He could've paid someone. Hell, he could've paid someone to do all of it—the flowers, the cat, the bricks, and the break in." But it didn't add up.

"Yeah..."

"You're not buying that any more than I am."

"The window deal and the flowers maybe, but the break-in and the cat... Those were personal. He's angry. He wants Wren to know he can get to her anywhere."

Tucker nodded his agreement. "Exactly."

"So where does that leave us?"

"It leaves me wondering if we're looking at the wrong man."

"I've been thinking the same thing." Ethan sighed. "I didn't want to go there."

"You're not joking." The situation was a little less complicated when Rex was their prime suspect. His high-profile lifestyle was easy to keep tabs on. "I think we need to start asking ourselves who else might be behind this." The question left him unsettled. The facts were falling into place, and it appeared less and less likely that Richardson was Wren's stalker. They needed to find their mystery man before he found Wren. "I'll call Owens again later. I want all the I's dotted and T's crossed before Richardson's officially scratched from the list. If he's in the clear, we'll have to look at other options and go from there."

"Let me know what Owens says."

"I will." The floorboard creaked in the next room. "Wren's awake. I should go." He'd been waiting for her to get up. Apologies were definitely in order after last night. He'd been an asshole. His struggle with being here was his problem, and he'd made it hers.

"One second. I want to thank you again for helping me out, man."

"No problem."

"I didn't realize...the Utah house... I never put two and two together..."

He knew where Ethan was going. "No problem," he repeated wanting to end this right here.

"It's a big deal, Tucker, and I'm grateful for all you're doing."

"Wren's a good woman. She doesn't deserve what's happening to her."

"Yes, she is and no, she doesn't."

"Then that's the end."

"Okay. Call me when you have something."

"I will." He disconnected and shoved his cell in the elastic waist of his pajamas as he made his way into the hall. Wren's door opened, and he stopped as she stepped out in black yoga pants and a white long-sleeved top. She looked good enough to eat with her sleepy eyes and hair pulled back in a ponytail. "Good morning." He tried a friendly smile.

"Morning," she responded coolly, then made a beeline for the kitchen.

He winced. She was still pissed, and he couldn't exactly blame her. He stopped in the doorway as Wren opened cupboards at random until she found the coffee mugs. She tugged the fridge door open and pulled out a one-shot coffee pod and small glass creamer.

"Did you sleep okay?"

"Mmm." She placed the pod in the designated spot in the coffeemaker, pressed the dispenser down, poured a few drops of creamer in her mug, and shoved it beneath the spout.

He walked to where she waited for her brew and leaned against the counter next to her, arms crossed against his bare chest. Sometimes the best way to deal with a cold shoulder was to play with fire. Wren definitely had her fair share of fire. "Heard you up for quite a while. Get a lot of work done?"

"Not nearly enough." She whirled away, grabbed the loaf of whole-wheat bread, and shoved a piece in the toaster. Strawberry jam appeared from the refrigerator next, then a knife from the drawer. The toast popped up, and she pulled it from the slot, spreading jellied fruit around the bread, and grabbed her coffee as it finished dripping. She stepped toward the hall, but he stood in her way.

"Where you going?"

"To my room. I have stuff to do." She took a bite of her toast and tried to skirt around him.

He moved to the left as she did. "It's Sunday."

"So?" She dodged to the right.

He followed her dance and stepped forward, leaving her no choice but to back up. He advanced again, and she bumped the counter. Coffee sloshed to the rim of her cup. "Easy, Cooke. You're going to spill." He took the mug and brought it to his lips, sipped, groaned. "Good stuff."

Frowning, she took the cup back. "Make your own."

"I will." He rested his hands on the cool granite countertop, purposely boxing her in. Hints of her perfume teased his nose as he leaned in close. "You look damn good in the morning, Cooke." He wrapped one of her silky curls around his finger. "All sexy and rumpled."

"Rico's back, I see." She smirked.

He lifted his brows. "Huh?"

"Decided you're going to be friendly again?" She sipped her coffee, measuring him.

"I want to apologize again for last night. I was a jerk. I really am sorry, Cooke. It won't happen again."

Still eyeing him, she took another bite of her toast.

"Truce?"

She swallowed. "On one condition."

"What's that?"

"You tell me where the washer and dryer is. I'm completely out of clean clothes."

"I can do better." He grasped her wrist, guiding her piece of toast to his mouth, and bit in. Holding her gaze, he chewed and swallowed. He wanted out of this house, and now he had the perfect excuse. "I'm taking you shopping."

"Shopping? I don't have time to shop. I have a business to run."

"I bet you could sneak away for a little while—couple hours will do us both some good."

"I can't." She set the coffee cup down and placed a hand on his shoulder, giving him a gentle shove.

He moved to let her by and looked to his right, catching a glimpse of downtown in the distance. Cars drove along the busy streets, and early-bird skiers took advantage of the quiet resort slopes. There was fun to be had among the bustling shops and crowded restaurants. He snagged her hand. "Wait."

She turned. "Tucker, I have laundry and work to get to. Patrick has two big meetings to cover tomorrow. He and I have a lot to go over. I still have several mockups to create and orders to fill, not to mention concept bids to generate for new clients."

He pulled her to the windows as she spoke and stood behind her, bringing her back up against his chest, gripping her shoulders gently. "Look at the view. It's like a fairyland."

"It's beautiful, but I really have to call Patrick." She took two steps before he yanked her around to face him.

"Come on, Cooke. Two hours." Now that the idea was firmly planted, it was suddenly vital that he share the town he once loved with her. "You know what they say about all work and no play..."

"Yes, they say it's productive."

He grinned. "Your laptop will be here when we get back, and you need some warmer clothes. We could be here for a while. Besides, Ethan Cooke Security's paying for this little block of retail therapy."

"Does my brother know about this?" She stood on her tiptoes, studying his wound, gently touching the tender skin around the bandages. "Looks sore."

"Ow." He pulled his head away from her probing fingers. "He'll know when he gets the bill."

"Well if Ethan's buying..." She smiled. "It's tempting, but I—"

He pressed his finger to her soft lips, sensing another refusal. "Hold up. Listen."

Her eyes darted left, right, then met his. “What?”

“Do you hear it?” he whispered, moving closer, still looking in her eyes.

“No.” Her brows furrowed as she concentrated. “What?”

“The clothes. They’re calling your name.” He grabbed her hips and nestled his lips close to her ear. “‘Wren, come buy me.’”

She scoffed, swatted his arm, then reluctantly laughed. “You *idiot*. Why on earth did Ethan send me away with you?”

He chuckled. “Because you’re just that lucky.”

She laughed again.

“Come on, Cooke, you know you want to.”

“Oh, all right.” She pulled his hands from her waist and backed up. “Two hours and *only* two hours, then I have to get back to work.”

“Deal. We’ll meet at the door in thirty minutes.”

“I only need twenty.”

“Twenty, it is.” He watched Wren walk away, then glanced toward town again. For the first time in fourteen years, the idea of walking the streets of Park City was actually appealing.

Wren took the steps from the garage into the house, loaded down with shopping bags. “Whew. I had no idea I got so carried away.”

Tucker stepped in behind her, closed the door, and locked it. “You’re definitely a champion shopper.” He set down his own bags and tugged the beret from her head.

“Thanks.”

“No problem. You want help bringing those to your room?”

“Nah. I’ve got it.”

“I guess I’ll heat up lunch.” He shook the deli box he held. “You’re in for a treat. Nobody makes a calzone like Tony.”

She breathed in Italian spices and smiled. "Smells amazing. I'm starved."

"That makes two of us."

"I'll be right back." She headed toward her bedroom, more relaxed than she had been in a long time. It was after one—well past the two hours she'd allotted herself for a quick trip to town. She needed to call Patrick and get those orders in by five if she wanted on-time delivery next week. And she was behind on the new client bids that absolutely had to be completed by this evening, but she couldn't regret the much-needed break. For the first time in months, her shoulders were free of tension and the constant nagging headache was nowhere to be found.

She'd had a good time—a great time actually—wandering from shop to shop, with Tucker at her side. He was the first man—besides Patrick—who didn't seem to mind sitting in a chair by the dressing room while she tried on clothing options.

He'd been funny and charming, flashing her his slow, sexy grin when she swiped the curtain back, modeling her attire, looking for second opinions on potential purchases. He'd even helped her pick out t-shirts and other little knickknacks for Kylee and Emma and bought a couple things for himself. And he'd been a good sport, trying on the clothes she threw over his curtain.

She chuckled, shaking her head, remembering the cowboy attire she'd tossed at him and his, "You've gotta be kidding me, Cooke." After several minutes of her coaxing and teasing, he shoved the curtain aside and strutted out in the plaid shirt, skintight jeans, boots, and Stetson, posing. Numerous women had stopped to stare at his muscular body filling out his clothes in all the right places. His mischievous eyes had stared into hers while he grinned, and she'd fought not to swallow her tongue as her hormones shot into overdrive. The outfit had been meant as a joke, but he'd had the last laugh when he chased her around the store calling her 'little lady' and forced her into a spirited dosey doe. Then they'd both laughed as they clung together, spinning round and round.

Her smile faded. She wanted that moment back. Tucker was quiet again. As soon as they piled into the Jeep and started up the winding road to the house, his sense of humor vanished and the mysterious tension came back, robbing him of his gorgeous smile. He spoke more now than he did last night, but he wasn't the same.

What was it about this place that made him so unhappy? Surely there was something. She glanced around at the beautiful view through the large picture windows, the top-of-the-line furnishings, and spacious guest bathroom beyond, dumbfounded by how such a spectacular place could make anyone sad.

Shrugging off her curiosity, she took off her jacket and scarf and headed for the closet to put away her new items. She wanted to ask what was bothering him, but he made it more than clear that he didn't want to talk about it. Growing up with Ethan made her wise to the ways of men. Tucker would share if and when he wanted to. Bringing up his mercurial moods would be construed as nagging, so she would leave him alone.

She pulled glossy pine doors open and gaped at the enormity of the walk-in closet. "Wow," she whispered in awe as she glanced around at empty rows of shelving, drawers of various sizes, and the three-sided mirror tucked in the corner. Tucker's mother was serious about fashion. Wren's organized soul teemed with envy, and she made mental notes of the layout for potential changes in her own home.

Wren pulled pretty sweaters and slacks from bags and folded or hung them according to color, then she lifted the cumbersome box containing her new winter boots and shoved it on the shelf above her head. A paper fell, floating to the floor. Frowning, she bent down, picked it up, and turned it over. A picture. She glanced at the date stamped in the bottom right corner—*July 10, 1999*—and smiled as she stared at Tucker, wearing his swim trunks, standing by the pool, grinning for the camera with his arm wrapped around a girl's slim waist. Apparently Tucker never went through a gawky adolescent stage. He couldn't have been more than sixteen or seventeen in the photo, yet he was still muscular and gorgeous. He'd added bulk and height over the years, and his facial features had sharpened with age, but he'd been a head-turner his entire life. And the girl standing with Tucker, grinning his identical smile, had the same bold hazel eyes and black hair, though hers was much longer and tied back in a ponytail.

A knock sounded on the bedroom door. "Lunch is ready."

"Thanks." She glanced over her shoulder. "Come on in."

He stopped in the closet doorway.

"Look what I found." She turned, flashing him the picture, then studied it again. "I didn't know you have a sister. What's her name?"

"Staci."

"You look just alike. Must be pretty close in age."

"We're twins."

"Twins?" She beamed, studying Staci, more intrigued than before. What would it have been like to share a womb with Tucker? "Who's older?"

"Me."

"She's gorgeous—much better looking than you," she teased. "What does she do?"

"Nothing."

"Nothing?" She looked at him, puzzled. "I mean professionally."

"She's dead." He turned and walked out.

"Wha... Tucker." Horrified, she stared after him, unable to move. Dead? She looked at the grinning, vibrant, bikini-clad girl tucked against Tucker's side and shook her head in disbelief. Turbulent waves of guilt consumed her as she placed the photo back on the shelf and hurried to the kitchen. Italian sausage and hot, fresh dough scented the air, turning her stomach. “Tucker.”

He stood at the counter, cutting the calzone in half.

“Tucker. I’m—I’m so sorry.”

He stopped, glancing over his shoulder.

“I had no idea.”

He shrugged. “She’s been gone a long time.” He gave his attention back to the meal she no longer wanted.

She stood where she was, unsure of what to say or do. Tucker may have given her one of his casual shrugs, but he still hurt. Of course he did. How could he not? He and Staci had been close. One snapshot frozen in time made that clear.

“Let’s eat.” He brought two plates to the dining room table.

Wren hesitated, unsettled by the surprisingly powerful grief consuming her for a girl she’d never known and the heartbreaking anguish for the man who still lived. What must it be like to lose a sibling—and a twin at that? If anything ever happened to Ethan... She couldn’t bear to think of it, yet Tucker lived with the reality of loss every day. She followed Tucker’s lead and took her seat, placing a paper napkin in her lap.

Tucker breathed deep. “Smells good.”

“Mhm.” She gave him a small smile and stared down at golden folded bread.

“You gonna eat?”

“Yes.” She tore off a chunk of crust and nibbled a bite she didn’t want.

He reached across the table and lifted her chin with his thumb, meeting her eyes.

She blinked rapidly, fighting an unexpected wave of tears.

“Don’t.”

“I won’t,” she whispered, shaking her head, caught up in a well of empathy for the kind man staring at her.

“It won’t bring her back.”

"I feel so bad. I had no idea." She swallowed. "I'm just so sorry, Tucker."

"It's all right. You didn't know. Go ahead and eat some lunch. I'm certainly going to." He dropped his hand, picked up his calzone, bit in, and closed his eyes. "*Mmm*, just as good as I remember."

She picked up the loaded pocket and took a small bite. The kick of hot sausage and rich sauce twisted her stomach.

"Good, huh?" Tucker bit in again.

"Yes." She gave him another small smile as he wiped his mouth. She grasped for something to say, wanting to move past the moment. Tucker's shopping bags by the couch caught her eye. "I had fun today. More fun than I've had in a long time."

He swallowed. "Me too."

Minutes passed in silence while Tucker devoured the majority of his enormous half. He tossed the remaining crust on his plate and patted his stomach. "Ugh, I'm finished."

"Me too." She pushed back from the table.

"You hardly ate anything."

"I'll save it for later." She reached for his plate. "I'll take care of this."

"Thanks."

Wren walked to the sink, setting down the plates, and gripped the edge of the counter. Why did she feel like she was going to burst into tears? She *rarely* cried, yet she couldn't shake the need to weep. Tucker seemed to be at peace with his sister's passing—or mostly, but she wasn't. She couldn't stop picturing Staci's young, beautiful face. *She's been gone a long time. How long?* she wondered.

Wanting to be busy, needing to focus on something other than tragedy, Wren picked up the cookie sheet Tucker had used to heat their late lunch and scrubbed away the stubborn spots of burnt sauce and cheese. Finished, she dried the sheet, put it away, tossed the remaining food in the trash, and placed the plates in the dishwasher. With nothing left to do, she stepped into the dining area and stopped. Tucker stood by the large picture windows, staring out. Despite his tough build, he appeared small against the massive panes of glass—and very alone.

Wren pressed a hand to her heart, aching for the man she was just beginning to know, and walked to him. The instinct to comfort was stronger than her need to keep her distance. She wrapped her arms around his waist and rested her cheek against his solid back.

Tucker stiffened, hesitating, then covered her hands with his.

"This place makes you sad."

He didn't respond.

"The pool in the picture. It's the one outside."

"Yeah."

His family had come here since he and his sister were babies. Everything made sense now. "This house. It was special to both of you."

His grip tightened against her skin, and he turned. He held her gaze and brought her knuckles to his lips.

She closed her eyes in defense against his tender gesture and the invasion of staggering confusion it caused.

He pressed her palm to his cheek and she met his gaze. "You should go get some work done," he said quietly.

Swallowing, she nodded. "I'll be in my room if you need me."

He slid his thumb along her jaw as he glanced at her lips.

She ached to taste him. All she had to do was step forward, so she took a step back, turned, and hurried to her room, needing to escape whatever had just passed between them.

☙ Chapter Nine ❧

Fat snowflakes fell from the evening sky, catching the outside lights Tucker kept on. He applied deodorant as he glanced at the digital clock on the bathroom counter—six-thirty. There was plenty of time to take Wren out and be back before the latest snowstorm dumped the worst of its bounty on Park City. He walked into his room with his towel slung low around his hips and grabbed a pair of black slacks from the closet. He tugged on boxers, then his pants, and pulled a fitted white sweater from a hanger. He slid the shirt over his head and smiled as Wren's voice carried through the wall. She'd been on the phone or Skype with Patrick for a week running. Wren Cooke was the true definition of a workaholic. From sun up to well past sun down, she was at it, designing rooms on her fancy little computer, constantly scanning stuff, or in some sort of conference call. It was time for her to come up for air.

He walked down the hall, stopping by her half-open door, watching her pace about the space with her cell pasted to her ear. Damn, she took his breath away, even in jeans and a simple lavender long-sleeve v-neck.

"No. She chose the pale eggshell yellow." Wren huffed out a breath. "Patrick, we're not changing the color again. Tell her the fabric already arrived and the furnishings are being made. I've ordered over a quarter of a million dollars' worth of product for the room she okayed two weeks ago. I can't eat that type of cash just because she's decided she wants to change her mind again. Show her the plans. Remind her of how much she loves it." She pressed a hand to her forehead and closed her eyes. "I know. I know. She's a pain in the ass. Yes, you have to go back tomorrow." She grinned. "I'm too far away to bail you out." She chuckled. "Go home, pour yourself a glass of wine—the good stuff I bought you—and put your feet up. We'll go over the Movenbeck install again tomorrow after you've had a chance to relax. I'll call Shane and set up a mani/pedi for you. Yes I do, because I love you and value your sanity. Go home, Patrick. Okay. Bye." Wren disconnected and let loose a frustrated growl in her throat as she collapsed back among the debris covering her bed.

Tucker rapped his knuckles against wood and pushed the door open. "Rough day?"

She rubbed her temples. "I don't want to talk about it."

He set a huge binder of fabrics on the floor and sat on the edge of the mattress. "Mrs. Cartwright giving you a hard time?"

She stopped her methodical messaging and opened one eye. "How did you know?"

"I heard the last minute or so of your conversation. You were pacing, soothing Patrick's ruffled feathers, and dropped a 'pain in the ass.'" He shrugged. "I put two and two together."

She smiled. "Can't get one by you, Detective." She scrubbed her hands over her forehead. "That woman is driving me *crazy*."

Tucker lay beside her, pulling a pencil and another binder from under his hip. "We could drive to LA, kill her, hide the body and be back here before anyone was the wiser."

She chuckled and turned to her side. "Don't tempt me. If she keeps this up, I might take you up on your offer."

He rolled over, resting his cheek on his folded arm, facing

her. They'd barely seen each other or spoken over the last several days. He'd been closed behind the doors of his room just as busy with his work as she was with her own. "Why don't you get dressed up—Wren-Cooke-style—and I'll take you out."

She groaned. "I'd rather lie here and sulk."

He swept a long wispy wave behind her ear, and she inched away. "Rumor has it today's your birthday."

"No, it's not. Wait." Frowning, she sat up. "Yes, it is." She stood. "I can't believe I forgot my own birthday. And Patrick, he always remembers. Stupid Lenora Cartwright," she muttered, glaring.

"Ethan said he'll call you later. He sent me a text about an hour ago. He's been tied up on duty all day." He'd had no idea November first was Wren's birthday until Ethan clued him in.

She smiled. "He never forgets either."

She didn't say anything about her parents; obviously they hadn't bothered to call. Bastards. For that alone, he wanted to make tonight special. Tucker stood. "Since Patrick's not here and neither is Ethan, we'll have to celebrate on our own. Get dressed and we'll do it up right."

She wrinkled her nose. "I'm too tired, plus I have to go over plans for the Movenbeck install."

"There's nothing wrong with taking a little break."

She leaned over the bed, setting right the mess of sketchpads, pencils, color pallets, her laptop, and so forth. "I took time off last weekend when we went shopping."

His mouth dropped open, feigning shock. "Stop the presses. Wren Cooke took a morning off from work a *week* ago."

She sent him a wry smile. "This is a huge few days for my business, and I'm stuck *here*. Brice and Mindy Movenbeck are having a big charity gathering for their foundation in the new space I designed." She stacked furniture magazines on the dresser, then started to pace. "Tomorrow morning's the install; tomorrow night's the party. These are A-listers, as you know. This has to go right. Everything *must* be perfect. This is make-or-break, and I have to sit back while Patrick handles it all. Then there's Lenora's projects and the million other things that have to be seen to while I'm hundreds of miles away." She stopped abruptly, set her hand on her hip, sighing, her frustration and worry more than apparent. "This stalking crap couldn't have happened at a worse time." Her eyes were strained, her posture ramrod straight. She needed some time away, whether she was willing to admit it or not.

"Hey." He closed the distance between them, resting his hands on her shoulders. "You've gotta take a couple of deep breaths here, Cooke."

She stepped back from his touch. Wren had been careful to keep her distance since their moment in the dining room. Something had passed between them, something...powerful and intimate. He and Wren were just getting to know each other, but she understood him. Not many did. And she cared. Beneath her cool, guarded exterior lay a sweet, kind woman with a deep well of empathy for others. She'd struggled with her emotions at the dining room table while she mourned for him and a girl she'd never met. More than anything, he wanted her to let him back into that place where few people were allowed. Breaking through Wren's defenses wasn't going to be easy. He sure as hell had his work cut out for him, but as he stared at the exotic beauty with the cautious gray eyes, he'd never been more certain that she was worth the effort.

He advanced again, and she hesitated with another step back, then held her ground. He needed to touch her. He stroked a finger along her jaw. "You're beat, Cooke. A couple hours away with a decent meal will recharge your batteries." He moved his hand to her neck, caressing his knuckles along her soft skin, and she shuddered.

"Tucker—" She pulled his hand away. "I can't."

She could, and she needed to. He fiddled with her fingers. “Tell me you aren’t going to let Lenora Cartwright ruin your special day.”

She frowned.

“This is your last official year in your twenties. Put on something nice and let’s go—for a little while.”

She let loose a deep breath. “Give me fifteen minutes.”

He grinned. “See you in twenty-five.”

“Fifteen. Start your timer.” She walked into the guest bathroom and closed the door behind her.

Wren studied the gorgeous presentation of her dish as their suit-clad waiter set their meals before them. “This looks lovely.”

The waiter picked up the bottle of pinot grigio, adding to the crisp white Wren already sampled, then tipped more into Tucker’s glass as well. “Enjoy your meals.”

“Thank you,” Tucker said as he picked up his fork and knife.

Wren breathed deep and hummed her appreciation. “I can’t remember the last time I had a good piece of cod.”

“Looks like this could be your night.”

“It smells amazing.”

“Why don’t you go ahead and give it a try.”

She cut into the tender white fish, forked up a small bite, and closed her eyes, moaning as the subtle tastes melded beautifully on her tongue. “Oh my gosh. This is amazing. The hints of pesto are perfect.”

Tucker grinned. “Good.” He cut a sample of filet mignon and held the fork to her lips. “How about this?”

She held his gaze in the candlelight as she sampled the melt-in-your mouth morsel. “The chef is a genius. He’s earned every one of his five stars.”

He tasted his meal for himself and nodded. “Not half bad. I’ve never been to this restaurant. Ms. Hayes suggested it. She thought you might like it."

She glanced around at other well-dressed patrons enjoying their cuisine. Quiet violin music added to the stuffy fine-dining atmosphere. She looked back to Tucker again. This definitely wasn't his scene. He was more of a burger-and-beer kind of guy, yet he seemed just as at home here among Park City's upper crust as he did in his atrocious apartment. "Ms. Hayes was at the house today?"

He shook his head. "Yesterday. She stopped in to check on us—brought some fresh fruits and vegetables by. She asked where you were. I told her you were working. She said I should bring you here. When Ethan told me it was your birthday, I thought tonight would be the perfect opportunity to check it out."

"That's very sweet. Ms. Hayes takes good care of you."

"Always did."

"So, how long has it been since you've been back?"

"Fourteen-and-a-half years."

"A long time." Too many memories here, she assumed. Her heart broke all over again for the man sitting across the table, but she pushed away the unhappiness. He was trying to make tonight special. "Park City's a beautiful place." She looked out the window as pretty flakes fell. The slopes in the distance were lit up, and several enthusiasts were taking advantage. "Do you ski?"

"Sure. You?"

"Yes." She swallowed another heavenly bite. "It's been awhile, though. Several years, actually, but Ethan and I have had more than our fair share of races. In fact, that's how I broke my arm."

His brow shot up. "Some competition."

"He'll do anything to win."

Tucker paused with his next forkful. "Ethan broke your arm on purpose?"

"He says no, and Ms. Willa the same, but I've always had my doubts. I was about to cross our agreed-upon finish line and bam, he just happens to tangle his pole with mine, and I take a nosedive."

He grinned. "Sounds like a conspiracy."

She chuckled as he cut another piece of steak.

"Tucker Campbell? Is that you, son?" A tall older man stopped by their table.

Tucker stood, smiling, and held out his hand. "Mr. Follensby."

Mr. Follensby returned the handshake. "I haven't seen you in years. How are you?"

"I'm fine. Doing well."

The man smiled down at Wren.

"Mr. Follensby, this is Wren Cooke. Wren, Mr. Follensby is a good friend of my parents."

She took his hand. "Nice to meet you."

"And you. I hope you're enjoying your stay here in Park City."

"I am. This is a beautiful area."

"It certainly is." He patted her hand and returned his attention to Tucker. "I ran in to your pop awhile back in London. The missus and I stayed at the resort. The old man still runs a tight ship. Be sure to let him know his staff is still among the best. We were well taken care of."

Tucker nodded. "Will do. That's always great to hear."

"How's Melanie?"

"Mom's good. She's doing her charity work in Monterey."

"The missus needs to give her a call the next time we head that way. Well, I should go. I don't want to interrupt any more of your evening. It was nice to meet you, Wren."

"You as well."

"Good to have you back in Utah, son." He slapped Tucker's shoulder. "You take care now."

"I will, and you do the same."

Mr. Follensby left as quickly as he'd strolled up to the table.

Wren sipped her wine, following the older gentleman's

path to the exit. "Now *there's* a man with some energy."

Tucker settled himself in his seat. "He's always had plenty—used to work for my dad."

"I see." She'd learned more about Tucker's family in the five minutes he'd spoken with Mr. Follensby than she had in the week they'd been in his home. She wanted to know the man across the table. "He worked at the hotel your father runs in London?"

"No, Mr. Follensby oversaw the Northeast branches here in the States for...years. He's retired."

"Well that's a relief."

Tucker frowned. "I'm not following you."

"I was starting to think your father was Bruce Wayne and the off-limit wing at the summer home housed the bat cave." She took another bite of cod.

He grinned. "Sorry to disappoint you. Nothing as exciting as that."

"So, your father runs hotels in London and the U.S.?"

"Among several other spots around the world."

No wonder they had money. With a job like that... She picked up her wineglass and set it back down as she connected the dots. "Wait a minute. Campbell Suites."

He sampled a bite of creamy mashed potatoes. "That's us."

She gaped as she stared at the simple man across from her. "*You're* Campbell Suites?"

He shook his head. "My dad's Campbell Suites. I'm a bodyguard."

"But—this is—" She pressed a hand to her forehead, trying to digest this new development. If she'd ever been more shocked, she couldn't remember. "I can't believe this. You're family has piles and piles of money and you live in that crap hole by the water?"

He shrugged. "I like my crap hole by the water."

"Your family's main home is in Monterey?"

"Yes."

"Has your mother ever been inside your apartment?"

"No. She doesn't get out of Monterey much."

"That might be for the better. A shock like that could be unhealthy."

He chuckled.

She smiled at the absurdity of it all. "So, why aren't you a hotelier like your father?"

"That was the plan. Then things changed."

"Like what?"

"I decided I wanted to become a cop instead."

"From hotelier to justice seeker."

He shrugged. "Something like that."

His eyes were growing distant with every question she asked. He was closing up on her again. Why? Taking a risk, she reached out and touched his hand. "I'm not teasing you, Tucker. Criminal Justice is a very noble profession."

He smiled. "We're a noble breed. You just won't date us."

She wrinkled her nose and pulled back, caught in her own web of inconsistencies. Score one for Tucker. "Nope."

He reached forward and snagged her hand. "There's just one problem, Cooke." The troubled look was gone from his eyes, and the mischief was back. "We're out on a date right now." He rubbed his thumb over her knuckles, and she swallowed as a spark of heat followed the trail.

"This isn't a date." She tried to free herself from his grip as he sent his thumb on another journey, but he held her still.

"No?"

"Absolutely not."

"You're dressed up—look good enough to eat, by the way; I'm dressed up, we're drinking wine, candles are flickering while you stare into my eyes. Definitely a date, Cooke."

She wiggled uncomfortably in her deep red, clinging sweater-dress as his long, slow strokes continued to drive her crazy. "Sorry to disappoint you. We have a working relationship—nothing more. I'm just not attracted to you," she lied.

Shrugging, he shook his head. "You win some, you lose some."

She opened her mouth to respond, but snapped it shut. He was baiting her and having a hell of a time doing so. She was quickly losing control of this evening. It was time to go. "I don't know about you but I'm full." She pushed back her mostly empty plate. "I'm ready whenever you are." She glanced down at her hand, wanting him to let her go. His thumb alone was making her melt. What would the rest of him do?

"No cake?"

"Uh, no thanks. The fish and veggies were very filling."

"Ice cream?"

"I doubt they have Death by Chocolate."

"Probably not." He held up his free hand, signaling the waiter.

Minutes later, the heat puffed through the vents of the Jeep and the wipers batted away enormous flakes as they traveled down Main Street. Wren kept her hands in her lap, her fingers laced, afraid Tucker might try to touch her again. He packed a punch. Her skin still tingled from his last teasing assault.

He slowed and pulled up to a spot by the small general store. "I'll be right back. Keep the doors locked."

"Okay."

Tucker hustled inside, tucking his chin into his thick jacket. The wind was picking up, along with the precipitation. She watched Tucker through the large panes of glass, studying him as he moved about, bringing his item to the counter. Her heart picked up its pace as he spoke to the cashier and grinned. That smile was as lethal as any weapon. She scrutinized his gorgeous face and powerful build, searching for *any* flaw. There was none to be found. He was beautiful—perfectly so. And beneath the cockiness and sarcasm lay a kind man with plenty of sweet spots. All in all, Tucker Campbell was a dangerous package. It was wise to remember that. She still struggled to wrap her mind around the staggering wealth he came from. He was so basic—not a stuck-up, entitled bone in his body. She admired him more because of it. He easily could have sat back and coasted in his father's footsteps, but he'd paved his own path.

He gave the attendant a quick wave and pushed through the door.

Wren unlocked the driver's side for him. "What'd'ya get?"

He handed her the small brown bag. "Needed some shaving cream."

"Oh." She loved his constant five o'clock shadow.

He buckled in and waited for an ebb in traffic, then reversed back onto Main Street. He stopped at the four-way intersection and took a left up the twisting mountain road.

Wren pulled her phone from her purse as Tucker slowly maneuvered the sharp, slippery curves. Dinner had been enjoyable and a much-needed break, but now she had to get back to work. There were probably a million voicemails waiting for her. She slid her finger across the screen and stared. No new messages. No waiting texts. Surprised, she shoved the cell away. Patrick must've actually taken her advice and put his feet up.

"Everything okay?"

"Yeah. It's just weird not being bombarded by calls."

"Enjoy it while it lasts."

She wanted to, but the silence left her uneasy. Patrick was as obsessed with the business as she was. She grabbed her phone again, ready to give him a call, then put it away. Maybe he'd found himself a date—the new guy he met on the buying trip last week, perhaps. Patrick deserved a quiet night as much as she did.

Tucker pulled in the drive and stopped. "Brilliant. What the hell kind of plow job is that?" A good two feet of snow had been pushed up against the garage door.

"I guess they don't know we're staying here."

"Yeah, but it's the garage. Who *does* that?"

Shrugging, she shook her head. "I don't know what to tell you."

He backed up and pulled closer to the front door. "I'll have to call the company and get this figured out. I can't have the vehicle sitting out. It's not good for logistics."

"You never know when we'll have to make a speedy get away," she teased.

He smiled. "I think we're good here, but I like to be safe rather than sorry." He turned off the ignition and killed the lights. "Looks like we're going in this way tonight. Ready?"

"Yes."

"Wait right here." He snagged the bag from her lap, shoved it in his pocket, got out, came around to her side, and opened her door. "It's getting slippery." He offered his arm.

She was in heels, and the snow was piling up, yet she didn't want to grab hold. She was still churned up over a simple slide of his thumb. "Thanks but I think I'm good."

"You sure?"

"Yeah." She stepped out and slid. "*Crap!*"

He grabbed her around the shoulders, pulling her against him, catching her before she went down.

She clung to him, gripping his powerful waist. They stared in each other's eyes as their breath puffed out in white plumes.

"Wasn't kidding. How about that arm?"

His cologne clogged her brain, and her gaze darted to his lips just inches from her own. "Uh."

"It's freezing out here, Cooke. Walk."

She broke out of her trance and took a step toward the door. What was her problem? She'd never reacted to a man like this before. A few swipes of his fingers along her skin and he'd successfully tied her up in a ball of sexual knots.

He unlocked the door and she stepped inside, immediately untangling herself from his hold.

"Thanks for dinner," she said in a rush as she unbuttoned her coat. "I should probably get back to work." She needed to lose herself in the details of the Movenbeck install and pretend this whole evening never happened. Work would help her smooth out the worst of whatever it was Tucker was doing to her.

"Night's not over yet."

What did he mean by that? She narrowed her eyes as he put his jacket in the closet and walked to the fire, throwing more logs onto the sleepy embers.

"Wanna scoop us a couple bowls?"

"Huh?"

He tossed her the brown bag.

She caught the paper sack, peeked in, and couldn't help but smile. "Death by Chocolate."

"Gotta have it on your birthday."

"I thought you said you bought shaving cream."

"I didn't want to spoil the surprise."

How was she supposed to resist a man who made a special stop-off in crappy weather for her favorite ice cream? He kept throwing her off balance with his sweet gestures. "Thank you."

"You're welcome."

She held his gaze a moment, worried for the first time ever that her sheer determination to keep Tucker Campbell at arm's length might not be enough. She had few defenses against a kind heart.

"You all right?"

"Uh, yes. I'm going to...do this..." She waved the bag and turned, rolling her eyes at herself on her way to the kitchen. "Get it together, Wren," she muttered as she yanked two bowls from the cupboard. *Nothing* was happening here. She didn't feel anything more for Tucker than a healthy dose of lust. She glanced through the open space separating the kitchen from the living room and huffed out a breath. Did he have to stand there like that, looking all gorgeous and vulnerable while he stared into the fire?

She bit her lip as she fought the urge to walk to him and

soothe away his sadness. *No. This isn't happening.* More determined than ever to remain unaffected, she scooped up a small serving of creamy chocolate for herself and a large helping for Tucker. They were friends—if that. And he was her bodyguard. She was *not* about to be the clichéd damsel who fell for her protector. The idea alone almost made her chuckle. Calmer, steadier, she put the container in the freezer and grabbed two spoons on her way to the sitting area. She would enjoy her birthday treat with some friendly conversation, then get back to work. The end. "Here you go."

He gave her a small smile as he took the bowl and sat on the loveseat. "Thanks."

Determined to show herself that Tucker was nothing more than another attractive man, she took the cushion next to him. Heat radiated from the fire as she held the cold bowl in her hand and scooped up a bite of rich chocolaty sin. "Mmm. This is the best flavor ever invented."

"Pretty good," he said over a mouthful, propping his legs on the coffee table and crossing his ankles.

She rested her head against the cushion as she relaxed further. She'd completely overreacted. She could handle sitting next to Tucker while they enjoyed their dessert. "Look at the snow. It's really coming down."

"They're saying we should see a good foot-and-a-half by morning, maybe more."

"It's beautiful—peaceful. I'm rarely around snow, so this is nice." She finished her helping and put her dish on the side table. Copying Tucker, she rested her feet on the table, crossing them at the ankle. "Thank you for tonight—for making my birthday special."

He scraped up the last of his ice cream and set his bowl aside. "I wish I had a gift for you."

"Dinner out and Death by Chocolate was perfect."

"Wanna watch a movie?"

"I'm pretty content watching the snow."

"Snow, it is." He settled his arms behind his head.

"You don't have to stay."

"I want to stay."

She looked at him as firelight flickered across his face.

His eyes held hers, and she licked her lips as a surge of want flooded her veins. Who was she kidding? This wasn't a good idea. Sitting here like this with the fire crackling and the snow falling and a gorgeous man inches away. She rushed to her feet. "I'm—I'm going to take care of the bowls." She reached for hers, turned for his, and crashed into his chest. His hands snaked out, grabbing hold of her arms, steadying her. She cleared her throat. "Sorry."

"No problem." He held her gaze as he took the dish from her and set it on the table.

"I was going to put that in the dishwasher," she said as her heart kicked into high gear.

"I'll take care of it later." He skimmed his knuckles along her cheek and took a step closer.

She knew she should walk away. She needed to, but she stayed where she was, breathing in his cologne, lost in his eyes, savoring his gentle touch, yearning as he moved in and captured her lips, slowly, tenderly.

She clutched his forearms in defense against the rush of heat catapulting through her stomach as he brought his hands to her cheeks, caressing, and changed the angle of the kiss. He urged her mouth open and his tongue slid against hers, teasing, tangling. She clung now, completely seduced by his bold flavor and skill. Her fingers moved along mounds of biceps and firm shoulders and rested against the smooth skin at the back of his neck. Moaning, she urged him to take them both deeper, but he eased away, still holding her face in his hands.

Wren blinked her eyes open, completely undone by a not-so-simple kiss. Her phone started to ring, disturbing the quiet, yet she made no attempt to answer as she stared at Tucker.

"Your cell's ringing."

"I know." She reached down, grabbing it, and glanced at the readout. "It's my brother." She pressed 'talk.' "Hell—Hello."

"Wren? Are you okay?"

She was anything but. "Yes."

Tucker still held her close, stroking her skin, making it impossible to think. She stepped away, hoping to break whatever this power was he had over her.

"Ethan, can I call you back?"

"Sure. Kylee wants to talk to you."

"Tell her to give me one second." She disconnected and gripped her phone, still unsteady. What should she say? She couldn't think with her heart pounding. "I'm going to go—I'm going to go to my room. I have to call Ethan back."

"Okay. Happy birthday."

"Thank you. For everything." She turned and headed down the hall toward the safety of her room.

"Hey, Cooke."

She stopped.

"Tonight was definitely a date."

Staring straight ahead, she started walking again. She had a phone call to make, then she needed to sit down and think long and hard about this unexpected turn her trip to Utah was taking.

Tucker sat on his bed, gripping his phone as he stared into the dark. His conversation with Owens left a ball of dread in the pit of his stomach. They had problems—big problems.

Sighing, he dialed Ethan. It didn't matter that it was after one. He would want to know now.

"Cooke," he said groggily.

"Sorry to call so late."

"What's wrong?"

"I just got off the phone with Owens."

"What's going on?" Ethan's voice tightened with concern.

"Owens concluded his investigation into Rex Richardson. He's not our man. They're one hundred percent sure."

Ethan sighed.

"A couple of officers responded to a call at Cooke Interiors right around closing time tonight. Apparently after Patrick got off the phone with Wren, he went to lock up and found a dead black cat on the front step—decapitated; the guts were scattered all over the damn place. Patrick reported the incident immediately. He was pretty shaken up. He's not going to tell Wren."

"Good. She doesn't need to know; it'll only upset her. We'll send Collin over to install cameras around the building first thing in the morning. Son of a bitch. I never should have let her talk me out of putting them up. She said they messed with her ambiance or some shit like that the last time we had the conversation."

"Sounds about right." Ambiance was going to have to take a backseat to practicality now that the stakes were higher. Tucker rubbed at the painful tension squeezing his shoulders. "There's more. The cops went over to Wren's house after they finished at her office, just to check things out. They found another dead cat—guts everywhere again, but he wrote 'MINE' all over the siding in blood. Her tires are slashed. He drove over to my apartment, took care of the Jeep too. Left another carcass on my hood; keyed 'YOU'RE NEXT' along the side."

"He's ballsy and escalating."

"That's for damn sure. He can't find her, and it's pissing him off. He's no longer running the show." A dangerous combination. Tucker clenched his jaw. "We can be certain he knows she's still with me."

"Looks like it. We'll get the paint and tires fixed and have someone bring your vehicles to my place."

"Thanks."

"Owens is *positive* Rex isn't behind this?"

"His alibi is solid for the bricks and break-in. And he's not in LA right now. He left for Australia after his police interview."

"Damn. I don't even know where to start on this one. She's my sister, and I don't know how to help her."

No one understood better than Tucker the helplessness of not being able to protect someone so important. "I'm at a loss myself. I'll talk to Wren when she wakes up and ask her if she's had trouble with anyone else. There has to be something. This guy knows her—maybe a former client or someone she dated. He feels betrayed. We just have to figure out who the bastard is."

"If we don't know who the hell we're looking for, how can we be sure you're safe where you're at?"

"Honestly, we can't, but we could say that about any place. He could track us down in Hawaii, at any one of my family's resorts, or in Europe. The only place safer than Park City is your house, and it's being ripped to shreds for the next few weeks. No one knows about the house here in Utah—or hardly anyone. Everyone assumed my father sold after Staci's murder. Dad would have, but Mom wouldn't let him."

"You're right. It's just—"

"She's your sister."

"Yeah." He sighed. "Keep me up to date if Owens gets anything new."

"You'll be the first. Not that you won't be checking in yourself." Ethan's hacking skills had broken through many firewalls before. "I'll keep her safe, Ethan."

"I know you will."

Tucker disconnected and stood, looking out the window into the endless dark, listening to the wind howl as Park City was pounded by the worst of the storm. The pretty falling flakes of hours before now fell in torrents, while violent gusts tossed them about mercilessly.

The power was out—had been for a while. Tucker flipped on his flashlight, walked to his closet, and grabbed his duffel bag. He unzipped the side, pulled out his Glock, and pushed a loaded magazine into the clip. For the first time since they arrived, he felt the need to keep his weapon close. They officially had no idea who they were messing with and how this man was connected to Wren's life. It was highly doubtful Wren's stalker would find them here, but nothing was out of the question.

He slid the gun into the band of his pajama bottoms and stepped from his room, ready for his nightly walkthrough of the house. With his flashlight in hand, he wandered about, inspecting the windows and doors, hesitating when he reached the forbidden hallway. Reluctantly, he started down the endless corridor. *Last one to their room is a rotten egg. Go! I'm the fair queen and you're her enchanted stallion. Get down so I can ride on your back.* He clenched his jaw, moving faster as painful memories consumed him. He checked the glass terrace doors, giving them a firm tug, and turned, stopping at the second door on the right, placing his unsteady hand on the knob. He wanted to turn it as much as he wanted to run away. *Love you, Tuck.* Staci's last words echoed in his mind, and he stepped back, continuing on to the living room, hating the hell out of this place.

A swift wave of anger washed through him as he made his way to the stack of logs by the living room fireplace. Why did he insist on torturing himself by heading down that fucking hall every night? The house had a fully functioning alarm system—or it did when the power was on. If someone tried to get in, the damn thing would let him know. But that wasn't how he did things. Wren was depending on him to keep her safe. Part of his job included routine inspections of their surroundings, whether he loathed them or not.

Ready to put the worst behind him—for tonight anyway—he grabbed an armful of wood and brought the load with him to his parents' old room—Wren's room now. Quietly, he closed her door, locked it, and brought the logs to the fireplace. The house would lose most of its heat before too long.

Within minutes, he had a fire crackling in the grate. He pulled the throw from the back of the chaise lounge he, Staci, and his mother had piled on more times than he could count and made himself comfortable. He set the gun on the floor, well within reach, covered up, and stared at Wren asleep in the firelight. She was beautiful, stunningly so, as the flames cast shadows over her breathtaking face.

He focused on her lush lips, and his pulse quickened as he thought of their tender embrace. He'd wanted a taste of that sassy mouth since the moment he saw her barrel into Sarah's hospital room all those months ago. Wren had been everything he'd imagined and then some.

It had been hard stepping back from her when all he'd wanted to do was carry her to his bed. Wren would have been his willing partner for one night, then she would have had the perfect excuse to push him away. He would have been nothing more than exactly what she'd expected—a guy looking for a meaningless roll in the sheets. He had no intention of being what Wren expected. He wanted more. He wanted it all. He wanted her surrender.

The log shifted in the fire, casting embers around the grate. He reached out, touching his gun again as he glanced from Wren to the dark. Eventually she would understand that he was different. He had every intention of proving it while he kept her safe.

☙ Chapter Ten ❧

Wren opened her eyes, startled by another strong burst of wind battering the windows. If this kept up, the glass was sure to break. She'd never heard such powerful gusts before. And the snow—it fell in frenzied sheets. She stared out at the winter wonderland, fascinated by the billowing pines and the drifts as tall as she was. The forecasters had said a storm, but this was a blizzard—her first. Park City was being pummeled.

She rolled to her back and sat up, frowning at the small flames licking the remains of three logs in the fireplace and Tucker asleep in the chaise lounge. When did he come in and how did she not hear him start a fire? She studied him as he slept. He looked uncomfortable with his long, powerful legs hanging off the edge and his head resting against his arm in the crook of the chair. He had to be freezing; his blanket lay pooled on the floor. Her eyes wandered over the dark scruff of his beard and mile-long lashes, his chest and stomach—all that smooth, muscled skin. No one had a right to *look* like that.

Her gaze trailed back up, locking on his mouth, and a rush of heat washed through her belly as she remembered his firm lips pressing against hers and the unhurried way their tongues tangled. No one had a right to *kiss* the way he did.

Tucker Campbell was lethal—more so than she'd first imagined. He'd destroyed her with a few teasing swipes of his thumb and a sensual meeting of lips. What would he do to her if she let him have his way? She shuddered out a deep breath as the liquid pull of desire started between her legs. She blinked and shook her head, shocked by where her thoughts were roaming. What was her problem? Yanking her covers back, she stood.

This was ridiculous. *She* was being ridiculous. Tucker had kissed her. So what? She was acting like a teenage girl with hearts in her eyes. At wits' end, she shoved the sheets up, then the comforter, smoothing out wrinkles with violent swipes. It was just one lip-lock, and her unexpected reaction to it didn't have to mean anything. It *didn't* mean anything. It's not like Tucker was the only man who'd ever rung her bell...sort of. Okay, so maybe he was the only guy who'd ever turned her into a puddle of sexual mush, but that was beside the point.

She grabbed the pillows and tossed them to the head of the bed. She needed to get laid, that was all. But *not* by him. Perhaps the thought had crossed her mind while she clung to him during their stupid embrace, but she was over that. It had been a while—a long while—since she'd allowed someone to take her to bed. Work hardly left her time to think of her libido, and none of the men she'd dated lately had been worth the emotional investment. Respect and some level of affection were necessary in a partner. She respected Tucker and on many levels liked him a lot, but she wasn't going there. She had little doubt he would more than scratch her itch, but he was so damned complicated. She had enough to deal with right now.

So that was it. Tucker Campbell was a hell of a kisser, and she'd been more affected than she expected due to her sexual drought. She just needed to keep her distance, make sure he kept his lips to himself, and her problems would be solved.

In the dim light of the early morning, she tossed the pretty blue shams among the pillows, relieved that this little issue had a simple solution. Now she needed to get to work. The Movenbecks would be expecting Patrick at eight with the truck full of furniture and the accents arriving moments later. She picked up her laptop as she glanced at the bedside clock, and swore. "You've got to be kidding me." No electricity meant no Internet. She sure as hell didn't have time for this. Yanking up her phone, she slid her finger over the screen and stared in disbelief. *No Service*. This was not happening. She sat on the edge of the bed as a rush of panic surged through her system. How was she going to check in with Patrick and make sure everything was going as planned?

Rushing to her feet, she hurried over to Tucker, barely registering the warmth of the fire as she scanned the hardwood floor, looking for his cell phone. It wasn't there. She settled her knee on the edge of the chaise lounge, peeking into the dark recesses of the areas his solid body didn't fill, then she patted at the pockets of his pajama pants.

Tucker eyes flew open as he suddenly sat up. "Cooke, what the hell are you doing?"

She pulled the blanket up and kicked something solid beneath the chair. "Ow." She dropped into a crouch, catching sight of the black item. Bingo. "I need your phone."

"Huh?"

She grabbed hold and pulled out a gun. Her smile of triumph vanished.

"What are you doing with my pistol?" He plucked the weapon from her hand.

"What are *you* doing with your pistol?" Her communication issues with Patrick ceased to matter as she stared at the Glock. "Why do you have that?" A wave of terror washed through her as she glanced over her shoulder toward the huge panes of glass. "Is he here? Did Rex find me?" A warm hand gripped her wrist, and she gasped.

"Relax, Wren." He tugged her down next to him. "As far as

I know, he has no clue where we're at."

"Oh." Her heart still thundered as she pushed herself more fully on the seat. "Then why?"

"The power was out when I went to sleep. The alarm has a battery backup, but they don't last forever. Like I said—better safe than sorry."

"Oh," she said again and took a deep breath of relief as she pressed a hand to her chest. "You scared me. I was half expecting to turn around and see Rex out the window."

"Wren." He sighed and took her hand.

She eyed him as her stomach pitched. Tucker never used her name, but he had—twice in the last three minutes. "What?"

"I got some news early this morning. Rex Richardson isn't the guy messing with you. He's not your stalker."

She shot up from her seat. "Yes, he is. Of course he is." Of all the things she'd been expecting him to say, this wasn't it.

Tucker shook his head. "No, he isn't."

She balled her hands into fists and rested them on her hips. "I *knew* this was going to happen. I knew they were going to sweep this whole thing under the rug." Rage and a sharp sense of betrayal drowned any remaining embers of fear. "So much for protecting the innocent."

"Rex is as much a victim as you are."

Her eyes widened in her shock. "How can you look at me and say that?" She turned to leave.

He snagged her wrist. "Wait a minute, Cooke."

She yanked her arm, trying to break free. "Not right now."

He gave her a hard tug, pulling her down next to him. "Sit down."

"I don't enjoy being manhandled." She tried to stand again. "I said not right—"

"Shut up and listen for five damn seconds," he said as he wrapped an arm around her waist, holding her in place.

She pressed her lips firm, sending him the look of death as he sidled himself closer.

"Some stuff happened yesterday."

Immediately the sinking feeling came back. "What?"

"My car was vandalized, as was yours. They found a couple more dead cats. Rex didn't do it. He's been out of the country."

"But it has to be him. Who else could it be?"

"That's what we need to figure out."

"I don't..." She shook her head, struggling to wrap her mind around the latest turn of events. "I have no idea who else would want to send me messages, kill cats, and ruin our cars."

"So we'll make a list of all the men you've had contact with over the last six months."

"Six *months*? I can't even tell you all the men I've had contact with over the last six weeks. I'm a business figure in Los Angeles. I interact with men every day."

"Okay, so three months. Start with the people you see on a regular basis: Patrick, the date you brought to Ethan's party...Mike, JT. Start with people like that and move back from there."

"Why do you keep bringing up Patrick? It's not him anymore than it is JT or Mike." She smiled as she thought of boring Michael Collins. "The only things Mike obsesses about are stocks and bonds."

"Probably, but the name of the game is elimination. We'll give Owens and Ethan your list. If the individuals on it have nothing to hide, they'll be cleared. I want everyone, Cooke, even if you think it couldn't be them."

"What about you? I've been spending a lot of time with you lately, and things keep getting worse."

His brow rose. "Are you implying I'm your stalker?"

"Suggesting Patrick, JT, or Mike could be is just as absurd."

"They're just names to check off; it's that simple."

"All right. I'll make you a list." The idea of including people she loved and trusted on that list left her unsettled. The possibility that it could actually be one of them made her ill.

"Precautions." He slid his thumb along her jaw. "That's all."

Nodding, she moved back. The last thing she needed right now was Tucker tying her in more knots. "He could be—he could be a stranger, right?"

"Could be."

"But it's not likely."

"In most cases, victims know their stalkers."

"Sarah didn't know Ezekiel."

"I said in *most* cases."

She rubbed her temple. "I truly don't have any idea."

"We'll start by eliminating who we can, then we'll go from there."

"Figuring out who he is could take months." She closed her eyes and sighed, overwhelmed by the realization. "Somehow I thought this was going to be simpler."

"If Rex had been our man, it would've been a little easier."

The beautiful pine walls suddenly felt as if they were closing in around her. "I can't stay in this house indefinitely. I have a business to run and a life to live."

"This is a temporary solution to a problem. Once the renovations are finished at Ethan's, we'll get you settled in there."

"Okay." There was no point being upset with Tucker; he was just doing his job. But what about now? "I'll make you the list, but first I need to use your phone. I have to get a hold of Patrick. The Internet is out, and my cell suddenly has no service."

"The cell towers are probably down too. The wind is howling like a bitch." He handed her his cell phone anyway.

She slid her finger over the screen and read *No Service*. "Damn it." She shoved the phone back in his hand as she stood. "I don't have *time* for this." She walked to the window, utterly frustrated, and watched the snow fall and the wind blow. "I can't run Cooke Interiors like this."

"I'm sure we'll be up and running in a couple days."

She whirled. "A couple days? I don't have a couple days, Tucker. I have right now. Today's the big install at the Movenbecks. We have half a million dollars' worth of furnishings and accents to place before the charity event tonight. Brice and Mindy are expecting perfection, and for what they've paid me, they damn well should get it. Patrick and I should be dealing with this together. I should be there handling the majority of this. But I'm here while some sick bastard ruins our cars and kills poor, defenseless animals because he can't get to me." She turned back to the chaos out the window—a perfect representation of her life as of late—and pressed her forehead to the glass.

"Hey." He pulled her away from the window and took her chin between his fingers. "I know this sucks, Cooke. I know it does, but everything's going to work out fine. Patrick can handle today. Cooke Interiors means just as much to him as it does to you. He'll pull this off."

"I hope so."

"He will. As to the rest... We're going to get this figured out. I want you to feel safe. You *are* safe here with me. No one's going to hurt you; I'm promising you that."

Her life was falling apart. Somewhere out there, an obsessed, crazy man hunted her, but as she stood in front of Tucker, staring into his determined eyes, she'd never felt more secure. She rarely believed the promises of others, but she believed his. "Okay."

The snow had finally stopped, and the sun was attempting to peek out from behind the clouds. Tucker had seen his fair share of winter storms in Park City, but this one had been a doozy. They would be lucky if they got plowed out by tomorrow. Thank God he'd been able to get the Jeep in the garage before the worst of the blizzard hit. He set down his card. “Draw two, Cooke.”

She took two cards from the deck. “So how much longer until we have power?”

Tucker shrugged and played a yellow eight. “Uno. Could be an hour, could be days. The electric company will take care of downtown before they get to us up here in the boonies.”

Wren glanced at her phone. “How long do you think it will take them to fix the tower?”

He grinned. She’d asked him the same question at least twice since this morning. “The answer hasn’t changed since the last time—probably a day or two. I’m sure Patrick’s fine.”

“I just wish I could check in.”

This was eating her alive. Mother Nature couldn’t have picked a shittier day to flex her muscles. If the phone and Internet situation were any better downtown, he would find a way to get her there, but the residents of Park City were on their own until the road and utility crews were able to get their jobs done—and they sure as hell had their hands full. “I wish I could help you, but unfortunately we’re out of luck.”

“What if Lenora keeps calling him with suggested changes for the pool house while he’s busy with the Movenbecks? She’s bound to send him over the edge.” Wren changed the color to blue with another eight. “He’s meeting with her after he finishes the install. How am I supposed to talk him down from a murderous rampage if I can’t even make a call?”

He chuckled. “We’ll have to hope he resists the urge. When the plow guys come through, we’ll get an update on things downtown. If they know of someone with a functioning landline, we’ll get you to it.”

“When will they be by?”

“Probably tomorrow at the earliest.”

“*Tomorrow*?”

“Yeah.” He set down the winning card. “Beat you again.”

She threw down her remaining hand in a huff. “I’m officially convinced the deck is rigged.”

“Sore loser.”

"Losing gets a little old after the sixth or seventh time."

Cranky too. She needed a distraction before she went over and tried the light switch for the umpteenth time. She was definitely a city girl, and a frustrated one at that. "I'm going out to get firewood. We'll need it tonight. Why don't you come help?"

She looked out the window. "The snow is taller than I am."

"In some spots the drifts are taller than me, but I still have to get wood." He shrugged. "Never pegged you for a whiner, Cooke."

She glared. "I'm not a whiner."

He stood and turned, biting his cheek. "Could've fooled me. Haven't heard much of anything else since this morning." He closed her bedroom door behind him, catching the tail end of her mutterings—something about his anatomy. If he knew her, and he was starting to, she would be ready to wade through the drifts by the time he was in his coat and hat. He'd called her a whiner, but she wasn't by trade. She was just restless and worried and had every right to be.

Tucker opened his closet and pulled his new winter garb from the shopping bags. As he sat on the bed and tied his boots, he craved the palm trees and ocean views of home. The piles of snow were far less exciting than they had been to him and Staci all those years ago. But he was here now, so he would have to make the best of it. Fully dressed, he started down the hall, pulling on his hat and thermal gloves as he walked.

"Wait for me."

Grinning, he stopped and turned. He definitely had Wren's number.

She closed her bedroom door and hurried to catch up, dressed like a sexy snow bunny in her new red ski pants and black jacket. "Guess it's a good thing we went shopping when we did."

"Guess so."

She pulled the black warmer over her ears and slid a slick

pair of gloves on her hands. "I'm ready."

Goddamn, he wanted the hell out of her. "Let's go." He opened the door to a violent slap of wind and gritted his teeth against the cold. "Looks like we're going to have some good old-fashioned Utah fun."

She sent him a doubtful look. "Oh goodie."

He smiled. "I'll go first and make a trail."

"Super. We'll be just like the pioneers." She feigned excitement, then rolled her eyes.

He laughed. "Has anyone ever told you you're a hot ticket, Cooke?"

She grinned. "Maybe."

"Just step where I step so we can get this over with." He started into the drifts, sinking once before he made it to the dip where the wind had blown most of the snow away. He glanced behind him and chuckled as Wren fought her way forward. They weren't even a quarter of a way to the woodpile, and she was already huffing and puffing. "Keep up that pace and we should be back inside by midnight."

"What's that phrase Ethan says? Oh right—kiss ass, Campbell."

Roaring with laughter, he shook his head and turned to concentrate on the next leg of their journey. Luckily, the rest of their trek wouldn't be quite as bad. The house blocked the remainder of the slope from the worst of the winds.

"Hey, Tucker."

"Yeah." He turned and a solid ball of snow thwacked him on his temple—thankfully the one that wasn't bruised. Blinking, he absorbed the shocking surprise and cold.

Wren burst out laughing, her big bold laugh he would never get enough of, as he stared at her and swiped the worst of the stinging chill away. "What the hell?"

"That was for calling me a whiner." She tried to pull herself together, but a snort of laughter escaped, and she leaned forward in her mirth. "You should've seen your face. It was priceless." She wiped at her cheeks. "Oh, I think I'm actually crying."

"Hey, Cooke."

She glanced up, still chuckling.

"Better run." He darted toward her as fast as the snow would allow, and she turned, screaming, doing her best to beat him back to the house. He gained on her quickly and tackled her to the ground, laughing.

"Don't even think about giving me a whitewash!"

"I think a snowball—" A handful of powder blinded him as Wren swiped her glove his way.

She scrambled up, shrieking through her bursts of laughter as he wiped at his eyes and spit away the worst of the latest attack.

"Oh, it's on now." He grabbed for her boot and missed, then crawled forward and captured her leg. She fell, and he shimmied up her body, snatching up her wrists, yanking her arms over her head, and lay on top of her. "All's fair in war, Cooke," he panted out.

"Be nice," she puffed, winded, grinning and batting her lashes.

He chuckled. "Sorry, but you have to pay." He kept her wrists pinned with one hand and used the other to form a sloppy, misshapen ball. "Any last words?"

"Tucker," she warned, screeching as small chunks of snow fell on her cheeks from the makeshift weapon he moved closer to her face.

"That's my name." He chuckled sinisterly and smooshed the ball in the center of her forehead.

She bucked under him and let loose a bloodcurdling scream. "Damn it! That's cold!"

"Snow usually is." He grinned down, enjoying himself immensely as he wiped the worst of the mess away.

She struggled to free her arms. "Truce."

"Oh, now she wants a truce."

"Yes." She chuckled. "Very much so."

"I don't know. I have you right where I want you." He

pulled off his glove with his teeth and skimmed his fingers along her chilly jaw.

Her smile vanished. "What are you doing?"

She was beautiful, with her gray eyes bright, her cheeks rosy, and her wild black curls spread out over the blinding white. "I don't think I've ever wanted someone the way I want you, Cooke."

She struggled to free her hands again. "Let me up."

He let her hands go but kept her pinned to the ground. "Cooke—"

"I already told you, I'm not attracted to you." She pushed at his chest.

"Bullshit. You were plenty attracted last night."

"No." She shoved again, rolled out from under him, and stood. "That was a mistake. Last night was a mistake. That kiss didn't mean anything." She walked to the house as quickly as the drifts would allow.

Damned if he was going to let this go. He got to his feet and followed. "Wait a minute."

She moved faster.

"Hey, Cooke, I'm talking to you."

"I don't want to talk to *you*."

He caught her as she reached for the doorknob and spun her to face him. "Wait."

"What?"

"If you don't want to roll around in the sheets, that's fine. I'll get over it." *Maybe.* "But don't stand here and tell me last night didn't mean anything. You're only lying to yourself. There's something here. There's something between us whether you like it or not."

"No." She tried to pull free.

He yanked her against him. "Yes."

"No," she whispered again as she clutched at his jacket.

He brushed his thumb over her bottom lip. "Yes, Wren." He would say it until she stopped denying what they both already knew.

Her breath shuddered out as they held each other's gaze. "This can't happen. I can't—we can't..."

She was saying no, but her eyes were saying yes. He couldn't take it anymore. He had to have her. He crushed his lips against hers and dove in, instantly invading her mouth.

She moaned, and her gloved hands were in his hair, bringing him closer.

He reached out, found the doorknob, and twisted. They walked through, still clinging, and he kicked the door shut. Whirling them around, he pressed her to the heavy wood and pulled the warmer from her ears, never taking his mouth from hers. She took off her gloves, tossing them to the floor as he kicked off his boots. He unzipped her jacket, yanking it down her arms, and tossed it aside.

He reluctantly eased back, breath heaving as he tugged at her sweater. He impatiently worked his way through the layers of clothing to get to her soft skin. He'd wanted to touch her for months; now that he could, it wasn't happening fast enough.

She discarded his jacket and thermal top, casting them aside in between fevered kisses. He pulled her turtleneck off and groaned as he stared at her black bra over her small, firm swells. "My God, Cooke, you're gorgeous."

She responded by pulling his mouth back to hers, nibbling and tugging at his bottom lip as she unsnapped his ski pants and eased them over his hips. He shoved them further down and stepped his way out like a marching soldier.

Her eagerness revved him higher, and finally he cupped her breasts through the silk, making her shiver. "I've gotta get you out of the rest of these clothes," he panted, picking her up. She wrapped her legs around his waist as he rushed to the bedroom. Her tongue traced his ear and glided down his neck, driving him crazy.

He opened the door, slamming it behind them, and laid her on the bed. He tugged off her boots, tossed them over his shoulders and made a beeline for the snap on her ski pants. He peeled them off, taking her yoga pants and black lace panties with them. He'd never seen anything so spectacular as Wren mostly naked in the fading sunlight.

"Come here." She held out her arms, inviting him to her.

He crawled to her and their mouths instantly collided as his hands went on a frantic journey, brushing along her smooth arms, the sides of her slender waist and hips. He pulled at the front clasp of her bra, releasing her beautiful breasts. "Cooke," he groaned as he touched and traced, then lapped and suckled at her aroused nipples. She arched, whimpering as he inched his way down, kissing her stomach, ready to turn up the heat. He moved to the floor, kneeling by the edge of the bed, and grabbed hold of her legs, yanking her forward and she gasped. He lifted her hips and invaded her with his tongue.

She jerked and moaned, and her thighs contracted. "Tucker. Oh my God, Tucker."

He'd never heard anything better. He plunged again, and her fingers clutched in his hair as she cried out long and loud, spasming, pouring around him.

Her gasps filled the room as she rode out her orgasm, and he slid his fingers along her hot, wet skin, tracing, exploring the most secret spots of Wren as her stomach clenched and her muscles shuddered with each hurried breath. He continued his discovery, using teasing strokes, waiting for her to come down from the first high.

She relaxed, and her hands slid to the bed. Their eyes locked, then he shoved two fingers deep and used his mouth, revving her up for the second time. Her brows furrowed and she gripped the comforter, arching her back, tipping her head, and went flying. Writhing, bucking, she called for him.

He started his way up, leaving open-mouthed kisses over her hips and waist, between the valley of her breasts, wanting the rest of her. Their gazes met again as she cupped his face, drawing his mouth to hers. The kiss started slow but quickly turned urgent as she slid her palms down his back and clutched his ass through denim.

He ground himself against her, savoring the feel of Wren's breasts pressed to his chest and the rest of her hot body beneath his. She reached between them, pulled at the snap on his jeans, and unzipped, tugging his clothing past his hips.

He helped her slide his pants off and tossed them to the floor. She stroked him, cool fingers against hot skin, and he hissed out a breath, resting his forehead on hers as a rush of goose bumps covered his skin. He'd wanted this, Wren's hands all over him, but there was more. "Wren," he groaned. "I need you."

She brought his mouth back to hers, and he pushed himself inside her, fisting his hands against the bed as he moved slowly, savoring her hot, tight wetness.

She clutched his shoulders, whimpering as he held her gaze and thrust deep.

She moaned as his movements grew hurried with the urging of her hips. She slid her hands along his sides and her fingers curled against his waist, clutching as her breathing grew rapid. "I'm going to—I'm going to... Oh, *God*."

He pumped faster, and she stiffened, crying out. He captured her mouth once more as he pushed deeper, consumed by a rush of heat. Grunting, he exploded, falling with her.

Minutes passed while he rested his head in the crook of her neck, breathing in her sexy scent while she caressed the skin along the back of his shoulders, and their hearts pounded the same rapid rhythm. He lifted his head and looked into her eyes, smiling as he brushed away the damp hair along her forehead. He'd wanted her from the first moment—exactly like this—but never did he imagine it would mean so much. "Cooke, I—"

The wind kicked up with a powerful gust, and they both jumped.

"It's snowing again," she said in utter amazement.

He glanced over his shoulder. "Looks like it. Probably will off and on over the next couple days."

She let loose an incredulous laugh. "I don't think I've ever seen so *much*."

"Welcome to Utah."

She smiled as she touched the fading bruise at his temple. "We never got around to the firewood."

He grinned. "I think we kept each other plenty warm."

She chuckled. "I can't argue with you there."

"I'll go get enough to get us through tonight." He kissed her chin, then nibbled. "How about you stay here just like this?"

She smiled again as her fingers wandered to his hair. "How about you get the wood and I'll make dinner? Ms. Hayes brought more than fresh fruits and vegetables when she stopped by. I think I saw fixings for beef stew."

"And that's the beauty of cooking with gas. You've got a deal." He rolled off her, untangling himself from her warm body. "Who needs electricity anyway?"

"*Me*." She sat up and wrapped her arms around her knees.

He studied her, watching as she pulled back. Even after what they'd shared, he was going to have to work for her trust. "Hey." He reached out, gripping her chin between his fingers. "Don't do that."

"What?"

"Push me away before the sheets have even cooled."

She eyed him as he moved to stroke her jaw.

"I'm not going anywhere. There's something here. There's something between us." He leaned forward and kissed her lips. "You might want to get used to that." He got up, grabbed his clothes, and left the room. She needed time to think about what he'd just said.

The light flickered and the kitchen plunged into darkness...again. Wren sighed as she scrubbed at the soup bowls, trying to finish the dishes before the water she'd heated turned cold. The thirty seconds of power had been the longest stretch yet—long enough for her to get her hopes up that the electricity might be here to stay. She *needed* the Internet or her cell signal back. Either would do; she just had to talk to Patrick. The Movenbeck party was well underway at this point. The agony of not knowing how the install had gone was driving her crazy. She could only pray everything went as planned—hopefully better. The Movenbeck project and Lenora's pool house were worth fifty grand to Cooke Interiors, and word of mouth from a job well done was priceless. She'd had several new referrals in the weeks since Lenora's impromptu get-together in the newly renovated library.

Wren turned on the tap and rinsed away the suds with icy cold water, then dried the items she'd washed. The light winked on, then off just as quickly. "Oh come *on*." She eyed her phone in the candlelight as she shoved away the last of the dishes. Unable to resist, she picked it up, checking for service as she'd done several times throughout the past twelve hours. Still nothing. "Damn it." How was she supposed to *work* like this?

With a frustrated huff, she set down the cell and grabbed the washcloth submerged in the warm, soapy water. She wrung it dry and wiped down the counters, pausing as the floor creaked in one of the rooms beyond. The flicker of candlelight cast shadows about the kitchen, and she shuddered. The house was so quiet, and the wind still howled, pounding at the glass, giving her the creeps.

Tucker left her some time ago to complete his nightly walkthrough. He was somewhere among the maze of rooms, checking windows and doors, making certain the house was secure. Despite all that, tonight she had the willies.

It was tempting to seek him out and make conversation to drown out the worst of the relentless winds, but the afternoon had changed things. She'd tried to keep the evening light while they enjoyed beef stew by the fire, but it had been a struggle.

A wave of flutters erupted in her belly as she thought of their sexy romp—again. Her dry spell was definitely over and her itch officially scratched—and she wanted more. "Stupid," she muttered, scolding herself as she plunked the washcloth back in the suds, then wrung it dry to attack the stubborn beef broth on the stovetop.

She shouldn't have slept with him, plain and simple, but she'd quickly lost her resolve to keep her distance when he captured her mouth by the front door. The gentle kiss of last night had been replaced with urgent heat. Desire had instantly consumed her, and she soon found out that Tucker was the best damn lover she'd ever had.

Now that everything was said and done, she could only regret that hormones had overruled practicality. If she could take today back, she would. It would've been better to go through life wondering how sex with Tucker could be, but now she knew what it felt like to have his lips brand her skin and his powerful body cover hers. But more than that was the way her heart had flip-flopped as he stared in her eyes while he moved inside her. She'd never felt as connected to anyone as she did in that moment.

The lights flickered again, and she sighed. It wasn't supposed to *be* like this. Sex was supposed to be mutually satisfying and uncomplicated—at least it always had been, but this entire situation was growing thornier by the second. She'd never been in search of romance or a deep, emotional connection, yet Tucker had given her a taste of both, and she craved another sample.

Sighing, she gave the washcloth a final rinse and pulled the stopper from the drain. Why couldn't he keep it simple? Why did he have to insist there was more here? There wasn't. She refused to get mixed up with any man. Game over. The end. She and Tucker were not the next Sarah and Ethan or Morgan and Hunter. What her family and friends had was rare, and something she had no interest in.

More often than not, relationships were built on lies and

infidelity. She'd witnessed her parents' farce of a marriage firsthand. If Grant and Rene Cooke had ever been faithful to one another... They hadn't. So what was the point? Never ever would she put her heart in someone else's hands for them to discard so easily. Alone was better—always. She was too busy with her career for anything more than a simple date and casual roll in the hay every now and again.

So, maybe Tucker made her feel something powerful and intimate and *terrifying*, but she would get over it. They'd had sex—nothing more, nothing less. Tucker said he wasn't going anywhere, but he would move along quickly enough when he realized they'd had a one and done. Sure, they had heat, there was no doubt about it, but eventually heat burnt itself out. Where would Tucker be when the flames cooled? She wasn't willing to stick around and find out, so their intimate relationship was going to stop right here.

They needed to talk and reach an understanding before this situation got any more out of hand—and there was no time like the present. He was bound to be finished with his walkthrough by now. He'd been gone a while. She blew out the candles scattered around the kitchen and living room, carrying the flashlight Tucker had left with her. Where was he, anyway?

"Tucker?" She walked past the bathroom, home gym, and office, searching, but he wasn't there. "Tucker?" she called again, but received no answer. Frowning, she moved through the dark, stopping at the dim glow of light coming from the forbidden hallway. "Tucker?"

He still didn't answer.

Swallowing, she glanced over her shoulder, growing more freaked out by the second, and dashed down the long hall, despite his requests that she not. She slowed as she spotted him standing in the doorway of the second room on the left, staring. "Tucker?"

His gaze snapped to hers in the shadows of their flashlights.

"What's wrong? Are you okay?"

"Yeah," he replied dully.

"What are you doing?"

"Nothing."

She scrutinized his distant, devastated eyes before he turned his attention back to the room. Curious, she moved to his side and studied the pink-and-white striped bedding and pale, mint-green walls. Funky white painted letters spelled out S-T-A-C-I along the side of a closet, and photographs decorated dressers, the nightstand, and a large portion of a writing desk. A teenage girl's bedroom frozen in time.

The light in the hall blinked on, casting a strong glow into the room. "This was your sister's room." She stated the obvious because she didn't understand. All of the pictures she could see were of Staci and Tucker and their parents, she assumed, or groups of teenagers. In none of the photos did Tucker or his sister look older than sixteen or seventeen—like in the picture by the pool. How old was Staci when she died? Why did his parents keep a shrine to their daughter? "Tucker?"

He looked at her again, but he didn't see her. He was lost somewhere in his memories.

Despite her plans to keep her distance, she took his hand, unable to stand his obvious anguish.

He squeezed her fingers. "I finally made myself open her door. I haven't been able to."

"I don't—"

"She was everything good. She was the best part of us. A part of me died right along with her."

Her heart hurt for him, and she pressed his palm to her cheek.

"I heard a bump, but I kept on listening to my music. I thought she was just being clumsy as usual." A smile ghosted his mouth. "Mom always said they should've named her Grace. I didn't set the alarm that night. I should've checked on her, but I didn't know. Everything might've been different if I had known."

She had no idea what he was talking about. "How old was Staci when she died?"

"Sixteen. Just a couple days after the picture was taken."

She studied the numerous photographs in the room, struggling to decipher the one he spoke of. "Which one?"

"The one in the closet."

She glanced at the closed closet doors. Tucker wasn't making any sense, but then she understood. The picture by the pool she found the other day. "The one in your parents' room?"

"Yes."

She took a startled step back from the bedroom as everything finally made sense. Staci died in Park City. Right here in this room. "What—what happened?"

"We were supposed to meet JT and Jasmine at ten. She wasn't up yet. She was always awake before me. I made us bagels and opened her door and...she was dead."

"Oh, God, Tucker." He'd not only lost his sister but discovered her lifeless body. "I'm so—I'm so incredibly sorry." Stepping forward, she closed the door, as if that would somehow banish his pain, and pulled him away from the room. "I'm so sorry," she repeated as she enveloped him in a hug, laying her head on his chest.

He wrapped his arms around her, holding her tight, clinging.

The lights blinked once, twice, sending them into the dark.

She looked up, into his eyes. "Come on. Let's go down to our room." She wanted him away from here.

He nodded.

She held his hand, and they walked away from the dread of the forbidden hallway.

☙ Chapter Eleven ❧

THE JUKEBOX ROLLED INTO ANOTHER COUNTRY SONG as Tucker plucked up the last enormous beer-battered onion ring on his plate and took a bite. "This was a hell of an idea, Cooke. A hell of an idea," he said over his mouthful of greasy heaven.

"I know." She grinned and bit into her own golden-crusted ring. "I couldn't stand the thought of being trapped in that house for another second. I'll never take electricity for granted again." She tipped her cell phone up, glancing at the screen in the candlelight.

"Anything?" He gestured to her phone.

"No."

Their waitress came by with a pitcher of water. "How is everything?"

"The burger's great." Tucker smiled as he glanced at Beth's nametag. "Have you heard any updates on the power situation?"

"The question of the day." She smiled.

Tucker grinned. "I bet."

"Word is it shouldn't be much longer, thank the good Lord above." She picked up the glass, poured water, and set it back down. "The power crews are making progress. Rumor has it the resorts might be up and running later this afternoon and hopefully the rest of town by this evening." She repeated the process with Wren's glass. "The boys back in the kitchen are fed up with the generators and our limited menu. The dishwasher has to hand-wash everything, and I'm about finished with serving food by candlelight. I think if Bobby told us we couldn't run the juke I might quit." She winked.

"See, Cooke? You should be up and running by tomorrow."

Wren tipped her phone up yet again.

"Cell tower's damaged, Honey."

Wren wrinkled her nose. "I've noticed."

"Heard they're working on that too. You know, a couple ladies were able to get off a few texts when they were in earlier."

"I tried that." She picked up her phone. "But I'll try again."

"Signal's pretty weak. If you go stand over by the window, you might have more luck."

"Thanks." Wren immediately got to her feet and made her way to the window Beth had pointed to.

"You folks about finished here, or can I bring you some dessert? We don't have much—hot chocolate and maybe a couple pieces of apple pie left."

"I think we're good with the check."

"Sure thing, honey." Beth wandered away to stop at her next table as Tucker watched Wren's thumbs type rapidly. He was as ready as everyone else for electricity to be restored. He hadn't had a chance to check in with Owens or Ethan for almost forty-eight hours—definitely not ideal. He'd feel better if he knew what was going on with Wren's case.

Wren started back to the table, grinning. "I was able to get one bar. I got a text through." She took her seat. "The Movenbeck job went off without a hitch, and Lenora's behaving herself. Well, sort of."

"That's good stuff, Cooke."

"Heck yeah, it is." She picked up another onion ring and took a big bite. "I've been so worried," she said with her mouth full.

"I know."

She tipped her head back and let loose a relieved laugh. "I can't even tell you how much weight just lifted off my shoulders." She wiped her hands on her napkin. "Patrick has a breakfast meeting with Lenora and her gardener in the morning, but I'm not going to think about that right now."

Beth brought the check by. "Here you go."

"Thanks."

Wren plucked the bill from his hand. "My treat."

"If that's the way you want it."

"It is." She grabbed her purse from the chair and rifled through her bag, unearthing a twenty from her wallet. "There." She placed the bill on the table, and he snagged her hand.

"Thanks, Cooke."

"No problem."

"Not just for lunch. For the whole day, and last night too." Wren had been everything he needed when she found him by Staci's bedroom. She'd walked with him back to the room they were sharing for the time being, tucked him into her bed, and held him, stroking her cool fingers along his skin, banishing the worst of the dread. He'd fallen asleep breathing her in and woke with her still wrapped in his arms. He never should've opened the damn door. It had messed him up all over again.

"You're welcome. I had fun." She squeezed his fingers and freed her hand.

"Me too." On a whim, he leaned over the small table, gripped her chin, and brushed her lips with his, testing.

She pulled back. "What are you doing?"

"I'm pretty sure that's called kissing you."

"Why?"

He shrugged. "It was part of the 'thank you.'"

"Kisses aren't necessary. I wanted you to smile today. That's what friends are for."

He nodded, studying her until she looked away and stared at the jukebox across the room. Wren had made reference to their *friendship* several times throughout the day: at breakfast when they stopped off at his favorite diner; at Peak Adventures when they took breaks from careening down the steep, snow-packed hills on tubes, laughing as he and Staci had laughed that long ago Christmas; and again just now.

Wren didn't seem to mind casual affection, like the arm slung around her shoulders as they walked along Main Street, heading for the sports bar. She'd wrapped her arm around his waist, grinning while they talked the entire way. Intimacy seemed to be their problem. She wanted nothing to do with it, even after they destroyed each other in the sack and she comforted him through the night. "We back here again already, Cooke?"

Her gaze met his. "Back where?"

"Don't give me that."

Beth came to the table and took the bill and cash. "Let me get you some change."

"Thank you," he murmured, never taking his eyes off Wren's. "If I had a dollar for every time you dropped *friend* or *friendship* into our conversations today, I'd be a rich man."

"You *are* a rich man," she scoffed.

He grinned. "You got me there."

She smiled. "What's wrong with friends?"

"Not a thing, but we're more than that."

She shook her head. "Don't complicate this."

"Cooke—"

"I don't want anything more than that." She pulled her jacket from the back of her chair, put it on, and zipped it up.

"Too late."

She sighed wearily. "Why can't you leave this alone?"

"Because I want you."

"Well, I don't want you." She stood, slung her purse over her shoulder, and started toward the exit.

"Wait a minute, Cooke."

She kept walking.

Beth came back. “Here you are, sir.”

“Keep the change,” he said as he grabbed his jacket and hurried after Wren, snagging her arm as she reached the door. “I said wait. You’re not happy with me. I get that, but I’m still in charge of your safety.”

“Exactly.”

They stepped out into the crowds and made their way to the Jeep. “So, that’s the new angle? I’m the bodyguard and you’re the principal?”

She slid him a scathing glance. “I don’t need an angle.”

“I agree. I have feelings for you; you have feelings for me. It can be as simple as that if you let it.”

She stopped in her tracks. “Don’t tell me about my feelings. I don’t want to talk about this. Let’s get back to the house. I have work to do.”

Work. Her safety net. He almost called her out on it, but let the subject go. They weren’t going to solve anything on the sidewalk. He unlocked her door and went around to his side.

He took his seat and turned the ignition while Wren buckled her belt. She glanced in his direction, then looked away.

“What’s up, Cooke? Are we gonna talk about this or let it fester?”

“There’s nothing to talk about.” She turned her body and stared out the window.

“So, that’s it?”

“Pretty much.”

Not even close, but he’d wait until they were home to settle this. “You got it.” He shifted into reverse and inched his way into the busy traffic.

Wren pushed past Tucker as he unlocked the door and

tossed her jacket toward the closet in her attempt to hurry to her room and shut him out before he could follow. She had no doubt he would follow. The car ride home had been short but tense. She didn't want to talk about the conversation he started at the restaurant. Why did he have to mess up a good day? They'd had fun racing down the snowy peaks, laughing as she hadn't…ever. Why couldn't he leave it there?

"Cooke."

She walked faster as his long strides ate up the distance between them. "Leave me alone, Tucker. I said I was happy to let things fester." She stepped into the bedroom and swung the door closed, but not before he caught it, came in, and shut it behind him.

"Well I'm not." He pulled off his coat and threw it on the bed.

"I have stuff to do. Lots of work." She couldn't do much of anything with her laptop's battery low, but Tucker didn't need to know that.

"Work can wait." He whirled her around to face him.

"Why are you doing this? Why won't you let this be?"

"Because yesterday meant something—and last night and today. I care about you."

"I care about you too. Can't that be enough? Can't we leave it right there?"

"Why? Because it's safe."

Bull's-eye. "Because that's the way I want it."

"So that's the end?"

"Yes. We're friends, Tucker. Leave it there." She walked toward the bathroom in a last-ditch effort at escape.

"Are you attracted to me?"

She stopped, turning. "What?"

"I asked if you're attracted to me?"

"You're a gorgeous man."

"I'll take that as a yes. Do you have fun when we're together?"

"Sure. I guess."

"You were laughing as much as I was today. We have fun when we're together."

"Okay, so—"

"I'll ask the questions, you answer." He moved closer with every word. "Do you think about me when we're not together?"

She stepped backwards as he advanced, colliding with the wall. She swallowed a tingle of nerves as she realized he'd effectively boxed her in. She couldn't take a breath without inhaling his cologne. "We live in the same house."

"Does your heart beat a little faster when I touch you?" He skimmed his finger down her throat, pausing on her hammering pulse point, then continued his teasing journey.

"Tucker." She gripped his hand, stopping his movement before she did something stupid and caved in to her desires.

He laced their fingers. "Because you destroy me, Cooke. Every time you look at me with those gray eyes or that smile."

She pressed her free hand to his chest as his heart thundered against her palm. "Don't."

"*Why*?"

"Because I'm not what you're looking for."

"Don't tell me what I'm looking for, Cooke. I know exactly what I want."

"I'm not good at this. I don't do relationships. My job—"

"Is safe."

She frowned. "Is demanding. Are you implying I hide behind my work?"

"Swatches and paint chips won't let you down the way people do."

He knew her so well, understood too much. She tried harder to push him away, terrified by how much she wanted him to stay. "I ha—"

"I want more than just a roll in the sheets. I want you to let me in, the way you did when we moved together and you were too caught up to be afraid."

She wanted to believe him as she stared in his eyes—more

than anything. “I’m sorry, Tucker. I can’t give you what you’re asking for. I wanted to talk about this last night.”

“So we’ll start as friends.”

“And end as friends.”

He shrugged. “If that’s the way you want it.”

She blinked, then narrowed her eyes, studying him. What was he up to? He’d let that go too easily.

“But I want one last kiss.”

She scoffed and shook her head. “You’re unbelievable.”

“That’s not so much to ask. One meaningless kiss before we let this go.”

He had no idea how much he asked. “Fine, then friends from here on out.”

“You got it.”

She leaned in, ready to end this rollercoaster ride, and gave him a peck. “There you—”

“Not so fast, Cooke.” He captured her face in his hands and stared into her eyes. “I want a kiss. I want you to think about what you and I will both be missing every time you look at me.”

“Tucker...” She pressed against his chest, realizing her mistake. She didn’t need any reminders of what she was going to miss. Yesterday would be seared in her mind for some time.

He brushed his lips over hers, rubbing, teasing, while he stared in her eyes.

Butterflies danced in her stomach and she tried to pull back. “That’s enough,” she whispered.

He held her still. “We’re just getting started.” He nipped and nibbled her bottom lip and traced with his tongue until her fingers clutched the sleeves of his shirt and her eyes fluttered closed.

He eased back, ever so slightly, their breath mingling, and her mouth sought his, wanting more. He captured her lips with the slightest of pressure, and she groaned, eager for the invasion of his tongue. He deepened the kiss by degrees, and her hands slid up his arms, along the back of his neck and finally wandered into his hair as she drowned in Tucker's taste and her own desire.

He plunged and plundered, and she whimpered, struggling not to slide down the wall and pull him with her.

He brought her under again, then eased away.

"Wait," she protested with a murmur, moving in for more.

He groaned, diving, once, twice, looking at her as he pulled back. "Just friends, Cooke?"

How could she possibly respond when he'd undone her so completely? "I don't know." She shook her head as if breaking out of his trance. "I don't know, Tucker."

"I do. I'll be right here waiting while you figure it out."

He stood among the trees watching through his binoculars as Wren and Tucker mouth-fucked. Could Prince Charming shove his tongue any further down her throat? He shook his head. Don Juan might be pretty, but he lacked finesse.

He'd searched long and hard to find Wren, and he sure as hell didn't come to see this. He ground his teeth as her beautifully sculpted hands wandered up his muscular arms and tangled in his thick black hair. They'd been all over each other all day—at Peak Adventures, tubing down hills like foolish teenagers; walking down Main Street wrapped around one another; *now*.

Tucker Campbell was proving himself to be some bodyguard—probably should've followed Pops into the hotel business and left protecting the beautiful to someone more interested in safety than getting off. Wonder what Ethan would think.

Smiling, he dropped his binoculars and pulled from his bag the camera already equipped with the long-range lens and snapped away, looking forward to sending his work along to clue in big brother. Surely fraternizing with baby sister was against some sort of rule. After all, there was a lunatic on the loose. He snickered at his own wit and zoomed in, capturing a particularly excellent close up of Pretty Boy's tongue darting into Sissy's mouth. So graphic. The image really sent the point home that a lot more than door and window checks were going on around here. Bastard.

Nothing would please him more than to cause the handsome prince a few problems. He deserved them. And Wren... She lied. They were both going to have to be taught a lesson. He couldn't stand liars, but even more, he hated Tucker Campbell. For that alone, he would make it good. He shoved the camera back in his bag and pulled his binoculars free, peeking through one last time as Tucker and Wren held each other close, talking as if no one else mattered, but he was here now. They were going to start paying attention. In fact, the games were just about to begin.

☙ Chapter Twelve ❧

Wren rolled over and opened her eyes to the flashing digital clock on the table. "*Yes!*" She tossed the covers back, scrambled out of bed, and screamed as Tucker grabbed his gun in a two-handed grip and sat up, pointing his weapon in her direction.

Wren gasped as she pressed a hand to her racing heart. "What are you *doing*?"

"Jesus, Cooke," he said at the same time. "Why the hell are you rushing out of bed like that? You scared the shit out of me." Blowing out a deep breath, he set the pistol on the table and lay against his pillow, eyeing her the whole time.

"The power's back on. I need to see if we have Internet."

His brow shot up as he crossed his arms above his head and settled in against his elbow. "I'm going to have to kill you if you do that again."

"Mission almost accomplished. My heart's still pounding."

"Profit margins aren't worth dying for."

"Point taken. I'm sorry I startled you, but I have to get to work. Patrick has his breakfast meeting with Lenora and her gardener. I'm really hoping I can check in—maybe lend a little moral support and remind him of some of our key points. He must be exhausted."

"I thought he was handling everything."

"He is—really well, actually, but like I said a couple days ago, this is a huge week for us and he's on his own. The Movenbeck Project went well. Now we need to finish strong with Lenora and several of our smaller projects I haven't been able to work on without power."

"You guys are doing fine. The Movenbecks' shindig was a success, and Lenora's not bitching."

"For now. If we want the trend to continue, I need to put mockups together for her master suite and get a look at the rooms Patrick took pictures of for our new clients. I'm two days behind. I don't have a lot of time to chat." She grabbed her laptop, cell phone, and their accompanying chargers and raced toward the dining room, escaping.

Tucker looked good enough to eat with those sleepy eyes, disheveled hair, and dark scruff of beard. And that chest of his. She blew out an unsteady breath as she remembered hot, sweaty skin rubbing against hers, pressing her into the mattress.

Work. She needed to work and avoid any more alone time with him for a while. They'd been in each other's way for two days straight. *Swatches and paint chips won't let you down like people do.* She dismissed Tucker's theories behind her obsessive dedication to her profession—even if there was an uncomfortable stirring of truth behind his words.

And so what if there was? She'd been living her life just fine, content to follow her own rules until Tucker entered the picture and started messing things up with his sexy grins and heart-stopping kisses.

She plugged her electronics into the socket with more gusto than necessary as she glanced toward the hall leading to their bedrooms. Hopefully the power was here to stay. Tucker could go back to his own room, and she could actually sleep instead of stare at the ceiling while he lay next to her in nothing more than his boxers, churning her up.

Tucker Campbell was turning her upside down and inside out, confusing her, making her feel things she didn't want to feel. He'd given her some space last night after he proved his point with another mind-numbing kiss—plenty of time to stew in her own sexual juices while he checked the house and worked out in the home gym, but then he'd come back and stripped down to almost nothing while he held her gaze and helped himself to half of her bed.

She'd wanted to tell him to get out, the words had been on the tip of her tongue, but he'd continued to stare at her in the firelight, challenging her with those smug eyes, so she'd clenched her jaw, tugged off her pajama bottoms, and had the satisfaction of watching him swallow while she walked to the bed in skimpy panties and a clinging spaghetti-strap sleep-top. The move had been childish, and she'd been playing with fire, but she'd be damned if she was going to suffer alone.

But that was over now. The turmoil would end today, damn it. It was time to get things back to normal around here—or close enough. She powered on her laptop and phone, holding her breath, waiting for them to boot up, and smiled her triumph as her cell screen showed four bars of service and her computer linking into the Internet. "Thank you, thank you, thank you."

She signed into her e-mail account and was immediately inundated by pages of unopened messages in her inbox. She would be swamped for *hours* trying to play catch up, but first she needed something quick to eat and a cup of coffee... after she texted Patrick.

I know you're busy with breakfast ☺ . Give me a call when you finish up and we'll schedule a Skype, or if you need me beforehand, just holler. Looks like we might be back in business.

"Please, dear God, let us be back in *business*." She turned on the small countertop television on her way to the bread bin, pulling two whole-wheat slices from the bag as her mind raced through the list of objectives for the day. Return e-mails, check in with the Movenbecks, then she had to get to Lenora's master suite. Somehow she had to tinker with one of the weight-bearing walls, which wasn't going to be easy, but she would find a way to give Lenora what she wanted or switch it around some and make Lenora want what was actually feasible. The Cartwright job and potential clients from the Movenbeck renovations were bound to keep Cooke Interiors busy and comfortably in the black well into next year. Patrick was definitely due a raise.

"...tragic death of someone so young right here in Park City."

Wren whirled as the toothy blonde's words caught her attention. She turned the TV up louder.

"The town is in shock as word spreads of sixteen-year-old Alyssa Brookes' untimely passing. Details are still emerging as we bring you this breaking news. At this point, we know Alyssa and her family are full-time residents of Park City. She was a cheerleader and president of the Sophomore Class at Park City High."

Tucker stepped into the kitchen, hair damp, smiling. "I'll never take hot water for granted again."

"Shh. The news..."

"What—"

"Shh. There was a murder. Sixteen-year-old girl. Details are still coming in."

Tucker's eyes changed, sharpening as he stared at the television.

"...unconfirmed sources are saying Alyssa was found in her bedroom by her mother, strangled. The motive behind this beloved community member's violent death is still unclear. Park City's Police Chief and the town's mayor will be addressing the public at a ten o'clock press conference. We'll continue to bring you details as they become available. Chuck, back to you in Salt Lake."

Wren pressed a hand to her chest as her heart broke for

the mother of Alyssa Brookes. "That poor girl. That poor family."

Tucker grunted as he turned to the refrigerator and pulled a coffee pod from the box. He grabbed a mug from the cabinet and a banana from the fruit bowl, peeled it, and bit in.

Wren watched him as he doctored up his morning java, pouring cream into his cup, swearing when chunks of spoiled milk floated to the top. "We'll have to go to the store. Everything in the fridge is probably bad."

A young girl had been strangled to death somewhere in the town limits, and he was worrying about food. "Tucker."

"Yeah." He dumped the undrinkable contents down the drain and looked at her.

"What—why...the girl. She's been murdered..."

"What do you want me to say?"

She blinked, taken aback by his indifference. "I'm not sure. Maybe nothing, but you act like you don't even care. Of all people, you should know..." She stopped herself as his eyes heated and cooled just as quickly.

"I should know what?"

"Nothing. I'm sorry," she murmured as she reached for her toast.

He gripped her wrist, stopping her. "No, go ahead. What should I know?"

"Never mind."

"I should know what it's like, right? I should know what it's like to open a bedroom door and find the person you love most in the world dead and staring up at nothing?"

She flinched. "Tucker—"

"Do I have to grieve for all of them? A sixteen-year-old was found just like Staci; she won't be the last. I understand exactly what that girl's mother is going through. Am I a bad person because I shut it off, because I don't want to relive the pain again and again?"

"No, of course—"

"I spent seven years of my life trying to save the world,

trying to take killers off the street so they couldn't do to others what someone did to my sister."

What was Tucker talking about? Who did what to his sister? "Tucker, I don't know—"

"That's right. You don't, so leave it alone." He dropped her hand, turned, and left the room.

She stared after him as he retreated down the hall. What just happened? She'd never seen him angry before. Did he think she was judging him? And Staci? What exactly happened to Staci? He'd never said. She shuddered as she glanced toward the forbidden hall, realizing she knew nothing of the story. Shaken, she walked to the dining room table and sat down in front of her laptop, staring blindly at a screenful of mail.

Her laptop dinged loudly, alerting her to a new e-mail, startling her out of her thoughts. She glanced at the sender, groaned, then puzzled over the subject line. *Extremely Dissatisfied!* She sighed and rolled her eyes. "You're never satisfied," she muttered as she hovered the mouse over the unread mail, hesitating as she glanced in the direction Tucker had walked. She wanted to go to him and make sure he was all right, but she doubted he had any desire to see her now. Pressing her lips firm, she clicked on Lenora's message.

Wren,

I'm writing to express my deep dissatisfaction with our business relationship as of late. You abandoned me mid-project and apparently Patrick has done the same!

Wren frowned. *What*?

I believe I've been very accommodating with Patrick's illness, but to miss our breakfast meeting without even a word is abominably rude and unprofessional. I am beyond displeased with our current arrangement and will no longer require your services. You can expect to hear from my attorney...wherever you are!

Lenora Cartwright

She reread the message several times, waiting for Lenora's ramblings to somehow make sense. What the hell was going on? She ex'd out of the e-mail and searched her inbox, spotting numerous messages from Brice Movenbeck. She pressed a hand to her sinking stomach as she glanced from subject line to subject line. *Still waiting for Patrick* was sent at 9am on November second. Then *Wrong furniture!* at 10:30am. *Please contact me ASAP!!!* had come in at 4:45pm. Her hand trembled as she clicked on the last message.

Wren,

I don't know what in the hell is up, but Mindy and I are beyond frustrated and quite frankly surprised with the disaster you and Patrick have left us to deal with. Patrick never showed up, the wrong furniture was delivered (which took several hours to correct), and our room is still in shambles while Mindy and the help try to put everything to rights with less than an hour until guests arrive. Contact me immediately.

Brice

"No." This wasn't right. She frantically searched for the last correspondence Patrick sent at 7pm on November first, scanning it. He said right there that he would meet with Brice and Mindy first thing in the morning, then head over to Lenora's as planned. He attached two files of photos for new client rooms.

She yanked up her phone, trying to reassure herself this wasn't really happening. She reread Patrick's return text she received at the bar and grill yesterday afternoon.

Install perfect. Party fabulous. Lenora tolerable. Ready for breakfast meeting.

"This doesn't make any *sense*." She stabbed Patrick's number on her speed dial as her breath heaved out in her shocked anger. Missed appointments, losing their biggest clients, potential litigation. She pressed her fingers to the vicious throb in her forehead.

"Hey, you've reached Patrick. Leave me a message and I'll get back to you."

"Patrick, it's Wren. I just received an e-mail from Lenora Cartwright. Apparently you called in sick yesterday and missed the meeting this morning. And you never showed up for the Movenbeck install. I don't know what's going on, but it better be good. How could you do this, Patrick?" Her voice shook with tears and she cleared the emotion away. "We just lost our biggest client, and I don't even want to know what Brice and Mindy are going to say." She disconnected and rushed to her feet, almost knocking over her chair, as a spurt of panic grabbed her by the throat. What was she going to do? She moved about, pacing away the bright, hot fear. Everything she'd worked for. Everything *they'd* worked for.

She stopped in her tracks, listening to the violent pounding of her own heart. "This isn't right. Something isn't right."

She picked up the cell phone and dialed the Cartwrights. Screw Ethan's rules about outgoing calls.

"Cartwright residence."

"Ms. Cheri, this is Wren Cooke. Is Lenora available?"

"I'm afraid she's in her session with Willamina."

"Do you think you could interrupt her? It's urgent."

"She gave me strict instructions that she isn't to be disturbed."

Damn it. She bit her lip. "Okay. Can I leave a message?"

"Certainly."

Then a thought occurred to her. Patrick had been in the Cartwright mansion every day since her abrupt departure. "Ms. Cheri, did you talk to Patrick when he called in?"

"Of course, madam."

"How did he—how did he sound?"

"Different."

"What do you mean?"

"His voice was a bit...muffled I would say."

"Muffled?"

"Yes, Madam. He said he was dog sick and would return tomorrow, which would have been yesterday. He called in yesterday and said he would be here today, Madam."

She frowned. "He missed two days?"

"Indeed, Ms. Cooke."

"And he said 'dog sick'?"

"Precisely."

'Dog Sick.' Patrick wouldn't say 'dog sick.' He would say 'under the weather' or 'ill', especially to a client. She fell back into her chair as a new wave of dread washed through her. Something was wrong with Patrick. "Ms. Cherie, how did Patrick look when you saw him last?"

"Quite fine, actually."

"Okay. Thank you. Would you please have Lenora call me at this number?"

"Yes, Madam."

She hung up and immediately dialed Patrick's number with a trembling finger.

"Hey, you've reached Patrick. Leave me a message and I'll get back to you."

"Patrick." She gripped the cell phone tight. "Patrick, please call me. Something's wrong. I can feel it. I'm not mad about the meeting or the install, but I am worried—very, very worried. I don't care about our business right now. We'll figure that out later. Just call so I know you're okay. Please."

She hung up and hurried down the hall, looking for Tucker, listening to his murmurs through his bedroom door, and stopped. *What am I doing?* She was *not* about to go running to Tucker with her problems. *Her* problems. She turned back, shocked that her first instinct had been to seek his help. She didn't need him or anything he had to offer. Hurrying to her laptop, she punched "LAPD" in the search engine and dialed the number for non-emergencies.

"LAPD non-emergency."

"Yes, my name is Wren Cooke. I need to speak with Detective Owens immediately. He's involved in my stalking case. Please, it may be life or death."

"Please hold, Ms. Cooke, and I'll see what I can do."

Seconds passed, but it felt like hours while she listened to the canned elevator music buzzing in her ear.

"Ms. Cooke, this is Detective Terrance Romero. Can I help you?"

"Yes, I need to talk to Detective Owens."

"He's out at the moment."

She huffed out a breath. "Detective Owens has been handling my stalking case. I really need to speak with him."

"I'm familiar with your case, Ms. Cooke."

"You are? Okay. Good. Good. I think something happened to my business partner, Patrick Stone. He's missed two important meetings and he's called out sick two days running." She nibbled her lip. "This is going to sound strange; I can hardly believe I'm saying it out loud, but I don't think he's the one who called in. Can you send someone over to his house to check on him?"

"When was the last time he was seen?"

"I don't know. I'm not in Los Angeles. The last time I talked to him personally was the evening of November first." Three days. Anything could have happened in three days.

"What makes you think someone would want to impersonate Mr. Stone?"

She sighed, beyond frustrated. She didn't have time for this. She needed to know Patrick was okay. "Our client's housekeeper said he sounded different, and he said something Patrick wouldn't say. I've known him for several years. He's my best friend. I'm telling you, something's *wrong*. He's never sick—ever—and he wouldn't blow off a breakfast meeting with one of our most important clients."

"I'll need an address."

"Thank you." Relief swamped her and she blinked back a sudden wave of tears. "He lives at 722 Beverly Drive. Bungalow B."

"We'll call you back after we check this out."

"I can't even begin to thank you, Detective." She hung up and stared out the window as she attempted to wrap her mind around the last twenty minutes. Did she really just call the LAPD and tell them someone was impersonating her best friend? She picked up her cell again and reread the text he sent yesterday. None of this made sense. The message came from *his* phone; he had to have sent it. He had to have called the Cartwright mansion and spoke with Ms. Cherie. Was he mixed up with drugs and she'd missed the signs?

Her e-mail dinged with another incoming message from one of her suppliers. She closed her eyes, already finished with the day as she pushed in, closing the gap between herself, the table, and her laptop. The screenful of unanswered mail was no longer an exciting escape from her feelings for Tucker, nor was it a personally rewarding motivator to get caught up. Each bold line in her inbox was an overwhelming reminder that she was slowly drowning in a life over which she no longer had any control.

She needed to call Brice, but first she had to talk to Patrick and find out what in the world happened. Desperately struggling to keep *something* together, she opened the last e-mail Patrick sent and clicked on the photo attachments. The first picture popped up and her eyes filled again as she grinned—Patrick cheesing it up for the camera. That silly, handsome man in his designer top was the friend she recognized. He wouldn't have left her high and dry without a reason. "Be okay, Pat. Please," she whispered, clicking to the next picture of a boring, ugly space. Despite her distress, she was immediately flooded by ideas on how she would fix it. And she *would* fix it—somehow...from hundreds of miles away.

She opened a Word document in a side-by-side screen, ready to begin her concept notes, then stopped, letting loose a hopeless, humorless laugh as she shook her head and a tear she couldn't keep at bay fell. Who was she kidding? Cooke Interiors was dead in the water. She could make the wretched space on her screen shine, but without anyone on the LA end to help bring her visions to life, her business was over. Everything she and Patrick had worked for...

"Like hell this is over." Despite the hundreds of e-mails that needed her attention, she brought up Design 101 and began the tedious yet comforting task of transforming a drab space into the spectacular.

Tucker added his final thoughts to the preliminary site assessment he was typing up for Jackson. He'd spent the last two hours on Google Maps scrutinizing the one-block radius around the penthouse suites the diplomats would use for their weeklong stay next month, searching for potential weak spots and areas at risk for security breaches. He was officially on report duty until he and Wren were able to head home. His phone rang as he attached the file to his latest e-mail and pressed 'send.' He answered on the second ring. "Campbell."

"Tucker?"

He frowned. "Yeah, who's this?"

"Terrance Romano."

One of his old partners in crime. He smiled. "Hey, Romano. Didn't recognize your voice. What's up?"

"We checked into Patrick Stone. He's been life-flighted to General—damn mess. He's critical."

Tucker shook his head. “Wait. What? What the hell are you talking about?”

“Ms. Cooke requested a welfare check at Patrick Stone’s residence. She was pretty rattled. He didn’t show up for an important meeting this morning. Couple of officers stopped by the house, peeked in a few windows, found him on the living room floor with his skull bashed in. Somebody beat the fuck out of him with a lamp—shards of pottery all over the place. Blood’s matted and dried on the walls and area rug. Looks like he’d been laying there a couple days.”

“Goddamn.” Tucker closed his eyes as he rested his forehead in his hand. This was going to crush Wren.

“Owens is on his way here. We’re processing the scene now—can’t find his wallet, but all other valuables seem to be in place.”

Tucker’s eyes flew open. This wasn’t just a simple robbery gone bad. The coincidence was too much. “How sure are you on the timeframe?”

“CSI says spatter’s about forty-eight hours old. It’ll take us a little time to nail down an exact timeline.”

“What about his cell phone? Did you find Patrick’s phone?”

“Don’t think so. Hold on.” Romano’s muffled voice filled Tucker’s ear as he murmured something. “Nope. No cell phone found either.”

“He sent her a text yesterday afternoon—or someone did, using Patrick’s phone.” How long had Wren been communicating with the wrong man? Had she slipped up and said anything about where they were staying? Tucker shot out of his chair and stood by the windows, scrutinizing the shadows among the snow-covered trees.

“We’ll call his provider, see if we can triangulate a signal.”

“Call me back if you get something. I need to know where the bastard is. And I want an update on Patrick as soon as you have one.”

“Will do.”

Tucker hung up and sighed. All hell had broken loose, and Wren never bothered to fill him in. What was he going to say to her? How the hell was he supposed to tell her? She adored Patrick—had defended him viciously the two times he'd brought him up as a suspect. He shoved his phone in its holder and made his way to the dining room.

He stopped in the doorway, studying her. Her cheeks were pale and her shoulders tense—her movements jerky while her leg bobbed up and down under the table. She looked so small and vulnerable in her oversized red sweater. He clenched his jaw and steamed out a breath through his nose. "Cooke."

Her gaze whipped to his, and she froze, then looked down at her laptop again. "What?"

This wasn't going to be any easier after the way he'd left things a couple hours ago. He'd handled the news of the Brookes girl's death poorly. The details of her murder were strikingly similar to Staci's. He rubbed at the tingle along the back of his neck and dismissed the troubling clench in his gut. Similar didn't mean there was a connection. Seven years in Homicide taught him that no matter how hard he chased down leads, he wasn't always going to catch the bad guy. He'd never gotten justice for Staci. God knows he'd tried, searching the DNA databanks every six months for years, but there had never been a match. He'd learned to distance himself from the day-to-day sorrows of violent death, thank God, but Alyssa Brookes' murder got under his skin. "We need to talk."

"Can't. I'm working." She glanced at her phone, then back at the computer.

"Detective Romano just called." That got her attention.

She stood. "He said he was going to call me back. Why did he call you?"

"Wren."

"Don't." Her voice quaked with fear, and she pressed her lips together. "Don't call me that. You never call me that."

Her eyes filled. “Don’t look at me like you’re sorry.”

His heart ached for her as he walked to her and brushed his hands down her arms.

“What’s wrong with Patrick?”

He tucked a strand of hair behind her ear. “Sit down.”

She jerked away. “Just tell me what’s wrong with Patrick.”

“He should be at the hospital by now.”

“Why?” She clutched her arms across her chest. “What happened? Is he going to be okay?”

“They life-flighted him—”

“Life-flighted?”

“Yeah, to General. He’s critical.”

“Critical,” she whispered as she gripped her sleeves tighter.

“He has a head injury.”

“He fell.”

He wanted to let her believe what she chose, but the truth would come out eventually. It was better to give her the facts all at once. He shook his head. “No.”

“Then what else?”

“He was hit over the head with some lamp in his living room.”

Her eyes grew huge. “The blue urn lamp?”

“I’m not sure.”

“Yes, it has to be. It’s so heavy.” Her voice broke and she pressed her fingers to her lips.

He took a step toward her, wanting to comfort. “Wren.”

She took a step back. “The man who’s stalking me—he did this?”

“We’re not sure.”

“Yes, you are. You’re as sure as I am that it was him.” She strained to talk over the emotions clogging her throat. “This is all my fault.” She turned away as she fought to control her ragged breathing.

“Wren.” He walked up behind her and gripped her shoulders. “No.” She struggled to step away.

He held her firm, wrapping his arms around her waist as he pressed his cheek to hers. "This is not your fault."

"I ran for safety and left him to deal with the rest. Why wouldn't Patrick be a target?" she choked out. "The text yesterday. He didn't send me that message. And he didn't call in sick to the Cartwrights either."

"Did you ever tell him where you were?"

"No, but I should have. I should have brought him with me. How long had he been laying there?"

He clenched his jaw, feeling helpless as Wren fought to keep herself together.

She whirled. "How *long*?"

He took her hands, holding her gaze. "They think a couple of days."

"My *God*." She closed her eyes and tears spilled down her cheeks. "I need to—I need to..." She gestured toward their rooms.

He nodded. "I'll come with you."

"Alone." She tugged to free her hand.

He held tight. "Cooke."

"*Alone*."

He released her, and she grabbed her phone as she walked away. "Son of a *bitch*." He bunched his fists at his sides, trying to respect her need for space, but her dark, devastated eyes and ghostly white cheeks wouldn't let him. "Screw this." He started down the hall after her, gave a quick tap of knuckles against the door, and turned the knob, letting himself in when she didn't answer. Her back was to him as she pulled open a drawer and set a small pile of shirts on the dresser top.

"I need to speak with Grant please. Wren." She shook her head. "Cooke. His daughter. Yes, I assure you he does have a daughter and a son. I need to speak with him immediately. It's an emergency." She closed the drawer and opened the next. "Dad. My assistant, Patrick Stone, was life-flighted to General a few minutes ago. Head trauma. I need you to check on him and tell me if he's going to be okay." She cleared her throat, fighting to keep her voice steady. "Yes, right this minute. Your meeting can wait. I've never asked you for anything, but I am now. Just this once, pretend to be my father and help your daughter. Thank you." She hung up and stood perfectly still, clutching her phone in a white-knuckled grip.

"Hey."

She whirled. "I said I wanted to be alone."

"I heard you."

She sniffled and brought her clothes to the open suitcase on her bed.

"What are you doing?"

"Going home to Patrick."

He sighed, understanding that this wasn't going to end well. "No, you're not."

"Yes, I am. I'm all he has." A tear fell and she wiped it away.

"He has parents and a sister."

She glanced up and held his gaze. "How did you know—ah, your investigation." She shook her head. "I'm sure Detective Owens missed the part about his family disowning him because he's gay." She turned, heading for the bathroom.

Tucker followed, watching as she tossed makeup into a sapphire-colored travel case. "I'm sorry for Patrick, Wren. I'm sorry for you. I know how much he means to you, but you're not going anywhere."

She flung her toothpaste and toothbrush in the case. "Don't tell me what I will and won't do. I'm leaving." She grabbed her shampoo and conditioner from the shower.

"Your safety is my responsibility, and I'm telling you we're staying put."

"Not anymore," she scoffed as she zipped her case and skirted around him. "You're fired."

"I'm fired? I'm *fired*? Are you fucking *kidding* me?" He caught her arm and yanked her around. "I'm not your goddamn employee, and you're not going anywhere."

She threw her travel case among her clothes, zipped her luggage, and headed for the door with her suitcase in hand.

"Watch me."

Enough was enough. He walked forward and pulled the Samsonite from her grip. "Give it up, Wren."

She whirled. "Give me my bag."

"Drop the tough-as-nails act. Go sit down and *think* for a minute."

"I am thinking—about Patrick."

"And I'm thinking about you."

"I don't need you to think about me. I don't need you at all."

Her shattered eyes and trembling lips told him different. "Maybe, but you're stuck with me."

She yanked up her purse and walked out of the room without looking back.

He dropped her case and hurried after her, breaking into a half jog, realizing she was almost to the door. "Damn it, Cooke." If she made it to the Jeep before he got to her… He grabbed her and she turned, shoving him back a step.

"I said I don't need you!" She reached for the doorknob.

He yanked her back against him.

She fought his hold. "Let me go."

"That's enough." He turned her to face him and braced her up against the solid wood.

"Let me *go*." She shoved and punched as her breath heaved in and out.

He captured her wrists and pinned them against the door, shoving his face close to hers. "*Enough*, Wren."

She froze, gasping, looking into his eyes as tears raced down her cheeks.

"Enough," he said gently, still holding her in place.

She fisted her hands, fighting herself more than him. "I need to go," she shuddered out before she couldn't hold back the torrents of emotion any longer. Powerful, racking sobs burst from her body, and she pressed her forehead to his heart.

He wrapped his arms around her, holding tight as he brushed his hand down her soft hair.

"Oh, God," she cried against his chest, completely undone.

"Come on." He gathered her up, walking to the bedroom, sitting in the chaise lounge close to the fireplace, cocooning her against him.

"He needs me, Tucker. He needs someone to be there with him," she said between sobs.

He traced circles along her back. "We'll make sure someone's with him."

"But it won't be me."

"No, not for now."

"What if he doesn't make it?"

"He's receiving the best care possible."

"Please take me home, Tucker." She lifted her head off his chest and held his gaze. "*Please.*"

She was breaking his heart. "Don't do that, Cooke. Don't look at me with those devastated eyes and ask for something you know I can't give you."

"Please." Her lips trembled, and another tear fell.

He slid his finger along her jaw. "There isn't much I wouldn't do for you." He kissed her temple and pressed her palm to his heart. "You got me, Cooke. But I can't take you home. We can't risk it. I can't risk you."

Nodding, she bit her lip, suppressing the trembling. "I'll never forgive myself if he dies alone."

He wanted to tell her Patrick was going to survive, but he just didn't know. "He won't be alone." He pulled his phone from its case and dialed Jerrod Quinn.

"Quinn."

"It's Campbell. You keeping an eye on Abby today?"

"No. She and Alexa are with Jackson."

"Good. I need a favor."

"What's up?"

"Wren's friend, Patrick Stone, was attacked. He was life-flighted to General about an hour ago. Last we heard, he was critical. Can you go stay with him—bring your badge, tell Detective Owens I sent you over on behalf of Ethan Cooke Security. He'll go with the flow."

"Yeah, man. I'll head right over."

And that's what friends were for. Jerrod was fairly new to the Cooke team, but he fit right in, making a great addition. "Thanks, man."

"No problem."

Tucker hung up and slid his phone away. "Jerrod's heading over. We'll find someone to stay with him tomorrow and every day after until we can get home."

Her breath rushed out on another sob as she wrapped her arms around him. "Thank you."

"You're welcome." He returned her embrace, content to stay like this for as long as she was.

"Thank you for staying with me."

He rested his cheek on the top of her head, breathing her in. "Don't want to be anywhere else."

"I—" She lifted her head and met his gaze. "I need you."

"I know."

"You scare me."

He winked. "I know that too. I meant what I said when I told you you've got me, Wren." No one had ever tangled him up the way she did.

She closed her eyes.

"Look at me," he said gently.

She met his stare.

"I'm not going anywhere."

She studied him as he spoke.

He touched his lips to hers, hopeful for the first time that she might actually believe him.

"What are we going to do?"

He wrapped her up again and leaned more comfortably in the chair. "Stay put until the authorities figure this mess out."

"That's not enough."

"No, it's not, but it's the best we can do for now."

She sighed and rested her head against his shoulder, clinging for the first time.

☙ Chapter Thirteen ❧

Wren put away the last of the groceries Ms. Hayes' grandson dropped off, desperately wanting to stay busy. The next order of business was preparing the pot roast—with all the fixings. She shuddered at the thought of eating, but making a meal was something to do.

She hadn't been able to settle since her father called back with an update. Patrick was in bad shape. If he survived the next few days, permanent brain damage was likely. She clutched the canvas grocer's bag, fighting another round of helpless tears. Patrick needed her more than ever, and she couldn't be there for him.

Tucker opened the glass-fronted door of the gym and stepped out, sweaty and gorgeous in his ratty shorts. "You holding up over there?"

"Yes." She gave him a small smile, knowing that's what he wanted.

"I'm going to shower off real quick. The alarm's set. Don't open the door for anyone."

"I won't." She stared after him as he walked down the hall, nibbling her lip, worrying. Tucker was becoming too important. She was starting to rely on him, and not just for her safety. Her life was careening out of control. One of the people she loved most was fighting to survive hundreds of miles away, and there was nothing she could do to fix it. Her business was falling apart, and she couldn't leave Utah. The weight of the last few days had finally crushed her to a pulp, and Tucker had been there, holding her while she cried like she never had before, being everything she didn't know she needed.

Her heart had done a wild flip-flop as she lay cradled against his firm chest and he told her 'she'd gotten him.' As she stared into his gorgeous hazel eyes, comforted by his strong arms wrapped around her, she'd wanted to be 'gotten.' For the first time ever, she'd been tempted to toss caution aside and see where things could go. That alone terrified her, but there was so much more. All these *feelings*... What would happen when she couldn't resist Tucker any longer? For surely it was only a matter of time before she was completely sunk—if she wasn't already.

Her eyes grew wide and she shook her head. *No.* She was being over-emotional. Her spirits were at an all-time low. She was vulnerable, that was all. Nothing had changed. Tucker was still Tucker, and she was the same old Wren.

In defense against her own thoughts, she preheated the oven and pulled carrots from the refrigerator, washed them, and peeled them within an inch of their lives. Petite red potatoes were scrubbed next, and onions quartered. She tossed them in a roasting pan, along with the thick beef round and a healthy dash of salt and pepper, then slid them on the rack.

Now what? She glanced at her computer, unable to bear the idea of work—another first. She'd tried to get back to the grind after she climbed off of Tucker, promising him that she was going to be all right, but after several of Lenora's friends e-mailed their thanks-but-no-thanks on proposed bids for new projects and her long conversation with Brice Movenbeck, she'd lost her motivation to fight a losing battle. Brice had been gracious and understanding once she explained her situation and Patrick's, but her insistence to refund her fees and deeply discount all furnishings and accents for their huge inconvenience had immediately put Cooke Interiors in the red. She would be eating several thousand dollars in lost profits, and with so many potential new clients turning her away, there wouldn't be many options to recoup her losses. A rush of nausea twisted her stomach as she thought of her bottom line and the amount of money she would have to cough up for her vendors and Lenora Cartwright. The quarter of a million in product alone for Lenora's unfinished pool house was going to destroy her.

JT had e-mailed moments after her conversation with Brice, sharing that his mother called him in a snit about the current situation. He assured her he was doing everything in his power to convince her to reconsider her lawsuit, but Wren already understood Lenora wouldn't back down.

At wits' end and no longer sure of what to do, she turned away from her laptop and stacked the canvas bags Ms. Hayes would come for tomorrow. She rubbed at the achy tension squeezing the back of her neck and looked toward the wing she and Tucker shared. Now what?

Business was off the table—at least for a little while, and dinner was well on its way. Perhaps she would follow Tucker's example and indulge in a shower. A long, warm soak was just what she needed. Hopefully the water would loosen the knots along her shoulder blades. She started toward her room, liking the idea of soothing steam and fragrant soaps more and more. Maybe she could find a radio station that played classical—not her typical idea of good music, but what the hell? Patrick always said it helped him relax, so she would give it a try.

She closed herself in her room and turned, gasping as Tucker stood in the bathroom doorway with a towel slung low around his hips. The tension clenching her shoulders squeezed tighter as the swift sexual punch effectively tied her up. "What... Why aren't you using your own bathroom?"

He shrugged. "My stuff's in here."

"Oh." She flexed her fingers on the doorknob as her gaze followed a drop of water from his solid shoulder, down the mound of his pec, along the bumps of his six-pack, and disappeared into white cotton. "I'm going to...I'm just going to... clean up."

"Okay. Did your dad call you back?"

"Yes."

"What's the word?"

She shook her head and stared at the floor. "It doesn't look good."

He walked to her and rested his hands on her shoulders. "I'm sorry."

She breathed in wafts of his soap as she looked up, meeting his eyes. "He was getting out of a CT scan when my father checked in. His skull is fractured. He has a large subdural hematoma. They need to do a craniotomy to alleviate the pressure on his brain. He's very unstable, but they have to attempt the surgery anyway or he'll die. If he makes it through, they believe brain damage is likely."

Tucker steamed out a breath as he enveloped her in a hug. "I don't even know what to say."

"This feels like a dream—all of it," she said as she returned his embrace, resting her cheek on his warm skin, listening to his steady heartbeat, comforted, then just as quickly pulled away. She couldn't keep doing this—relying on him to soothe away her worries. She took care of herself. And if she needed an ear, she had Ethan.

Tucker kept his arms around her waist, trapping her against him, easing back enough to look into her eyes. "Where you going?"

"I have stuff to do, and so do you."

"You've had a hell of a day, Cooke. There's nothing wrong with taking a little time to let things settle."

"I don't want to let things settle. I don't want to think, period. My best friend is fighting to survive, and my business has gone to hell. I don't want to dwell on the fact that some crazy bastard has ruined Patrick's life and wants to hurt you as much as he does me."

"Like I said, hell of a day—hell of a last couple of weeks. Your business isn't ruined, Cooke. Taking one more day to steady out isn't going to make or break you."

"Cooke Interiors is beyond broken. Patrick never made it to the Movenbeck install, I have vendors up my butt trying to find out what I want to do with the product that should have been delivered and now is just sitting there, unwanted, and Lenora pulled out of our project. She'll be siccing her attorneys on me and tossing my name through the mud every chance she gets."

"Have you explained the situation?"

"I did to Brice. He was very understanding. But Lenora... JT's working on her, but she won't call me back."

"She's a bitch."

"Yes, she is, but she and the Movenbecks are my biggest clients right now—or were."

He brushed his finger along her jaw. "We'll smooth this out."

She pulled further away as she digested his use of "we'll." There was no "we" in this equation. There was only her. "I'll have to see what I can do."

"No rest for the weary."

"Pretty much."

"No help either."

"I don't need any."

"Or not mine anyway." He shook his head. "Every time I think we're getting somewhere..."

He knew her too well. "I'm self-reliant, Tucker. Always have been."

"Another opportunity to point out that you don't need me."

She shrugged even as she remembered her confession to the contrary. "You said it."

He grabbed her chin between his thumb and finger. "You

don't *want* to need me, but you do. It drives you crazy that you're twisted up."

"There's no *twisting* going on here. I take care of myself. I had a weak moment a couple hours ago. I appreciate you being there. The end."

He tugged her closer. "You can try to keep shutting me out, but sooner or later you'll figure out I'm just going to keep getting in your way."

"Let me go."

He stepped closer. "You need me, Cooke, and I need you. You scare me as much as I scare you, but at the end of the day, I'm more afraid to let you walk than I am to try to make something work. Why don't you think about that while you take your shower?" Tucker released his grip and walked out, closing the bedroom door behind him.

She breathed in the remnants of his soap as she made her way to the bathroom, her heart thudding. Damn him. She didn't have any choice but to think of him and what he'd said, whether she wanted to or not. *I'm going to keep getting in your way.* She glared, realizing that had been his plan all along. He'd been in her way since she walked into Sarah's hospital room months ago.

The doorbell rang, and Tucker frowned. Tom already dropped off the groceries, so who the hell was here? He set his laptop on the coffee table and unconsciously brushed his palm over the holster clipped to his belt as he walked to the door and peeked through the security hole. His frown deepened as he instantly recognized two plainclothes cops. He twisted the bolt and turned the knob, staging himself behind the heavy wood, keeping his hand on his gun until he knew what was up. "Can I help you?"

"Detective Tucker Campbell?"

"Former Detective, but yes."

"I'm Detective Jasper Rogers," the portly, gray-haired fifty-something said, "and this is my partner Detective Peter Franklin." He gestured to the tall, thin, younger man with dark brown eyes. "We're with the Park City Police Department. Do you mind if we come in and speak with you for a few minutes?"

He was still waiting for an update on Patrick's missing cell phone, but something told him this had nothing to do with Wren's situation. "About?"

"We have some questions we'd like to ask you about the Alyssa Brookes case."

He knew exactly where this was going and reluctantly opened the door wider. "Come on in." He wanted to resent them for being here, but he couldn't. Alyssa had been found strangled in her bedroom just like Staci. The last aggravated murder in the area had been Staci's. The Brookes' home was less than a mile away. He should've figured on a visit. If he were still pulling duty, he would've knocked on this door too.

"Tucker? Is everything okay?" Wren's voice was tight with fear as she stood by the couch in her black yoga pants and snug long-sleeve white top. She'd twisted her mass of damp curls into a thick braid.

"Everything's fine." He gave her a small, reassuring smile. "I'll take care of this. Go ahead and do what you were needing to." He didn't want her here right now. The past was the past, and she had nothing to do with it.

"Is this about—has there been a change in my case?"

"Your case?" Detective Rogers' brow rose.

"This is my family's vacation home, but I'm here in an official capacity. I'm Ms. Cooke's bodyguard. I'm an agent with Ethan Cooke Security—Los Angeles branch."

"No, I'm sorry, Ms. Cooke. We're here on other business."

"Oh. Can I get you some coffee?"

"Wouldn't mind. You, Franklin?"

"Sure would be nice. It's colder than a bit..." He cleared his throat. "Yes, ma'am. Thank you."

"Let me get a tray." Wren held Tucker's gaze a moment, her eyes full of questions, then left. Cabinets opened, then the fridge as Wren got busy in the kitchen.

"Go ahead and have a seat."

The detectives sat on opposite ends of the couch.

Tucker took a cushion on the loveseat. "I'm not sure what I can offer by way of help with the Brookes' case, but I'll do what I can."

"We appreciate it. We're here, Mr. Campbell, because a few of our responding deputies were quite taken aback by how similar Alyssa Brookes' murder scene was to your sister's."

"The news reported a strangling in the bedroom."

"Yes, but it's more than that. I'm going to be frank here, Mr. Campbell, and say that whoever killed Staci Campbell took Alyssa Brookes' life as well."

His stomach pitched and his pulse accelerated as he stared in Detective Rogers' serious eyes. "My sister was murdered over a decade ago. That's a pretty quick conclusion to draw in less than a day."

"You would think. I didn't live in Park City when your sister died, and Franklin here was in high school up in Montana, but many of the officers still on staff remember Staci's murder. It's the only real violence we've seen other than a couple of domestics gone wrong. This kind of stuff doesn't happen around here."

"So why now, after fourteen-and-a-half years?"

"That's the question we're looking to answer. After several deputies mentioned the Staci Campbell case to Franklin and me, we spent a couple hours reviewing the files in Cold Case—studied crime scene photos, witness statements, so on and so forth. I think we have a problem here, Mr. Campbell."

Wren walked in carrying a tray of steaming mugs and a plate of store-bought chocolate chip cookies. "Here we go." She set the smooth carved wood on the table and picked up a mug. "Detective Franklin, how do you like your coffee?"

"Black."

"Me as well, Ms. Cooke."

She handed over the cups and sat next to Tucker.

"You don't have to stay."

"I want to stay."

"Cooke—"

"I'm staying, Tucker."

He stared at her for another moment then looked at Detective Rogers. "What sort of problem?"

"First off, I'm going to need to ask for your whereabouts last night."

Wren picked up her mug and set it back down. "What's going on? What is this about?"

Their question was procedure, but it burned his ass—the implication that he'd had something to do with Staci's death. "I was here all night. As I said, I'm on duty."

"We were both here all night. Tucker hasn't left my side." She scooted closer to him in an unmistakable gesture of support.

Tucker took her hand and gave a gentle squeeze, touched that she was getting defensive on his account.

"And during the midnight hours?" Franklin asked.

"I've been staying with Ms. Cooke. There's a fireplace in her guestroom. The power has been out since the storm—finally came back on this morning, as I'm sure you know."

"Are you both willing to sign an affidavit attesting to the fact that you were both in residence all evening?"

"Yes," they said at the same time.

"I apologize, Mr. Campbell, especially when we're going to ask for your help."

He shrugged. "Procedure's procedure."

"We understand you worked homicide for several years."

Tucker nodded. "LAPD."

"It's also noted you majored in Criminal Psychology as well as Criminal Justice."

He'd been determined to find the answers to Staci's murder from the moment the authorities deemed her case cold. "That's correct."

Wren looked at him in surprise.

"We have several qualified officers on staff as well as Utah Bureau of Investigation in on this, but we see a unique opportunity to get your take as former law enforcement and your close association to one of our victims."

Wren's fingers clutched his. "What?"

"I'll explain later," he said absently, ready to immerse himself in whatever the detectives were willing to share. If what they were saying was true, they might actually catch Staci's killer this time.

"We brought along pictures of the Brookes' crime scene as well as pictures from 1999. We're hoping you might be willing to take a look, maybe give us some ideas."

Fourteen-and-a-half years had passed since he walked in to find his sister dead. He'd never looked at the crime scene photos; there'd never been a need. He remembered every grisly detail—if he let himself—as if Staci had died yesterday. "Of course." He glanced to his right, realizing Wren still sat next to him—her hand in his. "Would you get the Detectives some more coffee?" He didn't want her to see this. Deep down, *he* didn't want to see this, but if there was any chance of justice for Staci, he would do what he had to.

"That would be great, Ms. Cooke." Detective Rogers held out an empty mug.

She opened her mouth and quickly closed it, hesitating, then withdrew her hand from his, trapped by manners. "Sure." She took the cups.

"Wouldn't mind a few more cookies either, if you have any to spare. The grocery store bakery makes the best chocolate chip in town."

"Certainly. I'll be right back."

Tucker waited for Wren to head into the kitchen, then nodded at the Detective. "Go ahead and lay them out."

"I think it might be best to do a side-by-side comparison."

"I agree."

Rogers laid down two photos of dark purple hands—one Alyssa's, one Staci's.

Tucker's shoulders instantly tensed as he recognized the gold and rubies Staci had always worn on her index finger. He stared at well-manicured fingernails and remembered how cold his sister had been while he clutched her discolored, stiff fingers, waiting for help to arrive. But there'd been no help for Staci.

Tucker systematically shut himself down as he studied the ligature marks dug into both victims' wrists. Victims—not Staci Campbell and Alyssa Brookes, but two sixteen-year-old white females who had been brutally and methodically murdered. He wouldn't be able to get through this if he didn't distance himself all the way. "Same pattern. More than likely identical material used," he said more to himself than the men sitting close by. "Did he remove them post-mortem?"

"ME says yes. Perp tied her hands behind her back, then cut the nylon rope minutes after death."

The same as Staci.

Detective Franklin set out several more pictures—full crime scene shots and close-ups of naked, spread-eagle victims with their arms above their heads. Deep purple lines dug in at their throats; pinpoints of blood marring dead, staring eyes. Both victims had long black hair and pretty, slender bodies left posed in humiliating positions. Even in death, they hadn't been allowed their dignity. "The Brookes girl—was she raped?"

"Semen was found at the scene. We've rushed the kit off for DNA analysis. They'll do a comparison at the lab."

Tucker already knew there would be a match. "Perpetrator's point of entry?"

"Unknown."

Tucker's gaze flew to the detectives. Exactly the same.

The crime scenes were identical. "Fingerprints?"

"None that don't belong to anyone other than family and friends who are known to have been in the house."

What the fuck was going on? He needed to stand and pace away the worst of the adrenaline coursing through his veins, but he stayed where he was. This whole situation was…so many things: painful, disgusting, a potential beginning to answers for his parents and himself. "Goddamn."

"I'm assuming the Brookes family and friends have no one in common with the Campbell friends here in Park City?"

"If it were that simple, we sure wouldn't be here bothering you, Mr. Campbell."

Tucker nodded.

"Looks like we've got a serial on our hands. We've got a profiler heading in from Salt Lake. Ms. Cooke, thank you."

Tucker glanced up at Wren, pale and staring at the pictures spread over the table. He'd been so caught up, he didn't hear her come back. He rushed to his feet and took the mugs from her white-knuckled grip, handing them off, then pulled her several steps away. "Get out of here, Cooke." He didn't want her to see what had become of Alyssa Brookes and Staci. No one needed that horror stuck in their mind forever. He grabbed her chin, raising it until she finally looked at him and away from the photos. "I said get out of here. Go down to your room until I finish up here."

"No, I'm—I'm fine. I just didn't… You never told me. I had no idea Staci… I thought—I thought maybe—"

"Go get some work done."

Shock vanished and compassion filled her eyes as she clutched his wrist. "I'm okay. I can handle it. I'll stay with you."

Her sweet, steady strength was blowing gaping holes in the protective wall he'd built around himself. He took her hand and kissed her knuckles. "I'll be all right."

"Tucker." She touched his cheek. "Let me help you the way you've helped me." One gesture. One simple sentence undid him completely.

"Damn, Cooke," he sighed, closing his eyes. He wouldn't make it through this if he didn't shield himself again. "I need you to go."

"But—"

"I don't want you here." His voice sharpened as he pulled her hand from his cheek and dropped it. "I don't want you here," he repeated more gently, hating himself for causing the flash of hurt.

"Fine." She stepped away. "I'm sorry. If you'll excuse me," she said to the detectives and walked down the hall.

He clenched his jaw, understanding that any small gains he'd made with Wren were now lost.

Detective Franklin cleared his throat.

Tucker went to his seat, ruthlessly attempting to shove Wren to the back of his mind. He could only handle one problem at a time, and right now that was his sister. Staci's killer had struck again—fourteen-and-a-half years later. "Sorry about that."

"No problem."

He struggled to pick up where they left off. "You said you're bringing in a profiler?"

"Yes. She should be here in the next couple of hours."

"My parents paid for more than one profiler's opinion over the years. They've all said the same thing, and I concur. The guy's a sociopath. He's sick, coolly angry, and smart as hell. He blends well—could be a pillar of the community for all we know. But that's where the theory starts to unravel if we're connecting cases here. They've all said Staci's murder was personal. Her killer set out to terrify, humiliate, and ultimately end her life for a purpose. He was sending a message. As to what that was, we have no idea. Other than the identical killing, I can't find a connection between the two victims."

"There's definitely a connection, Mr. Campbell." Detective Rogers handed over two pictures of a torso glowing in the bold blue tint of a CSI black light. *SC* had been written on the stomach.

"What's this?"

"I thought we would save this for last—the only difference between Alyssa and Staci's cases. These are photographs of Alyssa Brookes' abdomen. The bastard wrote his message in his semen."

The wave of disgust left Tucker ill. "Fucker."

Tucker scrutinized the picture, then picked up the photos of both Staci and Alyssa's abdominal regions in standard lighting, studying.

"We can't say for certain what this means, but if we start drawing conclusions—"

"My sister's initials."

Detective Rogers and Franklin nodded.

Tucker struggled to concentrate on the details instead of the ball of rage twisting his insides. "So this man's back. We need to figure out what has provoked him out of an almost fifteen-year dry spell?"

"If he hasn't been killing somewhere else."

Tucker shook his head as he put down the pictures. "Although he's changed things up with this slight variation," He tapped the black-lighted photograph, "the method of murder itself hasn't. I've been running his MO through the databanks for as long as I've had access. There's never been a DNA or crime scene match before or after Staci's murder. This guy's methodical and enjoys his work. If he's done it since, we would know—kind of like now."

Rogers nodded. "Okay."

"Our man, he knows the area well. How long have the Brookes been residents of Park City?"

"About a dozen years now."

Tucker stared at the photos, struggling to find a parallel. "So Alyssa grew up here for the most part. She and Staci have similar traits—black hair and slim body types. Alyssa lived among this community for quite some time. It's not as if she was a visitor and the killer spotted her as his 'type' and suddenly had the urge to kill. That wouldn't fit his MO, anyway. He's not just killing at random. He selects and kills with a purpose." And his purpose appeared to be Staci.

"About now, I'm wondering why you gave up your badge." Detective Hayes set down his empty mug. "Must've been a blow to LAPD to lose you."

He shrugged. "Got sick of the game—sick of procedure."

"We're going to be reopening Staci's case. We'll work both hers and Alyssa's in a dual investigation."

He swallowed the sudden waves of emotion. For years he'd wanted to do this for Staci, but had been too bogged down in other people's crises to get the chance. "I'd like to help however I can."

"We plan to re-interview all witnesses, starting with your parents."

"Not my mother," Tucker said quickly. "You can speak with my father, but my mother's off limits unless there's something my father is unable to answer. You have her statements to go on. Dad and I can fill in the rest. Staci's murder destroyed her. She's never been the same. She finally started leaving the house again a few years ago to do her charity work. We're not going to fuck that up unless there's no other choice."

Detective Rogers grunted his reluctant assent.

Tucker pulled his phone from his hip and noted Franklin's glance at his weapon.

"What kind of trouble is Ms. Cooke in?"

"Stalker."

"Beautiful woman. LA, you said. She some kind of star or something?"

"No. Interior designer. We left Los Angeles for a while until things settle down." He pointed to the fading cuts and bruises on his temple.

"Oh?"

"Wren's been a target for the last three weeks. I got in

the way of a 'message' he sent through my apartment window. Guy's escalating. Her business partner was just found with his skull bashed in. We're thinking her stalker beat the shit out of him, took his phone, and has been playing games with her for the past couple days via text message."

"Hmm," Rogers said.

Tucker scrolled through his contacts and scribbled down his father's cell number, hating that his family was about to relive something they'd all put away. "Here you go. I'll let my dad know he should be expecting a call."

"We'll be in touch." Rogers retrieved the crime scene pictures, securing them in an acid-free bag. "I'm sure we'll have more questions."

"I don't see us going anywhere for a while." He glanced toward the hall, eager to move this along. He needed to talk to Wren and smooth things over.

Rogers and Franklin stood. "Thank you, Mr. Campbell."

"Thank you." He shook their hands and walked the men to their vehicle. Moments later he came back in, closed the door, and pressed his forehead to the solid wood. "Son of a bitch." He could hardly keep up with everything going on—Patrick, Staci, Wren. He sighed. Staci's case had new leads he needed to sort through, but first he wanted to talk to Wren...after he called his dad. She'd put herself out there—finally—and he'd pushed her away. Sighing again, Tucker rearmed the panel, waited for the double blink, and pulled his phone from its holder as he set off down the hall.

Wren sat on the chaise lounge, gazing into the fire as the horrid crime scene photos played through her mind. She shuddered, thinking of dark, bruising marks around pale throats and wide, staring eyes.

She'd seen death before—in fancy funeral homes, but not like that. A mortician hadn't had his opportunity to brush away Staci and Alyssa's horror with makeup and a pretty casket. The peace and comfort of eternal life was nowhere present in the dozens of photographs lined up on the coffee table.

A deep, weighing sadness consumed Wren as she remembered Staci's beautiful smile in the long-ago picture by the pool. Poor Staci. All this time, Wren had been sure Staci collapsed from some sort of undiagnosed heart condition, but Staci's fate had been far crueler. She died horribly right here in this house. And Tucker... Tucker found his sister naked, violated, and strangled to death. How had he survived? How had he been strong enough to go into a profession where he relived his nightmare every day? She admired him and ached for him, as much as she was leery.

There was a knock at the door, and she sighed. She didn't want him here when she was all mixed up.

Tucker peeked in. "They left."

She nodded. "Okay." What else could she say? Her first instinct was to get up and go to him, to offer any comfort she could, but she stayed where she was. Tucker didn't want to be soothed.

She studied him in the doorway, yearning, despite his weary eyes and tense shoulders, realizing she'd been right to keep her guard up. As much as she wanted to deny it, he'd hurt her when he pushed her away. He told her he needed her, but when push came to shove, it wasn't true. Tucker didn't need her the way she'd craved to be needed since she was a little girl, desperate for her parents' attention.

All her life she'd wanted to belong, to feel that cozy acceptance she experienced with very few. And maybe somewhere deep below the recesses of denial, she'd always hoped someone special would walk into her life and prove they were worthy of the affection she had to give.

Tucker Campbell was not that man. Perhaps for a foolish moment she believed he might be, but she'd been wrong. He had spoken of feelings, of wanting to see where they could go, but he was confusing lust with genuine emotion. In the end, Tucker wasn't any different from most everyone else out there.

I've never met anyone as completely jaded as you, darling, Patrick had said on more than one occasion. Maybe so, but she was less of a fool because of it. There was no such thing as a soul mate or happily every after, and this rude refresher was serving as her wakeup call. Tucker had almost worn her down and made her believe in possibilities, but no more.

"I'm sorry, Cooke, about earlier."

She shrugged. "No big deal."

"Yeah, it is." He walked to the chaise and sat next to her.

"We happen to be living in the same house due to a business arrangement." She stood. "That doesn't mean you're required to share your personal life with me."

"Damn it, Cooke." He snagged her hand before she could walk away. "I didn't want you to see that stuff."

She pulled free and moved further away. "I appreciate it. And I'm sorry for you. Sorry you've had to deal with so much. You're a good man."

"Why do I feel like you just told me you're sorry about my sister and to fuck off all at the same time?"

"I have no clue. I am sorry about Staci. My heart is broken for the beautiful girl I saw smiling in that picture by the pool. She should have had a full life. As to the rest..." She shrugged. "We'll call today an opportunity to put things back in perspective."

"Bullshit." He rushed to his feet, advancing on her.

She moved from the corner before he could box her in as he typically did. "I'm going to work for a while before dinner's ready."

"Hold up." He stopped in front of her.

"No, Tucker." She pushed at his chest and skirted by. "No more of this."

"Cooke."

"I don't want to play your games anymore. For some foolish reason, I thought you were different, but you have double standards just like everybody else. I'm supposed to cry on your shoulder, and let you into the deepest parts of me, but your pain and your problems are off limits." She opened the door. "Let's just go back to the way things were before we were stupid enough to sleep together." She stepped out and closed the door quietly, leaving Tucker no chance to respond.

Channel seven had been rehashing Park City's "tragic death" all day. The newscaster went through her latest spiel while he lay on his bed, listening. Tara Thompson's smooth voice speculated as to whether the heartbreaking Alyssa Brookes case could have a connection to the 1999 unsolved murder of Staci Campbell. He loved every second of it. But more, he loved that two officers had been by to visit with Pretty Boy earlier this evening.

Surely they'd asked the former detective about his sister, and because he was one of the good ol' boys, they probably shared the evidence found on scene—perhaps in picture form. A slow, cool smile curved his lips. He hoped the hell so.

After pulling free of Alyssa, he'd zipped himself back in his pants, untied her hands, and lay her arms above her head in just the right position—as if she were a prima ballerina. Then he propped her knees up and bent her legs, letting them fall open, exposing her to the world.

He'd gathered his nylon ties, shoved them in his pockets, ready to make his way through the house, but then an idea occurred. What if the cops were too stupid to figure it out? He walked back to Alyssa, crouched in front of her pretty posed form and dipped his finger inside her still warm body, retrieving his dripping juices to leave his message on her slender stomach. He scrawled *SC* with extra flourish, dip-ping time and again until he was certain everything was perfect.

He stood, admiring his work in the glow of his dim light, bending once more to fix Alyssa's hair and tip her chin up just a touch. Satisfied, he opened her door, creeping down the hall in the dark as quietly as he came.

Tweeledee and Tweedledum down at the precinct would surely put two and two together—and if they didn't, Super Tucker would help them out. It was time for the former detective to put those fancy degrees to work and catch a deranged killer—if the killer didn't catch him and the lovely Wren Cooke first.

~ Chapter Fourteen ~

"There's no change, Ms. Cooke."

"Okay, thank you." Pressing 'end,' Wren set her phone on the dining room table and rested her head in her hands. Had she really expected a different answer than the one she'd received this morning? Patrick was still in a coma, clinging to life after his harrowing late-night surgery. The doctors were successful in relieving the pressure on his brain, but they wouldn't know the extent of his injuries until he regained consciousness—if he did at all.

Her laptop dinged with an alert, and she glanced up, reading the sender. Her pulse pounded and her palms grew instantly damp. She'd been waiting for this e-mail since she spoke with her accountant yesterday evening. Henry promised her a no-holds-barred bottom line on Cooke Interiors' financial state by four o'clock. He'd delivered twenty minutes early. Holding her breath, she scanned his message, and her heart sank.

Wren,

Per our discussion, I adjusted your books to reflect several refunds on unrendered services and the payout to your vendors for undelivered furnishings and accents. After a bit of finagling, I was able to meet all of your obligations and keep you solvent, but just barely. I've set aside money for your quarterly taxes, which are due next month, and Patrick's salary for November, which leaves you with a low remaining balance.

Please note the breakdown provided and the outlines I've created with several options on how you may wish to proceed.

I was hoping to have better news for you. Give me a call with any questions.

Henry

Wren puffed out an incredulous laugh as she stared at her final balance—thirty-five dollars and twenty-nine cents. Was this some sort of bad joke? Six months ago, Henry informed her Cooke Interiors was on track for a record-breaking year; now she was on the fast track to bankruptcy.

How would she ever come back from this, especially with Lenora traipsing around town showing off pictures of her half-finished pool house, telling people that Wren Cooke and her rude assistant had left her high and dry?

Wren opened several e-mails this morning from concerned friends letting her know what was going on. And there wasn't a damn thing she could do about it.

Slamming her laptop closed, she gripped the edges of her chair and took several deep breaths, struggling to think past the insanity that was her life. She exhaled sharply, and her phone rang, startling her. She looked at the readout and groaned, then pressed 'talk.' "Lenora."

"Hello, Wren. Cherie gave me your message yesterday. Isn't it nice that you've decided to start contacting your clients again—or former client in this case."

And so it begins. "I would apologize—"

"As you should, but it's too late. You and your partner have demonstrated a complete lack of dedication to your own mission statement. 'Client-focused service at its best,'" she scoffed. "My needs have hardly been your first priority as of late. My pool house has no paint or furnishings, and what about my accents?"

Wren stood, clenching her jaw, and stared out the enormous panes of glass as Lenora's snotty tone set her temper burning. "Lenora, I realize you're upset with our business practices of late. I can only imagine how inconvenient it must be to have your renovations put on hold while I deal with my pesky little stalking situation, and it really was rude of Patrick to pick a time like this to have his skull fractured when you're waiting to have your curtains hung."

"Don't be dramatic, Wren. It can't be that bad."

"Yes, Lenora, it certainly is. While you've been perusing your samples over the last month, I've been dealing with dead cats on my doorstep, bricks being thrown through my windows, and threatening text messages."

"Well if you would have explained—"

"It wouldn't have made a damn bit of difference."

Lenora huffed. "Inconceivably rude, just like your assistant."

That capped it. "True, Lenora, definitely true. It *was* impolite of Patrick to lay on his living room floor, unconscious and mostly dead, when he should have been at your breakfast meeting playing referee while you drove poor Ricardo crazy with your landscaping demands."

"Of all the—"

"No, Lenora, Patrick isn't doing well, thanks for asking, but I'm sure he would want me to tell you to 'fuck off' on his behalf as well as mine. I'll look forward to your attorney's call."

"Why—what? I—"

"And Lenora, you go ahead and keep slandering mine and Patrick's names and you'll be hearing from *my* attorneys." Adrenaline surged through Wren's body as she pressed 'end,' cutting off Lenora's shocked sputtering. God, that felt *so* good. She turned, suddenly desperate for a drink of water, and slammed into Tucker. "Oh!" Reaching out, she grabbed hold of his arms, steadying herself as he clutched her waist, then let go. "I didn't know you were there." She released her grip and took a step back. This was the first she'd seen of him since yesterday. He had stayed out of her way and vice versa.

"I heard the last of your conversation." He lifted his hand to touch her but dropped it to his side.

"That was completely unprofessional on my part, but she had it coming."

"Can't say I disagree. You okay?"

She skirted around him, too unsettled to be dealing with the effects of breathing him in. "Yeah, I'm fine." She took a glass from the cupboard and snapped on the tap.

"Not that you'd tell me otherwise."

Weary to the bone, she sighed and looked at him. "Don't. Not right now."

"Cooke—"

"I'm fine. Please leave me alone."

He stood where he was for several seconds, holding her gaze, then walked off, closing himself in the gym.

She set down her glass, staring at the granite, wishing everything wasn't so *complicated*. In less than a month's time, she'd lost complete control of her life. Her heart began to pound as her self-righteous streak vanished and reality started sinking in. What had she done? Had she lost her *mind*? She rushed to her phone, yanking it up, wanting to call Lenora back and apologize. Telling Lenora where to go had been amazingly satisfying; Patrick certainly would approve, but she might've been able to salvage the Cartwright job with a bit of finesse and finagling. She should have tried to appease Lenora's ruffled, bitchy feathers, but she'd been rash and foolish instead. And now it was too late. Cooke Interiors might have been salvageable five minutes ago—more than likely not, but the business she'd worked so hard to build was certainly finished now.

What was she going to *do*? Her cash flow was about to

come to a screeching halt. She had a decent sized personal savings account, but her mortgage, car payment, and potential legal fees would quickly bleed her dry. And what about Patrick and his needs? If he survived and recovered, he wouldn't have a job to come back to. His long-term disability and health insurance would hardly cover all of his bills. The monthly costs for LA's best long-term care facilities were staggering. He couldn't afford that and now neither could she. Patrick's current hospital stay would decimate any capital he had. There was no way in hell she was going to watch him lose everything because of *her* crazy stalker.

The weight of the world settled on her shoulders as she stared out at Park City's bustling downtown under the darkening sky. For the first time in her life, she didn't know how she should move forward. There was no Plan B in the event of head traumas, psychopaths, and the loss of her business. Watching everything fall apart had never been part of the plan, but it appeared to be reality now.

She studied the sprawling homes lit up across the mountain as smoke plumed from pretty stone chimneys, and with the deepest of regrets, she knew what she needed to do. Her house. She was going to have to sell. And her sweet little Mercedes would have to be traded in for something more practical. Just like that, everything was gone.

Swallowing the useless lump of emotion, she sat in front of her computer, searching for Greta Holmes' contact information, then picked up her phone and dialed.

"Greta Holmes."

"Hi, Greta. This is Wren Cooke."

"Wren. My goodness, honey, how are you?"

"I'm doing all right."

"Sweetie, I've been trying to track you down. I've been hearing some things I thought you might want to know about."

She closed her eyes and tipped her head against the chair. "Let me guess, you ran into Lenora Cartwright."

"I'm afraid so, sugar plum. Let me tell you I didn't pay her one little bit of attention."

She smiled, appreciating her friend's unshakable allegiance, but the damage was done. Greta might have ignored Lenora, but many others would certainly listen. "Thanks."

"You let me know if I can do anything to help."

"You can, actually."

"Name it."

"I'm putting my house on the market."

"You want to put the... Are you sure, honey? We searched *weeks* for just the right place."

Her home *was* exactly the right place. As soon as she'd stepped through the front door, she'd known. She had never loved a space more. "Yes, I'm sure. I'm also hoping you might be able to help me locate an apartment—a one-bedroom." She winced as she thought of all of the beautiful furnishings that would have to go.

"But—"

"I'm out of town for the next couple of weeks," she interrupted. This was hard enough without Greta's questions. "But I would like to get this moving as soon as possible. If you would be willing to stop by my brother's office, Mia can get you a key. You can take pictures when it works for you and scan me the necessary contracts."

"This breaks my heart, honey, but if this is what you want."

Greta's heart couldn't be breaking more than hers. "It is."

"I'll get the pictures, and look into fair market value by the close of business today. I'll have a sign in your yard by tomorrow." Greta's thick drawl and classic southern beauty disguised a sharp-minded business shark.

"Excellent."

"I'll start looking into apartments as well."

"I really appreciate this."

"Happy to help, honey. I'll draw up contracts and scan them over to you within the hour."

"Perfect."

"Bye now."

"Bye." Wren hung up and pressed her fingers to her temple, absorbing the huge emotional blow. Patrick, her business, her home. How much more would she lose? She glanced toward the glass door of the gym as Tucker walked from one weight machine to the next, and looked away, ignoring the sweep of longing to run to him. She did *not* need Tucker. She was exhausted, that was all, and emotionally drained.

She'd slept little last night, worrying about anything and everything. The constant stream of problems was almost more than she could bear; the stress and pressure were tearing her apart, but she would handle it. Ethan was going to be angry when he realized she put her house on the market, but she refused to allow big brother to fly in and rescue her. They had always been able to count on one another, but she wasn't about to have him pay for a lifestyle she could no longer afford.

Somehow things would work out. They always did, but she wondered how. Her career was ruined—her reputation damaged. It would be close to impossible to find clients or a firm willing to take her on in the LA area. Nibbling her lip, she sighed. Maybe this whole nightmare was an opportunity for a fresh start—somewhere else. She could put a resume together and send it around to a few of the companies she'd worked with in the Santa Barbara area over the last few years. If she moved up the coast, she would be an hour-and-a-half from LA—close enough to be involved in Kylee and Emma's lives and visit Patrick, but far enough away to start over. Her gaze wandered back to the gym. Distance would be a good thing. And it didn't have to be forever—maybe a year or two. Long enough to let things blow over and gain a solid handle on her emotions again.

For the first time in almost a month, she felt like she had the answers. Relocating was exactly what she needed to do. She picked up her phone and sent off a text to Greta.

Change of plans. The house is still a go, but I'd like to look at apartments in Santa Barbara instead of the Palisades. Thanks!

Bolstered by her idea, she scooted in and opened a blank Word document. Her fingers flew over the keys as she added her experience, education and numerous qualifications to the first draft of her resume. She smiled as she read through her impressive list. She'd be gainfully employed in no time as long as no one contacted Lenora or her several other unhappy clients.

Her smile dimmed a bit as she thought of working for someone else. Never ever did she think she would be back here again, but this was where she was at...for now. "Santa Barbara or bust," she muttered as she saved her work, closed the lid, and looked out at the snow coming down—big fat flakes, the only kind that seemed to fall around here. They were in for another foot by morning, according to the forecast.

She studied the outline of white peaks in the distance and tall dark pines surrounding the house—her prison, for surely that's what this place was starting to feel like. The unceasing precipitation and frigid temperatures were losing their appeal as the days carried on. Even the charm of the town lit up at twilight did little to abate her constant restlessness. She was trapped; her life was suspended in time while they waited for answers that never seemed to come.

Edgy again, Wren stood, catching sight of a small piece of the pool railing jutting from the mounds of snow. Her mind immediately flashed to Staci in her cute bathing suit, grinning next to her brother—alive. Then she thought of Staci pale and staring, bruised and abused, dying a death that had been so horribly *wrong*.

Wren glanced at Tucker as he sprinted on the treadmill, and on a whim, headed down the forbidden hall, stopping at the second door on the left. She twisted the knob, stepping in, and her eyes were immediately drawn to the floor where Tucker had found his sister's body. She had no idea what compelled her to be here or why she felt a connection to a girl who'd died so long ago. But she did.

Nothing had changed. Staci's room was exactly as it had been in the crime scene photos. Curious, she walked further in and wandered from picture to picture in the oddly fun and breezy space.

She studied carefree summer days through the eyes of a sixteen-year-old. The Campbell twins had had so many friends. She smiled as she recognized JT and shook her head as she realized Tucker had his arm slung around a different girl in almost every shot. Most of the photos were from here in Utah, but a few had California palm trees in the background. Staci had appeared to be as outgoing and fun as Tucker was athletic and cocky.

She stopped at a full headshot of Tucker with his baseball cap worn backwards. Frowning, she moved in closer, studying him. He was different—lighter before the crushing tragedy of his sister's death. She'd never realized how distant and weary his eyes were until now. *A piece of me died right along with her.*

One moment in time had altered his life irrevocably. Wren finally understood why he didn't follow his father into the hotel business. He'd spent years searching for justice, trying to make sense of something that was impossible to understand. Who would Tucker be if Staci had lived? Would there still be that light in those gorgeous hazel eyes? She stepped back, her heart heavy, as she sat on the edge of Staci's bed.

"Ms. Wren."

Wren's gaze flew to the door, and she gave Ms. Hayes a small smile as she stood. "Hello. I'm sorry. I didn't mean to intrude."

"You're fine, honey, just fine." She stepped into the room. "This space has been empty for so long. This home used to be such a happy place. All the laughter and noise." Ms. Hayes smiled sadly.

"What—what was she like?"

"She was beautiful. All the Campbells are. Staci was as sweet as she was pleasing to the eye. And she had spunk." She chuckled. "She kept Tucker on his toes, and he did the same in return."

"They were very close."

"Yes—a blessing and a curse when you lose someone so suddenly."

"What was he like...before?"

Ms. Hayes studied Wren. "He's a special man. Despite it all, he's still kind."

"Yes."

"He's smitten with you."

"Oh, I don't—"

"Used to be smitten with all the girls, and my, did they flock to him."

"I'm sure." Wren rolled her eyes.

Ms. Hayes laughed. "He's grown now. Something tells me my little Tuckey's more choosy."

She doubted it but nodded anyway.

"He sure likes to look at you. Maybe you like to look at him too."

"It's...complicated."

"I'm sure, dear, but complications have a way of working themselves out." Ms. Hayes took her hand. "He was very different. He laughed more. His grief is still heavy. Bless his heart."

"I want to help him, but I don't know how." For some reason, it was easy to be honest with the sweet older woman.

"You're doing just fine."

"But I haven't done anything."

"You've done more than you know."

"I mostly give him a hard time."

Ms. Hayes laughed again. "He needs a bit of that."

Wren grinned for the first time in days.

"He hasn't been back since. I wasn't sure he would ever come. This was their place. They loved it here. Seems like you might be just what he needs to sweep away the worst of the pain."

"I'm not so sure."

"I am." She squeezed Wren's fingers. "I have a feeling Tucker wants to help you as much as you'd like to help him, but letting others in isn't easy for some of us." She winked knowingly. "Trust is a hard thing to surrender when the world has let us down. But sometimes we have to be daring enough to allow someone special into our hearts so they can help us through the worst of things. And there are few more special than Tucker Campbell, my dear." She kissed Wren's cheek. "Now, come enjoy a cup of tea with me before I head home."

"I would like that." What else could she say when she was so confused? She shut Staci's door behind them, and they started down the hall, heading toward the kitchen and two steaming cups of chamomile.

Tucker flipped from Google Maps back to his Word document, typing up yet another report for Jackson—this time for the New Year's Eve shindig in Time Square. Thank God this wouldn't be his duty; it was bound to be a damn mess.

By some miracle, he'd actually scored the night off. He'd wanted to do something with Wren to ring in 2015, but as things stood, he would be sitting on his ugly couch, watching his coworkers freeze their asses off while one of America's favorite pop icons counted down the final seconds to the new year.

It was doubtful he and Wren would be doing much of anything together any time soon—like ever. She'd been right when she called him out—brutally so—but right just the same. He had expected her to trust in him and share her emotions, but his feelings were off limits, at least where Staci was concerned. How could he ask for her complete faith when he was unwilling to give his in return? It had been a long time since he'd confided so much in another. The thought of opening up like that again scared the hell out of him. He doubted it was much different for Wren.

Sighing, he leaned back in his chair, resting his head on the plush leather cushion. Wren wasn't going to allow him to fix this. She'd been *waiting* for him to let her down, and he'd obliged her quickly enough. In her mind, she'd given him a chance—sort of—and he'd blown it. The end.

Let's just go back to the way things were before we were stupid enough to sleep together. He winced as her bitter words hit the mark again. He'd made several mistakes over the last few days, but taking Wren to bed wasn't one of them. It bothered the hell out of him that she regretted something that meant so much. He didn't want to be just another man who'd bedded her and disappointed. They'd shared a connection, whether she wanted to admit it or not. He wanted that back. There had to be something he could do.

The phone rang, interrupting his thoughts. He picked up, answering without glancing at the display. "Cooke."

"We traced the signals," Owens said.

Tucker sat up. "And?"

"He sent us on a hell of a fucking chase. Made calls all over the damn place—northern California, Nevada, Idaho, Utah."

Tucker clutched the phone. "He's here?"

"Last ping was from that text to Wren. He's in Park City. Or was as of forty-eight hours ago."

Tucker swallowed the news and stood. "Well, he sure as hell didn't fucking leave. How the hell does he know we're *here*? How the fuck does he know, man?"

"He's done his homework."

"But no one knows about this place."

"Your sister... Her murder made headlines way back when. It's not like Utah's top secret."

"Pretty damn close. Very few people are aware my father kept this place."

"Well, somehow this guy does."

"Guess we need to figure out how he figured it out." Tucker walked by the windows, staring into the dark. Somewhere out there, Wren's stalker was watching. He would bet his last dollar on it. He opened his door and hurried down the hall, sighing his relief as Wren sat at the dining room table, typing away on her laptop. He walked to the alarm, reassured by the double blink.

Wren glanced up from her computer and their eyes met, held, then she looked down at her screen and continued with her work.

"We'll alert the authorities up in Park City. Probably wouldn't hurt to check in with them yourself."

"We've been in touch." Tucker clenched his jaw and went back to his room. How the hell was he supposed to have this conversation and keep an eye on Wren? "There was a murder last night—a lot like Staci's. Identical, actually. They think it's the same man who killed my sister. I know it is."

"I'm sorry, man."

He shrugged. "Maybe we'll finally get him this time."

"Let me know if I can do anything to help."

"Thanks. I will."

"I'll put in a call to the local PD and give them our update."

"I guess that's all we can do for now." He wanted to get Wren out of here—now—and on the first plane to Los Angeles, but snow was falling in sheets and it was dark. They were better off staying put until daylight. "We're heading back to LA in the morning. This place isn't safe anymore. We're out in the middle of nowhere. The house is more glass than timber. There are picture windows all over the damn place. The bastard's having a fucking field day. He's peeping right now;

I can feel it. We'll catch the next available flight tomorrow."

"Sounds like we'll see you soon."

"Yeah. Keep me in the loop if anything else comes up."

"Will do."

He hung up, flung his phone to the bed, and rubbed at the instant tension along the back of his neck. "Son of a *bitch*." Now what? His first instinct was to shut off the lights and barricade Wren in the bathroom—one of the only rooms in the house without windows. He couldn't stand the thought of the bastard watching her, but hiding Wren away was a bad idea. Nothing good would come from tipping their guy off. The longer it took him to figure out the authorities were on to him, the better. Wren was mostly safe until morning. If her stalker could have taken him out, he would've by now, so they would play this as if nothing had changed.

He grabbed his laptop and cell and made his way down the hall, settling himself on the couch within eyesight of Wren. He opened his company e-mail account and started composing a message to Ethan. He couldn't exactly call while Wren sat mere feet away. There was no use frightening her, but her brother needed to know.

Ethan—

His cell phone rang, and he glanced at the readout this time. Speak of the devil. "I was just e-mailing you."

"No kidding. I was about to send you something too. A package came into the office this evening. Mia scanned a few items for me."

Tucker frowned at the edge in Ethan's voice. "What's up?"

"Why don't you tell me?"

Tucker's e-mail dinged with an incoming message.

"Should be there by now. Go ahead and take a look."

Tucker clicked open the mail from Ethan and downloaded the attachments. He stared, speechless, at a picture of him and Wren tangled together in a deep, searing kiss. Wren's fingers were in his hair while he clutched her close. "You've gotta be fucking kidding me." He flipped from one photo to the next, disgusted that a moment that had been for him and Wren alone now played out on his computer screen.

"What the hell is going on up there, Campbell?"

"None of your goddamn business," he bit off.

Wren stopped typing and looked at him.

He slammed his laptop shut and marched his ass to the bedroom as his blood boiled.

"He's *there*, Campbell."

"Obviously." He shoved his door closed. "I just got off the phone with Owens. They triangulated the signals to Park City a few minutes ago. He's been here for the last forty-eight hours."

"Son of a *bitch*. I trusted you. I trusted you to take care of my sister, man, not to use this as an excuse to get your hands down her fucking pants."

"Fuck off, Ethan. I'm doing my job. I'm taking care of Wren."

"Yeah, I can see that," he scoffed.

"This has nothing to do with you. What you saw in those pictures, that's personal."

"There's no such thing as personal in close protection, especially when I'm paying your salary and *especially* when your tongue's down my sister's throat when there's a fucking sicko staring in your bedroom window."

"Goddamn, you're an asshole. I had no idea he was here. I had no fucking clue he would find us."

"Maybe if you were following procedure—"

"Following procedure wouldn't have changed one fucking thing, and you know it. I'm not going to sit here and defend myself to you. I'll get Wren home in one piece. After that, you can take your salary and shove it."

Wren flung the door open and rushed into the room. "What's going on in here?"

"Nothing," he said to Wren, then spoke to Ethan. "We'll

be on the first available flight back tomorrow." Clenching his jaw, he pressed "end," and shoved his phone in the holder before he gave into the desire to chuck it.

"Tucker." Brows furrowed, Wren took several steps closer. "Was that Ethan? Did you just quit your job?"

"Looks like it."

"*Why*?"

He shrugged. "Apparently this whole bodyguard thing isn't going to work out. Go ahead and pack. We're leaving in the morning."

She shook her head. "Since when?"

"Since fifteen minutes ago."

"Did they catch the guy? Did they find the man doing this?"

He steamed out a breath, holding her gaze.

"Oh God." She pressed a hand to her heart. "He found me."

Her terrified eyes darted to the massive panels of glass. "He's out there." Cringing, she stepped back.

This wasn't how he'd wanted to tell her. "Sit down." He gestured to the bed.

She glanced toward the windows again, shuddering.

"Come on." He took her hand, pulling her down the hall to her room and into the bathroom.

She shut the door and rested her back against it. "How long has he been here?"

He leaned his hip on the counter "Looks like the last couple of days."

"He's been watching us. He's standing out there in the dark, isn't he?"

He could lie and deny it, but for what purpose? "Probably."

Her breath rushed out as she crossed her arms tight across her chest.

"Hey." He leaned forward, snagged her wrist, and tugged her to him. "Hey."

"What?"

"Everything's going to be all right." He pulled her into a hug, and to his surprise, she held on. "I won't let him touch you." He rubbed his hands down her back. "I'm promising you he won't touch you."

She nodded.

"We're leaving tomorrow. As soon as I can get us out of here."

She eased back enough to look him in the eye. "Then what?"

"Then we go home. You'll probably stay with Austin or Hunter until the renovations are finished at your brother's."

"What about you? What about your job?"

He shrugged. He didn't want to think about that right now. "Let's figure this out first."

"What happened? I heard some of your argument."

"Then you got the gist that Ethan's not real happy with the way I've been handling things around here."

She shook her head. "I don't understand."

Telling her about the pictures would only frighten her further, but if Ethan mentioned something before he did... "The man following you, he snapped a few photos of us when we were kissing."

Her eyes grew wide as she clutched at his waist. "He *what*? How?"

"Long-range lens would do the trick. He was nice enough to send them along to your brother. Ethan's not pleased."

"It's none of his business." Temper heated her voice.

"I agree, but he doesn't see it that way."

Wren yanked up the hem of his shirt and pulled the cell phone from the holder.

"What are you doing?"

She said nothing as she dialed.

He took her arm. "Cooke, what are you doing?"

She freed herself from his grip as she put the phone to her ear, her eyes glittering. "*Bastardo*!" she spat into the phone.

Tucker's brows rose as Wren turned away and continued her rant in fluent Italian. She paced about the large space, punctuating key words—swears, he was almost certain—with a gesture of her hand. Her cheeks pinked as her temper blazed. Her long waving curls flowed about each time she whirled.

Wren was *pissed* and absolutely stunning.

"Fine. I will. I love you too." And just like that, the storm was over. She pressed "end" and held out the phone. "Here you go."

He stared at the gorgeous spitfire in front of him and couldn't help but grin as he took his cell phone back. "What the hell was that?"

She swiped a strand of hair from her cheek. "Difference of opinion."

My God, was there anyone more perfect than this woman? "I know Ethan speaks several languages. You too?"

"I'm bilingual. Our nanny was from Italy. We spoke Italian before we did English."

"Huh." He pulled her closer, enjoying the simple fact that she was talking to him again. "I appreciate the sentiment," He put his phone back in its holder, "but I was going to talk to Ethan tomorrow after we'd both had some time to cool off."

"Good, I hope you do." She traced her finger along the bold black and red Ethan Cooke Security insignia on the breast of his t-shirt. "You're very good at your job, but I did that for me. I told him to mind his own business, more or less." She gave him a sassy smile.

"Damn, Cooke." He pressed his hand on top of hers, stopping her finger in its path along the "E." "How am I supposed to walk away from you?" Her smile vanished, and he wanted to bite off his tongue. Why couldn't he get this *right*?

She stepped away, turned, and hesitated with her hand on the doorknob.

"Wait a minute. Let me get the drapes." Her bedroom was

one of the only spaces with a barrier of privacy against the outdoors. This would be their first night since they arrived that they wouldn't watch the stars twinkle or the snow fall. Tucker opened the door and walked to the enormous windows, systematically shutting out the world beyond the four walls. The gauzy fabric was slightly see-through, but it was better than nothing. "All set."

Wren stepped out of the bathroom.

"We'll keep the fire going and the lights off. I'll get your stuff from the dining room."

"Thank you."

He walked to the well-lit great room, grabbed Wren's cell phone and laptop, then headed back. "It's late. Do you want a sandwich or something? We can eat in here and kinda camp out."

She shook her head. "I'm not hungry."

"I'll make you something anyway." He left again and made his way to the kitchen. What the hell were they going to have for dinner? He opened the refrigerator, perusing their options, and spied the cold cuts in one of the bins. "Perfect." He grabbed plates, bread, mayo, deli meats, and cheeses and began the process of building two sandwiches while he replayed their conversation in the bathroom. She'd smiled at him and voluntarily *touched* him, then he'd pulled out the serious card and ruined everything. "Fucking fatal error there, Campbell," he muttered to himself, disgusted with his own stupidity. He should've kept things light. Wren relaxed and opened up when feelings and emotions didn't enter the picture. So that would be the game plan for the rest of the evening—maybe a little TV and some meaningless conversation. He wanted her to smile at him again.

Tucker slapped two pieces of bread on top of roasted turkey and provolone and put the condiments and meats back, grabbed two waters, a bag of chips, and apples from the fruit bowl. He glanced at the steady blink of the alarm and shut off the lights on his way to the bedroom. Time to settle in and wait 'til morning. There was nothing more they could do. He walked in the room. "Dinner is served," he muffled around the corner of the chip bag in his mouth.

Wren glanced up from her laptop. "Looks like a feast." She leaned over from her side of the bed and took the plate from his hand. "Thank you."

He pulled the bag from his mouth. "No problem." With his hand free, he walked to the door, locked it, and joined her on his half of the mattress, taking his gun from the holster and set it on the nightstand close by. "Is it going to bother you if I turn on the television?"

"No."

He bit into his sandwich, powered on the TV, and settled himself among the pillows.

"Tucker."

"Hmm?" he grunted over his big bite.

"What's this? What is this stuff all over the side of my house?"

He swallowed. "What?"

"Greta just e-mailed me some pictures. She's recommending I hire a painter to do some touchups, and I can certainly see why. She made a comment to Mia about the marks when she dropped the keys back by the office. Mia said I should ask you about it." She turned the screen toward him.

Son of a bitch. Someone had done a shitty-ass job of handling the damage to Wren's property. The insurance company had assured Ethan the problem had been taken care of. He should've had Jackson or Jerrod or *someone* go over to double check. Tucker's stomach sank as he glanced from Wren's questioning stare to the various spatters and streaks of dark red still marring the pristine white. If he looked closely, he could make out *MINE* in a few areas. He sighed and met her eyes. There was going to be hell to pay for this one. Diversionary tactics were definitely worth a shot. "Why is someone taking pictures of your place?"

"Greta's my realtor. I'm putting my house on the market."

He picked up his sandwich and set the half back down without taking a bite. "Why?"

"I'm moving, hopefully to Santa Barbara."

"*What*?" If she'd slapped him, she couldn't have shocked him more. "Cooke, what the hell are you talking about?"

"Later."

"No, now. You love your house. You're only a couple of miles from your brother." *And me.* "Cooke Interiors—"

"Is a fiasco. My life is a mess. I need a change of scenery, so I'm leaving. Now, what's this stuff on the house?"

He wanted to talk this madness out until he convinced her she was making a huge mistake. Santa Barbara? She couldn't go. He wasn't ready to give up on them, even if she was. "That stuff?"

"Yes, Tucker, that stuff." She pointed to several streaks. "That was supposed to have been cleaned up."

"What is it?"

He gritted his teeth. "Blood."

She frowned. "Blood?" Her eyes widened. "But there's so much."

"Yeah." What the hell else was he supposed to say?

"What did he do?"

There was no need to ask who "he" was. "Cooke." He took her hand, stalling.

She pulled free. "What did he do, Tucker?"

Thanks a hell of a lot, Mia. "Remember when I told you about our cars being vandalized?"

"Yes."

"He didn't stop there." He sighed. "He killed a few more cats, left one on the doorstep at your office and another at the house. He wrote 'mine' on your siding with the blood."

"Oh my God. I can't even—" Wren covered her face with her hands. "That's so disgustingly sick."

He glanced toward the sheer curtains, knowing the man who "decorated" Wren's house more than likely lurked around in the dark.

"I should have known about this. You should have told me. Why didn't you tell me?"

"For what purpose? So you could be as upset as you are right now?"

"I had a right to know. You told me about the cars."

"That's a little less disturbing than someone writing all over your house with cat blood."

"I can handle it."

"I don't doubt it."

"No?" She raised her brow at him.

"Look, Cooke, I'm sorry. Ethan and I thought we were doing what was best for you."

"Doing what was best..." She yanked her computer back to her side. "Do you *hear* yourself? Do you have any idea how condescending you sound?"

"What good does you knowing do anyone?"

"'Anyone?' I'm not worried about 'anyone.' This is my *life*, Tucker, and I have no idea what's going on in it. You have no right to decide what should and shouldn't be kept from me."

"I'm sorry, Cooke." He took her hand again, holding firm. "We thought we were protecting you."

"Fine." She held herself rigid.

"No, it's not fine." He gave her fingers a gentle squeeze. "I really am sorry. From here on out, I'll share everything that comes down the vine."

"Thank you." She held his gaze, pulling her laptop on her legs.

"So, are we good here?"

"Yes."

"Okay." Tucker relaxed his shoulders, taking a deep breath, realizing he'd danced his way through a very dicey situation. He resettled himself among the pillows with his plate on his stomach and the remote in his hand.

"Oh my *God*. He was in my house?" Her shocked eyes met his. "My bedroom is trashed. Was he in my *house*?"

Shit. Tonight just kept getting better and better. He set his plate aside for the second time and sat up. "The guy broke in the same night he threw bricks through my windows."

"What—*Why*?"

"I can't rationalize a madman, Cooke."

"Look at my room."

She shoved the laptop in his face.

The comforter was missing, along with the pillowcases. Two drawers had been removed from the light oak dresser. Traces of fingerprinting powder remained by the French doors marring the pristine white trim. "The police took some pictures and gathered some evidence."

"They took my bedding and my *drawers* for heaven's sake. Why on earth would they do that?"

There was no way to pretty this one up. "He messed with some of your stuff—got in your drawers, sliced up your underwear, and laid it all over the bed."

"*What*?" She rushed from the bed. "This is *unbelievable*. My worst nightmare, and I had no idea. What else, Tucker? What else has he done that I don't know about?"

"That pretty much covers it."

Her nostrils flared as her eyes sparked with temper. "Don't talk to me in that tone. I have every right to be angry. Every right."

"I already told you I was sorry. We did what we thought was best at the time. I can't take it back. We were thinking of you. We didn't want you to worry."

"You didn't want me..." she laughed. "Did you think sparing me from two incidences was going to cure my worries, Tucker? I hardly do anything *but* worry. I barely recognize my life anymore. There's a sicko beyond those windows who wants to hurt me. Patrick is more or less dead. Cooke Interiors is ruined," she tossed at him as she paced. "You thought ripped panties and another disgusting message was going to break me?"

"I wanted to protect you—Ethan too. Why is that so wrong?"

"The thought was well-meaning, but your method sucks. This right here," she made a circling motion between the two of them, "this is another perfect example of why you and me would never have worked."

"Are you serious?" It was his turn to leap off the bed. "What does any of this have to do with you and me?"

"*Everything*. It has everything to do with you and me. I'm a strong woman, and you don't seem to recognize that. I can handle a lot. I'm handling it right now, aren't I?"

"This is bullshit, Cooke." He walked to her, stopping toe-to-toe. "You're grasping at straws, and you know it. The reason you and I don't work is because you don't want us to, plain and simple. This is just another excuse to push me further away. That's what you've been doing from the start."

"That's because my life doesn't *work* when you're in it."

She aimed a perfectly painful blow. "It works just fine, or it would if you'd let it, but you're too afraid to try."

"Damn you for saying that and damn you, Tucker, for messing everything up. I was doing fine until you came along."

"Maybe, but deep down you know we make each other better."

"No."

"Yes." He gripped her arms. "You're one of the strongest women I know, but you're a coward when it comes to your heart."

She gaped at him. "How dare you. How can you stand there and say that to me when you're no different? How ironic is it that the man out there," she jabbed a finger at the curtains, "wherever he is, he's trying his damndest to break me, but I refuse to let him. *Refuse*. But you, Tucker, you just might." She yanked back, walked into the bathroom, and slammed the door behind her.

He could hear water filling the tub as he sat again, staring into the fire, wondering who in the end would break the other first.

He chuckled as he stood to the side of the window, listening to the muffled shouting Her Highness and Pretty Boy fired back and forth. Trouble in paradise—perfect. This alone had been worth the risk of getting caught. Not that he would. Mother Nature was on his side tonight. He looked up, blinking as the snow poured down. There were plenty of inches left in this storm. His tracks would be filled by morning, just in time for all hell to break loose. He could hardly wait.

He leaned in just a tad, wanting another peek. Wren was even more magnificent when she was angry, and she was *raging.* He grinned as she ripped ol' Lover Boy a new asshole and struggled to contain a burst of laughter when she yanked herself from Sir Studly's arms and hurried to the bathroom, slamming the door behind her. Did it get any better than this?

His good mood fell away and his eyes narrowed as he stared at the Campbell Golden Boy easing himself to the bed. Poor, pathetic Pretty Boy wasn't used to women turning him away. Prince Charming would have to mop it up, because his string of bad luck was just getting started. In fact, it was about time for the next round of fun to begin. He back stepped in his snowshoes, turned, and walked toward the cluster of huge homes, enjoying the idea of Tucker suffering when the latest news hit.

He made his way through the twists and turns of pines, eventually stopping at his destination several houses away. The place was dark as expected except for the flashes of television in one of the windows on the second story. She was still up—excellent.

Crouching down, he gathered his items from the small bag he left by the tree earlier in the evening, freed himself from his snowshoes, and hustled to the front door. He used the key he'd helped himself to and punched in the code, deactivating the alarm as he stepped into the warmth of the spacious entryway. So far so good.

He made a beeline for the stairs and started up, halting, ducking, as a bedroom door opened and she stepped out, flipped on the light, and closed herself in the bathroom. This was definitely his night. He rushed up the remaining steps and went into her room. The movie playing on the small flat-screen cast a blue glow about the space. Hints of bubblegum and perfume wafted in the air. Academic awards hung on the walls and trophies scattered several of the shelves. Brainy.

The toilet flushed. Moments later, the bathroom door opened and the light shut off. Showtime. Chloe walked in and gasped.

"Don't scream."

Her eyes, wide and frightened behind her thick glasses, darted to the hallway.

He pulled the gun from his jacket pocket. "Close the door."

She hesitated.

"I assure you, you don't want to wake your family. It wouldn't be good for their health."

Her hand trembled as she complied, shutting them in for their own little party.

"Very wise choice. Now come over here."

"What—what do you want?"

"You."

"We have—we have money, lots of money. My dad's an investor."

He smiled and shook his head. "Unfortunately I'm not looking for money. Now come here."

She did as she was told, stopping in front of him.

Chloe Wright was sheer perfection, with her long black hair and slim body, but the glasses would have to go. "Lose the glasses and take off your clothes."

"No," she whispered, trembling.

"Okay." He shrugged. "I guess I'll ask your mother then."

"No." She held up a hand to halt him. "I'll—I'll do it."

"That's the right attitude. The glasses."

Chloe took off her black-framed coke bottles, and tears spilled down her cheeks.

"Much, much better. Now your top."

More tears fell. "Please."

"Might as well dry 'em up. Crying doesn't affect me. The top." He gestured to her shirt with his gun.

She pulled her light blue sleep shirt over her head, exposing small perky breasts. Spectacular. When he'd spotted her walking out of the library yesterday, he knew she would do.

"Pants and panties."

Quietly weeping, she slid them off and stood before him, beautifully naked.

He grew hard as his gaze traveled over her subtle curves. "I certainly know how to pick 'em. Now come closer and put your hands behind your back."

"I want—I want my mom."

"And I want you. Turn and put your hands behind your back."

She reluctantly did as she was told as her breath heaved violently.

He pulled the black nylon from his pocket and took a moment to palm Chloe's soft warm breasts. "Very nice," he whispered next to her ear as he slid his fingers down her arms. "Lock your hands."

Her whole body shook as she clasped her fingers together.

He tied the nylon at her wrists, knotting the slippery fabric firm.

"Lay down on the floor over by your bed—on your back. And spread your legs."

"Please don't—please don't make me do this." Her teeth chattered and her voice rose in her panic.

"Uh, uh, uh, you're going to wake your parents, then they'll have to die. Do you want them to die, Chloe?"

"No."

"Then do as I say."

She lay back on her bound hands and spread her legs as instructed.

His breathing grew ragged as he remembered the first. She'd looked and cried just like that while she waited for him. He gripped the rope in his fisted hand and slid out of his jacket, then freed himself from his jeans, ready to begin.

Kneeling in front of her, he rammed himself inside her, and she yelped, jumping. As he worked himself up, he no longer saw Chloe Wright. Staci Campbell stared back at him through terrified dark hazel eyes, and he thought of revenge. That was all he'd ever wanted.

☙ Chapter Fifteen ❧

Tucker threw the last of his clothes in his duffel and zipped it closed. He grabbed his laptop next and secured it in its case. They probably had three hours—four at the most—to make it to Salt Lake City International, secure two seats on standby, and take off before the next storm came in to wreak havoc on the region. All outgoing flights were either crammed full or canceled due to already shitty conditions. The clearing crews were struggling to maintain the runways with the endless blowing snow. Winter was here with a vengeance, and she wasn't letting up.

The Park City Festival wasn't making a quick exit any easier. Throngs of tourists filled hotels to capacity while they waited for their chance at a backlogged flight. All carriers were warning passengers it could be well into next week before everyone would get home, no matter their destination. That wasn't going to work. Staying here another day wasn't an option, let alone another week. Come hell or high water, he and Wren were leaving. He would bribe someone if he had to—a trip to any one of the Campbell Resorts—free airfare, spa packages, whatever the hell they wanted as long as they handed over their tickets and he and Wren were in the air today. But first they had to get to the airport.

He glanced out the window again at heavy gray clouds hanging low and worried about the drive. The highway was a mess, and the interstate no better, according to the early reports he'd listened to while eating his breakfast. Hopefully the road crews had made progress over the last couple hours. The ride was bound to be long and dicey, even with the Jeep's four-wheel drive, but his gut begged him to try anyway before Mother Nature trapped them here indefinitely. The longer they stayed in Park City, the more dangerous Wren's situation became.

Her stalker had been abnormally quiet, setting Tucker further on edge. Their guy was in Park City, so why wasn't he up to his typical games? No flowers, no carcasses, no messages written in blood. Patrick's cell phone hadn't triangulated a signal since Wren received the last text three days ago. The bastard got off on his power plays. He needed others to know he was running the show, so why wasn't he making his presence known? It was only a matter of time before he did, and Tucker wanted them long gone before their "friend" figured out he'd lost his latest advantage.

With one last look around the room, he shouldered the strap of his laptop case, grabbed his bag, and started down the hall, stopping as Wren stepped out of her bedroom with the original carry-on she'd arrived with and the new one she bought to accommodate the items they'd accumulated on their shopping spree in town several days ago. "Ready?"

"Yes."

Their first "conversation" in hours. The tension had been unbearable throughout the night while they'd lain next to each other in her bed. Wren had emerged from the bathroom long after she'd tossed the last of her angry words his way, smelling sinful from her extended bath. She had faced the wall while she unknotted her silky emerald colored spa robe and let it slide down her arms, revealing a simple spaghetti strap top and snug pajama bottoms that were unbelievably sexy, then she'd tugged the tie from her hair, sending thick black waves tumbling down her slim back. He'd gritted his teeth in defense against his *need* for her as she pulled the covers aside and lay down, settling herself in, never once looking in his direction.

He'd clenched his fist at his side, barely resisting the urge to reach over and slide his fingers along her soft skin and insist they make the best of a crappy situation. Luckily he'd come to his senses, keeping his hands to himself and his mouth closed, staring at the ceiling instead. There hadn't been anything left to say after their knock-down drag-out, so that's the way they left it.

"Were you able to get us a flight?" She asked stiffly.

"No. We'll have to fly standby. I'll pack up the Jeep and we'll get out of here."

She nodded, and they walked down the hall.

Tucker set down his luggage and stood back from the window as he looked out, searching for disturbances in the snow. If Wren's stalker was out there—and he more than likely was—he had the advantage. He could be hiding anywhere among the endless rows of thick pines. Tucker unfastened the snap on his holster and reached in his pocket, pulling out the keys. After a final scan, he turned to Wren. "I want you to lock me out and let me back in."

"Aren't you going to the garage?"

All three garage doors had several panes of ornately etched glass. His father had designed the Campbell summer home with luxury, aesthetics, and comfort in mind, not maximum security. If their man had the right weapon and shattered the right pieces of glass, he could gain entry faster than Tucker could get back inside. "Safe over sorry, right?" He twisted the valet key from the loop and handed her the remaining set. "Don't open the door until I'm standing in front of it."

"Do you think he's here, even with all the snow?"

He shrugged. "I'm not sure." He'd promised full disclosure from here on out, but telling Wren the man who'd been hunting her was probably among the trees less than twenty yards away wasn't happening.

"Maybe we should call the police." Her voice vibrated with nerves.

He reached for his bag, pausing. "Why?"

"Um, in case he's *here*." She gestured toward the windows and outdoors beyond.

"That's a nice thought, but the roads are shit. There are probably a few dozen accidents downtown. I don't think driving up a mountain road to walk me to my car is on their priority list right now." He checked his access to his weapon and grabbed his duffle, shouldering the strap and one of her suitcases, wanting to keep a hand free. "I'll do this in two trips. First for most of the luggage, then for you. Be right back."

"But if he gets in, he'll hurt you."

He reached for the knob, stopping as it registered that she was genuinely worried about him. Maybe not all was lost. Unable to stop himself, he stepped closer and skimmed her jaw. "That's why I have my gun."

She held his wrist. "But—"

"And you're going to do what I've asked, so worrying about you won't distract me," he said as he continued caressing, holding her gaze.

She leaned into his touch. "Yes, but—"

"I'll be fine, Cooke, as long as I know you're going to keep the door locked and shut yourself in your bathroom and call 911 if something should happen."

Frowning, she pulled at his wrist, stopping his gentle movements. "So I'm supposed to run for safety and leave you outside with a lunatic?"

And just like that, the tender moment was over. "Exactly. That's kind of how this job works." He stepped away, adjusting the strap on his shoulder, then turned and twisted the knob.

Wren grabbed his arm. "Tucker, wait."

His system was revving with adrenaline. He wanted to get them out of there. The next few minutes were make-or-break, especially if their man was waiting to make a move. "Cooke, we have to go now if we're going to beat the next storm. I don't want to be stuck here again without power."

She nodded. "Okay."

"Don't open the door—no matter what—unless you hear me give you the okay. I mean it."

She nodded again. "All right."

Tucker gave a last scan out the windows, searching for any movements in the trees, and stepped out into the chilly garage. "Lock it," he said, waiting for the bolt to slide in place.

Metal snapped as the lock turned and he made his way to the passenger's side, unlocking the door, lifting the lever and pulling the seat forward. He put the first two pieces of luggage in, constantly on the lookout for shadows outside the ornate glass. He started back, stopping suddenly, reaching for his weapon as something thundered close by.

"Son of a bitch," he muttered with his heart in his throat, realizing the loud noise was nothing more than snow falling from the roof. Puffing out a breath, he knocked on the door. "Cooke, open up."

Wren twisted the lock and he opened the door, stepping in, absorbing the warmth of the house as he closed them back in. "Do you have everything? I think we're all set."

"I'm ready. I need to see Patrick. Will you—will you take me when we get home?"

Was she asking because she needed the support or because he was still in charge of her safety until she was handed off to the next guard? "We'll go as soon as we land."

"Thank you."

He nodded and pulled his phone from the holder, typing an update to Ethan.

Heading to airport. Will let you know when we arrive.

"I called Ms. Hayes to let her know we're leaving. I didn't want her to come here by herself just in case he doesn't realize we've left for a couple of days."

He'd been so focused on getting them out of there he hadn't thought of that. "Good idea. Thanks."

She gave him a quick nod. "She—she said she won't come until next week, and when she does, she'll bring her grandson. She also wanted me to tell you that she's happy you came and that she loves you very much."

He struggled with the small clutch of regret as he glanced down the forbidden hall, realizing—as Ms. Hayes already had—that he would never come back to this place.

"Do you want to go down—one last time?"

Apparently Wren understood too. "No. There's nothing left here." He held her gaze, and something was suddenly different as they tried to work their way back from last night. Awkward silence filled the room, and she looked away.

Sighing, he looked out the window, watching clumps of snow fall from the heavy pine boughs. He didn't want to leave things like this. Once they were back in LA, she would box up her life and head to Santa Barbara with one of Ethan's guards. In a matter of hours, they would go their separate ways, mostly because that's what she wanted. It was unlikely they would see each other anytime soon, especially now that his employment was in question and she would live over an hour-and-a-half away. He was about to lose the one person who'd become as vital to his life as Staci had been. "We should go."

"Yeah. Do you think we'll get a flight out before the storm?"

"It's hard to tell." He just wanted to get them to the airport. Their odds could only go up once they were there. He grabbed Wren's carry-on. "I'm going to have you take the laptop cases, and I'll take this." He gestured to the luggage in his hand. "I'll put the bag in, then you get in. Quick and steady. If for any reason I pull you down, you go down."

She swallowed. "Okay."

He glanced outside, scanning quickly, as a Park City PD SUV pulled into the drive and his stomach sank. Why did he already know he wasn't going to like this? "Shit."

"What?"

"We have visitors."

Detective Rogers and Franklin got out and started toward the house.

Wren joined him by the side of the window. "Do you think they have news about my stalker?"

"Beats the hell out of me. Guess we should find out." Something told him this had nothing to do with the threat to Wren and everything to do with Staci's case. He opened the door, shielding Wren from the opening. "Morning, Detectives."

"Good morning, Mr. Campbell. Ms. Cooke." There was a barely perceptible edge to Detective Franklin's voice.

"Wren and I are just on our way out. We're heading to the airport. I want to beat the next storm."

"I'm not sure you're going to make it, Mr. Campbell." Detective Rogers glanced toward the heavy clouds.

Tucker narrowed his eyes at the tone. "My former colleague, Detective Craig Owens, contacted your precinct last night. Wren's stalker is believed to be here in Park City. I want to get us out of here before the snow traps us again."

"I'm afraid that's going to have to wait. We need you to come downtown."

This wasn't quite what he'd expected. "Excuse me?"

"There was another murder last night, Mr. Campbell. Half a mile from here."

"Oh my God." Wren pressed her fingers to her lips. "Another girl?"

"I'm afraid so, Ms. Cooke," Rogers answered, never taking his eyes from Tucker's.

The breath backed up in Tucker's throat, and he clutched the doorknob, absorbing the news, staring into Rogers' quiet intensity.

"We'd like to ask you some questions, Mr. Campbell."

"Same MO?" Tucker inquired, automatically flashing back to moments of his own personal hell, struggling to accept that another life had been lost to his sister's killer.

"Seems to be. We'd like for you to come with us."

"I'd like to help you out, but it's going to have to wait. I'm hoping Wren and I can get out on the next available flight. I'll jot down my e-mail; you can send whatever documents you have. I'll be happy to take a look."

"We appreciate your offer, but we'd like to speak with you now."

He shook his head. "I'm sorry. Wren's safety is my first priority. She's at risk the longer we stay." He grabbed the suitcase and started closing the door. "Wren, let's go."

Franklin put his hand against the heavy wood. "Mr. Campbell, this isn't a request."

Tucker stopped dead as the Detective's meaning sunk in. "Are you fucking kidding me?"

"Afraid not."

"Just what exactly is going *on* here?" Wren clutched Tucker's arm. "Are you implying that Tucker had something to do with these *murders*?"

"We're not implying anything, but the fact of the matter is we have two dead girls on our hands—three if we count Staci. Mr. Campbell is very familiar with the cases."

"Which is horribly tragic—"

"Cooke." He covered her hand and squeezed, touched that she was quick to rush to his defense. "Hold on just a second."

"We just want to ask a few questions, folks."

"Are you looking for my help, or have you decided I'm a suspect?"

"We want to clear a few things up."

The non-answer. He could get this over with so he and Wren could go, or he could start a pissing match and the good detectives here would flex their muscles and hold him for as long as they damn well pleased. "Wren and I will meet you at the station."

"Tucker." She clutched his hand. "You don't have to do this."

"It's okay." He gave her an easy wink despite his growing anger. "The detectives have some questions, so we'll let them ask."

"At least let me call an attorney. JT, he's the best. Let me call JT."

He squeezed her fingers again. "I don't need an attorney. I know my rights just fine," he turned his attention to the detectives. "Wren and I will meet you at the station," he repeated.

"Mr. Campbell—"

"I said I'll answer your questions, but I still have a job to do. Wren is still in danger. You're welcome to follow behind me, but unless you're charging me with something, we'll meet you at the precinct within the half hour and head to the airport directly after."

"We'll be happy to follow you," Detective Franklin said. "We'll need for you to remove your weapon."

The pissing match had already begun. "I'm a fully licensed bodyguard on duty, protecting my principal. Ms. Cooke's stalker is known to be in the area, as you are well aware. If you want to start impeding on my rights as well as my contracted client's, I'd be happy to call in the lawyers after all. We can make this as simple or as complicated as you want, Franklin, but don't forget, I know this game. I sure as hell have played it a time or two." He slammed the door in their cool, blank faces, threw the lock, and took Wren's hand as they started toward the garage. "Let's go."

Tucker glanced at his watch and rubbed his fingers along

his forehead, barely suppressing a sigh. He'd been sitting across from the detectives for two-and-a-half hours, answering questions and looking at dozens of crime scene photos, theorizing a lunatic's motives. They'd gotten nowhere.

"The only thing we can conclude is that the *SC* written on both Alyssa Brookes' stomach and now Chloe Wright's has something to do with Staci."

Tucker sat up straight, glancing at the glowing letters on the thin abdomens in two different photos. "As I said before, I agree. In my opinion, he wants to make sure law enforcement understands that he's responsible for all three killings. He's tying the murders together."

"But what's the motive?" Franklin asked as he sipped his third cup of coffee.

Wasn't that the million-dollar question? If they knew that, Staci's case would've been solved long ago. Tucker peeked at his watch again, growing more impatient by the second. This had been a complete waste of time. He could've just as easily tossed ideas around with Rogers and Franklin from Los Angeles via a conference call. And Wren would be a hell of a lot safer than she was here. They needed to *go*.

"That's what we need to figure out," Rogers muttered as he flipped through his notes. "Why don't we run through this one more time. Might as well cover our bases. We'll start with last night." He cleared his throat. "Ms. Cooke stated she was with you at all times except for the half hour or so that she took her bath."

"We've already established this."

"What were you doing during this time again, Mr. Campbell?"

Son of a bitch. It was all he could do not to reach over the table and knock out these dumb shits. If this was the type of investigating and interrogating that went on around here, it was no wonder Staci's murderer was still free. Beyond finished with this entire fiasco, he leaned in, looking both men in the eyes. "Let me break it down for you gentlemen, since we've discussed this at least a dozen times and you still seem to want to include me on your suspect list. Wren stormed into the bathroom right around ten thirty and didn't come out again until eleven, which means I'm officially unaccounted for for just about thirty minutes. It seems to me as though you're suggesting that in approximately half an hour's time, I not only left my client unattended while she sat alone and vulnerable in a bathtub when her stalker is *here*, but then I went out in a snowstorm, drove half a mile down an almost impassable road, broke into a residence, tied up and raped a girl at least two or three times, strangled her, then posed her, drove back home and was laying in bed like it was any other night for Wren to find me when she came back out?"

"Mr. Campbell—"

"I'm not finished. Did you even call the security company monitoring my home and ask if the alarm was deactivated at any time between ten thirty and eleven? Or better yet, did you ask me for access to my computer or cell phone where you would see that at approximately ten forty-five I received an e-mail from one of my co-workers and responded?" He shook his head and looked up into the camera. "You are capturing all of this, right? Because I can't wrap my mind around why these two still have a fucking job."

"Mr. Campbell, we have a duty to our citizens. This town hasn't seen a murder since July 1999, which coincidentally was the last time you were here. You come back to Utah, and two girls wind up dead, which is a damn screwy happenstance if you ask me. We wouldn't be doing our job if we didn't bring you in and ask."

"Maybe, but I don't know Alyssa Brookes or Chloe Wright, and I sure as hell didn't kill my sister. You're missing several key points here and wasting my time. Wren Cooke has been with me every moment since we've arrived in Utah, and she's attested to this in a sworn statement. But the biggest piece is the DNA. You should have Alyssa's results back by now. You and I both know the semen found on scene isn't fucking mine. You have a killer on your hands, Detectives, and it isn't me." He stood. "Unless you have anything else."

"We haven't dismissed you."

"But you will, because we both know this is teetering on harassment. I think we're finished here."

"We'll be in touch."

"Can't wait." He yanked the door open and stepped out of the room.

Wren rushed to her feet and hurried to his side. "Are you okay?"

"I'm fine," he snarled as he started walking, leaving her to follow.

She followed after him, catching up as he stopped at the kiosk for his holster and pistol. "What happened?"

He fished his permit and professional bodyguard license from his wallet and slid them under the small opening for the officer behind the glass to read. "Not a damn thing."

"What did they say?"

"That they don't know what the hell they're doing."

She rested her hand on her hips, and her eyebrows shot up on her forehead. "They did not."

"Okay, I told them they don't know what the hell they're doing." He looked at his watch again and struggled to bite back another swear. Almost noon. The likelihood of getting a flight out was beyond piss-poor.

"Tucker..."

The officer slid his gun and holster through the small door.

"Thank you."

"Tucker—"

"Let's wait 'til we get out of here." As they made it closer to the tinted glass doors, he stopped and closed his eyes, more than fed up with the day. "You've got to be *kidding* me." Snow fell in frenzied sheets. Forget the flight. They'd be lucky to get up the road. This was exactly what he'd been trying to avoid.

"What are we going to do?"

"Go back to the house and try again tomorrow." But it was doubtful they would be going anywhere for a few days. Weather reports had predicted two feet or more with this latest dumping, with another front moving in behind it.

"But what if we lose power?"

"We'll have to hope we don't."

Wren woke with a start, blinking in the dim light cast by the fire. She glanced at the bedside clock—11:40. Somehow she'd lost thirty minutes. Sleep fogged, it took her several seconds to realize the television had been turned off and Tucker no longer lay on his side of the bed. She sat up, spotting him on the chaise lounge, boxer clad, staring into the flames. His hair stood in short black spikes, and the stubble along his clenched, chiseled jaw was more pronounced in the flickering orange glow. Light and shadow accentuated his broad shoulders and muscular back, yet he appeared defenseless despite his powerful build.

Wren continued her study of the miserable man before her, contemplating whether to lie down or call his name. But then he rested his elbows on his thighs and placed his forehead in his hands in a gesture of utter defeat.

Despite the tension of the day and fight last night, she tossed the covers aside and walked to where he sat, unable to let him suffer alone. She stood in front of him, absorbing the radiating heat of the fire, having no idea what to say. They'd spoken some since their shouting match, but barely. After their dicey drive up the steep mountain road, he'd let them in the house, checked the panel, and gone to his room. She'd spent most of her time sitting on her bed, studying several apartment options Greta sent along via e-mail, listening to mutterings of Tucker's conversations with Detective Owens well into the evening.

Although Tucker never came right out and said so, she'd read between the lines, understanding that his two-and-a-half hours in the interrogation room had been hell. She'd paced about the hallway, feeling utterly helpless, her finger hovering over JT's number the entire time. She'd been ready to fight for Tucker. If the Park City police were going to be foolish enough to accuse Tucker of the absurd, she would have called in the best to defend him. The idea of Tucker harming anyone, much less the sister he'd adored, was nothing short of ludicrous.

He was hurting. She hated that he was in such pain, so she stepped closer. "Hi."

He glanced up, staring at her with pathetically miserable eyes. "Hey."

Her heart melted as she stared at him, yearning to wrap him in a hug. "Mind if I sit down?"

He scooted over.

She took her spot, and they looked into the fire. What now? What should she say when little more than twenty-four hours before they'd both shouted things better left unsaid? "Are you okay?"

"Yeah."

"Liar," she said without heat.

He met her gaze.

"I know we aren't exactly getting along... Today couldn't have been easy," she fumbled, then cut to the chase. "I wanted to help you. I still do."

He shrugged. "It's over."

But it wasn't—far from it. Nodding, she pressed her lips firm in frustration and stood. This was just another example of neither of them being able to fully trust in the other.

He took her hand in a viselike grip as she turned to walk away. "Wait."

She paused.

"I can't shut my mind down. I can't stop thinking about Staci and the other girls. I'm starting to wonder if this has something to do with me."

She frowned. "What?"

"The murders."

"That's crazy."

"I wanted to think so. For the most part, Franklin and Rogers have no idea what they're doing—small-time cops with three huge cases on their hands. But then Rogers said something about how there hasn't been a murder in Park City since Staci, then I show up and two more girls die."

"He's grasping at straws, Tucker."

"Maybe. Or maybe not. His comment bothered the hell out of me. I haven't been able to let it go. I needed to disprove it, so I called Owens when we got home. We started putting the pieces together the way we used to when we both worked homicide. We jumped back to July '99, starting with Staci's death." His hand flexed against hers, and his eyes grew distant. "By all accounts, her murder was personal. Someone studied her. They took the time to figure out how to get in the house without any of us knowing. According to the ME's reports, he raped her at least twice before he strangled her. He was very methodical, very cold. In his mind, Staci died for a purpose. Then there's nothing. Fourteen years pass, and Park City is a safe, quiet place until I come strolling back to town. Now Alyssa Brookes and Chloe Wright are dead."

"The timing has to be a coincidence." She sat on the hearth, still holding his hand. "How could there possibly be a connection between you and the three murders?"

He shook his head. "I don't know. I have no idea." He rubbed his free hand along his jaw. "I should. This is exactly what I went to school for. This is what I did for so long. My team and I, we closed so many cases, but I've never been able to help my sister."

She couldn't imagine the agony of always wondering, of never finding the answers he and his family needed most. "I'm sorry, Tucker."

Sighing, he closed his eyes. "I can't stop remembering. I

keep replaying our last conversation by the hot tub and the way she smiled as we said goodnight. I should have stayed with her. Why did I leave her by herself? I'll never forgive myself for going inside." He pulled his hand from hers and scrubbed at his face. "God. *God.*"

The agony in his voice brought tears to her eyes. "It's okay." She got on her knees in front of him. "It's going to be okay," she repeated as she wrapped her arms around him.

He pulled her close, resting his forehead on her shoulder as his breath rushed out in steamy torrents against her skin. "Is this what you wanted, Wren? Is this what you needed to see, me on my knees?" He gripped her tightly, clutching.

She held on to him just as strongly. "This isn't what I wanted, Tucker. This isn't what I meant."

"I feel like I've been ripped open, like she's dying all over again, like *I'm* dying all over again. I was supposed to protect her. She was my sister. My God, Wren, I loved her."

"Shh," she soothed as she played her fingers through his hair. "This isn't your fault. This isn't what she would want. Staci loved you as much as you love her." She kissed his cheek, desperate to ease his pain.

"I don't know what to do."

"I don't either," she confessed as she pressed her palm to his cheek, looking into his tormented eyes. "But I want to make this better." She kissed him, trying desperately to banish his suffering. "It's breaking my heart seeing you hurt this way." She touched her lips to his again. There was comfort here in their embrace.

Tucker slid his fingers along the small of her back, holding her gaze.

She moved in, capturing his mouth, slowly, tenderly. The kiss heated, deepening by degrees. Their tongues finally met as Tucker pulled her more truly between his legs.

"Cooke," he murmured, easing back.

"Shh." She touched her finger to the warmth of his lips.

He grabbed hold of her wrist, nibbling his way to the center of her palm as they looked in each other's eyes.

Shivering, savoring his touch, she pulled him back for more, and a small grumble escaped his throat. Electricity snapped in the air, humming along her skin, but there was no sense of urgency as there had been the first time they were together.

Tucker's mouth left hers, wandering to her temples, her chin, her neck as she ran her hands over firm shoulders and down his back.

"Wren." He skimmed his fingers along her jaw. "We're both pretty raw. I don't want to take advantage."

And because she knew he meant what he said, she couldn't hold back from giving him what they both longed for. She stood and held out her hand.

He reached out, accepting what she offered, and stood. "Are you sure?"

"You should know by now I don't do anything I don't want to." She smiled.

He gave her one of his slow grins. "I can definitely attest to that."

It had been so long since she'd seen one of those sly smiles. She hadn't realized how much she'd missed them.

His smile faded as he moved his fingers along her collarbone, sliding the strap of her nightshirt from her shoulder. He circled round her, slid the other strap free and the silky fabric cascaded down her body. He gathered her hair in one hand, wrapped it around his wrist, and tugged gently, tipping her head, exposing her neck. He nipped at her ear, sending tingles to her core, trailed open-mouthed kisses along her neck, her shoulder blades, and she whimpered, thoroughly seduced by the simple yet devastating gestures.

She reached her arms back, clasping her hands behind his neck and he slid rough palms down her elbows, her breasts, stopping, teasing, until her nipples hardened and she moaned, resting her head on his chest. He journeyed down her ribcage, her waist, stroking her stomach, making her muscles jump, then slid thumbs in the elastic of her pants, tugging, freeing her of the last of her clothing.

She attempted to face him, but he held her still, leaving circled caresses against her hips, her thighs, turning her legs to jelly, craving him. Moving her hands, she pulled at his boxers, and they were both naked.

Tucker walked them to the bed, gently pushing her forward on the mattress, nibbling and nipping at her shoulders as she crawled further on the sheets. His body covered hers, and he entered her from behind. She stiffened, moaning, eagerly welcoming him. He brought his hand around as he thrust, finding her with his fingers, teasing, rubbing, sending her over the top. "Tucker," she panted out.

As quickly as he invaded her, he pulled himself free. "I want to see you, Cooke," he said, winded.

She turned and sat in his lap, wrapping her legs around his waist. Lips met for a long, hungry kiss as he lifted her hips, and she took him in. They swallowed each other's groans as she rocked, sliding her hands along the hot, damp muscles of his chest, shoulders, his back.

He clutched at her ass, pressing her closer, pushing himself deeper as his steamy breaths puffed against her skin. He suckled at her breasts, lapping at sensitive skin, heightening the throb deep in her core. "I'm close," she whispered next to his ear, gripping his arms, ready for the stunning power to overtake her yet again.

"Not like this," he said, pushing her back so that she lay among the pillows. He broke their connection, changing their positions, nestling himself between her legs. She arched, ready to take him in, craving to ride the next wave as he pulled the covers over them.

She dragged at his hips in her attempt to guide him back as the liquid pull of desire churned her to the edge. "God, Tucker, I'm so close."

He entered her, slowly, torturously so, and she moaned, her body quaking, shuddering, her arms and legs trembling.

Gasping, straining, she reached, waiting, waiting. "Now, oh God, now."

He thrust hard—once, twice, three times—and a rush of heat rocketed through her system, destroying her. She cried out loudly, undone as the orgasm ravaged her. He held her jaw as she bucked and jerked, staring into her eyes, and she repeated his name again and again.

Her breathing steadied as she came down, and Tucker kissed her deep, no longer moving while he lay inside her. She rocked her hips, urging him to finish them both, but his mouth continued to capture hers. He eased back, staring down, caressing her damp temple. "This right here, the way you're looking at me when you're too busy feeling to think... You and me, we work just fine. You're what I want, Wren, what I need. I'm willing to wait until you figure out I'm exactly what you need too."

As she looked into gorgeous hazel eyes, intense with passion, she knew he was right. She traced his bottom lip with her thumb and kissed his brow.

"I need you, Wren."

"Tucker," she whispered, undone.

Their lips met once more, and he took her hands, clasping their fingers, pulling her arms over her head, and he began to move. Their rhythm was unhurried as they held each other's gaze. Soon the slow tugs deep in her belly grew to pulsing, and his breathing grew shallow, his hands clutching hers tighter.

She climbed as he did, whimpering. He pushed himself deeper, sending her flying as he shuddered and groaned. Sweaty, gasping, they smiled, and for the first time ever, she understood the true meaning of making love.

He walked among the trees, concentrating on the dim glow in Wren's bedroom windows. She was still up—perfect.

The hike from town had been a bitch in the bitter winds and blinding snow, but he had to see her—and him. The sweet taste of payback made the grueling two-mile trek a pleasure, despite his icy fingers and toes. Pretty Boy was in all kinds of trouble.

Park City was in an outright panic after another horrific murder. Poor Chloe Wright—such a smart, sweet girl. Rumor around Main Street was the police brought Tucker Campbell in for questioning. He grinned. Lord Campbell was having a rough month—shouting matches with the lovely Wren, interrogations at the cop shop, reliving his sister's tragic death time and time again. Ouch! What was a guy to *do* when everything was falling apart? The stress had to be taking its toll, and he looked forward to seeing it firsthand.

He skirted the last few pines and inched his way to the edge of the window. Moving closer, he peered through the small opening where the curtains met, staring, and a swift, hot rage consumed him. "You fucking bastard," he spat, watching Pretty Boy thrust himself into Wren beneath the ivory sheet pooling at his hips.

What the hell happened to the yelling and slamming doors? The asshole's movements suddenly stopped, and he brushed the hair back from Wren's face as he spoke. She brought her thumb to his lips, kissed his brow, and he took her hands, raising them above her head, and began fucking her again.

Wren had been mad as hell when he walked away last night. Pretty Boy was supposed to be miserable, sleeping on the damn chair with his gun at his side. The dick probably sent her one of his stupid-ass smiles, and she'd gone running back for more—they all did. "Bitch."

This wasn't *right*. He'd damn near killed himself getting here, and he sure didn't come for this. Where was Tucker's pain? Where was the *agony*?

The stud finished himself off, and by the stunned look on Wren's face, she'd finished too. He struggled to steady his breathing as they smiled at each other. Prince Charming said something, kissed her for a long fucking damn time, then rolled to his side, pulling Wren against him as she curled up in his arms.

His day of fun was ruined. *Ruined.* He glanced in once more and turned, ready to make his way back to town. It was time to show them all who was in charge. It was time to up the ante.

☙ Chapter Sixteen ❧

Tucker opened his eyes and stared down at Wren still asleep against his side. He loved waking up with her soft, warm body curled around his. If he had his way, they would wake like this every morning.

He moved his fingers through thick waves of black, sliding her hair back from her temple. Tucker studied her truly stunning face: long eyelashes resting against flawless skin, sharp cheekbones and soft, full lips. He'd meant what he said while he lay inside her, joined as closely as two people can be. He would wait for her, because there was no one else he wanted. Somewhere along the way, his utter fascination with the sharp-tongued beauty had turned into full-fledged love. He wasn't about to let her go. His job with Ethan no longer existed at this point, but he'd be damned if anyone else would be keeping her safe. If she was hell-bent on heading to Santa Barbara, he was going with her.

Wren could deny she had feelings for him and insist her life didn't work with him in it, but when they were together the way they had been just hours ago, he knew she lied to herself as much as to him. He wouldn't be declaring his heartfelt emotions anytime soon; Wren needed to catch up before they could move forward. She was still afraid, so he would give her time to get used to the way things were. Slow and light was the way to sneak past her guard, so that's how he would precede.

A gust of wind blew down the chimney, scattering embers, and he looked toward the window. Even through the barrier of fabric, he could see the snow stacked a quarter of the way up the glass. There was no way in hell they were going anywhere. Thank God they still had electricity. It was past eight—more than time to get up and check in with Ethan and Owens and answer any incoming e-mails he needed to finish up for Jackson. But they could wait a little longer. Before too long, Wren would open her eyes and pull away again. He'd take advantage of what he had right now.

Her hand stirred against his chest, and her eyes fluttered open.

"Morning."

She gave him a sleepy smile. "Morning."

"It's eight thirty, Cooke. Getting lazy."

"Mmm," she said as she flexed her arm across his body, stretching. "Do you think we'll get a flight today?"

"Uh, no. The snow's past the window frame."

"What?" She turned her head. "Holy *cow*. Look at all that."

He chuckled at her amazement. "That's nothing. Winter's just getting started around here."

She faced him. "I think I've decided I hate winter. I want my palm trees back." She grinned.

"Looks like you're stuck with pine for a while yet."

She groaned and settled her forehead against his chest. "I think I might hate pine trees, too."

He rubbed his hand along her shoulder blades, enjoying this little piece of casual intimacy. "Such a pessimist in the morning."

"No, just getting bored," she muffled against his skin, then looked up. "I need a conference call, an order gone wrong, mockups. I would even settle for a meeting with Lenora." She pressed her hands to his cheeks, moving in close, emphasizing each word in her mock desperation. "I like to be busy. I *need* to be busy."

He grinned and grabbed her chin, pulling her face another inch closer. "I can keep you busy, Cooke." He reached down and cupped her ass. "All you have to do is ask."

Her eyes turned from playful to mischievous in a flash, and her hand was under the covers, wrapped around him before he exhaled his next shaky breath. "Maybe I don't feel like asking."

"Hey, I can be flexible." He gripped her ass tighter, already revved from her hand working him. "God, Cooke," he sucked in through his teeth and pulled her closer, ravaging her mouth. There was no tenderness this morning, only blazing heat as she straddled him and took the kiss deeper. Her fingers were wild in his hair, and he gripped her waist, sliding his hands up her ribcage, hooking his arms around her shoulders, pressing her breasts to his chest. He tore his mouth from hers, leaving a trail of moist heat along her neck, then he dove again like a starving man, tangling tongues before she pulled back, breath heaving, staring into his eyes as she began a journey of her own—nips at his shoulder, lips and tongue over his pecs, curious fingers sliding down the sweaty skin of his abs. Then she journeyed lower, running her palms along his thighs, teasing as she moved ever closer to fulfilling him. She looked up from under her lashes, sending him a knowing smile as she stroked her finger up, circled, and made her way back down.

He clenched his jaw, waiting for the slide of her warm, wet mouth.

She continued her playful skimming until he thought he would beg. "Is this where I'm supposed to ask?"

His thighs shook as he tensed them. "You're killing me, Cooke," he choked out.

"So are you saying—"

He groaned his frustration. "Do it. Do it," he panted, sucking in and curling his toes, dropping his head against the pillow as she took him in. He groaned again, clutching at her hair as her hand and mouth destroyed him. “You keep that up and this is going to be over.”

She continued on until his stomach muscles danced with every breath, then stopped, leaving him dangling on the edge. She started her way back up his body, slowly, but he grabbed her under the arms, yanking her up, needing to finish what she began.

“In a hurry?”

“Turnabout’s fair play,” he promised.

“Not today.” She sat up and lowered herself on him. He grunted as she surrounded him in wet warmth, and she whimpered, grasping his shoulders. She began to rock, slowly and he played with her breasts, teasing purring moans from her throat.

Desperate to taste her mouth, he sat up, bringing them chest to chest. He kissed her deeply, clutching her hips, helping her hurried movements as her breathing grew more frenzied. He struggled to wait for her as she worked herself closer, then finally gasping, she froze as her muscles tensed and she throbbed around him. Jerking deep, once, twice, he let himself explode, muffling her cries as their mouths met and he grunted.

She rested her cheek on his shoulder, and he rubbed his hands up and down her back as they both caught their breath.

“I think we’re going to have to stay like this for at least a couple of hours. My muscles are officially jelly.”

He grinned. “I can see why.”

She lifted her head and smiled.

“Who knew the key to unlocking your inner animal rested in cabin fever? I’d threaten to keep you here indefinitely, but we would more than likely kill each other if we went at it like this all winter long.”

She laughed. “I’m game if you are.”

“Be careful what you wish for.” He wiggled his brows.

She chuckled and gave him a quick kiss.

These voluntary displays of affection pleased the hell out of him. He leaned back to the mattress, taking her with him. She collapsed against his chest, and he rolled, lying on top of her.

She reached up and played with the hair along his temple. "So what *are* we going to do today?"

"I thought we were going to drive each other crazy in bed."

She smiled. "I'm sure even you have your limits."

He feigned insult as he nipped at her collarbone. "You know how to aim right for a guy's ego."

"Gotta keep you in check."

He slid his finger along her jaw, debating whether or not to share the idea he'd been tossing around. As he stared into her eyes and moved his fingers over her skin, he realized this was the perfect opportunity to show her that he was willing to let her into the deepest parts of him. "I've been doing a lot of thinking since yesterday."

"What about?"

"Staci."

Her eyes sobered, and she touched his cheek.

"I'm going to reopen her case—unofficially."

"How do you go about doing that?"

"Basically, I'm going to go back to the beginning. Start from scratch, study all the evidence and see if I can flush out something that got missed."

"Is the police department going to cooperate?"

He shrugged. "Probably not, but I wasn't planning on asking. Luckily I know this computer geek who can hack his way through any firewall out there, and he doesn't have to follow procedure."

She traced his ear. "You're going to ask my brother for help."

"I'm not sure how enthused he'll be after we more or less told each other to fuck off, but at the end of the day, I need him if I'm going to find out who killed Staci. He's the best at what he does. These idiots here don't have a freaking clue."

"You and Ethan might be at odds, but he's still your friend." She kissed his chin.

"I know."

"He'll help you because you deserve to know the answers."

He nodded and grabbed her hand, kissing her fingers.

"I want to help you too."

He rested his forehead against hers.

She hugged him. "I want you to have some peace, Tucker. I want that for you more than anything."

"I guess today's the perfect day to go back to her room." He didn't want to. He didn't want to keep reliving her death.

"But it upsets you."

"I need to try to put the emotions away. I need to stop looking at this as her brother and look at this through a cop's eyes." Which would be a hell of a lot easier said than done.

"I'll come with you."

"You don't have to."

"Let me help you, Tucker."

He nodded. "Okay. Let's have some breakfast first."

"I need a shower—big time."

"Shower, then breakfast. Good idea."

"Separate showers." She drilled her finger into his chin.

He nuzzled her neck. "What's the fun in that?"

"I'm all finished with fun for the moment. Jelly legs, remember? I'll be lucky if I can stand up."

"I should definitely join you then. Safety first."

She grinned. "Nice try."

"Tough sell." He reached below the blanket and found her soft, tender flesh and began to stroke and circle.

Closing her eyes, she hummed in her throat. "Tucker. Showers."

"Are you sure I can't persuade you into letting me join you?"

"Nope. My mind's made up." She pushed at his shoulder.

Fighting dirty, he slipped a finger inside.

She froze, bit her lip, and moaned as she clutched at his

arm. “Unfair,” she shuddered.

“Maybe.” His finger moved about as he kissed her breast.

“Okay. You win.”

He grinned. “Baby, we’re both going to win. Wrap your legs around me. Your feet never have to touch the floor.”

She did as she was told, and he awkwardly got out of the bed with her twined around him. “Cold. It’s cold.” She clutched herself tighter.

“Only for a minute.” He grabbed his gun, captured her mouth, and locked the bathroom door behind them, setting the weapon on the counter. He twisted on the shower faucet, waiting for the steam, and walked them in to the warm spray. “Cooke,” he said against her lips as he pressed her to the wall. “We’re not leaving here until we both have to crawl.” He thrust himself deep and she groaned. “Better hang on.”

It was well after noon by the time they started down the hall toward Staci’s room. Wren was sorry to see the light leave Tucker’s eyes the closer they walked. They had a fun morning making each other crazy in the shower, on the bathroom counter, then back in the bedroom again, before they ate ravenously and laughed at the old sitcom playing on the small kitchen television.

Something had changed between them during the night as he held on to her, distraught over his sister. Their loving had been different—intimate, powerful—while they clung to each other in bed. In those moments by the fire, he’d given her his trust. She’d asked for it—demanded it—and he’d been willing to try. Now, as they walked together hand-in-hand, she understood she needed to do the same. Somehow after sharing what they did, the idea of giving Tucker everything wasn’t quite so scary...sort of.

They stopped in front of the closed door, and he sighed.

She gave his hand a supportive squeeze. “You don’t have

to do this."

"Yes, I do."

They both knew he did.

"I'll be right here with you."

He brought her fingers to his lips, kissed them. "You have no idea how much that means."

Probably not nearly as much as he was starting to mean to her. She pressed her palm to his cheek, touched by his sweet gesture. "Ready?"

He nodded and opened the door.

They stood in the doorway for several seconds, then entered the shrine to a beautiful life cut short. Tucker's jaw clenched as he stared at the floor.

This was a bad idea. Then she remembered him telling her that he had to stop looking at Staci's case through a brother's eyes. She desperately wanted him to click into 'cop mode' and escape some of his pain. "What—what would you do if you were still a detective?"

"I would talk to witnesses, study the crime scene photographs, try to get in the victim's and the killer's heads."

"You were the first witness."

He looked at her. "I was the only witness. My mom tried to come back here, but I wouldn't let her."

She bit her lip, unsure of what she needed to do to make this even a little easier. "I—she—that was for the best. What would you ask your witnesses?"

"I would want to know what they heard, saw, etcetera. This guy studied Staci. He knew her routine—all of ours." He rubbed at his forehead. "At some point, one of us had to have seen him."

"Here. Come here." She tugged his hand as she sat on the bed.

He hesitated. "I can't. We used to sit there and talk about everything or nothing at all."

She rushed to her feet. "I'm sorry."

"It's okay. I guess the best place for me to start is by asking myself the questions I would ask someone else."

She nodded. "Good idea."

"The night it happened, we had gone to a movie. Staci, me, JT, and Jasmine. We saw a Will Smith flick. I didn't care much about what was happening on the screen; I had the hots for Jasmine. I wanted the credits to roll so we could get to the part where I took her home and got to kiss her goodnight."

Wren rolled her eyes. "Why am I not surprised?"

He smiled, then it vanished. "It was my turn to drive. Staci and I had to share the car that summer—a small bone of contention. Anyway, I drove like a moron, trying to impress my girl. Pissed Staci off, but JT and I had a hell of a time."

"Did JT and Staci date?"

He shook his head. "Nah. They were just friends. Staci wasn't into the whole dating scene. She always told me I dated enough for the both of us."

"So what about JT?"

He shrugged. "I think he got around when he wanted to. He and I, we never talked about girls much—mostly sports and working out."

She glanced at the photos. "He was a pretty handsome guy—still is."

"Sure."

"Very successful and kind, despite his mother." She narrowed her eyes, shook her head. "Sorry. Keep going."

"We let JT off and set up plans for the next day—baseball game, then Jasmine suggested I drop Staci off first. She wanted me to walk her home."

"I'm sure she did."

He grinned. "Hey, I had moves."

He still did, but she scoffed for form.

"Staci went inside, and Jasmine and I walked to her house. She lived four houses down. We made a date for the lake, played a little tonsil hockey, and I left."

"Didn't it creep you out, walking alone in the dark?"

"I was a jock with a date to the lake. I wasn't thinking about anything but getting laid."

"It's just so *dark* here."

"Yeah. Good for stargazing. Staci loved—" His hand tensed against hers.

"What?"

"I forgot. I completely forgot until now."

"What?"

"There was something in the woods that night—scared the shit out of me. Ms. Hayes told us to be careful. A couple of cats had been seen in the area. I tucked tail and booked it the hell home, certain I was going to be a bobcat's next snack." His eyes sharpened. "What if it wasn't a fucking cat?"

She shuddered at the idea.

"Son of a bitch. Staci's killer had to know my father was gone. I was the other obstacle. But if it *was* him, why didn't he just off me instead of risk getting caught?"

"I don't know." This was so out of her realm.

He dropped her hand and pulled the pad from his jeans pocket, scribbling something down, and shoved it back.

"Did anything else happen? Were there any other noises?"

"No, just branches snapping. I hauled ass home, slammed the door behind me, told my mom I was home, and forgot about the whole thing. I was so preoccupied with the car and taking Jasmine to the lake. It was Staci's turn to have the Mustang the next day, and I needed it. I found her in the hot tub, staring up at the stars. We talked for a while. We made a deal with the car in which I got completely hosed, then I told her we should go in. She said she wasn't tired, we made fun of my dad a little bit, and she told me she loved me. I told her I loved her too, even though she was a brat." He steamed a breath through his nose and closed his eyes.

Wren stepped closer, slid her arm around his back, and rested her cheek against his chest.

He wrapped his arm around her shoulders. "If I'd stayed

with her, she would still be here."

"You didn't know. How could you have possibly known, Tucker?"

He shrugged. "I was thinking more about my dick than my sister."

"Which is completely normal. I'm sure Ethan thought more about his penis too, which is actually pretty gross, and I don't want to think about that."

A quick chuckle escaped him, and he squeezed her closer. "Damn, Cooke, I don't know what I'd do without you." He kissed her hair.

She looked up and smiled.

"I should have made her come in with me."

Her brow rose as she continued to look at him. "She told you she wasn't ready. If you had insisted, she would have dug in her heels. I'm a sister myself, Tucker."

"Yeah, I guess."

"You're looking at this in hindsight. There is no way you could have known what was to happen."

"I would give anything to change it."

She held him tighter, wishing she could change the outcome for him.

"I don't know what happened next. I crawled into bed, slid my headphones on, and put Pearl Jam on repeat. He must've waited a while after I went in. I think I dozed off, then I heard a loud bump in Staci's room. I didn't think anything of it. I closed my eyes and went back to sleep. My sister was being raped and strangled right here, and I slept through it." He shook his head and turned away from the spot on the floor. "I can hardly stand it."

Wren said nothing as she stared at his back. There was no use telling him everything was going to be okay, because it wasn't.

"He tied her hands behind her back, raped her, strangled her. She must have been so scared, fucking *terrified*. Why didn't she *scream* for me, goddammit?" He dropped to a crouch and pressed his hands to his face. “Why didn’t she fucking scream for help?”

Wren crouched next to him and hugged him, struggling to keep her tears at bay. He needed her strength right now.

“He probably threatened to hurt me and Mom, so she kept her mouth shut. Fucking bastard didn’t even give her a fighting chance. He was methodical and cruel—waited until he’d squeezed the life out of her before he freed her hands from behind her back. He cut the nylon from her wrists and neck postmortem, placed her arms above her head, left her naked and spread eagle.” Tucker rushed to his feet again and pressed his hands flat on the dresser. “Her shoulder was dislocated. The medical examiner said it was from struggling while he choked her to death.”

“Oh God, Tucker.” She’d never ached so much for another.

“We never did find her bathing suit or the rope. He fucking took them with him. His trophies.”

Not only had Tucker seen too much, but he knew too much—the hazards of the profession he had chosen. She tugged at his shoulder. “Come on. It’s time to go.”

He whirled. “How can I solve her case if I can’t even stand in this goddamn room?”

His venom startled her, but she took his arm and pulled again. His anger was with the situation, not her. “You’ve done enough today. You remembered the noises in the woods. You need a break.”

He yanked away. “A break? There’s no timeout from violent death, Wren. I can’t just put it away. There are answers here. There has to be, and I’m going to find them.”

Her first instinct was to tell him to go to hell as he lashed out at her, but she stood her ground. “They’ll be waiting for you after a breather. You’re upset, which means you aren’t thinking clearly.”

“Suddenly she’s a detective.”

She pressed her lips into a thin line, holding his angry gaze. “I’m sorry about Staci, Tucker, more sorry than you could possibly know. I can't even begin to fathom how hard this is, having to relive her worst moments, but you're being a jerk. If you would like me to leave, say the word."

"Things getting too emotional? I know how that trips you up." Misery swam in his eyes as he turned away again.

He was hurting and trying to hurt her in the process—it was working. "I'll take that as you want to be alone." She left the room, starting toward her own.

"Cooke."

She hesitated halfway down the hall but kept going.

"Cooke, don't go."

She stopped and turned as he walked to her.

"I'm sorry. I'm sorry," he repeated as he swept her up in a hug. "I'm sorry," he said again as he crushed her against him.

She returned his embrace, brushing her fingers through the back of his hair. "It's okay."

"No, it's not. Not even a little."

"This is hard, Tucker. I'm trying to help and understand."

"This is tearing me up. I don't know how to handle it. I never really have, but that doesn't mean you get to be the punching bag." He brushed her lips. "I'm sorry," he whispered once more.

"It's already forgotten."

"I need to talk to Ethan and have him get me everything in the files—local and FBI. I can't do much else until I have it."

"What can I do?" She rested her hands on his hips. "What else do you need?"

"You."

Her heart beat a little faster as he stared in her eyes. "I'm right here."

He leaned his forehead against hers. "Will you make us grilled cheese and soup while I put in a few calls?"

"Comfort food."

"There's nothing better than grilled cheese."

"I agree."

"Will you watch a movie with me? I want to feel normal, for us to *be* normal—just for one night."

The peace she so desperately wanted him to have—and to give him. "You're in luck, because I can deliver on all of these things. No crazy stalkers, no Staci talk. Just you and me, grilled cheese, and a funny movie."

"And maybe some sex? I can't get enough of you, Cooke."

She smiled as he grinned. "A completely normal night should definitely include sex."

He chuckled, hugged her tight, and they walked down the hall, going their separate ways.

He put the key in the lock, quietly opened the door, and punched in the code, closing himself in the dark. He crept further into the house, soaking up the warmth, straining his ears, listening for any movements down the hall. All was silent.

He turned toward the opposite wing, making his way through the great room, careful not to trip or bang into furnishings along the way. Excitement and adrenaline coursed through his veins as he moved past the kitchen. More than a decade had passed since he'd made this journey. Now that he was here, time vanished, and he was young again, eager and ready to follow through with his plan.

His heart pounded as he stepped closer and stopped at the second door on the left, his hand shaking on the knob as he let himself in. He paused, blinking, as he looked around. Everything was the same—the mint green walls, the letters spelling out her name, the dozens of photographs scattered about.

He walked to her side table and touched her beautiful face in the frame, stroking at her cheek as he looked into her smiling hazel eyes. His first. His best. *Staci.* She'd been perfect, so tight and warm, while he fumbled his way through.

And how she'd stared at him, those same eyes huge, while he squeezed the nylon, taking her last breath.

He shuddered, fully aroused as he pulled down her pink and white striped sheets, and freed himself from his pants, tugged, groaned, and left his present just for her. He dipped his finger in his mess and left his message, then took the ties from his pocket, kissed them lovingly, lost in his memories, and set them in their place.

With one last look, he regretfully shut the door and made his way back down the hall. That moment had been for him, but now he had work to do. This next step would end in one of three ways: him blowing Tucker away and taking Wren—he could live with that; Tucker blowing him away, which was less than ideal; or he would move forward with his plan and enjoy the show until he was ready to end it.

He walked to the east wing and stopped outside the closed door, grabbed his gun from his waistband, and clenched his teeth as he twisted the knob.

The door opened silently, and he peered in, breathing both of them in—Wren's French perfume and whatever the hell Tucker sprayed all over himself. Fucking Pretty Boy. As if his muscles and stupid grin weren't enough.

He wouldn't be grinning tomorrow.

He inched the door open, waiting for someone to move. Nothing. He shook his head in disgust—some bodyguard. Balling his hand into a fist, he stared at Tucker, naked and wrapped around Wren. She lay flat on her stomach, her cheek resting on his arm, their fingers intertwined as he cocooned her. Beauty and the Beauty. There was no fucking beast on that bed, and he hated Tucker more for it. He had *everything*.

He crouched closer, studying Tucker's muscled arm splayed on Wren's tiny feminine back among the yards of her black hair, the orb of her breast pressed against the mattress, and Tucker's perfect, chiseled form claiming ownership of the woman beneath him. The bastard loved her. It was plain as day.

His gaze wandered to the gun on the side table. Tempting, so fucking tempting, but what he had in store was so much better.

He stood, still scrutinizing them both, then left. Tomorrow was bound to be spectacular.

ଓ Chapter Seventeen ଓ

Wren turned on her back, stretching her aching muscles, and smiled. After yesterday's sex marathon she was fabulously worn out. Tucker was a tiger in the sack. She'd never been so thoroughly *ravaged*. Yawning, she arched and he pulled her to him, chest-to-chest, rolling so she lay on top of him. Her skin instantly puckered with goose bumps. "Hey, mister, it's cold up here."

He rolled again, trapping her under his body. "Better?"

She smiled. "Definitely warmer."

He nuzzled her neck. "What'd'ya say we start today off like we did yesterday?"

Her smile turned into a grin as she wrapped her arms around his waist and tilted her chin, giving him more access to her sensitive collarbone. "Sounds nice, and clearly you're raring to go, but I'd rather get up and try to make it to the airport."

"Every party's got a pooper."

She laughed and pinched his butt. "Guess that's me." She glanced toward the window, narrowing her eyes. "Is that... *No*."

"What?" His head whipped up, instantly on alert.

"It's snowing a*gain*. How can that *be*?"

He grabbed her chin, giving a firm squeeze. "Don't do

that, Cooke. You're lucky I didn't grab my gun and roll us off the bed."

She wrinkled her nose. "Sorry."

He studied the frenzied snow. "Goddamn. This is getting old."

"I strongly second that. We probably aren't flying again today, huh?"

"We'll have to catch the news and see if they've opened the airport, but I doubt it. At this rate, we're going to have to charter a plane."

"Sold." She tried to sit up.

He held her in place. "Don't get too excited. We have to make reservations, and conditions sure as hell have to improve before we can go anywhere."

"I know," she huffed. "How much longer do you think?"

"Tomorrow. Day after."

She groaned at the idea of being trapped in this house for another day.

"Whiner." He playfully sunk his teeth into her chin.

"Maybe a little." She slid her finger along his earlobe. "I'm just frustrated. I feel like our lives are on hold while we wait here. I want to see Patrick. Now that he's awake, I need to be with him more than ever. He's making small gains, but the doctors think he could be doing better."

He slid a strand of her hair behind her ear. "They also said he's in and out of it, and Morgan and Hailey have been stopping by to visit."

"And I'm grateful for their kindness, but—"

"It's not the same."

She bit her lip, nodding. "I just...I'm the only family he has. I want him to talk again. I want to hear his voice. Maybe if I'm there, he will."

"I get it, Cooke. I know how hard this has been on you." He kissed her forehead. "We'll be out of here soon."

She touched her lips to his, appreciating the fact that Tucker did indeed get it. He was one of the few people who understood her. "Thanks."

"Any time."

She gave him a small smile. "I guess this is the perfect day to stop procrastinating and submit resumes."

"Santa Barbara?"

"Yes." The idea wasn't as appealing as it had been a few days ago, especially now while she lay beneath him, warm, content, stroking his shoulder.

"Why not stay in LA?"

"Fresh start, remember?"

"Fresh start from what?"

"Everything—my house, my business. I hate the idea of living in an apartment miles from the home I spent two years making my own. And Cooke Interiors is ruined; my reputation is in the toilet. It'll take time to come back from that, especially after Lenora officially bankrupts me, which I have no doubt is her intention."

"I don't think it'll be as simple as that. Technically you've broken your contract, but not without just cause. You have a great track record and several clients who will vouch for you, I'm sure. Fleeing from a stalker is definitely an unforeseen circumstance."

He made everything sound so simple, but it wasn't. "Maybe, but attorneys aren't cheap and my business accounts are pretty close to empty."

"So I'll take care of the attorneys and anything else you need."

She dropped her hand from his shoulder. "No."

"Cooke—"

"No, Tucker. This is my mess. I'll clean it up by myself."

"But you *aren't* by yourself. You have me. And your brother and Sarah, Hunter and Morgan; the list goes on and on."

"I know but I like to take care of myself. It's important that I stand on my own two feet."

"And sometimes it's okay to let someone else carry you for a while."

She sensed his growing frustration. How could she make him understand? "I'm trying here, Tucker. I am, but I've been who I am for twenty-nine years, and mostly it's worked for me."

"I know." He kissed her nose.

"It's never been like this. *I've* never been like this with anyone."

"Cooke." He brushed his lips over hers, once, twice, deepening the kiss slowly, drawing out the tenderness until her heart overflowed and she was certain nothing would be the same again. Instead of pushing him away, she wrapped her arms around him, savoring the gentle pressure of his mouth moving over hers. He nibbled her bottom lip and eased back. "Guess you should get to those resumes."

She played her fingers through his hair, no longer wanting to leave this bed or Tucker's arms. "Guess so."

He pulled away and rolled to his back, resting his head on the pillow. "I'll take a look at the weather and figure out when we can charter a plane. Hopefully we'll be heading home in forty-eight hours or less."

"Sounds like a plan." She crossed her arms, suddenly cold as the heat of Tucker's body left hers. She studied him, lying among the pillows, perfectly relaxed with his eyes closed. Forty-eight hours or less. That's all they had left, then "real life" began again. She rubbed at the unexpected ache in her chest, trying not to regret that her time with Tucker was quickly coming to an end, but this was the reality of their situation. What they had here in Utah certainly couldn't last forever. She had a career to rebuild in Santa Barbara, and Tucker would be busy with his own once he and Ethan had a chance to talk.

Feelings would fade after a while, and she would move on. She fully expected Tucker to do the same. She would never have this again—the intimacy and trust they'd shared together, but it would only be foolish if she let herself believe that there was anything but an ending in store for her and Tucker.

She sat up, her shoulders heavy from her thoughts, and she reached for her robe, no longer wanting to think about Tucker, Santa Barbara, or any unwanted emotions that came with either. She slid the soft silk over her arms as the bright green and blue flowered fabric caught her eye. She blinked, staring. *What in the world?* Her eyes grew wide and bile rose in her throat as it clicked. Staci's bathing suit. The one she'd seen in the picture taken just days before the murder. "Oh, my God," she whispered as she clutched Tucker's arm. "Tucker."

"Hmm?" He grunted, eyes still closed.

"Tucker. The bathing suit."

"What?"

"Staci's bikini is on the floor."

He sat up, staring at her as if she'd gone mad. "Wren, what in the hell are you talking about?"

"Her bathing suit is on the floor, right next to my side. Look."

He leaned forward, grabbed the gun, and leaped up off the bed. "Fuck." He rushed to the door, locked it, reached for his pajama bottoms, and yanked them on. "Get in the corner." He pointed across the room.

She nodded and crawled across the bed, hurrying to the other side of the room, holding her body rigid, trying not to give in to her shaking.

Tucker dropped down on his knees, looking under the bed, then got to his feet. He padded over to stand to the side of the closet, yanked the door open, and whirled around, pointing his gun. He moved to the bathroom next, took the same stance as he had by the closet, whirled, and pointed into the bathroom. "Call 9-1-1, keep the door locked, and get under the bed. Stay there until I knock and say it's me. Don't you answer unless I say it's me."

"But—"

"Do it, Cooke. Now."

He stood behind the door, twisted the knob, waited, whirling into the hall with his weapon ready. Shutting the door behind him, he left her alone in the silence.

She secured her robe with trembling hands, staring at Staci's swimsuit, then glanced at the window. A murderer had been in the house—maybe he still was. She walked to the side table on watery legs, grabbed her phone, and shimmied her way under the bed frame. Dialing, she struggled to school her breathing. She could barely hear over the slamming thud of her heart.

"Nine-one-one, what's your emergency?"

"Yes, I need the police, immediately."

"What's your address?"

"Twenty-twelve Mountain View—the Campbell Estate. The murderer, he was here. My bodyguard is searching the house." She was rambling.

"Ma'am, what's your name? What murderer?"

"Wren Cooke. I'm Wren Cooke. The murderer. He killed Staci Campbell and Alyssa Brookes and Chloe Wright. He was here. He left Staci Campbell's bathing suit on my bedroom floor. I'm looking at it."

"Are you in a safe place?"

"Yes. I'm hiding under the bed. Please hurry and send someone. Tucker's by himself searching the house." She listened for him, waiting for him to call her name.

"Tucker who, ma'am?"

"Tucker Campbell. His family owns the house. He's my bodyguard. He's alone. Just get someone here."

"They're on their way, ma'am. Stay on the line with me until the police arrive."

She stared at the bathing suit Staci wore at the end of her life. Monsters. She and Tucker had two monsters on their hands—a stalker and a murderer. She thought of little else as the minutes ticked by in her agonizing wait.

"Cooke. Let me in."

Her heart shuddered with unbelievable relief as he called

to her. Wren scooched and shimmied her way out from under the bed and hurried to the door. "Tucker?"

"Yeah. Go ahead and open up."

She flipped the lock and flew into his arms, gripping him hard in a hug. "You're okay."

He hugged her back, clutching his arm around her. "I'm all right. Is that the police?"

"Dispatch."

He took the phone and put it to his ear, shutting the door behind him, locking them in the room. "This is Tucker Campbell. I need Detective Rogers and Franklin up here now." He sat on the chaise lounge, pulling Wren next to him, holding her tight against his side. "Yes, patch me through, please." His body was as rigid as hers, his eyes hard and distant as he looked at the horrid reminder of Staci. "Detective Rogers, Tucker Campbell. He was here. Staci's bathing suit is on the master suite floor, and black tethers are on the bed in her old room. I don't know. I'm armed; make sure they know that." He hung up.

She pressed her face to his chest, clinging, struggling to hold back her tears. "Are you okay? Are you sure you're okay?"

He grabbed hold of her chin. "I'm fine, Cooke. I need you to keep it together for me."

She nodded, swallowing, blinking the emotions away.

"He's not here."

"I don't care about that." She shook her head. "Yes, I do. Of course I do, but I was afraid for you. And that." She gestured to the floor. "I'm so sorry about that, Tucker." She cupped his cheeks and gave him a kiss.

"I'm in one piece."

"Just the way I like you best." She gave him a small smile.

He winked, but his eyes were strained and weary. "Did you touch anything?"

"No. Nothing. Just my phone."

"Go ahead and get dressed." He stood, dropping his pajama pants and pulled on his boxers and jeans from yesterday, then the snug black top that accentuated his build. "They'll be here soon."

She got to her feet and went to the luggage she never unpacked, took fresh jeans, panties, a bra, and her lavender shirt from the case. She unknotted the robe and dressed in front of him, not wanting to leave his side.

Tucker's cell phone rang. He glanced at the readout. Ethan. "Campbell."

"I just heard. Is Wren okay?"

He looked down the hall toward the bedroom. "Yeah. She was a little shaken up, but she's fine."

"I was stuck on duty and couldn't get away. What the hell happened?"

"Fuck if I know. There aren't any broken windows or busted doors, no foreign fingerprints, just mine, Wren's, and Ms. Hayes'. Somehow he got a key to this place." The idea sickened him as it did every time he thought of some demented fucker walking around his house, standing over the bed he and Wren slept in. "I just got off the phone with the security company. The alarm was deactivated at two thirty for approximately twenty-three minutes—same with the Chloe Wright Case."

"That's definitely worth looking into. What about Alyssa Brookes?"

"The cops are on it now, but according to Detective Franklin, the Brookes family didn't arm their panel the night Alyssa died."

"Hmm."

"He was in Wren's bedroom. He staged his fucking 'gift' on her floor and either before or after, stopped by my sister's room. He left black tethers and a message on Staci's sheets in semen—*SC equals TC*." He gritted his teeth, hardly able to stand it.

"Goddamn, man. I'm sorry."

Tucker shrugged. "At this point, I can only assume TC stands for me. He's tying me into the mix. I have no idea why or what this means." But it was going to eat him alive until he figured it out.

"Maybe he's telling you you're next."

"Maybe." But it didn't feel right.

"They need to get this bastard off the streets. We're lucky he didn't hurt Wren."

He'd thought the same thing. "Might've been part of his plan—unless that wasn't what he was after."

"What do you mean?"

"I feel like he's taunting me."

"You think this is about you?"

"It's crossed my mind."

"We have no idea what this guy's up to; until we do, I want Wren in your sight twenty-four seven."

"We've been together twenty-four seven. We were together last night."

Tense silence filled the line.

"Look man, I'm sorry you don't approve of me being with your sister, but that's the way it is. I don't plan on going anywhere anytime soon."

"What are you saying?"

"I'm saying I'm sticking around, so you might as well get used to it."

"That's my sister, Campbell."

"I'm well aware."

"My parents did a fine job of fucking us both up."

"You and Sarah seem to be doing all right. Doesn't Wren deserve what you two have?"

"Touché."

"I love her, Ethan."

"What about her? How does she feel?"

"She feels plenty when she doesn't think too much."

"You know I don't have anything against you personally. I think you're a hell of a guy. You're one of my good friends. I want Wren happy. You keep her happy, Campbell, and we'll be just fine. So, what's the plan now that we know a murderer has a key to your house and a code to your alarm?"

Apparently that was the end of their disagreement. "I'll reassign a code, but we're moving to the hotel until we can get the hell out of here. Luckily there are a couple of vacancies—guests can't get here in these conditions. The airport's closed. It's still snowing."

"Hunter said you said something about forty-eight hours."

"That's the best I can do."

"Then it'll have to do. I have the stuff you asked for—sent the file to Jackson too. I didn't think it would hurt to have him take a look. Text me when you're ready and I'll send it over."

He sighed, weary, tired, and more than half-sick after the emotional rollercoaster of the last several hours. "Will do. Hey, Cooke, what would you say if I said—" He stopped mid-thought as Wren stepped out of the room and walked toward him. He hadn't been able to shake the idea that Wren's stalking and Staci's murder were somehow connected. He'd wanted to bounce the idea off Ethan since the thought came to him earlier this morning, but now wasn't the time. "Never mind. Wren's heading my way."

"You sure?"

The idea was a stretch, but he couldn't let it go. "Yeah. I'll give you a call when we get settled in downtown. We have an officer following us, and someone will be assigned to our door until we can get out of here. Rogers spoke with the resort's security, so they understand the situation and know I'll be armed."

"Sounds like everything's under control."

"As much as it can be. I'll let you go."

"Bye."

Wren set her luggage down. "I'm ready."

He nodded.

"Have you heard anything new? What did the detectives say before they left?"

"Not much. It'll take time to process the items."

"Do you think—do you think the bathing suit was actually Staci's?"

"Yeah, I do."

"And the ties?"

"I'm willing to bet those are the ones he used on my sister."

"Tucker," she whispered, pressing her hands to his cheeks. "I don't even know what to say."

The compassion in her eyes went a long way to soothe him. He wrapped his arms around her waist. "You don't have to say anything."

"I wish I could take all of this away." She stood on her tiptoes and pressed her lips to his.

He pulled her closer, holding on tight, accepting the comfort she wanted to give. "We should go," he muffled against her hair.

"I'm ready." She stepped back and took his hand.

He turned to the two officers sitting on the couch. "We're ready."

"We'll follow behind you, Mr. Campbell."

"Thank you."

☙ Chapter Eighteen ❧

Tucker stared at the gruesome images of his sister in comparison to Alyssa Brookes and Chloe Wright, trying to find the connection between the three deaths now that he had Park City PD's and the FBI's files. Other than similar physical features and identical methods of murder, there was nothing consistent. He'd put in a call to his father, discussing the situation at length, triple-checking that their families had never met.

He rubbed at his tired eyes, glanced at Wren asleep in the next room, and flipped screens to the side-by-side layout Ethan had provided of each victim's family life, extracurricular activities, timelines, so on and so forth. Again, nothing popped out to grab him. Staci and Alyssa had been popular and extroverted. Chloe had been a quiet, brainy, bookworm. All three families had money, but not to the extent of the Campbell fortune.

He scribbled *Money?* on the mostly blank notepad next to him. Did finances somehow tie into this whole thing? He shook his head, immediately dismissing the idea. Ransoms never came into play. Nothing was ever stolen. Beneficiaries didn't gain more from death than life. "So, what the hell *is* it?" He scrubbed his hands over his face as the frustration drove him half-crazy. He'd been at this for *hours*. Jackson hadn't come up with anything he hadn't thought of already, and Ethan was still searching. He needed to shut it down for a while and come back with a fresh perspective. They were dead in the water until they figured out the killer's motive.

He stood, walked to the sliding glass doors, and moved the curtain aside, staring at the flurries in the glow of the streetlights. Hopefully this was the beginning of the end of the ceaseless pummel. Even the diehards had had enough. He slid the drape back, closing out the gray dawn, and looked at his laptop, unable to settle. His mind kept circling around to Wren's stalker and Staci's murderer being one in the same. The idea should have been ridiculous, but he couldn't shake it. Although it was possible two sick bastards taunted them simultaneously, it was highly unlikely.

Sighing, he went back to the table, knowing that sleep wasn't going to happen. He might as well play his theory out once and for all instead of standing around, driving himself crazy. Grabbing his pen, he wrote *Wren*, *Staci*, *Alyssa*, *Chloe*, and added *Park City* and *Los Angeles.* He drew three lines, connecting the victims to Park City and one from Wren to Los Angeles. He stared at the small diagram, trying to make it all add up.

He swallowed, his stomach churning, his hands growing clammy as he finally understood. *He* was the link tying everything together. *This town hasn't seen a murder since July 1999, which coincidentally was the last time you were here. You come back to Utah, and two girls wind up dead, which is a damn screwy happenstance if you ask me.* Rogers' words had plagued him from the second they were spoken; now he knew why.

He scribbled *Tucker* on the sheet, needing to finish this out, and drew lines from his name to Staci, Wren, Los Angeles, Park City, Chloe, and Alyssa, adding question marks next to the latter two names. He didn't know the girls or understand his part in their deaths, but his sister's killer had connected them together in a roundabout way with his 'message' on Staci's bedding. Jackson had initially suggested that the killer tossed Tucker's initials into the mix to throw the investigation off course, but this made more sense as he studied his detailed graph with his forehead in his hands, his suspicions confirmed on the paper before him. Wren's stalker and Staci's killer certainly could be the same person, and he was somehow at the center.

But how? Why?

He sat back, his mind racing. Staci's death had been methodical, cruel, and filled with purpose—a purpose no one understood. Wren's stalking wasn't all that different...dead cats, texts, flowers and bloody messages that made sense to no one but the individual sending them. He looked at his name on the sheet, then at Wren's. Her problems had started almost immediately after he became a visible part of her life. Alyssa and Chloe's lives ended shortly after he came back to Park City. Did they die for nothing more than that?

But what about the timeframe? Fourteen-and-a-half years separated Staci's murder and his interest in Wren—if that was even the angle. He jammed a hand through his hair, clenching his jaw, grappling to come up with another explanation. That didn't make sense either. Wren certainly wasn't the first woman he'd dated since Staci's death, so why would she be a target? Because she was the only one who mattered. But how the hell would anyone else know that when he'd just recently figured it out himself?

And that's where the theory started to unravel—a killer who murders for...who the hell knows why, then takes over a decade off only to come back for the love of his life and kills two more girls while he's at it? There were too many gaping holes to add up to something plausible.

He rubbed at the knots in his shoulders. Maybe all of this was a big coincidence and Jackson was right: The killer was smart. He very well could have added Tucker's initials to throw them all for a loop. He'd just spent a good half-hour spinning his wheels. He waited for the flood of relief as he glanced at his disproven theories, but the lead ball in his belly still weighed heavy. Why couldn't he let this *go*? Why couldn't he chalk this up to a bad case of paranoia and move on to something that actually made sense?

Because somehow among the mismatched pieces and inconsistencies, this *did* make sense. He ripped his paper from the notebook and rewrote his diagram on a fresh sheet, taking his ideas to the next step regardless of the discrepancies. This time he added a box with his name, the three victims', and Wren's in each of the corners and *Who?* in the last empty space. That was the huge question. If this was somehow right, past and present were colliding—Park City and three innocent girls, Los Angeles and one innocent woman, Tucker and a crazy fucker.

Making two columns, he scribbled 1999 and 2014 and began a list of everyone he and Staci knew in Park City, then he jotted names under the 2014 side, including individuals he and Wren were both acquainted with. He hated adding his friends, but they were names that could be quickly eliminated. He stared at the small roster and sighed. Nothing.

He dropped his pen, rubbed at the tension once again, and thought back to the weeks leading up to the chaos. He'd worked, worked some more, and tried to make a little time with Wren at Ethan's shindig. His fingers paused against his skin. Michael Collins? No. Michael Collins wasn't a blast from his past. Then his heart kicked into high gear. JT. JT fucking Cartwright. Big-time Los Angeles defense attorney.

He shook his head, wanting to deny the possibility. Cartwright and Staci had been incredibly close, and Wren was very fond of him. She and JT had gone to the gala together. His stomach shuddered as he thought of the young man who'd been there for him during the worst days of his life, the friendly man who'd offered to buy him a beer just weeks ago. Despite it all, Tucker wrote *JT* by the question mark. So far he was the only name that fit. He picked up his phone even though it was still shy of six. Ethan would want in on this as soon as possible.

"Cooke," Ethan answered groggily.

"Hey, sorry to call so early."

"Is everything okay? Is Wren all right?"

"Yeah, she's sleeping. I need you to do something for me. I need you to run JT Cartwright."

"JT Cartwright? I'm still half-asleep. Why does that name sound familiar?"

"Defense attorney. Son to Wren's former pain-in-the ass client."

"That's right. That's right," Ethan said, his voice changing, straining as he obviously stretched. "Why?"

"I've been playing with an idea. I didn't want to say anything until I had some time to turn everything over in my head. What if—what if Wren's stalker and Staci's murderer are the same person?"

The line stayed silent.

"I know this sounds like a stretch, but if you think about it, maybe it's not. Wren's being stalked, we head to Utah, and all the sudden my sister's killer is striking with a vengeance."

"Maybe, man, but I don't see it. Owens ran JT. He came up clean. I'll go back and double-check his whereabouts, but he didn't raise any red flags the first time around."

"I think there's something here. The killer has linked me to the murders—"

"Or you're a great opportunity to throw them off the trail."

"Hear me out. Staci was my sister; Wren and I are involved. There hasn't been a murder in Park City since Staci's death, then I come back to town and two girls die in an identical way to my twin."

"Definitely big coincidences, but what's the angle?"

He shook his head, still unable to figure that out. "I don't know. Revenge?"

"For what?"

"I don't know, Ethan. Like I said, a stretch."

"And you're thinking JT Cartwright's your man?"

"Not necessarily. He's the only name I can connect to my past and present. He was one of Staci's good friends, and Wren really likes him. We'll start with him until I can come up with someone else."

"I'll have something for you by tonight. I've got a crazy-ass schedule today. We're trying to wrap things up here and get back to LA. Sarah's new studio is finished."

"Sounds good."

"You still good to head home tomorrow?"

"I think so. The snow seems to be stopping. I'll call to confirm our flight at nine. As long as the airport reopens, we should be airborne by two."

"I'll talk to you later."

"Later." He hung up, set his phone down, and looked at the bed, craving to lie down and rest his weary head. He wanted to pull Wren against him and pretend everything was like it had been yesterday morning before they'd found Staci's bathing suit and a potential new lead to a case that might revolve around him. *Might,* he reminded himself. Ethan didn't seem sold on the idea, but they would see what they would see and move from there.

Suddenly exhausted, Tucker glanced at the security latch flipped in place on the door and stood, heading to the bedroom, pulling off his holster, shirt, and shorts. Perhaps he would catch an hour or two of shuteye now that his mind was less bogged down. He slid the covers back and settled himself against his pillow, hesitating as he reached for Wren.

What if he was right? What if all of this did circle around to him? Would Wren be so willing to stand by him if he was the reason for Patrick's injuries and the loss of her home and business? Maybe she'd been right. Maybe her life didn't work with him in it.

Unable to stop himself, he slid his finger along the soft warm skin of her arm, wondering if all the obstacles he and Wren had worked through might have been for nothing.

Wren rolled over and smiled at Tucker, who was sleeping soundly. His mouth hung slightly open as his chest rose and fell with each deep breath. Poor guy was exhausted. He'd been sitting at the table in their tiny kitchenette, staring at his laptop, frowning when she'd dozed off sometime after one. He must've studied the files Ethan sent for quite some time, trying to piece the new developments in Staci's case together.

She touched her finger to the deep purple circles under his closed eyes, aching for him. Yesterday had been nothing short of devastating. She'd seen Staci and Alyssa's horrid crime scene photos spread about the coffee table, yet the bikini, tethers, and crude 'message,' as Tucker had called it, on the bedding had somehow seemed crueler. She didn't need Tucker's psychology degree to understand that Staci's killer wanted him to suffer. The kind man lying beside her didn't deserve the punches he'd been dealt, yet he was handling them.

Wanting him to rest, she carefully pulled her side of the covers back and eased herself off the mattress, tiptoeing her way to the glass sliders in the next room. She slid the curtain aside several inches and blinked against the bright sunshine. "*Finally*," she whispered, grinning, never happier to see the sun's blinding twinkle reflecting off the massive snow banks and throngs of tourists cramming Main Street in the distance. Park City had been a ghost town yesterday when she and Tucker made their way to the resort through the storm, but the crowds were out in full-force today. She studied men, women, and children bundled in their winter attire, bustling about, and craved to be part of the action. Sitting idle was driving her *crazy*.

"Cooke?"

She whirled as the urgency in Tucker's voice registered

and rushed toward the bedroom, slamming into him as she turned the corner.

He grabbed her around the waist, catching her before she fell.

"What's wrong?" She eased back enough to look him in the eye, realizing he was still half asleep. "Are you okay?"

"Yeah. I didn't know where you were. I didn't hear you get up."

"I'm sorry." She hugged him, listening to his heart thunder. "I didn't want to wake you. I was hoping you would sleep."

"It's okay. I guess I went out harder than I thought I would."

"Come on." She took his hand and tugged. "Let's get you back to bed. You're exhausted."

He didn't move. "I just need some coffee."

She gave him another tug. "Snuggle up and I'll make you a cup."

He walked with her to the bed. "Five-star treatment. I guess I should stay up all night more often."

She smiled, studying him as he lay back down. Despite his attempt at joking, his eyes were still distant and weary. What she wouldn't give for him to flash her one of those slow, sexy grins. She crawled on the bed next to him, wanting to make this better. "Here, sit up."

"You just told me to lie down."

"Trust me."

He sat up, and she scooched behind him, pulling him back against her. She wrapped her arms around him and nuzzled her face in the crook of his neck, breathing him in.

He turned his head and kissed her lips. "This is much better than coffee."

"Mmm." She held him tighter, absorbing his warmth, hopefully lessening some of his troubles. "What time did you come to bed?"

"Around six."

"*Six*? Tucker, you've hardly slept at all."

He grunted as he laid his head on her shoulder.

"What on earth were you doing?"

"Studying the hundreds of pages of documents Ethan sent me."

She took his hand, lacing their fingers. "I'm sorry this is so hard on you. Is there something I can be doing?"

He shook his head as he brought their joined hands to his heart. "This works for me."

She rubbed her cheek against his soft hair. "How are things going? Do you feel like you're making some headway?"

"Not really. I've been tossing around a couple of theories that don't seem to take me anywhere."

"You'll get it. Why don't I—" Her cell phone rang, cutting her off. "Hold that thought. She leaned toward the side table and grabbed the phone. "Greta," she said as she glanced at the readout. "Hello?"

"Hi, Wren. I'm sorry to call so early."

"No worries. I'm up."

"I wanted to let you know I have two showings today, and one couple seems *very* interested. My gut's telling me we're going to move this house immediately."

Her heart sank. "That's wonderful."

"The little touchup to the exterior and a comforter for the master suite was all we needed. The inside is gorgeous, but you know that."

"Yes."

"All right. I'll let you know how things go. The eager couple has a three-thirty appointment. I'll call after we finish up."

"Sounds great. Thanks."

"Bye, honey."

"Bye." She hung up, struggling to suppress a sigh.

Tucker tilted his head, catching her eye. "Everything okay?"

"Yeah." She tried a smile. "That was my realtor. She thinks

we might have a buyer. She's very optimistic about this afternoon's showing. The couple's excited."

She could hardly stand the idea of anyone else living in her home, but her grim financial situation hadn't miraculously rectified itself in the last five days. "This is a good thing. A really good thing," she told herself as much as Tucker.

"Then why do you look so bummed?"

She shrugged. "I don't know. I'm not. The money will go a long way toward helping Patrick with some of his medical expenses and getting me settled in up in Santa Barbara."

"Wren, we can find a way to keep the house."

She shook her head, not even wanting to entertain an impossible idea. "No, I can't. I don't want to talk about this."

He held her gaze, then turned back to rest his head on her shoulder.

Her cell phone rang again.

"When did we wake up in Grand Central Station?" Tucker said.

She picked up the phone. "Los Angeles General." Her stomach knotted as she answered. "Hello?"

"Ms. Cooke?"

"Yes. Is everything all right with Patrick?" The line stayed silent, and she clutched her hand against Tuckers. "Hello?"

"Wren," a garbled voice said.

"Patrick?" Her eyes widened, instantly filling. "Patrick?"

"Wren," he said again.

"Oh my God." She'd been terrified she would never hear him speak again. "I miss you. I'm coming home to see you tomorrow."

"Wren," he repeated.

She swallowed the lump of emotion in her throat.

"Ms. Cooke, Patrick wanted to surprise you."

"Well he absolutely did. He said my name." Her lip wobbled.

"It's the first word he's spoken."

She closed her eyes, trying to keep her tears at bay. "So,

what does this mean?"

"That he certainly remembers you."

She grinned.

"Patrick is still improving every day. He's staying awake longer and working hard with his Occupational Therapist. The Speech and Language Pathologist will be in to observe him later today."

"Do the doctors—do the doctors have any idea of a long-term prognosis yet?"

"Well, honey, they were pretty sure he was going to be vegetative, but Patrick has different ideas. It's really hard to tell. We'll keep at his daily therapies and see where we go. Having you home will be a good thing. You'll be a great motivator. He loves hearing that you call to check on him every day."

"Good. Will you tell him I'm coming to see him as soon as I step off the plane? And tell him I love him, please."

"You bet. We'll see you soon, Ms. Cooke."

"Okay. Thank you for the call."

"Absolutely, honey."

Wren hung up, set the phone down, and pressed her lips firm against the rush of emotions wanting free.

"Sounds like some good news."

She nodded, unable to speak, as a tear fell down her cheek.

"Hey." Tucker sat up. "Hey," he said again as he turned and pulled her against him.

"He talked to me," she shuddered out. "He said my name."

"I know." He eased her back, looking her in the eyes. "That's damn good stuff."

"Yes, it is." Another tear fell, and she tried to turn away.

He forced her back to the mattress, weighing her down, covering her body with his, pulling her arms over her head, lacing their fingers. "Don't do that, Cooke."

She looked up into his face. "I hate crying," she sniffled.

"Yeah, I know."

"But I can't help it. I've been so scared. I wasn't sure he

would ever talk again or do much of anything. I'm so happy."

He planted a quick kiss on her lips. "This is big stuff."

"Really big." She tried to free her hand. "I need to wipe my cheeks."

He slid his thumb along the damp trails. "I can wipe away your tears."

And it felt good to let him. "Thanks."

"No problem."

She sniffed again. "I'm trying not to get my hopes up. I want Patrick to be who he was before all of this, but that might not happen."

"Sounds like he's got a lot of work to do, but he's making strides."

She smiled. "He certainly is."

"I'm sorry."

Her smile vanished into a frown as his tone grew serious. "For what?"

"For what Patrick's going through. For what you're going through."

"It's not your fault. I'm trying to remember it's not mine either. He's making progress. Five days ago, he was battling to survive. Today he's talking." She hugged him as the burst of excitement consumed her. "He said my *name*." She loosened her grip. "You're still coming with me to the hospital, right? I want Patrick to meet you."

"Yeah, I'll come."

"Good. Eye candy's always an excellent motivator." She sent him a playful wink.

He gave her a pained look. "Jesus, Cooke."

Laughing, she pressed her palms to his cheeks and pulled his face to hers, giving him a kiss. "There's nothing wrong with appreciating, no matter your preference. And Tucker, there's plenty to appreciate about you." She kissed him again as he tried to pull away. "Where are you going?"

"I have no idea."

She laughed harder, realizing he was completely embarrassed. "Mr. Campbell, you must know you're gorgeous."

"I don't really think about it."

"I do." She brushed a finger along his jaw. "A lot. Aren't I lucky you're all mine?"

"Getting possessive." He slid a strand of hair behind her ear.

"Definitely." She snagged his lip with her teeth.

"Are you telling me you only like me for my looks?"

"No." She skimmed her hands down his sides. "But they're an excellent bonus."

"You trying to get laid, Cooke?" He grinned.

She grinned back. "You're the detective. I'll let you figure it out."

He palmed her breasts, hardening her nipples, then traveled down, sliding his fingers under pajama bottoms and panties, invading her.

She arched, gasping as delicious tingles fluttered in her belly.

He kissed her neck and changed the pressure of his stroking, sending her reeling. "I'm going to go with my gut here and say you're definitely up for a roll in the sheets." He yanked her pants to her ankles, freed himself from his boxers, and entered her.

She gasped as he hissed out a breath and set a hurried pace. Skin grew damp and flesh slapped flesh as he rammed himself deep again and again.

"Tucker," she cried out, gripping his shoulders as he took her up and over with a quick flash of staggering heat.

He captured her mouth and thrust harder, emptying himself on a long grunt.

Their breath mingled as they stared at each other.

She slid the hair back from his forehead. "What was that?"

He shrugged. "You got me worked up."

"I guess so."

"Are you all right with that?"

"I'm pretty sure I didn't hate it."

He smiled. "Good."

"As much fun as we've just had, I should get up and shower."

He rolled off her and flopped to his back.

"Are you going to get some more rest?"

"Nah. I have stuff to do—phone calls to make."

"Do you think we might be able to go out for a little while?" She glanced at the window and the sunlight beyond. "The festival's still going on, then we could come back and take a nap."

He rolled to his side, looking at her. "We should probably stay in."

She barely suppressed a sigh at the thought of being cooped up again. "Okay."

He took her hand. "I wish I could throw caution to the wind and tell you yes, but it's better to stay close to the resort. We only have one more day."

"Of course. You're right." She pulled up her pants and got off the bed, looking toward the burgundy curtains.

"How about a compromise?"

She lifted her brow. "Let me guess, it involves shower sex."

He chuckled. "Not quite. I can't take you around town, but there's plenty of stuff to do right here at the resort. Why don't you pick something and we'll check it out."

Her mood immediately brightened. "I saw an arcade in the pamphlet, or there's the pool. I think there's a bowling alley too." She wanted to be busy doing something—at this point she hardly cared what it was. "We could get massages at the spa."

"You pick."

She wanted him to have fun too—the way they did the day they went tubing. "How about I kick your behind in the arcade, then show you how it's done at the bowling alley? Loser buys lunch, so don't forget your wallet."

He sent her one of his slow grins. "Definitely sounds like a challenge."

“Better believe it.”

He got out of bed and walked to where she stood. “Thanks for being cool with staying inside.”

“I don’t care whether we’re inside or out, just as long as we get out of this *room*.”

He pulled her against him, wrapping his arms at her waist. “I would give anything for this to be different.”

She studied the intensity in his eyes. Where was this coming from? “Of course you would. We both would. Tucker—”

His phone rang, cutting her off. “Why don’t you shower up? Then we’ll get out of here for a while.”

She nodded, still puzzled as he turned and headed toward the table to answer.

☙ Chapter Nineteen ❧

Wren released the ball and watched the dark pink orb roll down the middle of the lane. "Come on. Come on," she muttered as the ball stayed its course, then turned at the last second, landing in the gutter. "No! You've got to be *kidding* me." She whirled as Tucker muffled a snort. "Shut up."

"So close." Tucker held up his thumb and index finger an inch apart. "Maybe next time," he encouraged, then bit the inside of his cheek.

She narrowed her eyes in his direction, her competitive streak in full swing. He'd showered her with similar positive sentiments each time her ball did the same thing, which was *every* damn time. The score was 267 to zero. "Go bowl your damn ball so we can get out of here." She plunked herself on the bench, fuming. Tucker had kicked her butt throughout the day—air hockey, skee ball, pool. The list went on and on.

He stood. "You still up for lunch after this? You're buying, right?"

She glared. "It's a good thing I'm too much of a lady to get up and kick your ass. You might outweigh me by a good hundred pounds, but I swear I could take you right about now."

A slow grin spread across his gorgeous face. "You're a damn scary woman, Cooke."

She looked away, huffing, unwilling to be affected by his charm. "Do your thing already."

"So is that a yes to lunch or no?"

Her gaze whipped up to his, and she couldn't help but smile. "You're obnoxious."

"Just looking for a little clarification. I work best when I know what's going on."

She gave him the finger.

He burst out laughing and bent close to her face, capturing her cheeks in his hands. "I'm absolutely crazy about you."

She gripped his wrists, staring in his eyes as butterflies fluttered in her stomach. The feeling was mutual, even though he was pissing her off.

"Let me finish up this frame, then you can buy me something to eat."

She wrinkled her nose. "I guess a deal's a deal." She twisted his ear as he let her go.

"Ow!"

"Nobody likes a bragger," she smirked.

"Vicious." He walked away, rubbing the side of his head, picked up the black ball, and slid it down the lane. Ten pins knocked against the back, and he glanced at her, wiggling his brows.

And that was the end of that. Shaking her head, she looked down, hiding her smile. *Jerk.* Wren tugged off her borrowed socks and shoes and shoved her feet in her black flats.

Tucker joined her on the bench, saying nothing as he changed into his sneakers. "You ready?"

"Definitely. Where do you want to eat?"

"I'll let you pick."

"Winner's choice, and you were certainly the winner today." She swallowed the disappointment of annihilation as they dropped off their returns and Tucker pulled open the door for them.

"Aw, Cooke, you're a winner in my book." He tugged her

against him, wrapping his arm around her waist.

"Nobody likes a brownnoser either." She returned his embrace as they smiled at each other.

"How about the café? We could do soup and sandwiches."

"That sounds really good, actually."

"I agree." He wrapped her tighter, bringing her closer. "You know, you were a pretty good sport." He kissed the top of her head. "Kind of."

She smiled again as he grinned. "No, I wasn't. I hate losing."

"Huh, I couldn't tell."

She pinched his waist. "Despite losing every single game, I did have fun. It was so nice to get out and *do* something."

"I'm sorry about the festival. I know you wanted to go."

"This worked fine. And we stayed warm."

They walked past a swank bar and lounge that was closed until evening. "Beautiful décor. Hints of urban chic while staying true to the rest of the resort's rustic theme. I give the designer an A-plus."

"Definitely nice."

They entered the busy café and helped themselves to one of the booths with a spectacular view. A waitress immediately swooped in with menus.

"Good afternoon. I'm Mona. Can I get you something to drink?"

"Water, please," Wren said.

"I'll second that," Tucker added with a friendly smile.

Mona blinked at Tucker. "I'll, uh, I'll be right back."

Wren sent the pretty college-aged girl a wink, understanding Tucker's potent affect fully, then studied the menu. "So many choices." She flipped to the next page. "Everything sounds so good, but I think I'm going to have to go with the broccoli cheddar soup and a side salad." She glanced up when Tucker didn't respond.

The weary look was back as he stared out the window. She'd seen the tension and worry more than once throughout the morning as he scrutinized the people around them. Reaching over, she took his hand. "Hey, you, are you all right?"

"Yeah. Just taking in the view."

"You're worrying." She squeezed his fingers gently.

"Nah."

"I was under the impression we were safe here."

"We still have to be careful, but we're certainly better off here than at the house. There are video cameras all over the place and security on staff. If your stalker's hanging around, he knows that."

"And that's a good thing."

"Definitely. Video surveillance is always a deterrent."

"So what's on your mind, then?"

He held her gaze. "Nothing."

She nodded, knowing that wasn't true.

He opened the menu with his free hand. "Wow, hell of a selection."

She'd just said so moments ago, but he'd been lost in his own thoughts.

"The Club sounds good."

"Mmm." She didn't want to talk about sandwiches; she wanted him to tell her what was weighing so heavily on his mind.

Mona came back with two waters. "Are you ready to order?"

"You ready, Cooke?"

"Yes. I'll take the broccoli cheddar soup in the bread bowl and a small salad with oil and vinegar on the side."

"I'll grab a club on whole wheat and take the salad as well."

"I'll be back with your order."

"Thank you." Wren stared out at the majestic mountains and bright blue sky. Tomorrow she would be staring at palm trees and the Pacific, and everything would be different. She would officially begin the process of closing Cooke Interiors' doors, start packing and selling off her things, job searching, and slowly ease herself away from Tucker. A clean break was probably better, but they would go their own ways soon enough.

"What are you thinking about?"

"Home."

"Then why are you frowning?"

She looked from the window to Tucker. "I didn't know I was."

"Definitely frowning, Cooke." He pressed his finger between her brows. "Still are."

She shrugged. "There are a lot of changes coming."

"There doesn't have to be."

She ignored his comment. "Is the plane still set to leave at two tomorrow?"

"When I called them this morning, they said we were good to go." He slid his thumb over her knuckles. "What's really up?"

She jerked her shoulders in another shrug. "Nothing."

His brow rose.

She pulled her hand from his. "I guess I'm trying to figure out why I'm supposed to be an open book while you get to stay silent."

"What are you talking about?"

"You're eyes are troubled. Yesterday couldn't have been easy, yet you say nothing." She lowered her voice to a hissing whisper and leaned in as she glanced at the man and woman looking at her from the next table. "You get to wipe my tears and listen to my problems, but you handle yours alone."

"How can you say that? I've leaned on you plenty over the last few nights."

"That was then, this is now. You've been staring off all day and making small cryptic comments. The stuff with Staci...my stalker... This entire situation must be wearing." She shook her head. "Just never mind."

"No. Finish it up."

"I want you to confide in me the way I confide in you. I

want your trust, Tucker. I want you to trust in me the way I trust you. And not only when your troubles are so huge you're about to fall apart. I want to know about the big stuff and the little things."

"I do trust you, Cooke." Holding her gaze, he snagged her hand and gripped her fingers. "I *absolutely* do."

"Sometimes I'm not so sure."

"You want to know what I was thinking?"

"*Yes.*"

"I was thinking that I want all of this to be over. I want my sister's case put to rest. I want you to be able to walk down the street without looking over your shoulder."

She closed her eyes. "I want those things too. For both of us."

He got up and moved to her side of the booth, scooting in until their legs bumped. He raised her chin, staring into her eyes. "Understand me, Cooke, when I tell you there's no one I want more, no one I trust more than you. Got that?"

She nodded and kissed him, reveling in the ability to believe in what he said. "Me too."

"Good." He brushed his lips against hers. "I want to take you out tonight."

She blinked at the abrupt change in conversation. "You do?"

"Mmhm. It's our last night in Utah. We're both getting dressed up. I'm bringing you to the fancy little lounge down the hall."

She smiled at the idea. "Okay."

"Um, sorry to interrupt."

Wren pulled away as she and Tucker both looked at their waitress. "You're fine."

Mona put their meals down with several extra glances at Tucker.

"I'm actually going to move back to the other side."

"Oh," Mona slid his plate across the table. "Enjoy your lunch."

"Thanks." Tucker turned to Wren after Mona walked away and gave her another quick kiss. "We good here, Cooke?"

"Yes."

"Then let's eat." He went back to his side, picked up a quarter of his sandwich, and bit in. "Mmm. Good stuff."

Wren smiled as she blew on the creamy broccoli cheddar.

Tucker was taking another bite when his cell phone rang. He pulled his phone from the holder, glancing at the readout. "I've gotta take this."

"Be my guest." She took her first bite, savoring pure heaven.

"Campbell. Yeah. What'd you get? Are you sure?" Tucker steamed out a breath. "No. I thought I was onto something. I'll let you know if I do." He hung up and shoved his phone back in its holder.

Wren glanced up from her meal, covering Tucker's hand with her own as he looked out the window.

He met her gaze, giving her a small smile, and picked up his sandwich, taking another bite.

She gave his fingers a gentle squeeze, enjoying the contentment of their last cozy lunch in the Park City mountains.

Tucker slid his finger along Wren's naked shoulder as they sat huddled in the corner at the bar. She smelled like sin and looked even better in her sleeveless clinging dress, which stopped mid-thigh. Her impromptu stop-off at the resort's boutique had been well worth the half-hour he'd followed her around as she perused her options, ultimately choosing the sapphire blue frock on the discount rack. And she'd done something fancy with her hair, twisting it all up so that her long, graceful neck was exposed.

He tucked a stray strand of wavy black behind her ear, bumping his Glock concealed beneath his sport coat. With every brush of his arm against his weapon, he remembered

Wren was still a target and their nightmare wasn't over. He'd struggled to stay in the moment throughout the day, as he did now, while her pretty gray eyes held his and she fiddled with his fingers.

"This was a perfect idea. He's very good." She gestured to the man playing the piano across the elegantly decorated space.

"Yeah, he's not bad." During the two hours they'd sipped wine—or beer in his case—and nibbled at the sampler of hors d'oeuvres, he'd hardly paid attention to the notes flowing from the glistening baby grand. Candles glowed around them, and Wren smiled into his eyes, yet his mind stubbornly wandered to his tattered theories and phone calls with Ethan. JT Cartwright wasn't their man. Flight records and credit card trails proved he'd been spending his time in Vegas or Los Angeles, working on a case. So now what? He and Wren were leaving in less than twenty-four hours, and they were no closer to a resolution. He wanted this over so she could move on with her life—so they could move on with *their* lives. Wren had certainly relaxed where their relationship was concerned, but she was expecting an ending once they landed in California. He had no intentions of saying goodbye. Eventually she would figure that out.

"...beer?" Wren's brow rose as she stared at him.

"What was that?"

"I said I'm going to order one more half glass of wine. Do you want another beer?"

"No, this is good." He scanned the room as he did periodically, studying faces, making certain the lounge guests were more preoccupied with their dates and dinner than with Wren.

"...up. Hello?"

His gaze whipped to hers. "I'm sorry?"

"What is up with you?"

"Nothing."

"Do you want to go back to the room?"

He wanted to study his diagrams and play everything through again. "Do you?"

"Not really."

"Then we'll stay."

A bartender he hadn't seen before came from the kitchen, carrying plates. He set the food down in front of two guests, wandered down the long bar, stopping along the way to pour several draughts and talk with a few other patrons. Tucker frowned, trying to place him. He knew the clean-cut blonde. The man turned and their eyes met. Tucker grinned. "Nick Pellerin."

"Well what do you know? Tucker Campbell."

Tucker stuck out his hand. "How the hell are you, man?"

Nick grabbed hold, shaking firmly. "Not too bad. Not too bad."

He and Nick had played many soccer, baseball, and flag football games during their summers in Utah. "Wren, this is Nick. Nick, Wren. He and I go way back."

She smiled and shook his hand. "Nice to meet you."

"You too." He gave her a friendly wink, then turned his attention to Tucker. "So what brings you back this way? You still in California?"

"Can't imagine living any place else."

"It's like a Park City reunion around here. Everybody's making their way back to the old stomping grounds. I saw Jasmine and her husband last month. I guess they live in Florida now. Then I ran into Johnny Simmons a couple weeks ago and again the other night. I think they're living in Los Angeles."

"Jonathan and Lois Simmons?" Wren piped up.

"Yeah, I think that's his wife's name." Nick poured Wren another glass of wine, setting the stem on a fresh napkin.

"It's a small world. I decorated their home about six months ago. Super people."

Tucker's stomach clutched. Johnny Simmons was *not* a super person. He'd been a cocky little asshole for as long as they'd been acquainted. Their rivalry had worsened with every summer that passed. He and Johnny had exchanged blows the summer before Staci died, and JT had joined in.

Cartwright had despised Johnny too. Their dislike for one another had turned brutal the summer of Staci's death. JT had never mentioned why he detested the creepy bastard, but Johnny and JT had definitely loathed one another.

Tucker gripped his pint glass as several dots lined up. He had known Johnny growing up, and Wren knew him now. The coincidence was too huge to dismiss.

"So what are you doing now, Tuck-Man?"

"Uh, I'm a bodyguard. I work for Wren's brother."

Nick nodded. "I could see that."

He itched to pull out his phone and call Ethan, but wrapped his arm around Wren's shoulders instead, trying to keep up with the conversation. "You and Angie still together?"

"Absolutely. We have our second baby on the way. I'm picking up a few hours here a couple nights a week with Christmas coming. Teaching doesn't exactly provide the life of luxury." The small pager on Nick's belt buzzed. "Got an order up. I'll leave you guys to enjoy the rest of your evening. Nice to see you again, Tucker. Nice to meet you, Wren."

"You too," they said at the same time.

Wren leaned into his chest. "He seems nice."

"We had some good times."

"I recognized him from several of the pictures in Staci's room."

"We all hung out. He's a local. His dad owns one of the ski shops in town."

"I'm sure they're doing a brisk business with all of this snow."

"I don't doubt it." He slid a finger down her neck. "So, you know Johnny Simmons."

"Yes, I guess I do. He and his wife are very sweet, and their living room is *gorgeous*." She smiled teasingly.

He returned it as his mind raced. "How long did you work on their place?"

"Mmm, about four or five weeks. We knocked out a wall, added more livable space, laid new floors, painted and refurnished."

"Sounds nice. What's Johnny doing now?"

"He and Lois own several upscale coffee shops in the Los Angeles area."

His brow shot up. Of all the professions he'd imagined Johnny doing—drug trafficking, pimping, hit man—selling fancy coffee hadn't made the list. "Seriously?"

She bumped his arm. "Yes, seriously. I didn't notice Jonathan in any of your sister's photographs."

"We didn't get along."

"Oh."

Tucker shrugged. "He was a prick."

It was Wren's turn to raise her brow. "Well, let me assure you, he's changed his ways. He's very much a family man." She kissed his cheek.

He doubted it, but kept his mouth shut.

The music stopped and Wren glanced toward the baby grand. "The pianist is taking a break. I want to go over and put a tip in his jar." She scooted off her leather stool.

"Stay where I can see you."

"Will do." She wandered over to the older man talking to several guests.

Tucker didn't waste any time yanking his phone from its holder. He hit Ethan on the speed dial and waited.

"Cooke."

"I want you to run Jonathan Simmons. Father's name is Markus. Mother's name is Eloise. They live in Aurora, Colorado—or did. I'm assuming they're still married. I knew him as a kid—fucking hated his guts as much as he hated mine. I just figured out he knows Wren."

"I'll run him."

He glanced toward the kitchen door as Nick came out.

"Let me give you another name. Nicholas Pellerin." He felt like a dick even thinking it, but better safe than sorry. "Father Lucas Pellerin. Mother is Krissy. They're locals. I don't think there's anything here, but check it out anyway."

"I'll get on it."

He looked at Wren, chatting with the man in his tuxedo. She sent Tucker a smile across the room, and his heart beat a little faster. "Thanks, man." He shoved his phone away and smiled back. What the hell was he doing? The gorgeous woman talking to the pianist was *his,* and he wasn't paying her a damn bit of attention. That would end now. There was nothing more he could do until Ethan ran the names. The rest of the night belonged to Wren.

She made her way back to him, stopping next to his chair.

He skimmed his fingers along her jaw. "Do you want your wine?"

"No. I want you."

The piano started playing. "Wanna dance?"

"In our room."

Desire curled tight in his stomach as he stood and took her hand. "Let's go."

They walked to the elevator, got in, and started up to the fifth floor. Wren's perfume crowded his nose as her thumb slid along his in slow, gentle strokes, driving him crazy. She smiled up at him and he reached over, pressing the red button, halting the car in its tracks.

Wren grabbed hold of his arm as the elevator jerked. "What are you doing?"

He wasn't exactly sure as he turned, taking her face in his hands and brushed his thumbs over her cheeks. "Did I tell you how beautiful you look tonight?"

She rested her hands on his waist. "Yes, when I stepped from the bathroom."

"Once isn't enough. You're beautiful, Wren." He captured her lips, gently, tenderly, enjoying her as he should have all along.

Her fingers slid up to his wrists, holding tight, as her mouth gave against his.

He deepened the kiss slowly, savoring her sweet taste, her scent, her petite body pressed to his.

"Wren," he murmured against her lips.

She eased back, staring into his eyes. "You have to let the elevator go."

"I know." He kissed her once more, undone by the swift wave of love moving through him. He wanted to tell her, wasn't sure how much longer he could wait. Instead, he took a step back and sent the car up.

"Thank you for tonight." She pulled his arm around her shoulders, twining their fingers, and pressed her lips to his knuckles.

"Oh we're not finished." If he couldn't tell her he loved her, he was going to show her.

She smiled. "Okay, then thank you for tonight, so far." She bit her lip. "You make me happy, Tucker. I didn't think I would ever be truly happy."

What could he possibly say? The door slid open, and he came to attention. "Come on."

They stepped out and started down the hall. Tucker shook his head, barely suppressing a sigh. The cop on door duty was asleep in his chair.

"Is he *sleeping*?"

"That's what it looks like to me."

"Some guard."

"That's why you've got me, baby." He grinned.

She chuckled.

His smile vanished as they stepped closer and he read the ugly red scrawl on the wall at the officer's side. SC+AB+CW+WC=THE SINS OF TUCKER CAMPBELL. "Shit." His pulse kicked into high gear as he yanked his gun from the holster. "I *knew* this was right. I knew this was exactly fucking right."

"Knew what? What are you talking about?" Then she saw

it. "Oh, God."

He pulled her closer and turned them so he could see down both sides of the hallway. "I want you to check his pulse—quickly, then I want you inside."

She nodded.

They stopped in front of the cop, and Wren pressed trembling fingers to the side of his neck. "He's—he's alive. There's blood in his hair and down the back of his neck."

"I know. I see it. We'll get him some help in a minute." He swiped the keycard, and pushed them through the door, closing it behind him. "Stay right here until I sweep the rooms." He yanked open the closet door in the small kitchen area, gun pointed, then did the same at every corner or space large enough to hide someone who didn't belong. He threw the latch to the glass sliders, slid the door open, barely noticing the cool slap of wind against his face as he swept the balcony. He came back in, locking up behind him. "We're good," he said as he turned, pulling his phone from its holder, looking at Wren. She stared at the floor, gripping her arms across her chest. "I'm going to phone this in, and I need to help the officer in the hall."

"Fine," she answered dully.

"I want you to call down to the front desk. Tell them to get security up here right away. Throw the slide over the door. Don't open for anyone unless it's me—not security, not another cop."

She picked up the resort phone, glancing in his direction with hurt and anger radiating in her eyes.

He took a step toward the door and stopped. "Wren, what?"

"Go help the police officer. He's bleeding." She opened a drawer and shoved a clean towel in his hand.

He wanted to stay until she told him why she was staring at him like that, but questions would have to wait. He opened the door, gun drawn, and stepped into the hall. No one was there. He dialed 911, looking at Wren once more as she shut him out and threw the latch in place. He glanced at the cryptic message as he pressed the towel to the officer's head wound, worrying about what all of this meant for him and the woman on the other side of the wall.

☙ Chapter Twenty ❧

WREN LAY AMONG THE PILLOWS SNUGGLED IN HER yoga pants and Tucker's huge gray sweatshirt, trying to stay warm. A cold slap of realization struck her as she'd read the ugly message scrawled along the hallway wall a couple hours ago; she'd been freezing ever since. Another wave of goose bumps puckered her skin as she thought of the bold red letters and the gravity of their meaning. She grabbed the soft navy fleece from the foot of the bed, covering her legs as Greta chattered away, struggling to pay attention.

"They wanted tonight to think on it, but I'm confident we'll have an offer tomorrow."

She closed her eyes, swallowing another blow. "That's great, really great."

The front door shut, and Wren opened her eyes as Tucker stepped in the bedroom. He'd been in and out of their suite, bringing the detectives with him. They'd hovered over his laptop or flipped through his notebook on the table, discussing Tucker's theories at length. He'd glanced her way numerous times from his seat in the tiny kitchenette, but they hadn't spoken since she'd locked him out to deal with the injured officer.

"I overheard them talking," Greta continued. "It sounds

like they're going to want to move on this fairly quickly."

She plucked at the blanket, her movements jerky as she felt Tucker's gaze boring into the top of her head. "Do you have an idea of what they're thinking of for a closing date?"

"I'm not sure, honey, but I'll let you know as soon as I do."

She darted a glance at Tucker, and her heart rate kicked up several notches as it ached. "Agree to whatever they want," she said in a rush. "The sooner, the better. I can be out in a week—two at the latest." She didn't want to leave her home, but as she peeked at Tucker from under her lashes, she knew she couldn't stay in Los Angeles any longer. The faster she got out and moved on with her life, the more likely she was to forget him.

"Honey, I don't know if we can move that quickly."

"Regardless, the house will be vacant as of December first, if not before. I'll be heading to Santa Barbara as soon as possible."

"All right. We'll get everything worked out."

She needed *something* to work out—desperately. "Thank you, Greta. Thanks for the call."

"You're welcome."

Wren hung up and fiddled with her phone, borrowing time to gather herself. Tears floated too close to the surface, as they had since the cryptic message on the wall changed everything. She'd had plenty of time to piece the instances of the last few weeks together while the police dusted for fingerprints and murmured back and forth. Staci's murder, Alyssa and Chloe's, her stalking, all of it circled back to Tucker. And he'd known.

"Wren."

She looked up, meeting his gaze as he leaned against the doorframe. He'd long since ditched the sport coat and now had his sleeves rolled halfway up his forearms, his holster and weapon still in place.

"We need to talk."

What could they possibly say? Tucker had made a fool of

her. She'd trusted him, and he'd lied. "I don't think there's much to say." She picked up the remote at her side and turned on the television, flipping from station to station, attempting to relieve her nervous energy, waiting for him to go away.

He walked over and snatched the remote from her hand, pressing the power button.

Swallowing, she sat up as the room fell silent and he settled himself on the corner of the bed.

"We need to talk," he repeated.

Wafts of his cologne tickled her nose as she played trembling fingers through the fringes of the soft blanket. "It's been a long day. Let's just call it a night so we can pack up and get out of here tomorrow." She'd never been so ready to leave.

"Cooke—" He grasped her ankle, tracing his thumb along her skin.

A rush of betrayal consumed her as he held her gaze and touched her as if he still had the right. She pulled free of his grip. "When were you going to tell me? When were you going to share that this whole thing was never about me?"

Clenching his jaw, he sighed. "I didn't want to say anything until I was sure."

"Did you think I wouldn't put it together, Detective?" She looked down, swallowing over the tight ball of emotion in her throat. "What happened to 'full disclosure?'"

"I didn't—"

"What happened to 'There's no one I want more, no one I trust more, Cooke,'" she scoffed, attempting to disguise the tremor in her voice.

"There *is* no one I want or trust more."

"How can you look me in the eye and say that?" More than finished, she pulled the fleece back and crawled across the mattress on her way to the bathroom—the only place she could escape.

"Wait." He reached over, snagging her elbow.

"Let me go." She tugged against his grip.

He did, but then hurried around to her side of the bed, standing in her way before she took two steps. "Not until we figure this out."

"There's not much to figure out." She breathed him in as she attempted to skirt around him. "We're going home tomorrow. I'm heading to Santa Barbara as planned, and you're not. Story over. The end."

"Just listen for a minute."

"I'm all listened out."

He stepped to the left as she did, blocking her way.

She huffed out a frustrated breath as they both moved to the right. "Damn it, Tucker."

"Wren—"

"We're finished here." She tried shoving past him, afraid she was going to burst into tears.

"Like hell." He grabbed her wrists, locking them behind her back, pressing their bodies together. "We're far from it."

She instantly stilled as he held her close.

"Please hear me out."

She stared into his eyes, desperately wanting him to tell her this was all some big mistake and that he hadn't purposely been keeping her in the dark. "How long have you known Staci's killer and my stalker are one in the same?"

"Since yesterday morning. Or I was running with the idea, anyway."

"Since yesterday morning," she repeated as the sinking in her stomach worsened. "So when I asked you what you were thinking about at lunch today, and you told me you wanted Staci's case solved and for all of this to be over, you kind of skimmed over a major point. I guess Staci's killer and my stalker being the same person wasn't important enough to share, even though it was clearly weighing heavy on your mind and very much affects my life."

"It's not that simple."

"Sure it is. It's exactly that simple. You lied, Tucker, right to my face. And worse, you followed up your evasions with your whole 'trust' spiel."

"Wren, I—"

"I let myself believe there was something real here." She pulled out of his grip and took a step back. "For one stupid second, I thought there might be something to this whole relationship thing, but then I saw the writing on the wall—literally—and understood you're no different than anybody else. A few pretty words here, a deep, meaningful look there. Those damn slow smiles of yours. You wanted what you wanted, and you got it." She laughed humorlessly, shaking her head as she stared down, chastising herself for her utter foolishness. "I sure as hell didn't put up much of a fight in the bedroom."

He gripped her chin, forcing her to look him in the eyes. "Don't go there. Don't pull that bullshit card on me."

"Bullshit card? No, I don't think so."

"There's more here than sex, and you know it."

"I wanted what... Ethan and Sarah..." she stopped before she humiliated herself any further.

"You want what Ethan and Sarah have, it's yours, but the thing is, I don't. I want what we have. We're pretty damn good together, Cooke."

"I thought so too, but then tonight happened, and I realized there's nothing here at all." Her heart crumbled in a way she never knew it could.

"*Everything's* here." He held her tighter. "You and me. This is everything."

"No." She shook her head adamantly. "You're making this worse. Just leave it where it is."

"I don't want to leave it where it is. I love you, Cooke."

Her eyes grew wide as the breath backed up in her throat. "Don't say that." She took a step back as jitters of panic set in. "Don't you say that."

"I do, Wren. I'm so far past in love with you."

"Stop." She turned away, pressing unsteady fingers to her trembling lips, utterly devastated, steeping in confusion.

He turned her to face him, gently this time, cupping her cheeks in his hands. "I love you."

She closed her eyes, hating herself for wanting to throw her arms around him and tell him she loved him too. "I can't do this." A tear fell, despite her efforts to keep them at bay. "I don't *want* to do this. You can't lie and break promises, then expect me to rush into your arms. I'm not that person. I won't be that person. Not for you or anyone else."

"I didn't lie—or not intentionally. I wanted the facts before I had to tell you that the man who killed my sister and ruined your life did so because of me. I was afraid you would walk away when you understood that your business, your house, Patrick's injuries are all my fault."

"Nothing that man has done is your fault. I could never be upset with you for some twisted person's crazy actions, but *yours* have hurt me, Tucker. You didn't respect me enough to confide in me your ideas, no matter how absurd you thought they were. You didn't have faith that even if the worst were true, I would stand by you. Those things—confidence, respect, faith, and trust—that's what a relationship is built on. That's all I've ever wanted; that's what I thought we had."

"I'm sorry, Wren." He took her hand, pressing her palm to his heart. "I didn't see it that way. I should have, but I didn't. I'm sorry," he repeated.

"It's not okay. I gave you everything, Tucker, everything I was never able to give anyone else, and you've thrown it in my face. I won't do it again. I can't." She took her hand from his and stepped away as another tear fell. "For the remainder of tonight and tomorrow, I want you to stay away from me. When we get back to Los Angeles, I want you to bring me to Patrick and wait for Hunter or Austin or whoever Ethan can get to cover me, then I want you to go away."

"Wren, please."

Shaking her head, she took another step back. "I believed in you, Tucker. I wanted it all. *You* made me want everything. Damn you for that." She shut herself in the bathroom, locking herself in the only place she could go to get away from his devastated eyes. She sat down on the toilet lid and let the tears pour down her cheeks.

Tucker sat on the bench in the kitchenette, twisting his half-empty beer bottle round and round on the table. It was tempting to tip the winter lager back, drain it, then grab the assortment of hard liquors from the minibar and drink until he couldn't feel the pain anymore, but he stayed where he was, staring at the wet imprints the glass made on the dark, smooth wood.

I believed in you, Tucker. You made me want everything. Damn you for that. He dropped his forehead in his hands, smothering in the heavy weight of regret as Wren's words echoed in his head over and over. He couldn't stop thinking of her wrecked gray eyes or the tears dripping down her cheeks as she backed her way to the bathroom.

He clenched his jaw, remembering the deafening silence after the door snapped closed, the blast of water in the tub, drowning out the worst of her sobs. It had taken every ounce of willpower not to barge in and make her listen to him, but she'd made it clear she was finished with the conversation—and with him.

He rubbed his eyes with the edges of his palms, still trying to figure out how everything had gone so damn *wrong*. He'd never meant for things to end this way. Hell, they were never supposed to have ended at all. They were supposed to go back to California, figure out who was destroying their lives, get married, and eventually do the whole kid thing. He wanted that more than anything, for Wren to be his wife and the mother of his children, but it didn't look like that was going to happen.

Tucker sank further on the seat and rested his head against the wall. He never meant to lie, not even by omission. He'd wanted the facts straight before he told her. That's how he worked—gather information, make it all make sense, and move forward. If Wren only understood that his approach had nothing to do with secrets or a lack of trust and everything to do with habits long ingrained. But she would never see it that way. As far as she was concerned, he'd been caught in a lie and his procedures were an excuse to deceive.

Wren had no tolerance for such misunderstandings, and he couldn't necessarily blame her. She'd grown up watching two masters play with marriage and deception. He never wanted to pummel Grant and Rene Cooke more than he did right now. Their lifetime of selfish, pathetic behaviors had destroyed a piece of their daughter, making a foundation of trust nearly impossible to build. He glanced at the door, understanding that any gains he and Wren had made were gone—more than likely for good. He'd had her. Wren had been his, completely, and he'd done a fine job of forgetting he still needed to take care. Despite her strength, there was a vulnerable woman beneath, waiting to be hurt.

The bedroom door opened, and his gaze flew to Wren's tear-swollen eyes and blotchy cheeks as she tossed his pillow and a blanket to the floor and closed herself back in the room without looking at him. His heart physically ached as he stood and walked to the door, placing his hand on the knob. All he had to do is twist, step in, and alienate her further by bugging her when she'd had enough.

Sighing, he grabbed the bedding and chucked it into one of the chairs, instead of punching the wall like he craved. The small jolt sent the silver disk Detective Rogers had slipped him to the floor. Reaching down, he picked it up, glanced at the bedroom door again, then plunked his ass back on the bench. If groveling wasn't an option, he might as well work and figure out who the fuck was destroying his life.

He pulled the CD from the clear sleeve and slid it home. Seconds later, the fifth-floor hallway popped up. He fast-forwarded through the first twenty minutes, watching the fifty-something cop sleep in the chair next to their door. "Didn't exactly make it hard for him now did you?" he muttered and pulled another sip from his bottle. The camera suddenly tipped up, showcasing a view of the coffered ceiling. One hundred and twenty seconds ticked by in the right hand corner of the screen, then the camera flipped down and refocused on the officer appearing to nap as he had two minutes ago. Tucker froze the shot, scrutinizing the wall to the right of the cop. It was impossible to see the message from the angle the camera faced.

Jotting down a note, he paused as the footage abruptly cut to the stairwell. A hunched man in a black winter hat and baggy jacket hustled down five flights of stairs and out a side entrance. His face was completely concealed and his build hard to estimate due to the bulk of his outfit. The cameras caught sight of him in the parking lot before he simply vanished into the dark.

Tucker studied the footage more than a dozen times, trying to find anything they could use, but the bastard didn't make one fucking mistake. He looked at the times he'd written down and where their mystery man had been in regards to him and Wren. They had exited the elevator mere moments after the camera had been flipped back into place. What if he hadn't been compelled to stop the elevator car? What if he and Wren hadn't shared a kiss? A chill shot down his spine as he thought of what could have happened had fate finally brought them all face to face.

The bed creaked, and Tucker looked to the door, watching the blue flickers of the television reflecting in the dim light beneath the crack, listening to the sitcom's canned laughter. Wren was probably snuggled under the sheets, dozing as she usually did this time of night. He gritted his teeth, physically craving to be with her. The idea of never holding her close again while he fell asleep stole his breath. The wave of mourning was no different than what he felt when he thought of Staci.

His phone rang, and he snapped up the merciful distraction. "Campbell."

"I ran Nick Pellerin. He's clean," Ethan said.

"Yeah, I know. We had a little action here tonight. Cops left about an hour ago."

"What happened?"

"Our guy made it to the fifth floor, knocked out the sleeping cop at our door, and left me a message—SC+AB+CW+W-C=THE SINS OF TUCKER CAMPBELL." He gripped his phone tighter. "I knew this was about me."

"I have to admit, I thought it was a stretch. I'm sorry I doubted you."

"I doubted myself."

"Is Wren okay?"

"Yeah, he was gone by the time we got up here."

"What about you? How're you handling this?"

"Some fucker tortured my sister and now he's after Wren. I'll let you decide." He huffed out a breath and closed his eyes. "Sorry."

"Don't worry about it. This is a lot of shit to be dealing with. What can I do to help?"

"I have no idea." He rubbed at the back of his neck as the television was powered off and Wren's room grew dark. "Ethan, I need to request a change of assignment. There should probably be someone waiting to take over when we land tomorrow."

The line stayed silent.

"Look, I know—"

"I'm trying to keep the big brother card in check, Campbell. I'm trying really fucking hard not to tell you to kiss my ass."

"Save your breath. Wren already took care of that. Let me make it clear that *Wren* wants the change, not me."

"What the hell did you do?"

"I didn't tell her about my connection to her stalker. She figured it out when she saw the writing on the wall. She thinks I lied."

Ethan sighed.

"It'll probably be easier all the way around if you switch things up. I'll cover someone else's duty and they can take over Wren."

"Is this what you want?"

"I already told you it's not. What did you get on Simmons?" He wasn't about to discuss his relationship with Wren, or lack thereof, with Ethan.

There was another long pause before Ethan spoke. "So far I'm not finding much. He travels a lot for business—all over the western US. I found record of one flight from LA to Salt Lake City recently, but everything else has been to Seattle and Northern California."

He sat up straighter. "Nick Pellerin said Simmons had been here at least twice."

"I've only found record of one flight there and back. He brought his wife. He could have driven the other time. I'll take a look at his credit card trails."

"What else?"

"He had a couple of brushes with the law the summer after Staci died—petty shit—shoplifting, vandalism, nothing hinting at a serial killer in disguise."

"Little punk bastard." Tucker picked up his beer and took a deep swallow.

"I'm about finished digging through his high school years. I didn't realize he and JT Cartwright spent some of their freshman year at the same prep school."

"Son of a bitch." He set his bottle down with a snap. "I forgot about that. I can't believe I forgot about that. JT never liked Johnny, but after that year, he despised him. He never did say why."

"Cartwright didn't return from spring break to finish out the second semester. His grades had slipped some, but I didn't see any infractions involving the two. Looks like Cartwright's father is alumni and still a huge supporter, even after they started sending JT to the private school in Beverly Hills."

"I guess not everyone's cut out for boarding school."

"Guess not. I'll finish running Simmons and get back to you in the morning."

"Sounds good."

"And I'll look into the reassignment."

He didn't want tomorrow to be the end. "Thanks."

"Unless you don't want me to."

"Wren does."

"You're putting me in a hell of a spot."

"She's your sister, Cooke. I get that. There are no hard feelings for doing what you need to do."

"I'll talk to you in the morning."

"Bye." Tucker hung up and drained the rest of his beverage. Simmons and Cartwright had gone to school together. How the hell did he forget a detail like that? What else had he forgotten over the years? It was time to find out. He reached for his wallet and pulled out the business card JT had given him several weeks ago. He dialed the personal line scribbled on the back.

"Hello?"

"JT, it's Tucker Campbell."

"Tucker. How are you?"

"Not too bad. I'm sorry to call so late."

"No problem. I've been burning the midnight oil lately—big case coming up next week."

Tucker winced, feeling instantly guilty for assuming his old friend was somehow mixed up in this mess. "I'll keep this quick."

"Don't worry about it."

"Thanks. So, I've been looking into Staci's case. I've reopened it, informally."

"Wow, I'm sorry. That must be hard."

"Not knowing what happened hasn't been easy, but I'm hoping this time around we might be able to find some answers. I'm looking at Staci's case from a new angle and may have come up with a few leads. I thought you might be able to help me out."

"Yeah, sure, whatever I can do."

Time to cut to the chase. "I'm looking at Johnny Simmons as a person of interest."

"You think Johnny Simmons killed Staci?"

"I'm playing with ideas here, and he's one of them."

"Holy shit, Tucker. I know the guy's a bastard but that's really messed up."

"It's definitely a bit farfetched, but I ran into Nick Pellerin tonight. He said he's bumped into Johnny a couple of times recently, and it got me thinking."

"Nick Pellerin? Are you in Park City?"

"Yeah, I have been for a few weeks. I brought Wren here hoping things would settle down."

JT sighed. "Wren. I feel awful about Patrick and the lawsuit. I tried to talk to my mother, but she won't listen."

"It's not your fault, man."

"Yeah, but it's not Wren's either. I'll try again after Dad and I get this case wrapped up."

"I'm sure Wren will appreciate it."

"Sorry to get off topic. What did you want to ask me about Johnny?"

Tucker picked up his pen, running the cheap plastic through his fingers. "You and Staci spent a lot of time together—with and without me. Did Simmons ever give her any trouble when I wasn't around? Threaten her or anything like that?"

"Not that I can think of off the top of my head. Simmons pretty much stayed away from me, and vice versa. He never came around Staci when I was there at least."

This wasn't getting him anywhere. "You and Johnny both went to that prep school in Denver, right?"

"Yeah, for a little while. I didn't like it, and my mother hated me being so far away, so I decided not to go back after

Spring Break."

"Did anything happen between you and Johnny while you were there?"

"No."

"I remember some pretty bad blood the last summer we were all together."

"No one likes a dick."

"Can't argue with you there." JT wasn't going to be able to help him after all. "I guess I'm looking at this from the wrong angle. I'll let you get to work."

"I'd still like to buy you a beer sometime."

He and JT had been pretty good friends back in the day. Grabbing a drink together didn't have to be about Staci or the past. "I'll be back in LA in the next couple days. I'll give you a call."

"I'm in Vegas until the end of the week finishing up a few depositions."

He clicked and unclicked his pen. "I can get seats to the Lakers if you want to catch a game. We pull duty for a few of the players."

"You've got a deal. Let me wrap up stuff around here and we'll make something happen."

"Thanks, man."

"Wish I could be more help."

He shrugged, despite the frustration. "If it doesn't play, it doesn't play."

"I hope something turns up. We'll be in touch."

"Later." Tucker hung up. Another dead end. He scrubbed his hands over his face. Johnny Simmons more than likely had nothing to do with Staci's death. Petty crimes and teenage rivalries were a long way from rape and murder. And by Wren's account, Johnny, or Jonathan in this case, was a stand-up guy with a wife, kids, and several successful coffee shops. Was he grasping at straws?

He added a question mark next to Johnny's name, unwilling to fully dismiss him, despite Wren's glowing reviews and

JT's surprise. There were still inconsistencies in his whereabouts. Nick had seen Johnny twice, and there was only one record of a flight. Why would he drive to Park City when it was so much faster to fly?

He pulled his laptop closer, searching through the Park City PD files, stopping when he came across the signed statement of Markus and Eloise Simmons, attesting to the fact that their son Jonathan had been home and in their presence the night Staci died. He'd said goodnight to his parents at eleven and had gone up to bed.

Mr. and Mrs. Simmons had always been nice enough people, but that didn't mean they wouldn't lie for their son or that Johnny couldn't have left without his parents' knowledge. Sneaking out, committing murder, and crawling back into bed was certainly a possibility. Stifling a yawn, he circled the question mark. There was nothing more he could do tonight. He needed to try to get some sleep. Tomorrow was bound to be a long day. He closed his laptop and stood as his phone rang. "Campbell."

"Tucker, it's JT. Sorry to bother you."

Tucker sat again. "No problem. What's up?"

"I've been sitting here thinking about our conversation, and something clicked. I almost don't want to say anything because I can't be sure it means anything."

The skin prickled along the back of his neck. "Go for it anyway."

"The summer after Staci died, I went up to your house on the first anniversary... That probably sounds weird..."

"No, you two were close."

"I still miss her."

Tucker clenched his fist with the fresh wave of pain. "We all do."

"I'd been thinking about her and how she always liked to sit in the hot tub and look at the stars. I started around back, half expecting to see her lounging around, and I bumped into Simmons. I think he might've been looking in her bedroom window, but I can't be sure. I asked him what he was doing. He gave me this little smirk and said he was checking out the view, then he walked off. I was going to ask him what he meant when I saw him at the next ballgame—figured he was making some sort of sick joke to piss me off, but his family packed up and left a few days later. I never did see him again, and I forgot about it."

Tucker's heart raced, and his hands began to tremble as JT spoke. "Simmons was at my place the summer after Staci died?"

"Yes."

Son of a bitch. It wasn't uncommon for serial murderers to go back to a kill site.

"Like I said, I don't know if this means anything, but now that I think about it, it seems like it does."

"I'll get right on this. Thanks, JT."

"I wish I had thought of this sooner."

So did he, but now was what they had. "No, this is good stuff. I'll let you go." He hung up and dialed Ethan.

"Cooke."

"It's Simmons. I just got off the phone with JT. He remembered seeing Johnny lurking around Staci's bedroom window the summer after she died. He's pretty sure it was on the first anniversary of her death. He made some comment about checking out the view. I want surveillance on his house and confirmation of his whereabouts for the last twenty-four hours and every night since Wren's problems started. I'll call Owens and Rogers here in town, but we're doing this ourselves. I'll be damned if anyone is going to screw this up."

"Almost everyone is in the field, except for Jerrod. Abby's staying with Jackson and Alexa tonight."

"Perfect." He couldn't have asked for anyone better. Jerrod was a former US Marshal; if anyone could track Simmons down and keep him in his sights, it was the newest member of their team.

"I'll call him and have him park his ass outside Simmons' house until we get some of this figured out."

"Thanks. I'm calling Rogers."

"I'll take care of Owens on this end."

"Sounds good." He hung up before Ethan could respond and immediately dialed the detective.

"Detective Rogers."

"Rogers, it's Tucker Campbell. I've come across some new information in Staci's case. I think we may have a person of interest—name is Jonathan Simmons. He currently resides in Los Angeles, but his family had a home here in Park City at the time of Staci's death."

"Name sounds familiar."

"You'll find it in your files. He and I didn't get along. His family was questioned briefly after my sister's death, but nothing came of it. I spoke with JT Cartwright just now—another former summer resident of the area and friend of Staci's and mine. JT said he spotted Simmons lurking around our property on the first anniversary of Staci's death."

"I don't remember seeing anything about that."

"He never reported the incident. It bothered him some, but he forgot about it. If we want to connect past and present and go with the theory we discussed earlier, he still fits. Wren decorated his family home approximately six months ago in LA. Another childhood friend of mine, Nick Pellerin, said he spotted Johnny in town on more than one occasion recently. We have several points that add up and a motive."

"I'll call Franklin into the station."

"If it is Simmons, he's either still in the area or on a flight putting some distance between himself and Park City."

"We'll get an APB out on him right away, check with the airport and local hotels here and in Salt Lake. I'll also contact Detective Owens out in Los Angeles."

"Sounds good. I'd like to go up to the house tomorrow—one last time before Wren and I head home. I want to piece all of this out and make sure it fits. It might be best if you and

Franklin come along. We'll all be on the same page should there be any follow-up after I'm back in LA." He wanted to make sure things were done right—and the backup wasn't a bad idea if Johnny was still in the area.

"I guess I don't have a problem with that. Never hurts to have an extra pair of eyes. Why don't you plan on having us ride along?"

"I'd like to head up around nine if that works for you. We'll have plenty of time to run through the ME's reports, make sure everything plays, then get to the airport."

"All right. We'll meet you in the lobby at a quarter to nine."

"See you then."

Tucker opened his laptop once more and rewound the video surveillance Rogers gave him, watching the man as he went down the steps in slow motion. Was that Johnny Simmons? Did he really kill Staci and the others?

His phone alerted to a text from Jerrod.

Parked outside Simmons' house. He's nowhere to be found, but his wife and kids are watching a Disney movie. Should be an exciting night.

It didn't surprise him that Simmons wasn't home. It was hard to be in Los Angeles and Park City at the same time. Tucker responded.

I owe you one.

He rewound the video footage again, scrutinizing the man in black's movements, trying to catch some small gesture that reminded him of the kid he hadn't seen in almost fifteen years. This wasn't getting him anywhere. Everyone was doing what they could at this point, and he needed to go to bed.

Frustrated, he closed his laptop and stood, stretching his tensed muscles. He couldn't afford to pull another all-nighter. Grabbing his pillow and blanket, he quietly opened the bedroom door and entered slowly, trying not to wake Wren. She didn't want him in the room, but she was going to have to deal. She would be rid of him soon enough.

"What are you doing?"

He stopped. "Taking the recliner."

"There's a couch in the sitting room."

He removed his holster. "Yeah, but I'm still in charge of your protection."

"We're on the fifth floor. He isn't coming in through the window."

"We're going to make sure." He unbuttoned his shirt, took it off, slid out of his slacks, and settled in the chair, pulling his feet up and stretching out.

Dim light filtered in from the kitchenette, and they held each other's gaze in the shadows. He wanted to go to her, to wrap himself around her. "Cooke, I don't want it to be this way."

"I do." She rolled over.

He stared at her long wavy hair against the pillow, trying to accept the fact that he and Wren were finished.

☙ Chapter Twenty-one ❧

Wren stepped from the shower and wrapped herself in a large cotton towel. She used her hand to wipe away the film on the mirror and stared at her pale cheeks and dull eyes as she stood among the wisps of steam. Was this what heartbreak looked like? Was the sickening dread churning in her belly what if felt like? And this overwhelming need to cry. She'd been mopping up stray tears since she backed her way into the bathroom last night. She thought she'd wept herself dry as she sat on the toilet seat, running a steady stream of water in the tub, hopefully masking the worst of her weakness. But the tears kept coming, coursing down her cheeks as she lay in the big, lonely bed, staring into the dark long after Tucker had settled himself in the chair.

He'd said he didn't want it to be this way as his voice and eyes radiated with misery, but his actions had spoken for themselves. Why did he have to lie? Why did he make a promise he had no intention of keeping? Sniffling, she pressed her hand to her lips, willing the next crying jag away. She hated this—*hated* it. Being in a relationship—even for so short a time—had made her weak and weepy. She'd let herself depend on someone other than herself—one of so many mistakes. Well, no more. This wasn't how she handled things, and she wasn't about to start now. It was time to be finished with this silliness and move on. Tucker wasn't everything. Or he shouldn't be. *Wouldn't* be, she amended as she straightened her shoulders and grabbed her brush, pulling the bristles through her hair. She just had to make it through the next few hours, then she would never have to see him again.

Her movements slowed, and she dropped the brush to her side as she thought of waking another morning without Tucker holding her or his lips never capturing hers. The sheer emptiness left her reeling.

What was she *doing*? She set her brush down with a snap. Tucker was just a man. There were a million more out there. This didn't have to be a big thing. She reached for the doorknob, then stopped. But it *was* a big thing. He told her he loved her, and maybe she loved him too—desperately—but how could she pretend everything was okay? He'd hurt her. She never wanted to feel like this again—like the world was falling out from under her. He'd promised his trust, and she'd given hers. He'd agreed to full disclosure and never followed through. Any building blocks to something more were irreparably eroded. There was more to a relationship than love, and Tucker couldn't give her what she needed—plain and simple. So that was the end. Time and distance would take care of the worst of the pain.

Bolstered by her own thoughts, she opened the door and stepped into Tucker's scent. He walked past the kitchenette doorway, talking on his cell phone, barefoot in snug blue jeans and no shirt, his hair still damp from his shower. She clenched her teeth against the violent longing to run her fingers over smooth skin and muscles, to hug him close and hang on. He was doing that on purpose, walking around shirtless—being too damn *sexy*. She turned away in defense, grabbed the outfit she'd forgotten and hurried into the bathroom. Today she would need every ounce of confidence she could muster if she was going to fight against Tucker and herself. It was time to put "relaxed Wren" away and step back into the real world. She was hours away from going home and starting over. Things had been different for a little while. She had let her guard down, and her career hadn't mattered quite so much. But it mattered now—more than ever. Interior design had seen her through tough times before, and it would again.

Craving to get back to the life she understood, she slid on her frilly black panties and put on the matching bra. Her cranberry colored cashmere sweater came next, then snug dark-wash jeans. She applied a soft application of makeup, playing up her eyes. She blow-dried and styled her hair and suddenly the vulnerable woman vanished and the ambitious career woman was back. "Much better."

Steadier, she gathered her items and stepped from the bathroom far more prepared to deal with the long day ahead. She zipped her cosmetic bag in her suitcase, sat down, and pulled on heeled brown leather boots. The extra inch added to her stingy height, boosting her confidence further. She took a deep breath and stood, smoothing down her top as she started toward the kitchenette. She paused in the doorway, meeting Tucker's eyes. Her stomach lurched and her heart slammed in her chest as she continued to the counter, perusing the small selection of bagels and muffins delivered fresh each morning.

"Let me call you back. Okay. Bye." Tucker hung up.

Wren reached for an oversized blueberry muffin, pulling back, too riddled with nerves to eat. She darted Tucker a glance, realizing he was staring at her. She pressed her lips firm, steeling herself, and turned to face him.

He leaned back in his chair, his long leg resting on the bench—the picture of relaxation, except for the clenched jaw and tensed shoulders. "Morning."

She clasped her hands, hoping he couldn't tell they were trembling. "Good morning." Swallowing, she took a step closer to the counter as he continued to hold her gaze.

"Sleep well?" he asked.

"Uh, yes. Fine."

He nodded.

Biting her lip, she turned back to the breakfast selections.

He stood, unfolding his powerful body from the chair, and started toward her.

"What are you doing?" She asked in a rush, backing up, slamming into the counter.

He paused. "I'm grabbing a muffin. Rogers and Franklin are coming by in a few minutes. We're going up to the house before we head to the airport."

"Oh." She closed her eyes and pressed her palms to the cool granite countertop, trying to pull herself together. "Sorry." "Professional Wren" wasn't handling this situation any better than "vacation Wren" had.

Big hands rested on her shoulders, and she jumped, whirling, staring up into hazel eyes, realizing she should have stayed facing the counter.

"Wren, please let me explain."

She breathed him in and itched to touch, to taste, to vanish the last twelve hours from her memory, but facts were facts. To give in now meant losing herself, and she was all she had. "No."

He stepped closer.

She pushed at his chest. "Leave me alone. Please."

He captured her hands and pressed her palms to his heart. "Don't make me walk away from you."

To her horror, her eyes filled.

"I made a mistake."

"Stop."

"Wren—"

There was a knock at the door. Tucker immediately dropped her hands and reached for his gun on the table.

"It's Detective Rogers," came a muffled voice.

"Step back," he said as he peeked through the security hole and opened the door. "Detective."

"I'm early. I know we said we would meet in the lobby, but I thought I should tell you Franklin called in sick—flu bug going around."

"We were just getting ready." Tucker opened the door wider. "Come on in."

"Good morning, Ms. Cooke."

Wren blinked her emotions back. "Good morning, Detective." She gave him a small smile, grateful for the distraction. "Can we offer you coffee and a muffin?"

"Oh, no, I'm all set." He patted his rounded belly. "My wife made a fine breakfast—still stuffed, in fact."

She nodded and looked at Tucker. "I guess I'll go get my stuff." She hurried away and picked up her suitcase as her cell phone rang. She lunged across the bed, reaching the side table, grabbing the phone on the third ring. "Hello?"

"Wren?"

"Yes."

"Wren, it's Clayton Mills from Clayton Designs."

She rolled over and sat up on the edge of the bed. "How are you? I haven't talked to you in *months*."

"It's certainly been awhile—the Rodeo project we collaborated on."

"We knocked their socks off." She grinned.

"We absolutely did. I'm going to cut right to the chase, Wren, and ask you if you would like a job here with us. I could hardly believe it when I saw your resume on my desk."

"Yes, well—"

"I heard about your situation."

She winced. "It's been difficult."

"I spoke with Lenora Cartwright myself. Luckily I rarely believe a word that comes out of her mouth."

"But others might."

"Perhaps, but then they'll see your work. I want you here, Wren. Top salary, full benefits as soon as you're available."

She pressed her fingers to her temple, hardly able to believe what she was hearing. Clayton Designs was one of

Southern California's top firms. "How can I possibly say no? Yes, of course I accept. I'm heading into LA tonight. I plan to spend a few days with Patrick and my brother and his family, but I'm all yours Monday morning."

"I was sorry to hear about Patrick."

She'd always wondered if she'd sensed a sexy vibe between Clayton and Patrick. "Thank you. He's making improvements every day. I'm hoping he'll be raring to go sooner rather than later."

"You'll have to be sure to tell him I said hello."

"I'm stopping by the hospital tonight. I'll be sure to give him the message. He loves having visitors."

"Maybe I'll make a trip down."

She smiled. "I think he would like that."

"Okay then, well, I'll scan the necessary paperwork and send it over; we'll get the ball rolling. I also have a couple of projects I would like your thoughts on. Do you mind if I send those along as well?"

"No, no, please do." Her system revved with excitement. "I have several of my supplies on hand. I'll get started right away."

"Sounds like we're all set. Welcome to Clayton Designs. My staff and I look forward to helping you settle in here in Santa Barbara."

"I can't wait. I'll have some mockups for you by this evening, and I'll see you Monday morning. Santa Barbara or bust."

Clayton chuckled. "I can already tell we're going to make history together."

"You better believe it. Bye, Clayton." She hung up, laughing as she fell back against the mattress. "I can't *believe* this." There was so much to do—mockups, packing, home sales, Patrick... First she would start with a call to Greta. She caught site of a movement and scrambled up, realizing Tucker was in the room.

He pulled his snug black sweater over his head as they

looked at each other. "Sounds like you're off to Santa Barbara."

She nodded. "Yeah, Sunday night."

"Congratulations."

"Thank you." She'd already told him she couldn't be with him, but somehow this felt like goodbye.

"We should go. Rogers and I want to check out a couple new developments." He grabbed a pair of socks and picked up his duffel bag, turning to leave.

Her enthusiasm for her new job vanished as a wave of loneliness overwhelmed her. She suddenly didn't want to work for Clayton or move to Santa Barbara. She wanted the man walking out the door. "Tucker."

He stopped.

What should she say? I love you, but I don't know if I can trust you? "I—I'll be ready in a second."

"Okay."

She clutched the edge of the bed as tears tried to escape again. Time, she reminded herself, would make this horrible ache go away. Her phone rang, and she ignored it. But what if Patrick's nurse was calling? She snapped the cell phone up, looking at the readout. Greta. "Hello?"

"We've got an offer."

"That's excellent—"

"Full asking price, plus payment for furnishings—everything but the master suite."

"*What*?"

"I got a call from the bank this morning. Some lady wants the house. She'll pay cash."

She shook her head, certain she didn't hear that right. "Cash?"

"*Cash*," Gretta confirmed. "She wants all papers signed by Thanksgiving."

"Good heavens my head's spinning."

"I understand."

"But what about the eager couple?"

"They haven't called me back yet."

"Who is it? Who wants my house and everything in it?"

"Honey, I have no idea. All the banker would say is she's some old rich eccentric. She saw the pictures of your place on my website and has to have it."

She hated the thought of some stranger having her things, but maybe this was for the best. This was her chance for a completely fresh start, and the extra money her furniture would bring wasn't a bad thing. "I guess—I guess she can have it."

"I'll call the bank now. You'll be staying with your brother for a while?"

"Until Sunday evening."

"I'll get some appraisals on all saleable items, and I'll drop the papers by tonight or tomorrow at the latest, and you can look everything over."

"Great. I have two more requests."

"Name it."

"I don't want the bedroom furnishings either. I would like to give them to charity—whichever foundation you prefer."

"Okay. I'll arrange for pickup today, if you'd like."

"Sounds good." She would never be able to sleep on the bed some sick man had touched. "Also, I accepted a position with Clayton Designs. I'm going to need an apartment sooner than we thought."

"Your head *must* be spinning."

"I want my new home to be right, so I don't mind staying in a hotel for a couple of weeks until we find what I'm looking for."

"I'll get right on it. I'll e-mail you what I can find currently available."

"Thanks." She hung up and stood.

Tucker stuck his head in "Cooke, we need to go."

"All right." She shook her head, still trying to take it all in.

"Everything okay?"

"Yes. My house... My house sold."

His eyes grew wide. "Already?"

"I know. I can hardly believe it."

"Guess you're on a roll."

"I guess so." So why didn't she feel like it?

Tucker drove up the steep road long since cleared after the last snowfall. He took the sharp curve, moving ever closer to twenty-twelve Mountain View, more than ready to get this over with. The next hour or so was bound to be hell while he and Rogers dissected the ME's reports, replaying his sister's final horrifying moments exactly as they happened—or as closely as they could estimate while they stood around Staci's old room.

Even with Johnny Simmons officially in police custody after a surprise seven-thirty a.m. LAPD swoop, Tucker wasn't about to miss this opportunity to see for himself that the authorities hadn't missed any vital details. Until hard evidence was found or DNA results came back officially placing Simmons at the scene, he would continue on with his investigation.

He passed JT's old house and glanced at Wren as she stared out her window. She was gorgeous and city-slick in her cream-colored beret and leather jacket—ready to take on the world, like the cool, career-focused woman he'd arrived with three weeks ago.

He barely suppressed a sigh as she pulled her phone from her purse, her thumbs flying over the keypad as she typed herself another reminder. She was slipping through his fingers, and there wasn't much he could do about it. In less than a week's time, she would be in Santa Barbara, starting a new life that had nothing to do with him. He gripped the wheel tight, wondering how he was going to let her go.

He glanced her way again, catching her looking at him. There was so much hurt radiating in those big eyes. Despite her best attempts, she could no longer hide all her sweet spots and hints of vulnerability—not after what they'd had.

Goddamn he hated this—categorizing their relationship as if what they shared was in the past. There was something *here*, right now—powerful and real whether she wanted to accept it or not. He planned to remind her as soon as their plane reached altitude and there was nowhere she could run to get away—a last ditch effort to repair everything that mattered. Perhaps his tactics were slightly underhanded, but too much lay on the line to play completely fair. But first he had to help Staci.

Slowing as they approached the house, he pulled in the drive, studying the glass and timber structure he once called home, looking toward his and Staci's wing, dreading the next little while. He waited, craving the moment when "cop mode" would kick in and his personal problems would disappear until he surfaced again.

Rogers parked his unmarked car behind the Jeep, got out, and met him at the driver's side door.

Tucker readied his weapon as he rolled his window down halfway, habitually sweeping the trees surrounding the property.

"Guess we should get on with this. It's damn cold out here." Rogers pulled his hat farther over his ears.

"Cooke, I want you to stay close. We're pretty sure our man's back in LA, but we're not taking any chances."

She nodded.

Tucker got out on his side and hurried around to Wren's door. The brutal winds blew strong, cutting right through the thickness of his coat. "Son of a bitch. We'll start inside."

Wren stepped from the Jeep, hunching against the unyielding chill. Tucker wrapped an arm around her shoulders, catching whiffs of her perfume as the three of them hustled to the entrance.

"I got a call from Detective Owens on the way here," Rogers said as he gripped the edges of his coat close to his cheeks. "He told me—"

Two blasts rang out, and Rogers crumbled to the ground, blood spurting from the wound in his neck, pooling from the hole in his face.

"Oh my God! Oh my God, Tucker!" Wren tried to turn away from the gore puddling on the pristine snow.

"Fuck!" He grabbed Wren, yanking her around and closer to his side, shielding her as he reached for his weapon, then he ran with her to the door. They were wide open. There was nowhere to go but inside. "Unlock the door!" He held the keys in his left hand, next to her elbow as he kept aim, pointing his pistol in the direction the shots were fired. Seconds passed like days as Wren's trembling fingers struggled to send the key home. "Come on, Cooke. Come *on*."

"I'm trying," she shuddered on wheezing breaths, and finally the key slid in the lock.

"Hit the panic button and head for the bathroom," he said as she twisted the knob.

Another shot echoed through the air, grazing the arm of his coat. "Goddamn. Get inside." He shoved her into the entryway as he caught sight of a figure moving in the trees. He fired twice, and a man fell with a piercing scream.

"Panic button," he said, slamming the door shut behind him, locking them in.

"Nice moves," JT said as he appeared from the coat closet, pointing a Glock 22 at Tucker's forehead, the muzzle mere inches away. "Very Rambo-like. I guess I won't have to pay him, not that I was planning to anyway. Don't press the button, Wren, or your boyfriend here will lose his pretty face."

"JT, what—what are you doing?" Wren asked, taking a step closer to Tucker.

"Executing a well-thought-out plan. I knew you'd come after I dangled Johnny in your face. Now drop your gun, Tucker, or I will shoot." He wiggled his index finger against the trigger, giving them a cool smile.

Hesitating, Tucker glanced at Wren. Her cheeks were

pale, her eyes glazed with terror as she stared at JT.

A blast echoed in the room, and heat tore through Tucker's shoulder. The gun fell from his hand with a clatter as the force and shock of the bullet knocked him back a step.

"Tucker! Oh God, Tucker!" Wren rushed toward him.

"No!" JT shouted. "Stay right where you are. I'm not going to have you bawling all over him, ruining my moment."

"He's—he's... You shot him."

"Is that what I did?" He aimed at Tucker's other shoulder. "I'll put another hole in him if you don't listen. We'll watch him bleed to death together."

Tucker sucked in air through his teeth, and sweat instantly beaded along his forehead as he clutched at the unspeakable burn just below his shoulder. Blood oozed despite the firm pressure he applied. "I'm okay, Cooke. I'm okay," he gritted out as the cell phone on his belt rang.

"Answer." JT said to Tucker as he moved his arm to point the gun at Wren. "Answer the damn phone and pretend everything's hunky-damn-dory, or I'll shoot her in the fucking head. And Wren, lose the coat and stay awhile."

Tucker stared into JT's cool eyes. There was no fear, no regret, not even madness. He would shoot Wren and not even blink. Pulling his blood-soaked hand from his shoulder, Tucker grabbed his phone and answered as Wren took off her leather jacket. "Campbell."

"Where are you?" Ethan asked.

"At the house." He fought to school his breathing and keep his voice steady. The pain in his arm was excruciating.

"Get out of there. Owens just called. Simmons isn't your man. He's been up in northern California fucking his mistress. It's Cartwright. They can't find him. They've put out an APB."

"Guess they should contact Park City PD."

JT rushed up to Wren and pushed the muzzle to her temple. "Don't think I won't. End the call—nice and smooth."

"Ethan, I've gotta go."

"What the hell do you mean you've gotta go? I still have information. Apparently Simmons and JT had a falling out at that prep school in Colorado. Jonathan caught JT peeping in some girl's closet. The headmaster kicked Cartwright out, but everything stayed hush-hush after pressure and promises of several lucrative donations. JT's been harassing Simmons off and on ever since."

"Hmm." What the hell else was he supposed to say as he looked from Wren's pleading, terrified eyes into JT's calculated stare?

"Owens put two and two together and they rushed to JT's apartment. He didn't answer, so management let them into his place. He's been using fake IDs to fly back and forth from Vegas to Salt Lake City."

"I'm getting twitchy." JT wiggled his finger against the trigger.

"Ethan, I'll call you back." He disconnected. "There. Now stop pointing that at her head."

"Makes you kind of nervous?" JT asked with mock sympathy. "You can rest easy, Pretty Boy. I'm not going to kill her like this. I'm going to strangle her the way I did Staci."

"You son of a bitch!" He lunged toward JT.

JT fired into the air, and ceiling particles showered over their heads. "Stay back by the door, and drop your phone while you're at it. Can't have you sneaking calls while you watch me rape and murder your girl. I mean, Wren *is* your girl, right?"

Tucker gritted his teeth as a tear slid down Wren's cheek.

"I asked you if Wren is your girl?"

"No, she's not. She called it off last night." He hoped to God that would take some of the thrill out of JT's desire to kill her.

JT's brows rose in surprise. "Wren, is this true? Did you dump Pretty Boy?"

Tucker gave her a barely perceptible nod.

"Yes. It wasn't working out."

JT hooted with laughter. “You went and got yourself dumped? Now that’s one for the books. Maybe you aren’t God’s gift to women after all.” He shook his head. “Have to admit, this kinda takes some of the fun out of it all.”

“Why?” Wren asked quietly. “Why are you doing this?”

“Because I can.” He shrugged casually. “Because I want to. There’s little that brings me quite as much joy as watching Tucker Campbell suffer. No one has a right to all that you have, Golden Boy.”

“You’re doing this because you’re jealous?”

JT’s eyes changed from amused to deadly in a flash. “I’m not jealous—just righting the wrongs of the world. Call it cosmic justice.”

“But *this* is wrong. You have to know this is wrong, JT.”

“You got me, Wren.” He pointed in her direction. “I *do* know it’s wrong. I just don’t care.”

“So then—”

“Cooke.” Tucker met her gaze and shook his head. “It’s okay.” She was trying to reason with a madman and make sense of all this, but she never would. He had to find a way to get them the hell out of there.

“You know what, Tuck-Man,” JT pressed his finger to his chin, contemplating. “It’s really not okay. *Nothing* about you is okay. Heir to the Campbell fortune; beautiful, doting parents; an adoring sister; a face and body that belong on fucking magazines; natural athleticism; a saintly need to do what’s right; and let’s not forget the women—any goddamn one you want. I mean you wanted him, Wren.”

“Not at—not at first.”

JT raised his brow at her. “Don’t try to kid a kidder, Wren. I saw the way you were looking at him the day *I* came to ask you out. I thought you two were going to jump each other right there in the library. Just proves my point further. You’ve got it *all*—always have. Everything you touch turns to goddamn gold, man. Gets tiresome, real fucking tiresome. I pretty much feel duty-bound to cause you as much pain as possible any chance I can get, but it has to be worth it. It really has to count." He slid a piece of Wren's wavy hair between his fingers. "And you definitely count, Wren. Watching you die will totally fucking count. Wouldn't you agree, Pretty Boy?"

Tucker stayed silent as he pressed his hand harder against his wound. He wouldn't be able to get them out of this if he lost too much blood.

"I'll take that as a yes." He glanced at his watch. "We should probably move this along. The cops'll figure out the good detective is dead sooner or later. Might as well have a decent body count when they arrive. I say we make this *epic*." He pulled Wren close. "How about you?"

Her breath shuddered out, and Tucker struggled to follow JT's order to stay put.

"Let me guess—you want to say goodbye to the love of your life before we have a little fun. Kinda loose, Wren, guy-hopping this way, but I'm a reasonable guy. Go say goodbye."

Wren's eyes filled as she walked to Tucker, folding herself around him.

He winced, attempting to return her embrace. "We're going to find a way out of this," he whispered against her hair, close to her ear.

She nodded, touching his cheek. "I'm sorry."

He held her gaze and skimmed his fingers along her jaw. They *would* find a way out of this. Like hell he'd leave her to die the way Staci did. "Don't give up on me, Cooke." He hugged her close again. "Do what I say when I tell you," he murmured.

"All right. Enough already. I think I'm going to puke."

Tucker's cell phone began to ring.

"We'll leave that behind. Let me set the alarm, then we're off to one of my favorite places."

Tucker watched as JT punched in the new code.

"Wondering about that, aren't you?" He chuckled. "Ms.

Hayes leaves all of her client's keys and codes tucked back in her writing desk. She really does need to be more careful."

"You hurt Ms. Hayes?" Wren asked, her voice tight with fear and unshed tears.

"That would be too predictable. Breaking and entering is much more fun. The old bat never even knew I was there on the several occasions I showed up. I wonder how she'll feel when she realizes her carelessness cost sweet little Chloe her life? Now walk in front of me." He gestured with his gun. "Wren first, Pretty Boy second. And don't try anything that's gonna get you killed before I'm ready." JT picked up Tucker's gun and shoved the weapon in the waist of his jeans. "Start down the hall. Second door on the left, but I'm sure you already know that."

Wren went first, then Tucker. He struggled to bury his dark rage and think of a way out of this as his gaze darted about, looking for anything he could use to disarm the crazy bastard.

JT shoved him forward with a boot to the ass. "Faster."

Tucker lost his balance, falling to his knees, sucking in a sharp breath when instinct had him catching himself with his tender arm.

Wren whirled. "Tucker."

"Keep going, gorgeous. He'll get up in a minute."

Tucker got to his feet slowly. "I'm good, Cooke. I'm good." But he wasn't. Sweat poured down his face as he fought against the unbelievable pain.

"No, you're not." She touched her fingers to his coat sleeve, pulling her bloodied hand away. "He's losing too much blood. He's going to pass out before too long, or worse."

"Ah, well, we can't have you dying before all the fun starts." He gave Tucker a pleasant smile. "Help him into the bedroom. We'll staunch him up some."

Wren guided him into the room, kneeling on the floor next to the bed where he sat, helping him ease off his coat. She pressed her lips firm, frowning as her worried eyes met his.

He touched a trembling finger to her jaw. “We’re good, Cooke,” he murmured.

“No, we’re not. You’re not. We need to get this stopped.” She looked over her shoulder as JT continued to hold them both at gunpoint. “I need scissors and a clean towel.”

“Oh, sure. Let me get you a pair. And why don’t I leave you alone for a few minutes while I gather up first aid supplies?” He chuckled. “Use the pillowcase.”

“It’s not sterile.”

“He’s going to die anyway. Just not until after you do. Pillowcase or nothing.”

Wren turned back to Tucker and tugged the pink-striped case from the down feather pillow, then leaned in, studying his arm closely. “I can’t get a look at your wound, but I can see the entry and exit point, so that’s something. I’m going to tie this off as tight as I can.” She wrapped the pillowcase around his lower shoulder, above his bicep. “Ready?”

He braced himself, nodding.

She pulled the cotton tight, squeezing until her hands shook from the exertion.

He clenched his jaw, breathing in deep as her efforts brought about a new kind of torture.

“Almost finished.” She wrapped, once, twice. “Can you feel your fingers?”

He gave them a wiggle. “Yeah.”

“Good.” She tied off her work with a knot.

“Perfect.” JT stood from his lean against the dresser. “Now, Wren, I want you to pick up the lamp.”

“What?”

“Pick up the lamp.”

She stepped over to the bedside table and did as she was told.

“Unplug it.”

She reached down and yanked on the plug.

“Pretty Boy, come sit down right here.”

Tucker resisted until JT aimed the gun at Wren.

"Now."

Tucker stood and sat on the spot JT pointed to with his foot.

"Wren, bring the lamp over to me."

"What—what are you going to do?"

"Just bring me the lamp."

She hesitated.

"You just mopped him up. Am I shooting again?"

Wren brought JT the lamp.

Before Tucker could turn his head, pain shot across his temple, and the world went black as Wren screamed.

☙ Chapter Twenty-Two ❧

Wren stared, frozen with horror as Tucker crumpled to the carpet. "Why did you do that?" She dropped to her knees, cradling Tucker, gently running trembling fingers over his skin, examining his injuries. A dark purple bruise had already bloomed, and blood oozed from the deep gash along his hairline. "Tucker, wake up." She grabbed his limp hand, squeezing it in hers, willing him to do as she asked. "Please, wake up."

JT stepped closer.

"Get away." She gripped Tucker tight against her, shielding him with her body. She'd be damned if JT was going to hurt him again. "You leave him alone."

"Oh relax. He'll wake up soon enough. I'm finished with him for a while anyway. Now I want you."

Her heart thundered, and she tried to ignore the outright fear surging through her as she continued stroking Tucker. He couldn't help her any longer. Somehow she needed to save them both.

"Besides, he looks a hell of a lot better than Patrick did after I finished with him." JT wiggled his brows, smirking.

She swallowed tears of powerlessness and rage as she thought of Patrick's daily struggles to recover. And Tucker, he was so...still and vulnerable. "You're disgusting. A horrible, disgusting coward."

JT crouched next to Tucker and pressed the gun to his head. "I'd stop and think about what you say before you make me angry, Wren."

She eyed the pistol jammed against Tucker's scalp. "I'm—I'm sorry."

"No, you're not." He shook his head dismissively. "Save your empty words." He stood. "Go ahead and leave Pretty Boy alone. It's time for us to begin."

She caressed Tucker's forehead once more as she stared at his gorgeous face, regretting, wondering if last night's conversation in the elevator were the last happy words they would speak.

"Why?"

Her gaze shot to JT's as his voice changed, growing cool. "Why what?"

"Better yet, let's go with what? *What* is it about this man that makes you look at him the way you do?"

She wasn't sure how to answer. She was terrified to say the wrong thing. "I don't—I don't know."

"Yes, you do. Unlock the mystery. Make me understand why no one can *ever* get enough of Tucker Campbell. I mean I know he's pretty, but..." He shook his head. "I don't get it."

"There's more to Tucker than looks. He's a good man—down in the bones good. He's funny and sweet and loyal, and he's smart."

"He's perfect. Got it. Sorry I asked."

"No. He's not perfect. He makes mistakes, just like you and me."

"He's got you wrapped around his finger."

"Nobody wraps me around their finger. I ended our relationship, didn't I?"

JT grinned. "You're a hot ticket, Wren Cooke. I really do like you."

"Then why do you want to hurt me?"

"Because he loves you. I said I *like* you. You're gorgeous

and smart—nothing wrong with a gorgeous, smart woman, but you became irresistible the day I discovered you and Tucker all snuggled up in my mother's library. I would've been okay with you turning me down because you 'weren't looking for a relationship.'" He rolled his eyes as he made air quotes. "But then I realized the truth. You weren't looking for a relationship with *me*."

"I enjoyed our friendship. You were one of my good friends, JT." She shook her head. "I don't understand this. I don't understand you. You're an attractive, successful man. Why do you worry so much about what Tucker does and doesn't have?"

"Because he's always gotten what I wanted—the loving parents, the adoring sister, the girls. Every year the Campbells would swoop in from Monterey, more bonded and beautiful than ever. I tried to make good ol' Lenora and Dave as proud of me as Tucker's family was of him, but Auntie and Uncle barely paid attention."

"Auntie and Uncle?" She frowned, confused by his ramblings. "What—"

"Yes." He put a finger to his lips. "Our little secret," he whispered, giving her a wink. "My mother couldn't handle my 'very unique needs.'" More air quotes. "A kid tries to light the house on fire and keep a few dead cats under his bed, and Mommy Dearest freaks and ships ya off to Uncle David and Aunt Lenora." He shrugged as if what he said was neither here nor there.

She swallowed her disgust, fully grasping just how sick JT was. "That must have been—that must have been tough."

"Such is life, Wren, such is life. My mother didn't want me, neither did my aunt or uncle, nor did any of the girls. They never gave me a second glance, because they were always looking at *him*. Do you know how many miles I ran, how many weights I lifted? It never fucking mattered. Get up."

She stood immediately with his lightning-fast change of

mood, afraid he might try to hurt Tucker again.

"Look at these pictures." He gestured to the photographs on Staci's dresser. "His arm around a different girl. Taylor." He tapped the pretty brunette clinging to Tucker. "Cheryl. Nora. *Jasmine*. And let's not forget Staci—sister extraordinaire. She was special." He stroked his finger along Staci's cheek in the photo. "She was my friend. I loved her—as much as I've ever been able to love anyone."

She struggled to suppress a shudder as his eyes transfixed on Staci. "Why did you do what you did? Why did you hurt that sweet, beautiful girl?"

"Because Jasmine chose Tucker. Because Staci loved him more."

She shook her head, realizing she could never possibly understand. "She was his sister. His twin sister. Of course she loved him more."

His finger stopped caressing as his eyes left the photograph to meet hers. "Don't talk to me like that. Don't look at me like you're judging."

Anger roiled deep, bursting through her veins. Fury was suddenly more predominant than her fear. "You ended her life in the most horrible of ways. She trusted you. And those girls—Alyssa and Chloe. You're disgusting—a predator who uses your perceived wrongs as an excuse to do the unthinkable."

JT's hand shot up, slapping her across the cheek. "Shut up."

She pressed her fingers to the sharp sting and took a step back.

"We're done chatting. Take off your sweater."

"No." She stepped back again on legs that shook and felt like jelly.

He pointed the gun in Tucker's direction, staring into her eyes. "Take it *off*."

She yanked the soft cashmere over her head.

"Mmm, *mmm*. I'm definitely going to enjoy this. Boots

and jeans."

She stood perfectly still, refusing, until he shook his head and aimed his gun at Tucker. "Wren, this is going to happen. I'm going to rape you—three, maybe four times, 'cause damn you're beautiful. Then I'm going to strangle you while Pretty Boy watches. I want Tucker to see what Staci went through—and you. I'll kill him after a while, but I want him to suffer first. Take off those jeans."

She glanced at Tucker, who still lay unconscious, and struggled with the zipper on her boots as her hands began to shake—the terror was back with a vengeance. Her stall tactics had proved useless. The cops weren't coming. Tucker wasn't waking up. She had to make a move; she had to do *something*.

She pulled one foot free, then the next, gripping the soft leather tight. Then she swung at his face with all her might.

The sharp heel connected with JT's cheek, drawing blood. Surprise registered as he clutched at his wound, swearing. Seeing her moment, she took it, racing to the door and down the hall.

"Stupid, Wren. Really stupid idea," he hollered as he chased after her.

She glanced behind her and screamed, realizing he had already caught up.

He hooked her around the waist, lifting her off her feet, and she used her elbows, ramming back at any part of his body she could reach.

"Let me go!" She kicked, hoping to connect with his balls. "Let me *go*!"

"I thought you were smart." He gripped her tighter, and she could hardly breath. "If you like it rough, that's all you had to say." He brought her to the room, slamming the door, and rammed her back against the wood. He grinned down at her cruelly. "I usually like to watch my girls get naked, but I'm happy to help." He held her in place and unbuttoned her jeans with his free hand. "Let's get you out of these." He pressed his firm body to hers, trapping her as he pulled her pants down her legs. “Black bra and panties. It’s almost like you knew you were going to get fucked.” He rubbed himself against her. “I’m tempted to take you right here, Wren, I really am, but it’s hotter if you’re tied up.”

“Monster!”

He took her face in his hands, squeezed. “I thought you said I was a predator.” He kissed both of her cheeks. “Make up your mind. Now let’s turn you around.” He forced her to face the wall as he grabbed a length of black nylon identical to the stuff they found on Staci’s bed along with his “message.”

“You do understand that this is his fault. Just like the night Staci had to die. He made me kill her. He made me kill my friend, because he stole Jasmine away. Kind of like how he stole you. I watched him walk her home and shove his tongue down her throat, just like I watched you in the library. I pretty much decided right then and there that you were going to have to die eventually.” He pulled the rope tight around her wrists until it was biting into her skin, then tied it off. Tears raced down her cheeks, and she clenched her jaw, afraid her teeth would chatter, realizing her chances for escape were officially gone.

He turned her around and yanked her to Staci’s bed. “Lay down.” He shoved her down to the spot where Staci had been laying in the crime scene photos. “On your back.”

With little choice, Wren lay on her tied hands.

“Damn, damn, damn, Wren. We’re talking centerfold material here. Where’s a camera when I need one? This is going to be the best one yet, and ironically perfect. Staci was a virgin when I had her. It was my first time too—sex and murder. This time around I’m plenty experienced, and so are you. And, Wren, I’ll be so much better than him.” He tossed Tucker a scathing look. “Like I said, this is going to be epic. I’m going to tie up Pretty Boy, and we’ll wait for him to come to, then…well you know what comes next, although maybe

I'll add a little foreplay. We'll get you good and wet before I take the plunge—never had time for that. It's always rush, rush, rush. If we're going to do this, we might as well do it right."

Wren looked away from the vile man grinning at her and stared at the flowery frame of Staci and Tucker smiling in a picture well over a decade old, praying that Staci's nightmare had been mercifully faster than hers was about to be.

Tucker lay where he'd fallen, arm aching, head throbbing, eyes closed, listening to JT's disgusting ramblings, waiting for his moment. He hated hearing Wren suffer, could hardly stand that she thought she was on her own, but they had one chance. He would either get this right or they would both die.

JT had knocked him out for mere seconds, but he'd remained still, devising his plan while Wren stroked soothing fingers along his forehead and clutched at his hand, begging him to wake up. He'd desperately wanted to give her a gentle squeeze and reassure her that everything was going to be okay, but their circumstances didn't allow for gestures of comfort. He knew what he needed to do; the opportunity just had to present itself.

"You know, I'm looking forward to helping you out of that underwear, Wren."

JT's footsteps started toward Tucker and stopped. "In fact, maybe we should work on that now after all."

"Please don't do this," Wren shuddered out as JT moved back in her direction.

Son of a bitch, he was ready to *end* this. Tucker clenched his jaw as a burning rage simmered in the depths of his being—for what JT was doing to Wren, for what he'd done to Staci, Alyssa, and Chloe. It was hell on earth knowing Wren lay mere feet away, helpless and terrified, but he didn't dare move; his head spun as if he were on a tilt-a-whirl, leaving him nauseous, and his arm lay against his side, heavy and useless, while blood saturated his shirt. He needed JT to come to him so he could finish this once and for all.

"I had the opportunity to watch you and Pretty Boy go at it—"

"You—you watched Tucker and I have sex?"

"Mmm, I did. His Highness is a real Casanova. Clearly he knows how to satisfy you. I'm eager to show you what I can do. Let's get to that bra, Sexy."

"No, JT."

"Oh, yes, Wren. Absolutely. I've been waiting a long time for this. Now stay still."

Her movements stopped, and she whimpered as JT groaned. "A slide off the shoulder. So *seductive*. Maybe there is something to this whole undressing your victim thing. Do you like being my next victim, Wren?"

"Tucker," she whispered. "Please wake up."

"Oh, he can't help you," JT laughed. "Even when he does wake up."

Goddamn, he couldn't take it anymore. Enough was enough. Taking a chance, Tucker moved his boot along the carpet and let out a grunt.

JT's crazy laughter stopped, and the room fell silent except for Wren's trembling exhales.

"Well, well, well. I think someone's coming around."

"Don't—don't hurt him."

"Aww, loyal to the very end." JT got to his feet and started Tucker's way. "That's touching, Wren. Nauseating, but touching."

Tucker's heart jackhammered, pounding in his arm, his head. This would either work, or he was dead.

JT knelt behind him, grabbing his wrist, pressing on his shoulder, attempting to push him face down. "Let's get you—"

Tucker reversed his grip, clamping hold of JT's forearm,

and rolled, fighting the wave of dizziness. He brought his good arm up, delivering a fist to the fucker's nose as Wren screamed. Using his moment of advantage as JT hollered out in pain, tears streaming from his eyes, hands pressed to his face, Tucker grabbed the gun from the floor where JT laid it, picked it up, and scooted himself back, using his injured arm to steady his poor balance. "Put your hands up, you son of a bitch, or you're dead," he panted out as adrenaline soared through his body.

JT pulled his hands from his nose, lifting them as blood fountained to the floor. "This isn't *right*! This isn't how this is going to end! You always ruin everything!"

"Game's over, asshole. Now shut your mouth and keep those hands nice and high before I decide to pull the trigger."

"Pretty Boy to the rescue." JT eyed him, smirking, and made a quick move toward the weapon in the waist of his jeans.

Tucker shot two rounds into JT's chest, and blood instantly bloomed as he collapsed back, hitting the carpet with a thud. He held his aim, his ears ringing with the deafening blasts, until he was certain JT wouldn't be getting up again.

"Tucker." Wren rolled to her side, her right bra strap draping off her shoulder, tears streaming, fidgeting her way in his direction.

He got to his hands and knees, blinking against the blurry haze, too dizzy to stand, and crawled to her, his arm protesting his every movement. "It's okay, Cooke. It's all right." He helped her sit up and fought with the knots, struggling to untie her. The nylon finally gave way, and she threw her arms around him, burying her face against his neck.

"Oh, God, Tucker," she choked out.

He enveloped Wren in a hug, pulling her in his lap, holding on as tightly as she did with his good arm. There were several minutes during the last hour he'd worried they wouldn't get out of this alive. "It's all over." He rubbed his hand over her back, breathing in her scent as her shoulders shook, and she sniffed, shuddering out hot breaths against his skin.

"I was so afraid." She pressed her lips to his, once, twice, and clung again. "I didn't know if you were going to wake up. I didn't want you to watch me die."

"We're both okay. We're both in one piece." His voice sounded weak and far away. Lifting his hand to caress her was suddenly a strenuous chore, as all of the energy left him.

"Tucker." Wren cupped his cheeks in her hands, her brows furrowed with concern. "You're sheet white." She scrambled out of his lap, her entire side smeared in his blood. Her eyes tracked down her own body, taking in the horror. "Oh, my... Here, Tucker, lie back." She helped him prop his arm up, making him wince, and pressed his hand to his wound. "You're—you—you need help. I'm going to call for help. I'll be right back." She rushed from the room. "Try to apply pressure, and don't go to sleep," she hollered down the hall.

Tucker lay still, struggling to do as Wren asked. Now that the worst was over and she was safe, all he wanted to do was close his eyes and succumb to oblivion.

Wren ran back with towels from the bathroom and his phone at her ear. "Yes, twenty-twelve Mountain View. Detective Rogers has been murdered and my friend has been shot." Her voice floated around him as she pulled his hand from the pillow sheet knotted above his bicep and immediately pressed the towel to the wound, pushing all her weight on his arm.

He wanted to holler out from the pain, but managed a dull groan, finding the effort to do anything more exhausting.

"Yes, he's conscious but concussed and he's lost a lot of blood. I'm not sure. I'm applying pressure now. I won't."

He had no idea how much time passed while Wren continued to hold the line and he drifted in and out. He blinked at the saturated hand towel and up at Wren's face, struggling to concentrate on her firm demand to open his eyes through the fog.

"...awake, Tucker."

Somewhere a door burst open, and officers rushed in. Wren dropped the phone she held in place with her shoulder as the cops waved the paramedics into the room.

"He's lost a lot of blood. He needs help right away."

The paramedics moved in, replacing her hands with their gloved ones, tight against his arm, taking over his care.

"Let's get the lady a blanket," someone said as Wren stood close by in her panties and bra.

Tucker held her worried eyes as an officer draped her in a blanket and tried to usher her from the room.

"No." She held her ground. "I want to stay with Tucker."

"I'm all right, Cooke," he mumbled. "Let them clean you up and take a look at your wrists." The paramedics rolled him onto the backboard and lifted him to the gurney.

"Blood pressure's dropping. Pulse is thready. Let's get him out of here." They yanked the gurney up.

"I'm going with you." Wren's worried voice floated through his ears.

"Ma'am, we have to go right now."

He heard nothing else as they whisked him away.

Wren sat by Tucker's side, gripping his hand, waiting for him to come around. He'd opened his eyes several times, but he'd been out of it. The machine above him monitored his vitals, but she pressed her cheek to his chest, reassured by the steady beat of his heart.

He was so pale; he'd lost so much blood, but he was going to be fine. Despite his concussion and the gunshot wound, the doctors were confident he would make a full recovery. He was young and strong, the surgeon had reassured her the dozen or so times she'd asked. Rest and a few weeks of physical therapy were on the horizon, but Tucker would be his old self again before long.

His parents were here. And Ethan. She knew she should let his mother have a turn with her son, but she couldn't go until she saw for herself that the doctors didn't make a mistake. Once she was sure, she needed to be on her way.

She'd had hours to think and reflect while Tucker went through surgery and slept off the worst of the anesthesia in Recovery. If she stayed, she might never leave, and that wasn't an option. She wasn't cut out for long-term commitments, and that's what Tucker wanted and deserved. He'd lied, but maybe somewhere deep down she understood that his mistake was the perfect excuse to push him away for good. She didn't know how to depend on others. "Happily ever after" was for Ethan and their friends. She lived her life alone and was stronger for it. She needed to leave, get on with things, and allow Tucker the same opportunity. By the time he was up to snuff and back in LA, what they had here in Park City would be a distant memory. He would soon forget his declarations, and that was for the best.

Tucker's fingers moved through her hair, and she gasped, sitting up. She clutched the hand she still held, pressed it to her cheek, and looked into his drug-fogged eyes.

"Cooke," he whispered and smiled.

"Tucker." Emotion clogged her throat as she smiled back. "You're going to be okay." She kissed his knuckles. "Everything's going to be all right now." She sniffled, fighting her tears. "Your parents are here, and Ethan. We've all been waiting for you to wake up."

"I got shot."

She nodded. "The surgeon said there's no permanent damage. Your mom and dad are going to take you back to Monterey for a couple of weeks while you recover."

"I'm tired."

"So rest."

"He's dead? JT's dead?"

"Yes." Poor guy was still out of it. "He's dead."

"I shot him?"

She nodded again. JT had been the worst kind of soul, preying on the innocent, destroying the lives of so many, and Tucker had ended him. Hopefully they could all move on now and find some peace. "You saved us."

"I'm tired," he repeated.

Smiling, she kissed his knuckles again and stood, leaning close to his face, brushing his hair back from the bandages along his temple. "Get some sleep."

"I love you." He closed his eyes.

Her heart ached as she bent closer and pressed her lips to his. "I love you too," she whispered.

He blinked up at her.

"I know you won't remember this." She shook her head, wiping away the tear rolling down her cheek. "That's for the best, but I needed to tell you before you go your way and I go mine." She touched his lips once more—for the last time—as he closed his eyes. "Goodbye, Tucker."

She settled his hand at his side, turned, and walked out of his life.

❧ Chapter Twenty-three ☙

Wren wove her way through the groups of people, with Emma snuggled in one arm and an apple pie balancing in the opposite hand. "Excuse us. Pardon us."

"Looks like your hands are full." Abby sidled herself next to Wren as they made their way from the chaotic kitchen to the crowded dining area. Thanksgiving—Cooke style—was in full swing.

She smiled. "Oh, we've got this. Don't we, Emma?" She nuzzled her niece's soft, baby neck.

Emma gave her a huge grin as her little fingers made a grab for warm, cinnamony apples in a golden flaky crust.

Wren pulled the pie further out of reach, and Abby grabbed hold before the dish crashed to the floor.

"Okay, then again, maybe we don't." She chuckled. "Thanks."

"No problem. I'll take this along to the masses." And just like that, Abby disappeared into the next room.

"Where'd she go with our dessert, Emma?" She lifted the pretty blue-eyed baby high, listening to her giggle.

"Do my turn, Auntie Wren. And Olivia too." Kylee tugged on Wren's gray slacks.

Wren crouched down to Kylee and Olivia's level, with

Emma on her hip. She missed seeing these adorable faces whenever she wanted. “Oh, sweetie, you girls are half as tall as me.” She gently tugged Kylee and Olivia’s matching side ponytails and brushed a finger down their little noses. “I don’t think I can lift you the way I can Emma.”

Kylee’s face fell.

“But I can push pretty princesses on the swings.”

Kylee and Olivia jumped up and down, clapping. Emma squealed, bouncing on her hip in her attempt to copy the older girls.

“Go tell your mommies or daddies that I’m taking you out to the swing set. I’ll grab your jackets.”

“Auntie Wren’s taking us on the swings!” Kylee screamed down the hall, with Olivia following.

She stood, laughing. “I don’t know, Emma, but I think they might be excited.”

Emma clapped. “Da, da, da, da, da!”

“Oh, you agree?” She glanced into the crowded living room, and her gaze locked with Tucker’s as he sat on the couch, a beer in his hand, his arm in a sling, shooting the breeze with Austin and Hunter. Her smile vanished, and her heart did a violent flip-flop. They’d caught each other’s eye all day—when he first walked through the front door with his parents, across the table during dinner, now.

He stood, unfolding his powerful body in khaki slacks and a white polo, starting her way.

She clutched Emma closer. “Oh God, what is he doing?” She’d systematically avoided conversation with him the entire time he’d been here. She took several steps backwards, hoping to vanish among the crowd of family and friends standing around, but it was too late. His cologne already intoxicated her as he stopped in front of her.

“Hey.”

She swallowed, her mouth growing instantly dry. “Uh, hey.”

“Happy Thanksgiving.”

She swept stray strands of hair behind her ear. “Happy Thanksgiving to you.”

“I haven’t had a chance to talk to you. You’ve been busy all day. How are you?”

“Good, good. Great. How about you?” She adjusted Emma on her hip.

“Hanging in there.” He gave her one of his slow grins as he gestured to his arm.

Dear God, why did he have to go and do that? Her stomach clutched as she glanced at his straight white teeth and stared into his gorgeous hazel eyes. “Well, the girls are waiting for me.” She took a step back. “It was nice seeing you again.”

“Do you mind if I hold Emma?”

She glanced from Emma to Tucker. “No. Of course not.”

He moved closer, his arm brushing hers as he swooped in for her niece. “Hi, beautiful girl.”

Emma smiled. “Da da da da!”

“Ah, wrong guy, kiddo.” He looked at Wren, grinning. “Must be the black hair.”

“Must be.” She couldn’t do this. “Looks like she’s settled in. I’m going to get Kylee and Olivia’s jackets. I’ll see you around.” Turning, she walked away before Tucker could respond and made her way down the hall, skirting guests, stopping short at Ethan’s office. She closed herself in the room and sagged against the door, savoring the quiet. One stupid encounter with Tucker and she was shaking—the awkward first ‘conversation.’ Thank heavens it was over.

Sighing, she walked to the plush leather couch and pulled off her black pumps. She’d been doing all right without him—kind of. She’d been too busy to miss him—almost. Her life had been utter chaos since she landed in LA two and-a-half weeks ago. She’d hit the tarmac running and hadn’t stopped. Between her back-and-forth commute from Santa Barbara to the Palisades, unending meetings, mockups, frantic packing, apartment hunting and visits with Patrick, she barely had time to sleep and eat, yet Tucker was never far from her thoughts.

She rested her elbows on her thighs and kneaded with stiff fingers at the tension in her temples. This wasn't how it was supposed to be. *Nothing* was working out the way she'd planned. Santa Barbara was beautiful, but she didn't love her new hometown. The dozens of apartments and small two-bedroom bungalows she'd looked at were all wrong. On more than one occasion, Greta told her she was being too picky. And perhaps she was. She just needed to *choose* a place and stop spending her nights in a hotel.

A rental didn't have to be forever. Her position at Clayton Designs wasn't either, she'd decided the first day she walked through his doors. Clients were already flocking her way. Six months, maybe a year, and she could try again here in the city. The Cartwrights had dropped their lawsuit and headed to Europe with their impeccable reputation in tatters now that word was out about their sociopathic nephew's decade-long crime spree.

Patrick was making huge strides every day. His speech was improving, as was his vocabulary, and he could dress and feed himself independently. He'd hit his final milestone yesterday—walking the entire unit with a cane. Now he needed a spot to open up at the private rehabilitation facility. The doctors had warned them both it could take weeks, but Wren had other ideas. Grant Cooke, General's Chief of Staff, would be calling in a favor tomorrow morning, and Patrick would be transferred over by Monday at the latest. Patrick would have the best. Her friend would be back, sitting behind his desk, whenever he was ready. His slight limp, more than likely permanent, wouldn't slow him down. She'd already promised him his job and a timeframe—motivation for both of them to work their butts off to get back to where they wanted to be. She had her best friend back—a little different than he used to be, but he was still her Patrick.

So why was she so unhappy? Why did she always feel

like she was on the verge of tears? She was no longer being stalked, Patrick was well on the mend, Tucker was back in the office on very limited hours doing paperwork because Ethan couldn't keep him away. Everyone was safe, everything was fairly close to normal, yet she couldn't banish her sadness. She missed Tucker; she knew she would, but she didn't know it would feel like *this*—like her heart had been ripped out of her chest, like she was forever unsteady.

Maybe she longed for him and dreamed of him every night; maybe she'd almost made the biggest mistake of her life when her car somehow drove to his apartment one evening on her way back to Santa Barbara. Luckily fate had been on her side when she sat at the stoplight, waiting to make the left turn into his complex. She'd stared in disbelief as Tucker and a beautiful blonde hugged in front of his Jeep and walked to his building, the lady's arm wrapped around his waist. A concussion and bullet wound weren't slowing him down, and neither was a broken heart.

She'd done the right thing for both of them when she walked away. Tucker may have declared his love and assured her that what they had was special, but the truth of the matter was they'd been in an intense situation, creating equally intense yet false feelings. Utah was long over, and so were they. Tucker had moved on as he had every right to; she was determined to do the same.

She stood, sliding on her heels, wiping at the foolish tear tracking down her cheek. Kylee and Olivia were waiting for their turns on the swings. She walked to the door, yanked it open, and almost crashed into Tucker's mother and father. "Oh, excuse me."

"Sorry to startle you, Wren," Travis touched her arm.

"Oh, no, you didn't. I was just on my way to grab jackets so I can take the girls out to play."

"Doesn't that sound like fun?" Melanie smiled. "We wanted to come say our goodbyes."

"You're leaving?"

"We have to get back to Monterey. We still have to see to the details for Staci's remembrance tomorrow. It would mean the world to us if you could be there."

She had an eight-thirty breakfast meeting with clients and no desire to bump into Tucker again, but as she looked into Melanie's kind hazel eyes, she couldn't say no. "Of course I'll come. I have an early meeting in Santa Barbara, but I'll be along directly after."

"That sounds wonderful. Go ahead and call me later for details." Melanie smiled as she pulled Wren into a hug. "It's been so nice seeing you again. Tucker speaks so highly of you."

Wren held on, ignoring the knife to her heart. "I've enjoyed seeing you as well."

Travis stepped in for a hug as Melanie moved back. "We appreciate your family's hospitality."

"Anytime. I know we're all so glad you could enjoy the holiday with us."

"We had a lovely time. I guess we'll see you tomorrow."

She nodded. "Definitely."

"Now we just need to find our boy and say so long."

"Oh, uh—" she scanned the crowded hall and met his eyes. "Tucker's right there by the living room."

"Ah, so he is." Travis took Melanie's hand. "Happy Thanksgiving, Wren."

"Happy Thanksgiving."

Tucker held her stare as his parents walked his way. Wren hurried off in the opposite direction, determined to find her girls and leave Tucker in the past where he belonged.

Wren hurried down the crushed seashell path as quickly as her heels and snug, black pencil skirt would allow, following the twists and turns through the beautiful gardens encompassing much of the Campbells' massive estate. The

Pacific winds whipped at her hair and plastered her white blouse to her chest as she walked closer to the rows of people seated.

Travis was up front, addressing the crowd. He finished speaking, and suddenly everyone stood and started toward the tents, where music played and waiters roamed. "Damn. I missed it." Sighing, she spotted Melanie among her guests and rushed ahead.

Melanie smiled as Wren moved closer. "Wren, you made it."

She gripped Melanie's outstretched hands and kissed her cheek. "I'm so sorry I'm late. My meeting ran way over, and traffic was a mess."

Travis stepped up to their side and patted her arm. "We're just glad you could be here to help us celebrate our beautiful girl."

"Staci was certainly special."

"That she was." Travis' blue eyes scanned the groups under the tent. "Tucker's around here somewhere." He looked out over the manicured lawns. "Ah, he's over by the trees."

Wren followed Travis' finger, watching Tucker stand with his back to everyone. He wore a black suit and stared out at the ocean next to the blond she saw him with at the apartments. She struggled to ignore the clutching sensation in her stomach. "Yes, I'll have to say hello."

"Please make yourself comfortable, Wren," Melanie said. "Have a glass of wine and some hors d'oeuvres. Ms. Hayes is looking forward to seeing you again, and I would love to introduce you around."

Wren gave Tucker's parents a small smile. "That sounds nice."

Melanie gently squeezed her fingers. "We're glad you can be our guest this evening. Let one of us know when you're ready to be shown to your room."

The idea of staying on the same grounds as Tucker left her uneasy, but on an estate this size, it would be easy to avoid him. The Campbell home made the Cartwrights' look like a shack. "Thank you."

"Oh, I think Tucker's spotted you."

She glanced his way. Even with the distance between them and his dark lenses covering his eyes, she absorbed the heat of his penetrating stare. "I'll go say hello. If you'll excuse me."

"Certainly."

Taking a steeling breath, Wren straightened her shoulders and started in Tucker's direction, down another crushed seashell path. Her heart pounded as the wind blew his thick black hair about and molded his clothes to his beautiful body. Two encounters in twenty-four hours was proving to be too much, but she'd come because Melanie asked, and she somehow felt a bond with a girl who died long ago. The next few minutes didn't have to be a big deal. She just had to say a quick hello, then she could head back to the tent and make the best of a horrifyingly uncomfortable situation.

She breathed in Tucker's cologne as the breeze carried his scent in her direction. The blonde's perfume mingled with his, and the fragrances fit well—like the man and woman standing in front of her. "Hello," she said to Tucker and nodded to the stunning blond with huge brown eyes.

"Hey." He slid his sunglasses on top of his head.

She wished he would put the barrier back so she didn't have to look into the hazel eyes she missed so much.

"Thanks for driving all the way up here. My mom was thrilled when you said you could come."

His mother was thrilled, not him. God this was agony. "I was happy to."

He nodded. "Wren, this is Casey Albright. Casey, Wren Cooke."

Wren shook Casey's sleekly manicured hand. "Nice to meet you."

"And you." Casey smiled. "I think I'll go grab us a drink."

"Oh, please don't let me interrupt."

"You're not. Excuse me." Casey walked away.

Now what? Wren looked past Tucker to the pounding waves, counting down the seconds until this hellish moment could be over. "How—how are you feeling?"

"Pretty good."

"Good." She clasped her hands together, squeezing. "And the arm?"

He flapped his sling about as if he were a bird. "Much better. Couple more days and I should finally be rid of this thing."

"That's great." She licked her dry lips. "This is a beautiful area, and a beautiful day to remember your sister."

He nodded again. "I'll always miss her and wish things were different, but I think we're going to be able to put some of the sadness behind us. My mom's going to Paris with my dad for a couple of days. She hasn't been since Staci died."

"That's wonderful." She touched his hand and quickly pulled back as the simple gesture proved to be overwhelming. "I hope you'll be at peace."

"Thanks."

Waves crashed in the background, and she grabbed at wisps of her windblown hair, struggling not to squirm while they both struggled through painfully polite conversation. "I should probably—"

"So, I got a new place." He jammed his hand in his pocket.

Her brow winged up. "Oh, yeah?"

"Mom sort of freaked when she brought me home a few days ago."

She chuckled as he grinned. "I take it the ugly couch is history?"

"No way. I couldn't get rid of my couch. That thing's too damn comfortable."

She smiled again.

"Ethan said you'll be hanging around the Palisades this weekend. You should come by and check out the new digs."

She shook her head. "I can't. I'm cutting my stay short."

Or she was now. “I have to grab the rest of my things at the old house and get back to Santa Barbara. I think I’ve finally found an apartment.”

“Maybe the next time you’re in town then.”

“Yeah, maybe,” she lied. This was too hard. He wanted to be casual friends, and she wasn’t there; she wasn’t sure she ever would be. “I really should get back to the tent. Your mother wants to introduce me to a few people, and I want to say hello to Ms. Hayes.”

“Thanks again for coming.” He enveloped her in a hard hug, and she hesitated, surprised by the sudden gesture. She clung to his solid body, absorbing the comfort and agony of holding him close, then stepped away. He was ripping her to shreds.

“Wren.” He stepped forward, closing the small space between them, and stroked a finger along her jaw.

She looked deep in his eyes as his thumb swept close to her ear and traveled to her chin. She gripped his wrist, drowning in regret, suddenly wishing all of his promises had been true. He was supposed to love her. He was supposed to have waited, but as she stepped back, Casey walked toward them, reminding her that what they’d had was gone—if it ever existed in the first place.

She pressed her lips firm, attempting to stop the trembling, and blinked as tears swam too close to the surface. What had she been thinking? She shouldn’t have come to Monterey. She didn’t belong here. “I’m going to—I should—I have to go,” she struggled to say as a well of emotion choked her. Turning, she hurried up the path, bypassing the tents, Tucker’s parents, and Ms. Hayes, making her way to the driveway and her car. She picked up her pace as she hit concrete and ran, desperate to be away from here.

Hopefully the five-and-a-half hour drive back to the Palisades would be long enough to ease this raw, tearing ache gripping her heart, and she could finally convince herself, once and for all—as she’d tried to do over the last two and a half weeks—that she absolutely did *not* want a lifetime with Tucker Campbell. She would stop off at Costas Drive, grab the remainder of her things, and spend the night with Ethan and his family before she made her trek to her new home in the morning and finally put this chapter of her life behind her.

Tucker sped south on the 405, rushing back to the Palisades in the dark. This wasn't exactly how he'd planned for everything to work out, but this is how it was. His cell rang, and he pressed 'talk' without bothering to glance at the readout. "Yeah."

"Everything's all set," Ethan said.

Tucker sighed his relief as a huge weight lifted off his shoulders. "I don't know how to thank you, man."

"Oh, I'll think of something."

He grinned. "I don't doubt it."

"Where are you?"

"About twenty minutes out."

"Taking forty-six was the way to go. You've got her by a good ten minutes."

"The Pacific Coast is prettier, but it's definitely not faster. Thanks again. I'll talk to you later." He hung up and glanced at the clock. A ten-minute lead wasn't much, but he was lucky to have that. He'd spent the last five hours barreling through traffic, gaining his slim advantage. When Wren looked into his eyes, tears brimming, her voice tight with emotion, telling him she had to go, he didn't realize she meant all the way home. He should have stopped her from rushing up the path, but he'd been too busy digesting the idea that Wren was hurting too.

For two-and-a-half weeks, he'd fought his way through the long days, angry and miserable, struggling to accept that Wren had walked away. She'd packed up most everything and headed off to Santa Barbara without a second thought, leaving him to stew in memories and regret while she carried on as if nothing ever happened.

Yesterday had been hell on Earth while he watched her hustle around Ethan and Sarah's house, beautiful and sweet, helping with the children, cooking, setting tables, smiling and laughing with everyone but him. He'd finally cornered her among the groups of people, with Emma on her hip, and she'd blown him off, but not before he caught the flash of grief in her eyes. He'd tried to find her again, wanting to be certain he didn't imagine the moment, but she'd done an excellent job of avoiding him. Eventually he had no choice but to leave and make his way to Monterey.

After another sleepless night and a sweaty five-mile run on the beach this morning, he'd convinced himself he didn't give a damn about Wren Cooke's grief; she could've gone to hell for all he cared. He'd been determined to show himself and her that he didn't need her, that he could move on and be just fine. He'd played the awkward moments by the cliffs fairly well—finding enormous satisfaction in her discomfort—until she touched his hand and wished him peace. The quick brush of her fingers, delivered with genuine sentiment, instantly left him yearning, and he couldn't take it anymore. Unable to stop himself, he'd pulled her against him, breathing her in, clinging just as tightly as she held on to him, not wanting to let her go. As she'd stepped away, looking into his eyes while he stroked her soft skin, something powerful passed between them. His anger vanished, as did the pain, and he only wanted them back the way they had been before everything went so damn wrong.

By the time he snapped out of his fog and started after her in a full-out run, he'd been too late, catching sight of her pretty roadster turning right as she drove away. He'd raced back to his parents, explaining what they already knew, got in his Jeep, and called Ethan, setting his plan in motion as he booked it toward the interstate. He'd be damned if he was going to lose her again.

Tucker merged off his exit and slowed to a stop at the first intersection, impatiently waiting to make a right on West Sunset. He turned, accelerating, and braked just as quickly as taillights glowed crimson in the chaos of Friday night traffic. "Son of a bitch. Come *on*." He was losing his lead. If he was lucky, he had five minutes on Wren, but he still had a good six miles to go. He tapped restless fingers on the gear-shift and weaved his way around other cars, finally taking his right, driving the last mile, pulling past the driveway.

Headlights shined far in the distance as he sprinted to the entryway, unlocking the door, slamming it shut behind him, and activated the living room lights with the security panel. He hurried to the kitchen for a beer, fumbling with the opener, finally popping the top, then dashed to the ugly couch, sailing into his seat, powering on the big screen to rehash the highlights from yesterday's game, waiting as he caught his breath. Moments later, a key turned in the lock, and he settled himself more comfortably.

High heels clicked on the hardwood floor and stopped. "Hello?"

"In here," Tucker hollered, his heart still pounding. This was it—make or break.

Her heels slapped faster as she picked up her pace. "I think there must be some confusion..." She stopped in the doorway, her eyes going huge. "Tucker? What in God's name are you doing here?"

He pulled a sip from the bottle, taking her in, and his pulse kicked into overdrive. Damn, she took his breath away. Despite her day in the car, she was tidy, gorgeous, and everything he couldn't live without. "Catching the highlights—Pats versus Ravens. Hell of a game." Not that he'd actually seen much of the Thanksgiving Day matchup; he'd been too busy watching her to worry about who was scoring touchdowns.

Brows furrowed, hands on her hips, she stepped further

into the room. "Why is your television in my living room? And that ugly couch? Dear God, and your *curtains*." She dashed to the window, batting at the retched orange monstrosities as she had when they hung in his apartment.

He shrugged as she looked at him with horror. "Sarah hung them for me."

"Sarah? As in my Sarah?"

"More like Ethan's Sarah, but I guess." He took another sip, struggling not to laugh as she stared at him as if he'd lost his mind.

"Why would she do a thing like that?"

"She offered when Ethan and Hunter said they would bring the couch."

"Ethan and Hunter—I—what—" She shook her head, pressing her fingers to her temple. "What the hell is going on around here?"

"Closing's not 'til Monday, but Greta didn't think it would be a big deal if I moved in a little early."

"Let me repeat myself: What the hell is going on around here?"

"It's not that big a mystery, Cooke. You're moving out. I'm moving in. The end."

"It's definitely not the end, Tucker. Your head injury." She walked to him, concern furrowing her brows as she crouched in front of him, turning his head from side to side, examining his pupils. "Equal and responsive," she murmured. "How much have you had to drink?"

"Three, maybe four sips." He held her wrist, breathing in her sexy scent as she continued to cup his chin. Hints of her perfume had clung to his clothes as he unpacked his bag from Utah. No matter how he tried, he hadn't been able to escape her.

"I should get you to the doctor."

He shook his head. "I got the all-clear Tuesday. I'm back to work full-time next week."

"Tucker." She attempted to pull away. "We need to get

your stuff out of my house."

"Wren, this is *my* house—the new digs I was telling you about."

She yanked away and rushed to stand over him. "That's impossible. Greta said some old eccentric woman was purchasing this place."

"Casey sure as hell isn't old, and I don't think I'd call her eccentric—unique certainly."

"Casey? The blonde I met today?"

"The one and only."

She turned away and left the room, climbing the stairs.

He got to his feet and followed, stopping outside the master suite, holding his breath as Wren stood next to the brand new sleigh bed, sliding her finger over the maple footboard. He clutched the bottle in his hand, nervous all over again. "So, what do you think?"

"I think it's beautiful." She continued stroking the smooth curves. "The white comforter complements the dark wood nicely. The plants are lovely too. Clean, elegant, yet relaxed and inviting. This is a gorgeous space."

"Patrick picked everything out."

She whirled. "Patrick?"

"I let him have a free hand—bedding, furnishings, accents, the whole deal. He thought you would approve."

She stared down, nodding, and walked to the corner where her remaining items waited.

His stomach sank. This wasn't the reaction he'd expected. "What are you doing?"

"Getting my stuff."

"Cooke—"

"I need to go, Tucker." She bent down and grabbed a suitcase. "I'm tired, and I'm leaving first thing tomorrow morning."

He snagged her arm. "Wait a minute."

"What for? I really don't want to create an awkward scene when your girlfriend comes home."

He blinked his surprise. "Girlfriend?"

"Yes, Tucker, the blond who bought my house."

"First off, I bought this house. Second, Casey was Staci's best friend."

"I hope you'll be very happy." She tugged out of his grip.

He grabbed her elbow. "She's also my attorney taking care of the sale."

"Congratulations." She freed herself and started toward the stairs.

He followed at her heels. "She's been dating someone for over three years."

"It certainly didn't look that way the other night."

"What's that supposed to mean?"

"It means it's none of my business, and I really don't care." She sailed down the steps to the entryway, twisting the doorknob.

He pressed a hand to the wood, shutting the door with a snap, fighting to keep cool through his rising panic. "Obviously you do, so spit it out."

"Tucker, I have to—"

"Yeah, I know, you have to go."

"That's right." She twisted the knob again, but he held the door closed.

"I don't want you to go, Cooke. I can't let you go."

"Don't do this, Tucker." She yanked harder. "I don't want to do this," she said on a strained whisper.

He caught the hitch in her voice and slipped off his sling, resting his hands on her rigid shoulders. "Please, don't go."

She stopped, turning, her wrecked eyes staring into his. "I can't do this with you again."

"There's still something *here*." He ran his hands down her arms.

"You're right. We helped each other through some of the worst times in our lives. We have a bond, nothing more."

"So that's the end?"

"Yes." She reached behind her for the knob.

Desperate, terrified she was walking away, he gripped her arms tighter. “Are you attracted to me?”

She blinked. “What?”

“I asked if you’re attracted to me?”

“You know I am, but—”

“Do you have fun when we’re together?”

“Tucker, I’m not foolish enough to go down this road again.”

His questions had worked in Utah; they sure as hell were going to work this time too. “Just answer my question.”

“Yes, we have fun.”

He took a step closer, trapping her against the door. “Do you think about me when we’re not together?”

She pressed a hand to his chest as tears welled in her eyes.

“Do you think about me, Wren, even half as much as I think about you?”

“Please,” she whispered, her voice trembling.

He stroked his fingers along her jaw, relaxing slightly, realizing she was fighting herself. “I can’t get you out of my mind. Day and night, you’re there.” He stepped closer, their bodies almost brushing. “Do you think of me?”

“Yes, I think about you.”

“Does your heart beat a little faster when I touch you?” He slid his thumb over her rapid pulse.

She pulled his hand away. “I’m going to Santa Barbara.”

He reversed her grip, linking their fingers. “Because you want to or because you think you have to?”

“I have a job.”

“You can have a career here—reopen Cooke Interiors. My mother can come down and help for a couple months until Patrick’s ready to go again. She’ll love it.”

“You have no idea how much I want… I can’t do this, Tucker. I’ve had a lot of time to think. I’m not good at this kind of thing—commitment, trust.”

“We were doing just fine until I made a couple of mistakes.” He gripped her chin. “I’m going to make mistakes—

probably a lot of them, but I can promise you I'll never hurt you on purpose. I never meant to hurt you, Wren."

Her breath shuddered out. "I hurt you too. You're such a good man, Tucker. You deserve so much more than what I can give you." A tear trailed down her cheek.

He wiped the warm drop away. "I know exactly who I deserve and exactly what I want. I've been waiting for you since the day you came plowing into Sarah's hospital room."

"But what about Santa Barbara?"

"If you want Santa Barbara, we'll go. We can sell the house, and I'll quit my job."

"But you love your job."

He shook his head. "I love you."

Another tear fell as she closed her eyes.

"Do you love me, Wren?" He'd been certain Wren told him so as he lay in his hospital bed, drugged out of his mind, but as the days passed, turning into weeks, he'd convinced himself he'd dreamt what he wanted to hear. "Wren."

She opened her eyes, staring into his. "Yes, I love you."

He smiled with the rush of relief, certain he'd never heard anything better. "Tell me again." He slid his fingers through her hair.

She leaned into his touch. "I love you, Tucker."

"God, I need to taste you. It's been too damn long." He pressed his lips to hers.

"Mmm." Her mouth warmed against his as she clutched his shirt.

He wrapped his arms around her, pulling her against him as her flavor flooded his system. He'd been starving for her; he wanted to eat her alive, but he kept the pace slow, savoring, teasing another purr from her throat as his tongue slid over hers.

Her hands wandered up, caressing his neck, her fingers brushing through his hair.

"Cooke." He tugged on her bottom lip and rested his forehead against hers. "I need you. Please don't walk away from me."

She continued to play with his hair. "I don't want to walk away."

"Will you stay here with me and live in our house?"

"Yes."

"Will you put me out of my misery and marry me?" He grinned.

She smiled. "Yes."

"Can we do the whole kid thing?"

She snagged his lip. "I definitely want to make babies with you."

"Right now?" He wiggled his brows.

Chuckling, she shook her head. "Not until Cooke Interiors is up and running again. But we can practice in our new bed." She undid the top button on his shirt. "A lot."

He grinned again. "I can live with that." He pulled her fingers to his mouth and nibbled. "You haven't asked about your ring."

"I didn't want to be rude."

He grinned, pulling the two-carat silver stunner from his pocket, and she gasped. "This belonged to my grandmother. Staci loved it. My mother was saving it for her."

She swallowed as her eyes filled. "It's beautiful."

"I think Staci would be happy knowing you're wearing it." He slid the square-cut diamond on her finger.

"I'll never take it off." She cupped his chin in her hands and kissed him.

He bent down, reaching for her.

She stepped back. "What are you doing?"

"Carrying you upstairs."

"No. You'll hurt yourself."

"Nah." He scooped her up, wincing, still a little stiff.

"See?"

"I'm fine." He started up the steps, holding everything he'd ever wanted.

"You know, I think this is going to be good. We're going

to be good."

"Baby, we're going to be great." He nuzzled her neck, making her laugh. "Welcome home, Wren."

"Welcome home, Tucker." She rested her head on his shoulder. "But your furniture has to go."

"Aw, Cooke, every party has a pooper."

Laughing, she kissed his cheek. "I guess that's me."

Chuckling, he turned down the hall, walking with Wren to their newly decorated bedroom.

Thank you!

Hi there!

Thank you for reading *Waiting For Wren*. What did you think of Wren and Tucker's story? Did you love it, like it, or maybe even hate it? I hope you'll share your thoughts by leaving an honest review.

I'll see you again soon when we catch up with another installment of the *Bodyguards of L.A. County* series.

Until next time,

~Cate

Justice For Abby

Turn the page for a preview of book six in the *Bodyguards of L.A. County Series*.

« Chapter One »

May 2014

"Abby, wake up. We're stopping in a second."

Abby stirred as Alexa's voice floated through her dreams. She blinked several times, yawning huge and stretching in the passenger's seat as the warm winds blew through her sister's open window. "Where are we?"

"About sixty miles from Hagerstown."

"Thank God." She sat up further, glancing out at lush green trees and the endless stretch of farmland, eager to be home. "It feels like we've been in the car for *hours*."

Alexa rolled her eyes, chuckling. "Ab, we've been driving for less than four, and you've slept almost the whole time."

She smiled. "Some of us require plenty of beauty sleep."

Scoffing, Alexa slid her a glance. "I've gotta make a pit stop. My eyeballs are practically floating. See?" She quickly turned her head, widening her huge, lake-blue eyes, illustrating her point. "Can you wake Livy?"

Abby peered in the back, her heart melting as sweet little Livy slept with her mouth hanging open, clutching her favorite stuffed frog while her blond pigtails danced in the breeze. "Let's let her sleep. She wore herself out. I'll stay with her while you do your thing."

Alexa looked in her rearview mirror and put on her turn

signal, preparing to take the exit. "It's getting dark. There aren't many cars in the lot."

Abby studied the mostly empty rest stop and thick tree cover blocking her view of the interstate, unfazed by Alexa's perceived sense of danger. She was too used to her sister's overly precautious nature to do more than glance Lex's way and blurt out, "Worry wart alert, worry wart alert," in her teasing robot voice, grinning when her sister tossed her a baleful look. "Just go pee, Lex. Livy and I'll wait here with the windows up and doors locked. Nothing's going to happen in the five minutes you'll be gone." She shook her head, rolling her eyes, and reached in her purse, grabbing her phone. "I'll even punch nine-one-one into my cell. I'll keep my thumb hovered over 'send' the entire time." She held up her cell phone with her thumb above the button in demonstration as Alexa pulled into a spot close to the bathrooms.

"I'm sorry, did you say you wanted to walk back?" Alexa smiled as she unfastened her seatbelt. "You sure you don't want to come?"

"Pee already, Lex," Abby said with an exasperated laugh. Lex was already wound tight, and their mini-vacation was barely over.

"Okay, be right back." She rolled up her window and secured the locks as she got out, gently shutting the door.

Wincing, Abby glanced at Olivia, making certain the quiet slam didn't wake her niece, and turned, huffing out a breath as Alexa hesitated, looking toward the car. "Oh, Lex, *go*." She made an exaggerated go-ahead motion with her hands. If her big sister wasn't worrying about something, she wasn't breathing.

Sighing, she watched Alexa pull open the door to the pretty brick building. Then she turned her focus to her cell phone, her thumbs flying over the keys, adding 'to-dos' to her growing list. The week away had been fun, but now she had a million things to take care of before her long-awaited flight to LA. Two more weeks and she was outta here, off to nail down her dream job with Lily Brand. Her college diploma was hot off the press, but she'd been preparing for this interview since she sewed her first stitch with Gran's old Singer years ago.

Lily Brand wanted her, and she was more than thrilled to work for one of the world's hottest designers and philanthropists...for the time being, but in three years everyone would be wearing Abby Harris designs. She would be a household name. Now she just needed to convince Lex to put her money pit on the market and move herself and Livy out to Los Angeles so they could all be together. Life would officially be—

Something tapped against the backseat window, interrupting her thoughts.

Frowning, she turned, gasping as she stared at the gun pointing at Livy through the glass. "Oh my God," she trembled as her phone fell from numb fingers. Her gaze darted from the mean eyes behind the black mask to the weapon.

"...door."

His mouth moved, yet she heard nothing but the rapid pounding of her heart as she struggled to think. Was this really happening? Yes, of course it was. Livy needed help. They *all* needed help. The police would—

The muscled man smacked the pistol against the glass, making her jump. "Open the door," he said in a thick Russian accent.

She was going to refuse, but then she spotted another hulking man skirting around the gray van parked in the next row, coming their way.

The masked stranger at the window struck the glass harder, settling his finger on the trigger.

"Okay. Don't hurt her," she shuddered out, groping for the handle, too afraid to take her eyes off the weapon mere inches from Livy's head. "Don't hurt her," she repeated, remembering to release the lock, and opened her door.

"Unfasten your seatbelt slowly. Don't try anything funny."

Swallowing, she complied as she darted a look at the keys in the ignition. If she could somehow get in the driver's seat... But the gun aimed at her niece left her no choice but to comply with his demands.

"Auntie Ab?" Olivia stirred in the backseat.

She didn't dare look at the groggy angel calling her name. "It's okay, Livy. Go back to sleep."

"Where are we, Auntie Ab?"

"Livy, go back to sleep," she struggled to say over the terror and tears clogging her throat. "Shut your eyes—" Before she could say more, the man grabbed her arm, yanking her from her seat. "Let me *go*!" She fought to free herself from his biting, meaty grip.

"Auntie Ab!" Olivia started to cry. "Auntie Ab, come back!"

Both men took hold, one gripping her shoulders, the other her ankles, whisking her away from Alexa's car. "Help! Help me!" she screamed uselessly, kicking her feet, twisting and turning, trying desperately to free herself.

"Shut up, bitch!"

She ignored the nasty demand and wretched stench of cigarette breath, fighting for her life as the restroom door opened and Alexa stepped from the building.

"Help me, Lex! Help me!"

Alexa stopped dead, blinked, then ran forward. "Stop it! Leave her alone! Abby! Abby, no!"

"Alexa!" She fought harder as the men moved closer to the open doors at the rear of the van. "No! Please, no!" she begged, trying to claw, bite, anything as they stepped up into the vehicle.

The man at her feet dropped her legs with a jarring thud and shut them in the dark, stuffy vehicle, silencing Alexa's terrified shouts.

"Let me *go*." Abby squirmed in her captor's vise-like grip while the other man hustled to the cabin, driving off with a screech of tires. "Let me go," she repeated, fighting to breathe as her abductor increased the crushing pressure of his arms around her chest, restricting her movements further.

"Shut up."

"Who are you? Why are you doing this? Please let me go. I won't say anything. I'll pretend this never happened."

"Shut *up*!" He squeezed her until she gasped, certain he would crack her ribs. He gave her a violent shake and shoved her to the hard, unforgiving floor.

Heated tingles surged through her elbow, numbing her entire arm. She cried out in unspeakable agony, clutching at the bone, holding her body tense against the pain and a strong bout of nausea. Taking several deep breaths, she gingerly bent the tender joint, finding a glimmer of relief when she realized it wasn't broken. All of her limbs needed to be in working order if she had any hope of getting away.

She glanced up as the man pulled off his mask, revealing short black hair and clean-shaven olive skin. He might have been handsome before the broken nose and jagged scar along his right cheekbone, but as he stopped his movements and stared at her through glaring brown eyes all she saw was a monster.

"You like what you see?" He sent her a cruel smile.

"Why are you doing this?" she whispered as she scooted further back against the side of the vehicle, wanting to put as much space between herself and the vile stranger as she could. "You have the wrong person," she struggled to say, fighting to school her rapid breathing in the stuffy confines.

"Don't talk."

"What are you going to do to me?"

He reached over and grabbed her jaw, squeezing. "I said shut *up*."

She did her best not to whimper as his fingers bit into her skin with punishing pressure.

"You listen to the things I tell you." He pulled his hand away.

Her face pulsed where he'd undoubtedly left bruises, but she didn't dare rub at the ache as he studied her in the shadows.

The driver said something in Russian and the van slowed. The man at her side answered in his foreign tongue, still staring at her. Seconds later the vehicle bumped down what could only be a dirt road, jostling Abby about. She sat up, glancing at the back double doors, trying to spot the release latch. There had to be one. There had to be a way out of this nightmare.

"You think you will escape?"

Her eyes darted to the vile creature close by.

"You will never get away. You should get used to this."

She *would* get away, or die trying. Surely she was dead if she did nothing at all. She looked back to the door as the van slowed, then stopped. A fresh wave of dread sent her heart on another race when the driver got out. What were they going to do to her, rape and kill her? Would they bury her so Alexa never found her body? Her sister's terrified eyes flashed through her mind, and she resolved right then and there to fight until they robbed her of her last breath.

She scrutinized the door again, finally making out the latch as she devised her plan. If she could just get the door open, she would run for her life. Her five-four frame was trim and compact. She could *move* if she had to, and she definitely had to.

Her captor at her side turned, reaching into the cabin, and she saw her chance. It was now or never. She scooted toward the doors and reached for the handle just as the back opened.

"Going somewhere?" Dark brown eyes smiled into hers. The driver's face was handsome but his eyes cruel—just like his partner's. "Dimitri, I believe we have a flight risk."

"*Nyet*. She will behave or she will be punished. She will never get away, because I will always find her." He bent low as he walked to the doors, eyeing Abby the entire way. He stopped in front of her, and his big hand shot out, slapping her.

The metallic taste of blood filled her mouth as she jerked back, crying out from the shocking sting on her cheek.

Dimitri gripped her face, pulling them nose-to-nose. "Do you understand, little bitch?"

She blinked as tears fell, breathing in stale cigarettes.

He squeezed harder. "I asked if you understand?"

"Yes," she choked out, sure her jaw would disintegrate if he didn't release her from his hold.

"Good." He nodded. "Now get in the car, or I will discipline you again."

She was afraid he would knock her unconscious if she didn't obey, so she walked along the rutted road, staring at the roof of a beautiful old farmhouse peeking over the trees less than a quarter mile away. Safety was so close, yet so far away as she moved closer to the black Honda with tinted windows, noting the Maryland plates.

Dimitri opened the back door, giving her a violent shove to her seat as he slid in next to her. She inched her way over to her side and slowly reached for the handle, ready to make her escape.

"It's locked, but this is a nice try."

Abby glanced at Dimitri as her hopes of running withered. With nothing else to do, she moved closer to her window, watching the sun vanish along the horizon, wondering if she would be alive when it rose again tomorrow.

"We are late." The driver got in, started the car, and drove away.

Late for what? Where were they taking her now?

Dimitri said something in Russian, and Abby strained to listen, catching the words 'Victor' and 'Hartwell' in his rapid speak.

The driver grunted, tossing something over the seat.

"Put this on your head," Dimitri demanded.

Abby stared at the poorly sewn black fabric he held up. How would she see where they were going? How would she get help, which was exactly the point she supposed.

"You do not listen well. They said you were beautiful and smart, but I'm thinking this might be wrong. Your mind does not seem as good as your looks."

She didn't know what he was talking about. Who were 'they'? "You have the wrong person," she tried again even though it was useless. She had seen their faces. For that alone, she would die.

"You are the right one. Trust me. Now put it on."

She hesitated, hating the idea of losing her ability to see where they were taking her.

He grabbed a handful of her waist-long black hair, yanking her face to his. "I said put it on."

She stifled her yelp, took the bag, and covered her head, blinking in the darkness. She gripped her clammy hands in her lap as the pitch black left her more vulnerable than she already was. Goosebumps puckered her skin as she moved closer to her door, not wanting Dimitri's large frame touching her exposed arms in her tank top or her legs in her denim short shorts. She was suddenly aware of how much of her was uncovered. A rush of panic tightened her throat, making it impossible to swallow in the stifling confines, so she breathed deep, concentrating on the bold, berry scent of her shampoo, finding comfort in the familiar.

"We will work on your listening." His big hand cuffed the side of her head.

She flinched and held herself rigid, ready, waiting for the next blow she couldn't see coming while the car remained quiet and time stretched out endlessly. An hour passed, or maybe two, her mind racing the entire time, trying to comprehend what was happening. Where did these men come from? Were Alexa and Olivia okay? Would she see her family again?

The vehicle slowed, turned right, and came to a stop.

"Keep the bag on your head and do what Victor and I tell you," Dimitri said close to her ear.

Her heart ramped up to slamming, and her eyes darted

about as the driver—Victor, apparently—got out. Seconds later, her door opened. "Out." Victor grabbed her arm and yanked her from her seat, pulling her forward. "Walk."

Abby tripped several times as she hurried along the uneven surface, listening to the crickets singing and children playing far in the distance. A car wooshed by somewhere beyond. The sounds reminded her of a quiet neighborhood on an early summer evening.

"Go up steps." Victor yanked on her arm.

She used her free hand to catch herself on the concrete before she fell.

"You idiot. Go up three."

She counted three steps and was brought inside, catching glimpses of glossy pine floors and gorgeous oriental rugs through the opening at the bottom of her makeshift mask. The soles of her sandals slapped against the solid wood as she kept her free hand out in front of her, afraid she would crash into something as she struggled to keep up with Victor's pace. Another door opened, and musty air wafted into the bag.

"Go down steps. Twelve."

She pressed her palm to the cool stone at her left, steadying herself as she was pulled down the stairs, counting as she went.

The black bag was ripped from her head, along with several strands of her hair. Abby blinked against the bold light of the naked bulbs hanging from the low ceiling. She glanced around the dingy space in shock as her gaze traveled from girl to girl—six young teens, dirty, bruised, and malnourished, staring up at her through bland eyes while they sat or lay on filthy mattresses on the dirt floor. "What—"

"In." Victor shoved Abby into a small, windowless room, slamming the door, locking her in with a rusty scrape of something sliding against the heavy metal barrier.

She walked on shaky legs to the wooden chair in the corner and collapsed to the uncomfortable seat, clutching her arms around her waist, shivering as she bit hard on her bottom lip while tears rained down her cheeks. Where *was* she? What was this place? She shuddered, remembering six sets of listless eyes holding hers. Nothing good was happening here.

She covered her face with trembling hands and gave into her sobs, relieving the worst of her dread, wishing for nothing more than to be home with Lex and Livy. Thinking of her sister and niece, she forced away her tears, taking several deep breaths of stale air. If she wanted to see her family again, she needed to pull herself together. She couldn't get herself out of this—whatever *this* was—if she didn't think. There had to be a way out. Her eyes darted around the barely lit space, searching for a weapon, another exit, anything.

The door opened, and she rushed to her feet as a tall, well-built man stood haloed in the beam of light from the room beyond. Abby blinked as he stepped forward. "Renzo?" She bolted from the corner and fell against her friend's firm chest as a wave of relief flooded her. "Oh, thank God."

His strong arms wrapped around her.

"I'm so glad you're here. I don't know what's going on. I need help. Can you help me?"

"What happened?" He eased her back some, but she refused to release him from her grip.

"My family—we were on our way home from Virginia Beach. We stopped at a rest area, and two men grabbed me and brought me here."

"You were with your sister and niece?"

"Yes, Alexa and Olivia. I think they're okay, but I need to call and make sure. Will you get me out of here?"

"Of course."

She could hardly believe she was leaving. "Thank you. Thank you." She hugged Renzo again as tears of gratitude flowed free. "I knew this had to be some sort of mistake."

"Come on, let's get you home." He wrapped his arm around her waist and walked with her to the door. "Oh, wait." He stopped.

"What?"

"I can't let you go."

"What—what do you mean?" She freed herself from his grip, studying Renzo's handsome Italian features and dark brown eyes laughing into hers as they had many times while they'd talked and joked at numerous fashion events. But something was different. Renzo was suddenly altogether different.

"You'll be staying here until we send you somewhere else." He shrugged, as if what he said was no big deal.

"Renzo, what are you talking about? I can't stay here. I don't want to stay here. My sister will be worried sick." Her voice started to rise, as did her fear.

He gripped her shoulders and yanked her forward. "Watch your tone."

"I'm stuck in some basement against my will with several girls who look like they're a breath away from death. Don't tell me to watch my tone."

He grabbed her hair close to the scalp, jerking her head back. "Speak to me like that again. I dare you."

She sucked in a shuddering breath through her teeth. Who was this man? Who was this stranger? "Renzo, I have to go. I have job interviews—"

"You have a new career. You can thank me later." He leaned forward, closing several inches of distance, pressing his lips to hers.

She moved back as far as his hand in her hair would allow. "Renzo, stop."

"Don't play shy, Abby. I've been waiting for a taste of you for the last five months." He released her hair and pulled her closer as he slid his hand down her back and over her ass. "*Fuck*, yeah. You feel just like I thought you would—tight, firm. You're fucking hot, Abby. Those dark blue eyes, all that long black hair, your body." He ground himself against her as he backed her to the wall. "Do you know what hot girls want?"

She pushed at his chest as he held her in place. "Stop, Renzo."

"You didn't answer the question, so I will." He caught her full bottom lip between his teeth. "You want to be fucked." He pulled her magenta top from her shorts and slipped his hand down the front of her denim bottoms, groaning. "Lace underwear."

She gulped air into her lungs as she attempted to squirm away, her terror growing as she stood pinned and helpless. "Don't. Don't. I thought we were friends."

He stopped his exploration just shy of invading her with his greedy fingers, laughing. "You thought we were friends?" He shook his head. "No, we're definitely not friends. You're a bitch, and that's how you'll be treated." He brought his mouth to her neck, sucking hard, making her gasp with the sharp pain. "I've been waiting for the right moment to bring you aboard. The first time I saw you at the Christmas show, strutting around the runway in those hot little clothes you designed, I knew you would be perfect."

She stared up at the person who'd fascinated her with his adventures as a fashion photographer, at the "friend" who had made her laugh and taken her to dinner, fully understanding that this man lording over her was the epitome of evil. "What are you going to do to me?"

He grinned. "So many things, but that's personal. Let's get down to business." He molded his palms to her small, firm breasts, squeezing.

"You're hurting me." She tried to pull his painfully probing hands away.

"You'll learn to like it rough." He squeezed again as he smiled.

She shoved at his shoulder. "Renzo—"

"You're going to be my personal assistant—take care of the books, dole out the girls to customers, make them dresses and costumes when we send them off to our high-paying clientele."

She froze, her stomach churning, as she digested the details of her new 'job.' "You want me to help you prostitute women?"

He shook his head. "Our clients don't like women."

She thought of the sickly teens in the room beyond, utterly disgusted. "No. No, I won't do this."

"You absolutely will." He slammed her against the rough concrete, scraping the skin of her back as his hands found their way under her tank top, shoving up her bra, holding her in place with his hips as she attempted to evade him. "You'll dance too and show off these magnificent titties." He pinched her nipples until she clenched her jaw. "You're mine. You'll do exactly what I say, when I say it." He yanked her away from the concrete blocks. "Because if you don't, we'll grab your sister and that brat you talk about all the fucking time."

Her fear magnified as she thought of Alexa and sweet little Livy alone and vulnerable in the tiny house tucked among the woods. "Leave—leave them alone."

"You remember the rules, do what I say, and they'll be fine. You've got yourself a great career with the ring. You even get a room upstairs if you behave. And no one else will touch you but me." He leaned forward and kissed her again, snaking his tongue into her mouth.

She cringed, turning her head.

"Kiss me."

She stood still, too terrified to move.

"You just don't learn, do you?" He slapped her and shoved her to the ground. "You *will* do what I say."

Abby held her throbbing jaw, quietly crying as she sat in the firmly packed dirt.

Renzo opened the door. "Better get some sleep. Tomorrow you'll be learning the ropes in the office and at the club." He locked her in the small, stuffy space with a slide of something against the door and shut off the light, leaving her huddled on the floor in the dark.

About The Author

Cate Beauman is the author of the best selling series, The Bodyguards of L.A. County. She currently lives in North Carolina with her husband, two boys, and their St. Bernards, Bear and Jack.

www.catebeauman.com
www.facebook.com/CateBeauman
www.goodreads.com/catebeauman
Follow Cate on Twitter: @CateBeauman

Morgan's Hunter
Book One: The story of Morgan and Hunter
ISBN: 978-0989569606

Morgan Taylor, D.C. socialite and wildlife biologist, leads a charmed life until everything changes with a phone call. Her research team has been found dead—slaughtered—in backcountry Montana.

As the case grows cold, Morgan is determined to unravel the mystery behind her friends' gruesome deaths. Despite the dangers of a murderer still free, nothing will stand in her way, not even the bodyguard her father hires, L.A.'s top close protection agent, Hunter Phillips.

Sparks fly from the start when no-nonsense Hunter clashes with Morgan's strong-willed independence. Their endless search for answers proves hopeless—until Hunter discovers the truth.

On the run and at the mercy of a madman, Morgan and Hunter must outsmart a killer to save their own lives.

Falling For Sarah
Book Two: The story of Sarah and Ethan
ISBN: 978-0989569613

Widow Sarah Johnson struggled to pick up the pieces after her life was ripped apart. After two years of grieving, she's found contentment in her thriving business as photographer to Hollywood's A-list and in raising her angel-faced daughter, Kylee... until bodyguard and long-time friend Ethan Cooke changes everything with a searing moonlight kiss.

Sarah's world turns upside down as she struggles with her unexpected attraction to Ethan and the guilt of betraying her husband's memory. But when blue roses and disturbing notes start appearing on her doorstep, she has no choice but to lean on Ethan as he fights to save her from a stalker that won't stop until he has what he prizes most.

Hailey's Truth
Book Three: The story of Hailey and Austin
ISBN: 978-0989569620

Hailey Roberts has never had it easy. Despite the scars of a tragic childhood, she's made a life for herself. As a part-time student and loving nanny, she yearns for a family of her own and reluctant Austin Casey, Ethan Cooke Security's best close protection agent.

Hailey's past comes back to haunt her when her long lost brother tracks her down, bringing his dangerous secrets with him. At an emotional crossroads, Hailey accepts a humanitarian opportunity that throws her together with Austin, taking her hundreds of miles from her troubles, or so she thinks.

What starts out as a dream come true quickly becomes a nightmare as violence erupts on the island of Cozumel. Young women are disappearing, community members are dying—and the carnage links back to her brother.

As Austin struggles to keep Hailey's past from destroying her future, he's forced to make a decision that could turn her against him, or worse cost them both their lives.

Forever Alexa
Book Four: The story of Alexa and Jackson
ISBN: 978-0989569637

First grade teacher and single mother Alexa Harris is no stranger to struggle, but for once, things are looking up. The school year is over and the lazy days of summer are here. Mini-vacations and relaxing twilight barbeques are on the horizon until Alexa's free-spirited younger sister vanishes.

Ransom calls and death threats force Alexa and her young daughter to flee their quiet home in Maryland. With nowhere else to turn, Alexa seeks the help of Jackson Matthews, Ethan Cooke Security's Risk Assessment Specialist and the man who broke her heart.

With few leads to follow and Abby's case going cold, Alexa must confess a shocking secret if she and Jackson have any hope of saving her sister from a hell neither could have imagined.

Waiting For Wren
Book Five: The story of Wren and Tucker
ISBN: 978-0989569644

Wren Cooke has everything she's ever wanted—a thriving career as one of LA's top interior designers and a home she loves. Business trips, mockups, and her demanding clientele keep her busy, almost too busy to notice Ethan Cooke Security's gorgeous Close Protection Agent, Tucker Campbell.

Jaded by love and relationships in general, Wren wants nothing to do with the hazel-eyed stunner and his heart-stopping grins, but Tucker is always in her way. When Wren suddenly finds herself bombarded by a mysterious man's unwanted affections, she's forced to turn to Tucker for help.

As Wren's case turns from disturbing to deadly, Tucker whisks her away to his mountain home in Utah. Haunted by memories and long-ago tragedies, Tucker soon realizes his past and Wren's present are colliding. With a killer on the loose and time running out, Tucker must discover a madman's motives before Wren becomes his next victim.

Justice For Abby
Book Six: The story of Abby and Jared
ISBN: 978-0989569651

Fashion designer Abigail Harris has been rescued, but her nightmare is far from over. Determined to put her harrowing ordeal behind her and move on, she struggles to pick up the pieces of her life while eluding the men who want her dead.

The Mid-Atlantic Sex Ring is in ruins after Abby's interviews with the police. The organization is eager to exact their revenge before her testimony dismantles the multi-million dollar operation for good.

Abby's safety rests in the hands of former US Marshal, Jerrod Quinn. Serious-minded and obsessed with protocol, Ethan Cooke Security's newest agent finds himself dealing with more than he bargains for when he agrees to take on his beautiful, free-spirited client.

As the trial date nears, Abby's case takes a dangerous turn. Abby and Jerrod soon discover themselves in a situation neither of them expect while Jerrod fights to stop the ring from silencing Abby once and for all.

Saving Sophie
Book Seven: The story of Sophie and Stone
ISBN: 978-0989569668

Jewelry designer Sophie Burke has fled Maine for the anonymity of the big city. She's starting over with a job she tolerates and a grungy motel room she calls home on the wrong side of town, but anything is better than the nightmare she left behind.

Stone McCabe is Ethan Cooke Security's brooding bad boy, more interested in keeping to himself than anything else—until the gorgeous blond with haunted violet eyes catches his attention late one rainy night.

Stone reluctantly gives Sophie a hand only to quickly realize that the shy beauty with the soft voice and pretty smile has something to hide. Tangled up in her secrets, Stone offers Sophie a solution that has the potential to free her from her problems once and for all—or jeopardize both of their lives.

Reagan's Redemption
Book Eight: The story of Reagan and Shane
ISBN: 978-0989569675

Doctor Reagan Rosner loves her fast-paced life of practicing medicine in New York City's busiest trauma center. Kind and confident, she's taking her profession by storm—until a young girl's accidental death leaves her shaken to her core. With her life a mess and her future uncertain, Reagan accepts a position as Head Physician for The Appalachia Project, an outreach program working with some of America's poorest citizens.

Shane Harper, Ethan Cooke Security's newest team member, has been assigned a three-month stint deep in the mountains of Eastern Kentucky, and he's not too happy about it. Guarding a pill safe in the middle of nowhere is boring as hell, but when he gets a look at his new roommate, the gorgeous Doctor Rosner, things start looking up.

Shane and Reagan encounter more than a few mishaps as they struggle to gain the trust of a reluctant community. They're just starting to make headway when a man's routine checkup exposes troubling secrets the town will do anything to keep hidden—even if that means murder.

Answers For Julie
Book Nine: The story of Julie and Chase
ISBN: 978-0989569682

Julie Keller relishes the simple things: hot chocolate on winter nights, good friends she calls her family, and her laid-back career as a massage therapist and yoga instructor. Julie is content with her life until Chase Rider returns to Bakersfield.

Bodyguard Chase Rider isn't thrilled to be back in the town where he spent his childhood summers. His beloved grandmother passed away, leaving him a house in need of major repairs. With a three-week timetable and a lot to do, he doesn't have time for distractions. Then he bumps into Julie, the one woman he hoped never to see again. Chase tries to pretend Julie doesn't exist, but ten years hasn't diminished his attraction to the hazel-eyed stunner.

When a stranger grabs Julie's arm at the grocery store—a woman who insists Julie's life isn't what it seems, Chase can't help but get involved. Julie and Chase dig into a twenty-five-year-old mystery, unearthing more questions than answers. But the past is closer than they realize, and the consequences of the truth have the potential to be deadly.

Book Ten Coming Soon!

Finding Lyla
Book Ten: The story of Lyla and Collin
ISBN: 978-0989569699

Made in the USA
Columbia, SC
30 November 2017